THE WIFE TRAP

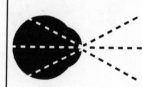

This Large Print Book carries the
Seal of Approval of N.A.V.H.

THE WIFE TRAP

TRACY ANNE WARREN

WHEELER PUBLISHING
An imprint of Thomson Gale, a part of The Thomson Corporation

Detroit • New York • San Francisco • New Haven, Conn. • Waterville, Maine • London

THOMSON
★ ™
GALE

ALL RIGHTS RESERVED

LIBRARY OF CONGRESS CATALOGING-IN-PUBLICATION DATA

Warren, Tracy Anne.
    The wife trap / by Tracy Anne Warren.
        p. cm. — (Wheeler Publishing large print romance)
    ISBN 1-59722-373-5 (hardcover : alk. paper)
    1. Aristocracy (Social class) — England — Fiction. 2. Large type books.
    I. Title.
PS3623.A8665W54   2006
813'.6—dc22   2006027173

U.S. Hardcover:
ISBN 13: 978-1-59722-373-7
ISBN 10: 1-59722-373-5

Published in 2006 by arrangement with The Ballantine Publishing Group,
a division of Random House, Inc.

Printed in the United States of America on permanent paper
10 9 8 7 6 5 4 3 2 1

With enduring love, to my father,
Richard Frank Warren, Jr.,
a voracious reader,
who never tired of learning.
Wish you were here to share my
adventures in publishing, to cheer me
on and ask me about each and every
detail along the way.
I think you would have
enjoyed the ride.
I miss you, Daddy.

To my editor, Charlotte Herscher.
Thanks for your insight and
encouragement, and for helping me
make this book even better.

Chapter One

Ireland, June 1817

Lady Jeannette Rose Brantford gently blew her nose on her handkerchief. Neatly refolding the silk square with its pretty row of embroidered lily of the valley, she dabbed at the fresh pair of tears that slid down her cheeks.

I really need to stop crying, she told herself. *This unremitting misery simply has to cease.*

On the sea voyage over, she'd thought she had her emotions firmly under control. Resigned, as it were, to her ignominious fate. But this morning when the coach set off on the overland journey to her cousins' estate, the reality of her situation had crashed upon her like one of the great boulders that lay scattered around the wild Irish countryside.

How could my parents have done this to me? she wailed to herself. How could they

9

have been cruel enough to exile her to this godforsaken wilderness? Dear heavens, even Scotland would have been preferable. At least its landmass had the good sense to still be attached to Mother England. Scotland would have been a long carriage ride from home, but in Ireland, she was separated by an entire sea!

Yet Mama and Papa had remained adamant in their decision to send her here. And for the first time in her twenty-one years, she'd been unable to wheedle or cajole or cry her way into persuading them to change their minds.

She didn't even have her longtime lady's maid, Jacobs, to offer her comfort and consolation in her time of need. Just because she had told Jacobs a little fib about her identity when she and her twin sister, Violet, had decided to exchange places last summer was no cause for desertion. And just because Jeannette's parents were punishing her for the scandal with this intolerable banishment to Ireland was no reason for Jacobs to seek out a new post. A loyal servant would have been eager to follow her mistress into exile!

Jeannette wiped away another tear and gazed across the coach at her new maid, Betsy. Despite being a perfectly sweet, pleasant girl, Betsy was a stranger. Not only that, she was woefully inexperienced, still learning about the proper care of clothing and dressing hair and recognizing the latest fashions. Jacobs had known it all.

Jeannette sighed.

Oh, well, she thought, training Betsy would give her new life purpose. At the reminder of her *new life,* tears welled again into her eyes.

Alone. Oh, she was so dreadfully alone.

Abruptly, the coach jerked to a tooth-rattling halt. She slid forward and nearly toppled to the floor in a cloud of skirts.

Betsy caught her; or rather, they caught each other, and slowly settled themselves back into their seats.

"Good heavens, what was that?" Jeannette straightened her hat, barely able to see with the brim half covering her eyes.

"It felt like we hit something, my lady." Betsy twisted to peer out the small window at the gloomy landscape beyond. "I hope we weren't in no accident."

The coach swayed as the coachman and footmen jumped to the ground, the low rumble of male voices filling the air.

Jeannette gripped her handkerchief inside her palm. *Drat it, what now? As if things weren't bad enough already.*

11

A minute later, the coachman's wizened face and sloped shoulders appeared at the window. "I'm sorry, my lady, but it appears we're stuck."

Jeannette's eyebrows rose. "What do you mean, stuck?"

" 'Tis the weather, my lady. All the rain of late has turned the road back to bog."

Bog? As in big-wheel-sucking-muddy-hole kind of bog? A wail rose into her throat. She swallowed the cry and firmed her lower lip, refusing to let it so much as quiver.

"Jem and Samuel and me'll keep trying," the coachman continued, "but it may be a while afore we're on our way. Perhaps you'd like to step out while we . . ."

She shot him an appalled look, so appalled obviously that his words trailed abruptly into silence.

What was wrong with the man? she wondered. Was he daft? Or blind, perhaps? Could he not see her beautiful Naccarat traveling dress? The shade bright and pretty as a perfect tangerine. Or the stylish kid leather half boots she'd had dyed especially to match prior to her departure from London? Obviously he had no common sense, nor any appreciation of the latest styles. But mayhap she was being too hard on him, since, after all, what did any man really know about ladies' fashion.

"Step out to where? Into that mud?" She gave her head a vigorous shake. "I shall wait right where I am."

"It may get a might rough once we start pushing, my lady. There's your safety to consider."

"Don't worry about my safety. I shall be fine in the coach. If you need to lighten the load, however, you have my leave to remove my trunks. But please be sure not to set them into the mud. I shall be most distressed if they are begrimed or damaged in any manner." She waved a gloved hand. "And Betsy may step down if she wishes."

Betsy looked uncertain. "Are you sure, my lady? I don't think I ought to leave you."

"It's fine, Betsy. There is nothing you can do here anyway, so go with John."

Besides, Jeannette moaned to herself, *it will be nothing new, since I am well used to being deserted these days.*

The gray-haired man fixed a pair of kindly eyes on the servant girl. "Best you come with me. I'll see ye to a safe spot."

Once Betsy was lifted free of the coach and the worst of the mud, the barouche's door was firmly relatched. The servants set about unloading the baggage, then began the grueling task of trying to dislodge the

13

vehicle's trapped wheels.

A full half hour passed with no success. Jeannette stubbornly kept her seat, faintly queasy from the vigorous, periodic rocking of the coach as the men and horses strained to force the carriage out of its hole. From the exclamations of annoyed disgust that floated on the air, puncturing the rustic silence, she gathered their attempts had done nothing but sink the wheels even deeper into the mire.

Withdrawing a fresh handkerchief from her reticule, she patted the perspiration from her forehead. Blazing from above, the sun had burned off the clouds but was doing little to dry the muddy morass around her. Afternoon heat ripened the air, turning it sticky with a humidity that was unusual for these parts even in mid-summer, or so she had been informed.

At least she wasn't crying anymore. A blessing, since it wouldn't do to arrive at her cousins' house — assuming she ever did arrive — looking bloated and puffy, her eyes damp and red-rimmed. It was humiliating enough knowing what her cousins must think of her banishment. A far worse ignominy to greet them looking anything but her best.

A fly buzzed into the coach, fat and black

and repugnant.

Jeannette's lip curled with distaste. She shooed at the insect with her handkerchief, hoping it would fly out the opposite window. Instead it turned and raced straight for her head. She let out a sharp squeal and batted at it again.

Buzzing past her nose, it landed on the window frame, its transparent wings glinting in the brilliant sunlight. The insect strolled casually along the painted wooden sill on tensile, hair-thin legs.

With equal nonchalance, Jeannette reached for her fan. She waited, running an assessing thumb over the fine gilded ivory side guard. As soon as the creature paused, Jeannette brought her fan down with an audible *thwap.*

In a single instant, the big black bug became a big black blob. Gratified by her small victory, she inspected her fan, hoping she had not damaged the delicate staves, since the fan had always been one of her favorites.

Catching a fresh glimpse of the squashed insect, she twisted her lips in revulsion before quickly flicking the carcass out of her sight.

"You've a deadly aim, lass," remarked a mellow male voice, the lilting cadence as

15

rich and lyrical as an Irish ballad. "He didn't stand a chance, that fly. Are you as handy with a real weapon?"

Startled, she turned her head to find a stranger peering in at her through the opposite window, one strong forearm propped at an impertinent angle atop the frame.

How long had he been standing there? she wondered. Long enough obviously to witness the encounter between her and the fly.

The man was tall and sinewy with close-cropped, wavy dark chestnut hair, fair skin and penetrating eyes of the bluest blue, vivid as gentians at peak bloom. They twinkled at her, those eyes, the man making no effort to conceal his roguish interest. His lips curved upward in silent, unconcealed humor.

Devilish handsome.

The description popped unbidden and unwanted into her mind, his appeal impossible to deny. Her heart flipped then flopped inside her chest, breasts rising and falling beneath the material of her bodice in sudden breathless movement.

Gracious sakes.

She struggled against the involuntary response, forcing herself to notice on closer observation that his features were not precisely perfect. His forehead square and rather ordinary. His nose a bit long, a tad

16

hawkish. His chin blunt and far too stubborn for comfort. His lips a little on the slender side.

Yet when viewed as a whole, his countenance made an undeniably pleasing package, one to which no sane woman could claim indifference. And when coupled with the magnetism that radiated off him in almost visible waves, he looked rather like sin brought to life.

And a sin it was, she mused on a regretful sigh, that he was clearly not a gentleman. His coarse, unfashionable attire — plain linen shirt, neckerchief and rough tan coat — betraying his plebeian origins, along with his obvious lack of manners before a lady. One had only to look at him to know the truth as he leaned against her coach door like some ruffian or thief.

She stiffened at the idea, abruptly realizing that's exactly what he might be. Well, if he was here to rob her, she wouldn't give him the satisfaction of showing fear. She might burst into tears on occasion but she had never been a vaporish milk and water miss. Never one of the frail sort given to wailing for her smelling salts at the faintest hint of distress.

"I am well able to defend myself," she declared in a resilient tone, "if that is what you are asking. Be aware I would have no difficulty putting a bullet through you should circumstances require."

What a fib, she mused, deciding it wisest not to mention the fact that she had never fired a gun in her life and had no pistol with her here inside the coach. The coachman was the one with the weapon.

Where was he anyway? She hoped he and the others weren't, quite literally, tied up.

Surprise brightened the rogue's eyes. "And why would you think you've cause to shoot me?"

"What else am I to imagine when a strange man accosts me in my own carriage?"

"Perhaps you might assume he's here to help."

"Help with what? Himself to my belongings?"

His eyes narrowed, glinting with a dangerous combination of irritation and amusement. "You've a suspicious mind, lass, painting me immediately as a thief." He leaned closer, his voice growing faintly husky. "Assuming I were a thief, what is it you possess that I might find of value?"

Her lips parted involuntarily, alarm and something far more treacherous quickening her blood. "I have my clothes and a few jewels, nothing more. If you want them they are in the trunks outside."

"If I were of a mind to want such things, I'd have them already." His eyes locked with her own, momentarily holding her prisoner before his gaze lowered slowly to her mouth. "No, there's only one thing I'm craving . . ."

Her breath caught in her lungs as he paused, leaving his sentence tantalizingly, frustratingly unfinished. Did he want *her?* she wondered. Did he intend to force his way inside her carriage and steal far more than belongings, perhaps kisses instead, and maybe other intimacies as well? Given the circumstances, she ought to be screaming her lungs out, ought to be terrified beyond measure. Instead she could only wait with her heart thundering in her ears for him to continue.

"Yes?" she prompted on a near whisper. "What is it you crave?"

The corner of his lips curved upward. "You, lass, hauling your fine backside out of this coach so your men and I can free it from the muck."

A long moment of incomprehension passed as his meaning gradually sank in. Surely she could not have heard him right? Had he actually told her to *haul her backside out of the coach?*

Her mouth dropped open, her shoulders

and spine turning stiff.

Why, the gall of the man! Never in her entire life had she been spoken to in such a disgraceful, disrespectful manner. Just who did he think he was?

"And what is your name, fellow?"

"Oh, my pardon for not introducing myself sooner," he said, straightening to his full, impressive height. He touched a pair of fingers to his forehead. "Darragh O'Brien at your service."

"Darr-ah?" She crinkled her brow. "Rather an odd-sounding name."

He frowned back. " 'Tisn't odd, 'tis Irish. Which you'd know if you hadn't just made the crossing over from England."

"And how can you tell that?"

"Well, you haven't a sign on your forehead but you might as well, since it's plain as the nose on your pretty face that you're English and new to this land."

He could discern all that from a couple minutes' conversation, could he? Well, at least he had the grace to offer her a small compliment even if it was wrapped around a criticism.

"Now then, lass, you know my name, so what's yours? And where is it you're bound? Your men didn't say."

"Nor should they have, since my plans are

really none of your affair, most particularly if you are indeed some sort of rogue."

"Ah, a rogue, am I now? No longer a thief?"

"That remains to be seen."

He barked out a laugh. "You've got a wicked tongue in your head. One that could slice a brigand to the bone and leave him fleeing in terror."

"If that is true," she asked with a teasing half smile, "then why are you still here?"

He flashed her an irreverent grin, obviously amused by her words. "Well now, I've never been one to run from danger. And I don't mind dipping my toe into an interesting spot of trouble when I chance upon one every now and again."

Up went her eyebrow at his salvo. Was he implying that *she* was just such a spot of trouble? Come to think of it, maybe she was at that.

"I stopped to offer my help, as I tried to tell you before," he explained. "I was riding past when I noticed the sorry state of your vehicle. Thought you and your men could do with an extra hand."

His words reminded her of her servants' conspicuous absence, some of her earlier suspicions returning. "And where exactly are my men?"

"Right there." He gestured with a hand. "Where they've been all this while."

She leaned forward and shifted on the seat, then looked over her shoulder through the window. And there they were, all four of them — coachman, two footmen and her maid — grouped around her luggage on a patch of dry road. She thought they resembled castaways on a small, deserted island, looking hot, bored and in absolutely no fear for their lives.

"Satisfied?" he questioned.

Clicking her tongue with a barely audible *tsk,* she settled back into her seat.

"Now then, I've shared my name. What might yours be, lass?" He leaned in again, resting both muscled forearms along the windowsill.

"My name is Jeannette Rose Brantford. *Lady* Jeannette Rose Brantford, not *lass.* I would prefer you do not refer to me in such familiar terms again."

His smile broadened at her lofty reply, his vivid eyes twinkling with a boldness that made her heart squeeze out an extra beat.

"Lady Brantford, is it?" he drawled. "And where would your lord be, then, this husband of yours? Has he sent you out traveling on your own?"

"I am presently on my way to my cousins'

estate north of Waterford near some village called Inis . . . Inis . . ." She broke off, racking her mind and drawing a complete blank. "Oh, fiddlesticks, I can't remember now. It's Inis-something-or-other."

"Inistioge, do you mean?" he suggested.

"Yes, I believe that is it. Do you know the place?"

"Aye, I know it well."

Assuming he was not a rogue — though she still had her doubts on that subject — she supposed he might be a decent sort. A local farmer or some such, a freeholder mayhap or possibly a merchant. Although she couldn't imagine Darragh O'Brien serving anyone, not with that brash, ungoverned attitude of his.

If he knew the village near her cousins' home, though, perhaps she hadn't too much farther to travel. Heaven knows, she longed to arrive at her destination so she could climb down from this coach and shake out her skirts.

"I am to stay with my cousins there," she said. "And though, again, it isn't actually any of your concern, my title is one of birth, not marriage. I am presently unwed."

The gleam in his expressive eyes deepened. "Are you not, lass? I always knew Englishmen were fools but I didn't know they were blind into the bargain."

A renewed ripple of awareness quivered in her middle. She buried it with a stern inner rebuke, reminding herself that no matter how attractive he might be, O'Brien was not the kind of man with whom a lady of her rank would consort.

"I believe I told you not to address me by the term *lass*," she said, her tone too breathless to sound much like a scold.

"Aye, and so you did." He grinned at her, visibly unrepentant. "Lass."

Then he did the most astonishing thing — he winked at her. An audacious, irreverent wink that sent a flood of warmth rushing through her veins like the unleashing of a rain-swollen dam after a heavy storm.

If she'd been given to blushing, the way her identical twin sister was, she'd be stained scarlet as a poppy now. But thankfully, blushing at every passing remark was one of the rare physical traits she and her sister, Violet, did not share.

The summer heat, she concluded, *that* was the cause for her untoward reaction. The steamy, unseasonable weather must be affecting her already overburdened senses. If she were back in London, she wouldn't have given him so much as a second look. Well, maybe a second, but not a third.

"Come along with you, then," O'Brien declared in a no-nonsense tone. "We've talked long enough and I need to get you out of this coach."

"Oh, I'm not getting out. Perhaps my coachman didn't mention it, but I have already had this discussion with him. We agreed that I would remain precisely where I am until the barouche can be set on its way."

O'Brien shook his head. "I'm afraid you'll have to step out, unless you've a wish to start living inside this vehicle. In case you didn't know, the coach is muck-mired up to its wheels and your men can't push it properly with you inside."

"If it's my safety you are concerned about, do not be. I shall be fine."

A bit queasy mayhap, but fine.

"It's more than your safety, though that is a concern. There's the matter of your weight."

"What about my weight!" Her eyebrows jerked high.

With a bold, assessing gaze, he scanned the length of her body, from the brim of her hat to the tips of her half boots. "I'm not implying you're fat or anything, if that's what you're thinking. You've a fine womanly figure, but even a few stone can make the difference between lifting this coach out of its hole or sinking it deeper."

She sat, momentarily speechless, his rudeness beyond measure. Imagine discussing her weight and her figure in nearly the same breath! Why, a gentleman would never dare. But then, this man was no gentleman. He was a barbarian. From his tone he might have been discussing farm animals that needed to be shifted from one pen to another.

A long moment passed before he continued. "Of course, if you'd rather, you can stay here while I ride on. I'll carry word to your cousins to let them know you're in need of help. I don't expect it'll take above four or five hours to set you on your way again."

Four or five hours! She couldn't stay in this coach that long. Maybe he was exaggerating, using subterfuge to lure her out of the vehicle. But what if he wasn't? What if her insistence upon remaining inside the barouche did make the difference between traveling onward or remaining stranded? Why, in four or five hours it would be dark!

She shivered at the thought. God only knows what sort of dreadful creatures might lurk in the vicinity, ready to creep from their hiding places after nightfall. There could be wolves — did Ireland have wolves? — or some other equally dangerous beasts. Hungry beasts who might not mind nibbling on a young lady.

Deliberately she kept her voice from quavering, trying one last argument. "If all this is true, why are you here telling me and not my coachman? I should think if things were so dire, he would be delivering the news himself."

"He was gathering up the nerve to tell you, as I understand it, when I happened along. He didn't like bearing the bad news, so I offered to deliver it myself."

She peered again at the surrounding ocean of mud. "But where would I wait? Surely you can't expect me to sit atop my luggage in the middle of this bog while the sun toasts me to a crisp."

The humorous gleam returned to his gaze. "Don't fret. There must be a spot of shade somewhere hereabouts. I'm sure we'll find one that suits."

She sincerely doubted it, but what choice did she have? Either she vacated the coach or risk still being here, virtually alone and unprotected, come eventide.

O'Brien shot her a sympathetic look, clearly aware of her dilemma and the internal war she waged. Opening the barouche door, he stepped forward. "Come along and save your stubbornness for another day. You and I both know the quicker we get you out of this coach, the quicker you'll be on your way."

"Has anyone ever informed you that you are impertinent?" Grudgingly, she climbed to her feet.

He chuckled. "A time or two, lass. A time or two. Now gather whatever it is you need and let us go."

She hesitated for a long, indecisive moment, then bent to retrieve her reticule where it lay on the coach seat. With it barely in hand, he reached inside and whisked her up into his arms. Shrieking, she almost dropped her purse as he swung her clear of the coach, his strength and balance the only things separating her from harm's way.

He cradled her against his solid chest, carrying her as though she weighed no more than a feather, despite his earlier remarks to the contrary. His nearness washed over her, engulfing her, surrounding her, the scent of fresh air and horses teasing her nostrils, along with something else, something indescribably, deliciously male.

Surreptitiously she tilted her head to catch a deeper whiff, the illusive fragrance uniquely his own, she realized. She closed her eyes and for the briefest second considered pressing her nose against his neck. Instead she held herself rigid in his arms, distressingly aware of the thick brown ooze that encircled them like a slick, squishy sea.

"Don't you dare drop me," she admonished, catching up the edges of her skirts to keep them from falling into the mire.

Methodically he slogged forward, mud slurping in noisy protest against his tall boots as nature fought to maintain its tenacious grip upon him. They were halfway across to the oasis where the servants anxiously waited and watched, when O'Brien teetered, his knees dipping precipitously downward for a sudden heart-stopping instant. She screamed and wrapped her arms around his neck, unprepared for the plunge into the tepid muck below.

But just as quickly as O'Brien faltered, he recovered, his feet as steady as if he'd never wavered at all.

Her heart threatened to thunder out her breast, her throat dry and tight. An instant passed as the truth slowly dawned. A glance at the wide, wicked, totally unapologetic grin on his face confirmed her conclusion.

"You beast." She cuffed him on the shoulder. "You did that deliberately."

"Oh, aye. I thought you could use a bit of jollying. You scream all high and funny like a girl, did you know that?"

"I *am* a girl, and that was not funny." Or it wouldn't have been if he'd miscalculated and actually dropped her. She tightened her hold.

He laughed again.

If only he knew who she was, he wouldn't laugh or taunt her. Back in England, before the scandal, she'd been used to gentlemen hurrying to do her bidding. Wealthy, refined men, who catered to her slightest wish, who fought one another for a chance to satisfy her most fleeting desire. She'd been the Ton's Incomparable for the past two Seasons. And she would be again, she vowed, once her parents came to their senses. It wouldn't be long before Mama missed her and Papa's temper cooled. Soon the pair of them would realize what a horrible mistake they'd made sending their beloved daughter away to this rustic frontier.

Until then, she supposed she would be forced to endure unspeakable indignities such as being carried about by disrespectful, provincial Irishmen like O'Brien.

Her servants stood in a mute cluster, their eyes round as planets when O'Brien set her on her feet amongst them. Betsy hurried instantly to her side, an act for which Jeannette was silently grateful, and made a shy attempt to pluck Jeannette's reticule from her grasp.

O'Brien moved to turn away.

"Are you leaving me?" Jeannette asked.

He paused, swung back. "Aye. I've got to help your men with the coach."

"But you promised me shade and a comfortable place to sit."

He planted broad hands on his narrow hips and made a show of scanning the area, then he locked his gaze with hers. "I'm sorry to say, but the only shade to be had is over in that little glade just there." He pointed to the spot, a small cluster of silver fir trees standing several yards distant. "And I suspect the ground beneath those trees is just as muddy as the ground here. If you've a parasol I'd have your maid open it out for you to keep you from the sun.

"As for the comfortable seat, I never promised you such, as I recall. If I were you, I'd sit on your strongest traveling case. Otherwise, you've a fine pair of feet on which to stand. After all the hours you've been in that coach, I'd think you'd be craving a good stretch by now."

With that he turned and strode back toward the foundered barouche. One by one, her men stole away after him, the warm summer stillness broken only by the undulating hum of insects singing in the fields.

Jeannette stood immobile, stunned to speechlessness. She didn't know whether to stamp her feet in frustration or burst into another noisy bout of tears.

But she wouldn't give him the satisfaction of seeing her so upset.

Dastardly man.

And to think she'd considered him attractive.

Aware no one was looking, she stuck her tongue out at O'Brien's turned back. Feeling slightly better for her childish act of retaliation, she turned to find a seat.

CHAPTER TWO

Lady Jeannette was a spitfire, Darragh Roderick O'Brien, Eleventh Earl of Mulholland, decided as he joined the men in search of flat rocks and tree branches, anything that might be useful as leverage to dislodge the trapped coach.

Proud and willful to a fault, a man might say. She reminded him of Queen Maeve of ancient Celtic legend — fiery, impulsive and determined to the core. He could well imagine her sending out an army of men to steal a prized bull for her own aggrandizement, just as Queen Maeve had done so many centuries before — Lady Jeannette was every bit as brazen and bold as her Irish counterpart.

Yet strong as her will might be, 'twas no stronger than his own. And like the fearless mythical warrior Cúchulainn, who had challenged Queen Maeve, he had no hesitation in taking a stand against Lady Jeannette.

He'd met her type before — spoiled, lofty English beauties certain of their own innate superiority. Likely another man would have taken offense, and perhaps the Irishman in him should have done so, but he wasn't one to rise easily to anger. Nor did he tend to hold grudges, at least not unless the offense was well and truly earned beforehand.

Besides, Lady Jeannette was just a girl, young and unsure of herself in a strange new land. Likely scared as well. Though he had to admit she didn't show it much, remembering the intrepid way she'd confronted him when she'd believed he might be a thief. He couldn't imagine any other woman of his acquaintance challenging him in such a manner. Having the nerve to brazenly threaten to put a bullet through him if need be. He could well believe she would have done it too, and sent up thanks he was no outlaw. The lady might be overbold but her words and actions bespoke a brave heart, and for that he could only feel admiration.

He thought again of her name — Jeannette Rose. A pretty, feminine appellation every bit as exquisite as the stunning young woman who bore it. Yet like that glorious flower, she came complete with a set of pernicious thorns. Wicked barbs she wasn't afraid to use to deadly effect. A man would do well never to misjudge her, else he draw away injured and dripping blood.

Aye, she was a regular little rosebush, he thought with a grin. Beautiful but sharp-tongued, just as he'd told her. Even now he could still feel the bite of the words she'd used back at the coach.

In the general way, outspoken females didn't bother him. How could they when he'd been raised in a house full of fiery-willed women? Females who'd long since taught him to respect their keen wit and laugh at the worst of their cutting words. Of course, it didn't hurt a man when he had the knack of knowing how to duck every now and again.

The Little Rosebush was just such a one and he had to confess he'd had a grand time sparring with her — a grand time indeed.

He glanced over his shoulder and caught sight of her sitting all stiff and proper on top of one of her trunks, her maid holding an open parasol over her head. Studying her, he realized he wouldn't mind going another round with her like a pair of linguistic pugilists. Then again, as a man in his prime, he wouldn't mind doing a lot of things with her.

She was pretty and there was no denying

the truth. Her skin creamy and soft as a blush peach. Her hair lush and silky, its pale golden hue cool like young winter wheat. Her eyes clear and vibrant as the shifting blue-green waves of a warm southern sea.

Desire ripened in his blood as he recalled the way she'd felt in his arms, delicate and female. The scent of her, sweet like apple blossoms and fresh as new-mown heather on a perfect spring day.

No mistake about it, she was a fine bit of femininity for all her determined ways and stubborn words. An easy thing it would be to kiss her, to press his lips to hers for the space of a few breathless moments. Of course, once the passion was through, she'd like as not snatch up that parasol of hers, or whatever else came handy, and cuff him for his presumption.

He grinned again at the idea and his foolish longings, then set himself more determinedly about his search.

A few minutes later, he rejoined the others, a pair of heavy stones in hand. Setting the rocks onto a dry patch of ground, he shrugged out of his jacket and rolled up his shirtsleeves in preparation for dealing with the mud-bound coach.

Good thing he hadn't worn any of his better clothes today, since they would soon enough be ruined by the task ahead. A gentleman architect, he'd been out scouting a nearby quarry for stone for a country house renovation he was undertaking, and had dressed accordingly.

Unlike English aristocrats, and many Irish ones as well, he didn't hold with the notion that a gentleman should not work. That a refined life must be one of entertainment, Society and idle sport, with a smattering of estate business and politics thrown in for variety. Of course, in his case he hadn't always had the luxury of excessive wealth. There had been a time years past when his family coffers had nearly come up empty. When he'd set himself to the task of keeping the Mulholland holdings together by sheer grit, relying upon nothing more than his intellect and the strength of his labor and nerve.

The lessons he'd learned then stood him in good stead now, and he was careful never to lose sight of them. He loved his work, was proud of his achievements and knew there was nothing shameful or lowering about wholeheartedly diving into a task, even if it quite literally meant getting his hands dirty.

The collection of stones and branches now positioned for maximum effect, he and the others took up places around the coach. With a silent prayer, the four of them set to.

Darragh pushed, his jaw locked in steely concentration, every muscle straining as he fought to rock the vehicle forward out of its pit.

"Mr. O'Brien, I would have a word with you."

Lady Jeannette's voice pierced the air, originating from somewhere behind him and to the left. For a second he thought he must be imagining things, then she spoke again.

"Did you hear me, Mr. O'Brien?"

Good Christ, she really was back there yammering at him. What on earth did she want? Couldn't she see he and the men were busy? Had the woman no eyes?

He closed his own and did his best to ignore her as he shoved with all his might. His hands slipped fractionally against the painted wooden boards of the vehicle, and for a brief, hopeful instant he thought the coach might be on its way.

"Ahem, Mr. O'Brien, your attention, please."

He huffed out a stream of breath. "I'm a might preoccupied at the moment, lass, if you'd care to notice."

Sweating, hot and muddy, Darragh shifted

his stance but knew the momentum had been lost. Biting off a curse, he twisted around to glare at her.

She came forward, careful to remain on dry ground. "How much longer is this going to take? The wait has become intolerable and my skin is beginning to burn." Her expression reflected her distress as she raised a hand and pointed a single gloved finger toward her face. "Betsy tells me my nose has turned distressingly pink."

He eyed the facial feature in question and thought it looked fine and white, even from a distance. Betsy, he decided, ought to learn to keep her opinions to herself. And Lady Jeannette should quit seeing mountains where there was nothing but tiny hillocks.

"I'm sorry for your malady," he said, striving for patience, "but if you'll have yourself a seat again, we'll get this coach on its way in a few shakes."

Jeannette frowned. "You don't look sorry."

"What?"

"About my nose. You do not look sorry about my poor burning nose. In fact, I think you are making mock of me."

His usually placid temper heated. He reined it in. "I am not making mock. Now, be a good lass and go sit on your trunks."

She marched closer, as close as the strip

of dry land would allow, halting just a few feet to the rear of the barouche. "Now you are patronizing me. I believe you forget yourself, fellow. For your information, I am the daughter of an earl."

And I *am* an earl, Darragh nearly shot back. Instead he decided it was easier to stop their useless bickering and simply return to the task at hand.

"I beg your pardon, my lady, if I said anything to upset you. Now, if you'd please, stand back so we can set this coach on its way again."

Without waiting for her reply, he turned back to the marooned vehicle.

With a sharp command from the coachman, the horses strained while Darragh and the other men pushed for all they were worth. He let out a roar at the intense strain, his muscles shaking. One more good shove, he thought. Just another inch or two.

Suddenly the wheels moved, spinning in a wild circle that geysered mud in a high, arcing flume. The barouche rolled forward and out of the bog onto the safety of dry ground.

Cheers and shouts erupted. Darragh grinned, joining the men as they slapped one another on the shoulders in pleased, prideful delight.

A scream shattered the scene — high and

shrill and female.

Darragh spun at the sound and froze at the sight that greeted his eyes.

Lady Jeannette stood, body quivering, her tiny hands clenched at her sides, her dress and face and figure completely splattered in mud.

For an instant, Darragh couldn't draw breath, the sight of her so utterly astonishing. She vaguely reminded him of a calico cat, her once immaculate orange gown bedecked with a patchwork of caramel-colored spots. Not even her hat had been spared, the jaunty white ostrich feathers on top drooping downward like a bunch of wilted flowers.

Clinging to the end of one of those feathers was a clump of mud that dangled precariously downward. Darragh watched in amazement as the bit of sodden earth suddenly went *plop,* landing right on the end of the nose Jeannette had so recently complained of sustaining injury. Her aqua eyes flew wide, her horrified expression nothing short of priceless.

A bubble of laughter rose into his throat, burst from his lips. Another followed, until he was consumed, helpless to restrain his mirth.

The servants, who up until this point had

remained mute and stunned, suddenly followed suit. One of the footmen snorted loudly then bent over double with hilarity. In a matter of seconds they were all convulsed. Even Betsy covered a grin with one hand before rushing forward to help her lady.

But plainly Jeanette was too angry to be helped, her face blistered with fury and embarrassment. To Darragh's way of thinking, the Little Rosebush looked as if she might burst into flames right where she stood.

He knew it was wrong of him to tease her when she'd been brought so low, but the imp inside him couldn't be contained.

"My lady," he said, "would you like me to carry you to your coach? There must be a spot or two left on your gown that isn't covered in mud."

If eyes were knives, the glare she shot him would have sliced him to ribbons. He saw her working up a retort but then she apparently thought better of the effort. Setting her chin at a regal tilt, she turned away from him.

"Load the luggage immediately," she ordered the servants. "I wish there to be no further delay."

As if she were taking a stroll in the park,

she picked her way through the muck to the coach.

He followed, waited until she and her maid had been assisted into the barouche and the coachman had closed the door.

Darragh leaned forward and smiled at her through the window. " 'Twas a pleasure making your acquaintance, Lady Jeannette Rose Brantford. Here's hoping we meet again one of these days."

Her sultry lower lip quivered. "The next time a blizzard starts in Hades will be soon enough for me." With a snap, she lowered the blind in front of his face.

She fought off tears for the next ten miles, pride the only thing that kept them at bay.

And anger.

Without the anger, she knew she would have crumpled into a whimpering, blubbering ball.

Ooh, that man, that Darragh O'Brien. She wanted to . . . well, she just wanted to punch him. In her whole life, she had never been subjected to such disrespectful treatment.

Thought he was funny, did he? Well, he was the least amusing man she'd ever known.

Her gaze landed on her skirt and one of the many encrusted patches of mud begriming the material. She sniffed, a fresh bout of tears threatening. Her beautiful, beautiful gown destroyed. Doubtless even the most skilled laundress would be unable to remove all the stains. Betsy wouldn't want the garment, nor any of the servants, the dress so far past salvation that even the lowliest maid would refuse to wear it. She had adored this gown and now it was fit for nothing but the rag bag.

With the exception of the day her parents had informed her she was being sent to live in this hinterland, today was undoubtedly the worst of her life.

Long minutes later, they finally arrived at their destination. One of the footmen hurried to assist her from the coach, casting his eyes respectfully downward. And well he should, she thought, remembering the way he'd laughed along with the rest of them. Then again, she supposed it would be wrong to put the blame upon him or any of the others. They'd only reacted to the moment out of normal, human surprise.

No, there was only one man responsible and the devil's name was O'Brien.

The shame of her humiliation welled afresh, raw and painful as a handful of blazing cinders. The feeling only increased when a tiny white-haired woman in a rather old-

44

fashioned mobcap and gown emerged from the house, her placid gray eyes widening to their utmost proportions as they encountered Jeannette.

The little woman paused in the driveway, a delicate hand lifting to cover the rounded O of her mouth. She blinked twice, then seemed to recover herself, rushing forward.

"Cousin Jeannette, is it you? Oh, my poor child, whatever has befallen you? Bertie and I were beginning to wonder if you would arrive today as expected since evening is nearly upon us, but never mind that now. I'm your cousin Wilda. Wilda Merriweather. Welcome to Brambleberry Hall."

The woman's kind greeting proved Jeannette's undoing, a tear running over her mud-smudged cheek.

Earlier inside the carriage, Betsy had done her best to clean her up, but without water the effort had been hopeless at best. Jeannette's face felt tight and dry, as if her skin might crack from its coating of grime. And here she had wanted to make an elegant first impression, only to arrive looking a complete wreck. Being red-nosed and puffy-eyed would have been preferable to this. Now she was red-nosed, puffy-eyed and splattered in mud!

"Was there a mishap, dear?" Wilda extended a sympathetic hand. "Come and tell me all about it."

More tears wet Jeannette's cheeks as she went childlike into the older woman's embrace. "It . . . it was terrible," she wailed as Wilda wrapped a comforting arm around her waist.

"The coach . . . stuck . . ." she said, trying to talk around her tears, ". . . man came . . . made me get out . . . sun burned . . . mud, mud, mud everywhere . . . beast laughed. Oh, my dress . . . and my pretty *boots.*" Then, to her complete mortification, she burst into a fit of messy sobs.

"There, there, child," the older woman hushed. "Everything will be set right, you'll see. Come inside and we'll get you straight up to your room for a hot bath and a lie down. You must be exhausted, simply exhausted after such a long trip. Why, the occasional journey to Waterford quite wears me through to the bone, right to the bone, so I can only imagine how fatigued you must be. You cry all you want, dearie, all you want."

Jeannette gave in to her misery, weeping copiously into her handkerchief as she let her cousin lead her into the house and up the stairs.

She'd barely gazed around the cheerful,

yellow bedchamber that, she supposed, was to be hers, when Betsy came forward to divest her of her ruined attire. A large tub was carried into an adjoining dressing room, steaming water poured into the bath by the bucketful. The room grew quiet as everyone left except her maid.

Sniffing, eyes swollen and undoubtedly as red-rimmed as she'd feared, Jeannette slid into the lovely warmth. Betsy soaped and rinsed her long hair, then left her alone to relax. Five minutes later, her head resting on the copper rim of the tub, she fell asleep.

Betsy awakened her with a gentle touch, wrapping her in a large fluffy towel the instant she climbed dripping from the tub. Sleepy and depressed, Jeannette sat in front of the fire, bundled into her warmest nightgown and robe. She sipped a comforting cup of hot tea, nibbled on the delicious buttered biscuits and cold sliced chicken that had been sent up to her, while her maid combed dry her waist-length hair.

Then it was to bed, the sheets crisp and cool and smelling sweetly of starch and lavender. She buried her face into one plump feather pillow and shed a few more tears.

She missed home. And England.

She missed her parents and sister.

She even missed her brother, Darrin, who seemed to do nothing these days but make a profligate young fool of himself.

Right now, she would trade anything to have them all back, to be at home in her own bed with things as they used to be. But nothing would ever again be the way it used to be, those days were now long gone.

She couldn't fathom why she felt homesick. Silly really, since she'd spent several months living in Italy with her great-aunt Agatha before her return to England a few weeks ago. She hadn't been homesick then. The trip part of the adventurous lark she'd enjoyed after trading places with her twin, when on the morning of her own wedding she'd refused to marry the duke to whom she'd been engaged. Violet had married him instead — pretending to be Jeannette. She supposed the deception had been very wrong of them both, but as it turned out, all had come right in the end. At least it had for Violet and Adrian, who were nauseatingly besotted with each other and expecting their first child later this year.

No, she was the one who'd suffered. She was the one who'd been sent away in disgrace and misery, and all for the sake of love.

Ah, Toddy, she sighed, *why did you have to*

play me false?

What a naive dupe she'd been to let an experienced cad like Theodore Markham toy with her affections. When she'd tossed Adrian over, she'd done so believing Toddy to be her one, true love. He'd whispered such pretty words to her, words of undying adoration and everlasting devotion, and like an idiot she had believed them. He'd flattered her, telling her how beautiful she was, all the while showering her with the kind of gallant, dutiful attention she had craved but rarely received from her own fiancé — Adrian, who was too busy with his duties and his friends and his own pursuits to see to her needs.

But Toddy had wanted her. Loved her. Or so she had thought until Italy, where he had learned there would be no fat dowry if he wed her. After that, he'd cast her aside like so much rubbish. Off, as she'd soon discovered, to hunt and seduce other, wealthier feminine prey.

She squeezed her eyes closed, fought as she had for so many long weeks to banish him from her mind. She no longer loved him; she was well and truly done with any tender feelings in that regard. But she had to admit he'd wounded something vital within her. Love, she now knew, could be unutterably cruel. Better not to love at all than to suffer such pangs and sorrows. Better to find solace in the things that counted for something in this world — wealth, position and dignity.

She would marry a title as she'd planned to do from the first. No charming cads this time to steer her from her course. Some rich old man perhaps who, if she was lucky, would die shortly after their nuptials and leave her a wealthy, young widow, free to live her life any way she chose. And once she returned to civilization she would set about finding him.

She'd ensnared one duke, she could surely catch another.

Sighing again, she snuggled beneath the bedclothes and forced herself to relax, forced herself at last to sleep. But her slumber was rife with dreams . . .

She sat alone in the stationary barouche, the wheels sunk deep into the mud. Without warning the carriage door was thrust open, a man's solid form blocking the sunlight that poured inside on a heated stream. Her breath caught on a sharp gasp as he took a bold step forward and leapt inside, and another as he slid up next to her on the seat. He stretched out a long, muscled arm and locked his hand around the frame of the opposite window. She burrowed backward into the corner as he crowded her close, blocking any faint chance of escape she might have had.

Meeting his intrepid blue eyes, she shivered, her blood humming with a mixture of fear and excitement, and yes, attraction. "What do you want?" she demanded. "My money? My jewels?"

She knew how his voice would sound even before he spoke, deep and musical, filled with the wild rhythm of the Irish hills. She waited for it and trembled in anticipation.

"Nay," he whispered, the word washing over her like a sleek, silken caress. "I've no use for such paltry trifles when there's far greater treasures to be had. So, what will it be, my lady, your virtue or your life?"

Her lips parted, her breath faint. "What choice do you leave me, sir? Pray do your worst."

The next instant his lips took hers, plundering her mouth with a primitive sweetness that made her senses swim, her limbs turn hot and malleable as wax. He thrust his tongue beyond her teeth and let her taste him, let her very pores fill with the intoxicating scent of his skin and hair until she could no longer distinguish her flesh from his own.

"Kiss me back, lass," he commanded.

And she did, losing herself in a forbidden

desire that she should not want but nonetheless did. Fingers aching to touch, she threaded them into his thick brown hair and pulled him closer, urged him on to take greater liberties, this thief of the heart.

He palmed a breast, her nipple peaking in immediate response as he stroked her with a knowing thumb. She sighed and quivered as he dropped a string of kisses along the column of her neck. Nipping her earlobe, he laved the spot with his tongue.

"Now, do you know what I want, lass?" he asked, his breath warm and husky in her ear.

She gently shook her head and waited, legs shifting restlessly against the aching want she needed him to assuage.

Abruptly, he set her from him. "You, hauling your fine backside out of this coach. Here, let me help."

And before she could voice a protest, he yanked her up off the seat, and with a push tumbled her out of the coach into the mud. He laughed at her from where he stood inside the barouche, beating a hand against the side of the vehicle over and over and over again.

The sound of his beating hand changed and grew louder, turning into a monotonous pounding that drew her up out of the dream.

She groaned and squinted against the

52

early-morning light, sleepy enough still to feel the wet mud, as well as the lingering desire, lying slick upon her skin.

She cringed and wrinkled her face against her pillow in mortification. How could she have had such an intimate dream, and about Darragh O'Brien of all people! How could she want such a man? What trick of her mind had led her to fantasize about him when he was no more than a commoner and well beneath her notice no matter how ruggedly handsome he might be?

Well, it was only a dream, she reasoned. Stupid and meaningless and utterly insignificant.

The dreadful noise continued.

For mercy sakes, what was that horrible racket? She leaned up on an elbow and peered across at the mantel clock above the fireplace.

Seven-thirty, the hands read.

Barbaric.

Appalling.

She never rose from her bed until ten, or sometimes even eleven if she'd had a particularly late evening the night before. Lord knows no sane, civilized human being would wish to wake any earlier. In her estimation people who purported to like rising with the sun needed a good physic, perhaps even a hearty bleeding to rid them of their bad humors and irrational behavior.

Moaning in exhausted misery, she stuffed a pillow over her head and tried to block out the cacophonous *thud, thud, thud* that echoed in the air like the drums of the damned. For a few scant seconds, the noise ceased. Forgetting all about her ignominious dream, she dozed off with a happy grunt, only to startle awake again moments later as the vicious pounding commenced once more.

She fought the battle of waking and sleeping for several more tortuous minutes before jerking upright on a snarled oath that would have made many a gentleman blush. Flinging back the covers, she hurried across to the windows.

She saw nothing out of the ordinary. Grass, trees, flowers, a bird singing on one of the branches. Only she couldn't hear his pretty warble, drowned out by the horrid, monotonous thumping.

What was that noise? *Where* was that noise? It sounded like . . . hammering or chiseling perhaps as she caught the metallic clang of metal striking metal.

Adam's apples, she inwardly cursed, *have I taken up residence in a madhouse?*

She crossed to the bellpull, rang for Betsy.

Obviously any further attempts to sleep would be futile.

Her maid entered looking a bit tired herself. "Good morning, my lady. Are you awake?"

"How could I be anything else with that infernal din going on outside? What in blazes is it, do you know?"

"Builders, my lady. It's my understanding that the west wing is being repaired."

"Repaired, you say? Hmm. You'd think they could show some courtesy and start a bit later. I shall have to speak with my cousins about this." Jeannette sighed. "Well, since I'm up and not likely to return to sleep, I suppose you may as well help me dress."

"Very good, my lady," Betsy said, dipping into a curtsey.

Half an hour later, still weary but feeling more herself in an exquisite day dress of pale pink spotted muslin and a sweet pair of primrose-colored slippers that she couldn't help but admire as she walked, Jeannette made her way through the house in search of the morning room. Since this was her first day in residence and she was awake so early, she decided she would break her fast with her cousins, who she was informed dined nearly every morning around this hour.

The house was large — though not as large as her father's house in Surrey — and done in the Palladian style that had been all the rage during the previous century. For her part, she found the architecture rather austere, with far too many unforgiving lines. Walking past a pair of Doric columns placed for dramatic visual effect — faux painted to resemble marble, she discovered with a casual touch — she finally located the morning room.

The infernal pounding eased slightly with the blessing of distance. *Heavens, how long will it go on?* she wondered.

She found Wilda seated at a linen-draped dining table, the furniture comfortably arranged for intimate family occasions. Attired in yet another sadly unfashionable gown, her cousin resembled a quaint country matron. Her fringe of short, curly white tresses were tucked beneath a frilly mobcap and lent her a curiously poodlelike appearance.

Jeannette hid a smile at the image.

At least the dress's color wasn't bad, she decided, the vibrant cornflower blue youthful enough to bring out the sparkle in her cousin's gray eyes.

As Jeannette crossed the threshold, Wilda laid her knife along the edge of her plate, strawberry jam shining berry-bright on the golden triangle of toast she held in her left hand.

Wilda beamed a smile. "Oh, good morning. Come in, come in. Do please take a seat."

Jeannette strolled forward and accepted a chair across from the older woman, murmuring a polite good morning in reply. A footman appeared, teapot in hand. With a silent nod, she gave her permission for him to serve her. He set a fresh cup and saucer before her, then poured the tea.

Her eyebrow went up of its own volition as she noted the color of the steaming brew — a dark, nutty brown that resembled coffee far more than tea. Obviously a different varietal than the pale gold, flower-scented Darjeeling she preferred. An Irish derivation, she supposed. Something that Darragh O'Brien would likely drink.

Forcing him from her mind, she reached for the sugar and cream, added healthy dollops of each to her cup.

"We breakfast casually most mornings," Wilda explained, pointing to a row of silver chaffing dishes on a nearby sideboard. "Please help yourself to eggs and sausages and kippers. They should still be warm. Or if you'd rather, we can send down to Cook for something else. Pancakes perhaps?"

"Eggs and toast will be fine, thank you."

When she made no move to rise, Wilda took the hint and nodded to the footman to prepare a plate. A second later, her cousin bit into the slice of toast still in her hand and chewed, tapping a nail against her teacup whilst she did so.

Was she making her nervous? Jeannette pondered. She supposed with her London manners it might be possible. Then there was the fact that despite her unmarried state she outranked the woman socially. Mrs. Merriweather might be a relation of her mother's on the Hamilton side, but the connection was inauspicious at best.

Cousin Wilda's father had been a mere baronet, and Mr. Merriweather, though descended from good stock, was no more than the younger son of a viscount. A rather impecunious viscount who hadn't had the means to provide adequately for his offspring in England. The reason her cousins Cuthbert and Wilda had moved to Ireland nearly forty years before.

The footman set Jeannette's plate before her. Improperly laden, she saw, with too many eggs, a blood sausage for which she had not asked and only a single square of toast. Oh, well, she was no longer at home and would have to get used to new routines and customs, she supposed. Lifting her fork, she tried a bite of scrambled eggs.

She had just swallowed when a loud crash reverberated through the house. Jumping an inch in her seat, her gaze winged across to her cousin. Wilda sat sipping her tea, apparently not in the least disturbed.

Wilda met her look. "And how did you sleep, Cousin Jeannette? Well, I hope?"

Hmm, how to respond? Particularly with the nearly constant round of banging and pounding that rang out more loudly than a harborful of shipbuilders.

"My room is quite comfortable, thank you, and the color most soothing."

Wilda's thin lips curved in a buoyant smile.

"There is the matter of the noise, however —"

"Good day, my dear, good day," boomed an older man as he burst into the morning room on a short but quick pair of legs.

A puff of pure white, his hair stood nearly straight up in a ring encircling his all but bald head. His eyes were dark as mahogany and every bit as opaque, slightly unfocused as if his thoughts were elsewhere. He wore breeches of brown worsted and a plain blue waistcoat and jacket, his ill-tied neck cloth clean but horribly wrinkled around his throat.

Barely glancing at her and Wilda, he made a beeline to the sideboard, clanged open one chaffing dish after another until he found what he was seeking. Plucking a sausage out of a pan, he ate the entire thing in a trio of bites. Jeannette watched in amazement as the odd little gent picked up a plate and began to heap eggs, scones, butter, jam, bacon and four more sausage links onto it.

He gathered up a fork and napkin, started back toward the door. "Can't stay, m'dear, ever so sorry, but I've got an experiment running and I mustn't leave it long."

"What sort of experiment?" Wilda asked, her usually even tones pitched high in suspicious alarm. "You haven't left a beaker of mercury heating again, have you?"

The man, who Jeannette concluded must be her cousin Cuthbert, turned an offended look upon his spouse as though her question had wounded him to the heart.

"Of course not," he said. "You know I promised I wouldn't ever do that again, not after what happened last time. If you must know, I'm timing the pollination cycle of my *Strelitzia reginae*."

"Well then," Wilda declared on a relieved breath, "your tropical flowers can wait a moment, long enough for you to meet your cousin Jeannette who's come to stay with us for a few months. Remember, Bertie dear, my telling you about her?"

His bushy white brows furrowed for a moment as his gaze settled upon Jeannette as if he'd only just then noticed her presence at the dining table.

The expression cleared as abruptly as it had come, then he smiled. "Of course, of course. Brantford's chit, eh? Jeannette, is it? Well, welcome to you, cousin. Most welcome, and pardon my lack of manners." He clipped off a quick but respectable bow.

Jeannette rose, curtseyed in reply. "Thank you, cousin, for inviting me to your home."

"From what I heard tell, it was your mother did the inviting and not the other way round. Edith always would have her way even when she was younger than you. Knew your mother in my youth and she always shot the fear of God straight up my spine. Worse than being chased by Diana with her quiver of arrows." He broke off, nodded at Jeannette. "Some sort of scandal, wasn't it, got you shipped off here?"

"Bertie," Wilda hushed, admonishing him

61

with a stern look.

"What?" he asked on a shrug. "She's the one involved in the dustup, so it shouldn't come as any surprise to her, what? Doesn't come as a surprise, does it now, girl?"

Jeannette paused, caught somewhere between affront and laughter. Humor won as she burst into the first laugh she'd had in a good long while. "No, no surprise at all."

"See, Wilda, she don't mind. Well, my eggs are getting cold and my *Strelitzia* awaits. Make yourself at home, Cousin Jeannette. Wilda, my love, I'll see you this afternoon at tea."

And with that he hurried from the room, breakfast in hand.

"Tea indeed," Wilda scoffed, "if he doesn't lose himself in one of those projects of his and forget the time like he always does."

Jeannette resumed her seat and let the footman refresh her tea.

"You'll get used to Bertie if you stay here long enough," Wilda continued. "He puts in an appearance for meals and not much else. Heaven knows why I continue to love that man. When he's not lost among his plants he's busy experimenting with his sun-image idea. Wants to make pictures of his flowers."

"Drawings, you mean?"

"No, dear. There are blind men who draw

better than my poor Bertie. Try as he might he's utterly helpless with a pencil or paintbrush, much to his eternal regret. No, no, he's taken the notion into his head to put images of living things onto a hard surface. He mutters on about it to me occasionally, talks about silver halides and such, but I don't understand the half of it. Thomas Wedgwood and some French fellow — Niépce, I think that's his name — are apparently busy attempting to beat Bertie out. They're all playing around with the same dangerous nonsense. I only hope those other men don't burn down half their houses like Bertie did."

Jeannette stopped buttering her toast in mid-stroke. "Burned the house?"

Wilda nodded animatedly, the lace edging on her cap fluttering at her movement. "Yes indeed. The silly man left one of his experiments heating over an open flame while he wandered off to the library to look up some fact or other. By the time he returned, his entire laboratory was engulfed. We were lucky only the west wing burned to the ground. If not for the local people setting up a bucket brigade down to the nearby stream, I fear we'd have lost the entire house."

"How dreadful," Jeannette sympathized.

"It was, and we've had workmen here ever since. Surely you've heard them racketing away?"

A fresh crash reverberated in the distance, followed by several indistinguishable male shouts.

Jeannette hid a grimace at the irony, set her knife and slice of toast onto her plate before politely reaching for the marmalade dish. She wondered if the older woman might be slightly deaf, since no one with adequate hearing could possibly miss the ongoing clamor.

"Yes," Jeannette agreed. "They are rather difficult to miss."

Wilda drank another swallow of tea, set down her cup with a delicate *clink* of china on china. "In the five months they've been here, I've gotten rather good at tuning them out. Barely even notice, these days."

Wilda angled her head to one side as if a new thought had just occurred. "They didn't disturb you this morning, did they, cousin? I asked the architect in charge most expressly to begin late today since I knew you would want to sleep in. They usually begin at first light, around six o'clock."

Sleep in! Jeannette marveled in horror. Wilda considered seven-thirty sleeping in? Obviously the woman had kept country hours for far too many years. She opened her mouth to correct her cousin's misconception, when she met the ingenuous expression in Wilda's eyes.

Now was her chance to complain, she realized, to unleash the barrage of displeasure that had been fairly burning a hole in her tongue for the past hour. But even as she opened her mouth to speak she realized she couldn't do it. Wilda would be hurt despite the fact that it was the workmen who were at fault.

Still, Jeannette knew she would simply die if forced to awaken every morning at the unholy hour of six. Perhaps some compromise could be reached.

She smiled. "Thank you for your consideration. I wonder, however, if I might beg a favor?"

"Oh, of course, child. However can I help?"

"Since the workmen started late this morning, do you suppose they could continue to do so? I have to confess, I'm used to keeping Town hours and I fear the strain of having to rise at dawn may prove unhealthy to my constitution. I imagine it is deleterious upon your health as well."

"Oh, I'd never thought," Wilda said in surprise. "You see, I'm long used to rising early. But if it will pose a misery for you, then I'll see what I can do. Be forewarned, however, we are dealing with men, and you know how contrary men can be."

The comment couldn't help but bring Darragh O'Brien to mind. With his face swimming in her thoughts, Jeannette finished spreading marmalade on her toast. Taking a savage bite, she chewed, swallowed and patted her lips dry.

"Yes," she murmured, "I know precisely what you mean."

CHAPTER THREE

Bored.

She'd been here less than a day and already she was so insanely bored she was all but ready to be bound and gagged and carried off to Bedlam, or whatever similar facility might exist here in this pitiful excuse for a country.

A light breeze played over her skirts, the sun bright, the sky blue, the temperature pleasant and not as warm as the day prior. As for the perpetual din that rang out in steady intervals from the construction site . . . well, she did her best to ignore that. She paused in her wanderings, used the toe of her slipper to nudge a few pieces of loose gravel on the path that cut through the gardens behind the house.

She heaved out a desolate breath.

She supposed she could read. A brief tour of the house had revealed the library — which thankfully had not burned down —

and the extensive selection of literary works it contained.

Yes, she decided, a book might well be her only salvation.

A half smile played at her lips as she thought how shocked those of her acquaintance would be if they knew she was even contemplating such an act. Even her own family believed her to be practically illiterate. But it wasn't true. Secretly she enjoyed reading now and again, especially the lurid romantic novels printed by the Minerva Press, though she rarely had an opportunity to indulge herself in such pastimes.

During the months when she'd been pretending to be her bookish twin, she'd had the opportunity to openly bury her nose in several volumes, including the Jane Austen novel Violet had been forced to abandon the day of their switch. The book had been quite diverting as she remembered, quite diverting, indeed. She wondered if there might be anything nearly as entertaining in the Merriweathers' library.

Unlikely. Wilda didn't strike her as the literary type, and Jeannette couldn't imagine Cuthbert taking an interest in anything but dry scientific and botanical tomes.

She crinkled her nose at the idea, already bored again.

Perhaps, on second thought, a book might not be the wisest choice. Just because she was away from home didn't mean she needed to fall into bad habits. As she'd learned long ago, ladies who wish to be admired by Society do not read, and if they possess a brain, they make sure never to reveal it — especially to members of the opposite sex.

She recalled a day years ago when her maternal grandmother, the Marchioness of Colton, had come to visit. A very great lady and undisputed leader of the fashionable set in her heyday, she'd made a rare trip upstairs to the third-floor schoolroom to visit her daughter's children — Darrin, aged nine, and the twins, Jeannette and Violet, not quite eleven.

Jeannette still remembered the silken rustle of her grandmother's magnificent jonquil gown, the soft click of her heels against the hardwood floor and the scent of the lily of the valley she wore that filled the space like a whisper of spring.

Usually bold, often to the point of folly, Jeannette had found herself stricken by an acute case of nerves. Quickly she'd lowered her eyes, praying her grandmother, whom she scarcely knew, would focus her attention upon the Wightbridge heir, Darrin. But her wishes crashed at her feet moments later when the marchioness strode over to her and reached out with an implacable gloved hand to raise up her chin.

The older woman, still beautiful despite her years, stared down at her out of critical lilac-hued eyes. She turned Jeannette's head left then right, inspecting her the way one might a horse or a dog. Abruptly, she released her.

"She's a pretty face, I'll grant you," the great lady pronounced, "as does the other one." She'd paused, cast a disapproving glance at Violet, whose nose was pushed as far as it would go into the book she held.

"But you'd be well advised, Edith," the marchioness counseled her daughter, "to curtail all but the most cursory of their education. Too much knowledge ruins a female, and if they turn bookish, well, it will prove their downfall. There'll be no marrying them off to anyone then, no matter how comely they might be. A woman's job, after all, is to learn to please a man so later she may have the luxury of pleasing herself. Put samplers and watercolor brushes in their hands now so they don't end up old maids."

Unlike her sister, who'd rolled her eyes and returned to her reading, Jeannette had taken her grandmother's remarks to heart.

Even at her young age she had known there could be no worse fate for a female than to end up on the shelf, unmarried and unwanted.

From that day forward, she'd taken only indifferent interest in her more academic studies, turning her attention to strictly feminine pursuits. And truly, the change had been no great hardship, since she genuinely loved fashion and furbelows, singing, playing the pianoforte, dancing and painting — all skills at which she excelled. Her grandmother had been an arbiter of style, an acknowledged leader of her set, and so too would she, Jeannette decided. If she needed to conceal the fact that she possessed a brain in order to achieve social success, then so be it. What, after all, was the loss of a few books along the way in comparison to having the fashionable world at her feet?

And once she married and married well, Jeannette knew she would be able to live her life as she chose to live it, just as her grandmother had foretold. If she decided at that time to reveal she wasn't quite as impervious to knowledge as some thought, then she would do so and give them all something new about which to gossip.

But for now she must bide her time here in this purgatory, bored, with no foreseeable relief in sight.

This morning while touring the house with Wilda, she'd inquired about local Society, anything to wile away the hours. To her consternation, Wilda had told her she and Bertie rarely entertained. Apparently the only assemblies were in Waterford, which was far too long a trip for people their age. Then she appalled Jeannette even further by telling her about the twice monthly get-togethers Wilda had with the vicar's wife, the squire's wife and a pair of local spinsters — not a single one of them younger than fifty. When Wilda invited her to join them when next they met, she'd swallowed her gasp of horror then very politely but firmly declined.

Ooh, she bemoaned, how could Mama and Papa subject her to such a fate? It was quite the meanest thing her parents had ever done.

She kicked another pebble and gazed in gloomy contemplation at a nearby cluster of vibrant scarlet poppies.

An exuberant round of barking filled the air, capturing her attention. She turned, gazed up just in time to watch a huge gray beast lope around the far corner of the house. She froze in shock as it sprinted toward her, lean and almost wolflike in ap-

72

pearance. Before she could flee, it lunged up onto its hind feet, set a pair of massive hairy paws onto her shoulders and toppled her backward.

She screamed as she fell amongst the flowers, then screamed again as the creature loomed above her, a great wet pink sponge of a tongue coming out to swipe her across the face. She shuddered and tried to escape, the scent of animal breath heavy in her nostrils. But the beast had her pinned, its weight and size heavy as a sack of stones.

"Vitruvius, off."

The creature tensed, having obviously heard the command. But it stayed long enough to get in one more good lick, while all she could do was whimper and roll her head in futile avoidance. Apparently knowing its time was up, the beast sprang away.

"Vitruvius. Bad dog. Very bad dog."

Dog? More like monster, she grimaced, swiping her hand across her lips in disgust, her face alarmingly sticky with slobber. *Ugh.*

"He's an ill-mannered brute. My apologies for his rudeness. Here now, are you all right?"

For a moment the only thing she saw above her was azure sky and lumbering white clouds. Then a face blocked them out as a man bent over her. She stared at his ruggedly appealing features, then lower, taking in his well-tailored though ordinary white cotton shirt, brown linen trousers and waistcoat, a navy blue silk neckerchief tied at his throat. How odd that he resembled that rogue Darragh O'Brien. How was it possible? Did all Irishmen look alike? Then the appalling truth struck her like a plunge into an icy winter lake.

He *was* Darragh O'Brien.

"You!" she accused.

"Lady Jeannette?" he questioned. "Is it really yourself, lass?"

"Yes, it's me. And for the last time, don't call me lass."

He quirked a smile and reached down a hand. "Here, let me help you up."

She slapped his hand away. "No, thank you."

Ignoring him, she rolled to her knees, climbed rather shakily to her feet. She beat at her mangled skirts while his beast animal sat watching, huge tongue lolling sideways out of its toothy mouth.

"That . . . that creature," she said, pointing at the dog, "is a menace. It should be kept in a cage."

"Don't take on so, lass. Why, he's naught but a puppy, too full of high spirits and exuberance to expect too much out of him.

He didn't mean you any harm. Did you, boy-o?"

Gazing down at Vitruvius, Darragh gave the animal an affectionate scratch on the top of his head. The dog smiled up at his master and flopped his tail against the gravel path.

"Puppy?" she said. "That beast is not a puppy, more like a bear or a wolf. Why, he could have ripped out my throat."

O'Brien snorted. "Not that one, no. He may be an Irish wolfhound, but he's docile to the core, despite the fierce origins of his breed. He's already done his worst to you, though I'll be the first to admit that tongue of his makes a fair and formidable weapon."

"Don't forget his paws. He pushed me to the ground."

A look of genuine regret passed over O'Brien's face. "He did, and for that you've my sincere and honest apology. Did he hurt you, lass?"

Lass. There was that word again. Did he not realize how disrespectful he was being? That he had an obligation to address her properly with the deference due her rank? Or was it merely that he did not care? She rather suspected it was the latter, but what recourse did she have when the infuriating man simply refused to obey? He and his

75

unmanageable dog quite obviously had a great deal in common.

As for her well-being, though she yearned to make a fuss and claim serious and lasting injury, she knew she could not justify it. Especially given the way she'd been able to climb almost immediately to her feet. Though she wouldn't be the least surprised if she awoke on the morrow to find herself literally riddled with a kaleidoscope of bruises.

She pulled out her silk handkerchief, wiped her face and hands before returning it to her pocket. "I'm as well as can be expected under the circumstances but my gown is not. It is ruined. Look at it, covered with paw prints. Great big huge muddy paw prints." She choked back a wail as the full realization hit her.

Oh, how could it be? Yet another of her favorite gowns destroyed and in the span of only a day's time. The injustice was not to be countenanced. The blame indisputable, resting squarely at the feet of one man. She didn't know what she'd done to merit such a series of calamitous misadventures at his hands.

She stared at him, forced to tilt her head back, way back, so she could meet his gaze. *Gadzooks, he was tall.* Until that moment she hadn't realized precisely how tall. Nor how lanky, his lean build betraying none of the muscled strength he'd displayed yesterday while carrying her from the coach.

She remembered the sensation of being cradled in his embrace, a disturbing fluttery tingle rippling through her middle. Disturbed by the unwanted reaction, she went on the offensive. "And what exactly are you doing here, Mr. O'Brien —"

"About that," he interrupted, reaching up to scratch the side of his firm jaw as if he was suddenly a mite uneasy. "You really haven't the need to call me 'mister.' Just plain O'Brien will do, or Darragh, since I've never been one for the formalities. Though if you insist, I suppose you can call me by my ti—"

"Mr. O'Brien shall do well enough." Encouraging intimacy between them, however innocently done, would not be proper. Nor would it be prudent, particularly considering the unwanted effect he had on her pulse. "So, why are you here? Have you business with my cousins? Or are you merely trespassing? You and that untrained hound of yours."

She cast a look of rebuke at the dog for his shabby manners. Though to be fair, the fault didn't really lay with the animal, but instead with his master for failing to control him.

For his part, Vitruvius was utterly unrepentant and unconcerned, his chin resting on one great paw, shaggy eyelids closed.

The dazzling blue of O'Brien's eyes lit up. "Ah, so you're the visiting relation, are you now?" He folded his arms over his chest. "I confess I'd been expecting an older woman, but I suppose you'll do."

The air rushed out of her lungs. "Suppose I'll do! Why, you really are beyond the pale."

He grinned. "Well now, as to that, we're a ways from the Pale." He jerked a thumb. "It's back near Dublin, or at least it used to be a hundred years or more ago when you English felt the need for fortressed territory."

She scowled at him, not liking the fact that she didn't have the slightest notion to what he was referring. She would make a point to find out later, she decided, a definite point. "So, you still have not said what you and your dog are doing on this property."

"Oh, that. I'm working for the Merriweathers, reconstructing that burned-down wing of theirs."

She bit the corner of her lip, struck by an inexplicable sense of disappointment. She had known he was a commoner, but some part of her had been secretly hoping otherwise. With his statement, he had just dashed that hope.

"So, you're a carpenter or some such," she remarked.

"No, I'm an architect. The one designing the new renovation and making certain it gets properly built."

The architect. Him? She hadn't even known the Irish had trained architects. Well, trained or no, her cousins ought to have sent to England for a proper man. At least such a personage, even if lowborn, would have known how to defer to a lady instead of baiting and badgering her at every possible turn. And sadly, his being an architect didn't make him a more suitable acquaintance for her.

Moments later, a fresh round of pounding rang out from the far side of the estate. She cringed. Hadn't they finished yet for the day? Would that infernal racket never end?

Abruptly it dawned on her. O'Brien was the architect, which meant he was in charge of that hammering. It also meant he was equally capable of stopping it.

"Oh, so *you* are the reason I cannot get a full night's rest," she said.

A tiny hint of a grin moved over his lips before he smothered it. "Woke you up, did we? The masons are working stone and they like to start early."

"They like to start barely after dawn. I am sorry, but it is most distressing and bad for my health. Since you are in charge, you can order them to begin later, starting tomorrow. Ten o'clock, shall we say?"

He looked shocked for a long instant, then tossed back his head and laughed. The sound erupted from his chest in a deep booming rumble so loud it startled a pair of red squirrels out of a nearby tree. Away they scampered across the grassy green lawn like a pair of bright flashes, while O'Brien remained convulsed with hilarity. The dog, roused by the noise, leapt to his feet and sprinted after the squirrels, barking repeatedly in his excitement.

Jeannette crossed her arms and tapped a toe. "I see nothing humorous in my request."

Chuckling harder again, O'Brien shook his head in a clear attempt to curtail his outburst, swiped a hand across the corner of one moist eye. "Ah, lass, you're a grand wit, you are. If you weren't a woman I'd invite you down to the pub of an evening and let you entertain us all."

"I was in no way jesting. I need my sleep. Without it, I shall soon look quite haggard."

"Ah, don't fret now. Even tired, I'm certain sure you'd look as beautiful as a perfect sunrise."

For a second, she warmed to his flattery. Then she realized he was trying to lure her away from the subject. Well, she thought, firming her shoulders, she would not be lured.

"Be that as it may," she stated, "ten of the clock is all the earlier I can afford to disrupt my natural routine. It is a pattern of long duration and cannot easily be altered."

He shook his head again, this time with a look of amazement. "Then you'll have a rough time, since a workman's day is best started early, when the temperature is cool and the sun isn't out shining full measure to bake him half to death. Besides, I promised Merriweather I'd have his house set right before the first fall leaves are lying on the ground."

"I'm sure my cousin would be willing to accept a reasonable delay."

"Reasonable, aye. Extra weeks to let you have your beauty rest, I doubt. Anyway, the work'll never be done if I give the crew near half the day to slumber away like some idle pasha or spoiled princess. If I did, the snow would be flying and the construction still not done."

Spoiled princess? Beauty sleep? As an Irish provincial, he obviously had no notion of the needs of a lady. No gentleman would ever be so cruel.

"Added to that," he continued, "this matter should be decided by your cousins. And excepting the morning just past, they've said nothing to me about changing the schedule."

"My cousin Wilda plans to do so," she said, stretching what she hoped would soon become the truth. "I've already spoken with her on the subject and she agrees."

"Agreed to ten, did she?" he said, shooting her a patently skeptical look.

Jeannette bristled under his gaze but stood her ground. Her chin came up, her voice steady despite her lie. "That is correct."

"Then you won't be minding if I nip into the house just now and have a word with your lady cousin?"

Their gazes locked, his own far too knowing, far too smug. *Devil take it,* she cursed inwardly. He'd seen through her bluff.

If there was one thing she hated, it was losing.

She held his knowing gaze for another long moment before hissing out a frustrated breath. Brushing past him, she strode toward the house.

She was halfway up the path when she noticed a rush of movement out of the corner of her eye. O'Brien's dog was racing toward her, its dish-sized paws even muddier than before. Hurrying faster, she prayed she could elude the creature but it caught up, trotting around her in an exuberant circle. Tail wagging, the animal rubbed his enormous body against her skirts, leaving enough hair behind to knit a coat.

Oh, dear Lord, what next!

Suddenly a whistle split the air. The dog froze, then turned.

"Vitruvius, come," O'Brien commanded in a stern tone.

The animal hesitated, clearly torn between his desire to accost her further and his need to obey. To her relief, the dog loped away.

Without another word, she headed once more for the house.

" 'Twas a delight meeting you again, Lady Jeannette," O'Brien called in a carrying voice. "Perhaps I'll be having the pleasure of it again early one bright and sunny morning."

And perhaps the sky would turn green and

the grass blue, she thought as she hurried into the house.

Darragh grinned, wincing as he listened to the terrace door slam shut at her back.

So the Little Rosebush was the Merriweathers' cousin come to stay for a while. He'd heard tell of her, together with the rumors. He didn't know all the particulars, but some whispered she'd been sent abroad after a dreadful scandal. Having met her, he could well believe it. Jeannette Brantford was the kind who likely kicked up trouble just by walking down the street.

Aye, she was a minx. Wild and willful. Whatever man decided to take her on, he'd have a devil of a time taming her. He'd have to be careful not to use too heavy a hand, gentling her to his touch and his will without breaking that proud, beautiful spirit of hers.

But it was safe to say Darragh wouldn't be that man, especially since he had no interest right now in taking a bride. Still, where would be the harm if he indulged in an occasional bit of teasing and flirting? It was just too much fun to be denied, watching her become more ruffled up than a hen caught out in a rainstorm.

He reached down, caught Vitruvius's jaw in his hand, angling the dog's face toward his own. "You're a naughty one, boy-o, and don't you forget it. 'Twas dead wrong of you to tumble her into the flower bed, though we're both guilty of enjoying the result. She's a pretty pair of ankles, I'll grant, but you'll need to mind your manners next time. I suppose I'll have to make amends as well. Hmm, I'll need to think on what will serve best."

He patted his hip, started back toward the work site. "Come on for now, lad. There's work yet to be finished today."

CHAPTER FOUR

By the end of a fortnight, Jeannette found she'd grown almost used to the incessant racket that echoed through the house from early morning to late afternoon each day.

Only on Sunday did silence whisper in like a refreshing breeze. The Lord's day one of true, blessed relief.

But *almost* didn't mean she liked the disturbance, not one jot. Nor did it mean she'd given up the effort to find a way to make the infernal noise cease. Or at least delay its start until a more civilized hour of the morning. Try as she might, though, she hadn't been able to come up with a means of achieving her ends.

And heavens above, she had tried.

She'd gone to Wilda first, bringing up the topic of O'Brien and his noisy minions over breakfast the morning following her alarming encounter with him and his rambunctious dog.

She had hoped for a sympathetic ear. After all, Wilda was a lady despite her lamentably dowdy appearance. Surely as a woman she would understand another woman's need for proper rest. And Jeannette could not get proper rest when she was roused to wakefulness at such a ghastly hour of the day. Only birds and mice and scullery maids bestirred themselves when dawn had barely broken across the horizon. Birds, mice, scullery maids and building crews, she amended.

The foul beasts hadn't even had the decency to wait until seven-thirty that morning, beginning work a full hour earlier, no doubt at the urging of O'Brien himself.

When she mentioned the problem to Wilda, reminding her cousin of her promise to speak with the architect-in-charge and request he begin work at a reasonable hour, her cousin informed her she had already done so.

"Oh, yes," Wilda confirmed. "I explained the problem and he was most sympathetic."

For a brief instant, hope rose inside Jeannette's breast. Just as quickly, it winked out as she remembered the exact hour at which she had been awakened.

"Was he indeed?" she ventured. "Then why did he and his men commence their labors at six-thirty this morning?"

Wilda gave her a look of helpless dismay. "Well, they must, dear. He explained how essential it is for the men to begin early. How even an hour or two a day will compromise their schedule. I am ever so sorry, but what can be done?" Then, like the helpless coward she so obviously was, Wilda tossed up her hands in defeat.

Jeannette next sought out her cousin Cuthbert in his temporary laboratory. As a man, she assumed he would be more easily able to state his demands and see to it O'Brien followed them.

Yet in spite of the plate of delectable breakfast foods she'd brought as a kind of culinary bribe — which he'd gobbled down like a starving orphan — Bertie had remained unmoved by her plight.

"Well now, can't interfere," her cousin said. "No, no, frightfully tired of being forced to conduct my experiments inside this storage cupboard. O'Brien's building me a specially designed laboratory, don't you know. Detached, with its own lightproof room and vapor chamber. Then there's to be a new orangerie. Oh, I can already see the *Dendrobium aggregatum* and the *Paphiopedilum faireanum* on display. The orchids came to me through an explorer chappie I know, all the way from India. Magnificent specimens, those plants."

He clapped his hands together. "And the new west wing, splendid, splendid design. O'Brien is brilliant, using quite the most up-to-date, innovative techniques and styles possible. Even Wilda can't wait for the renovations to be complete, since we're adding a new card parlor for her. She does love her cards, don't you know."

And with that, Jeannette found herself summarily ejected from the dark storage cupboard, where she'd spent ten minutes holding the oddest — and as it turned out, most useless — conversation of her life.

But the lack of success with her cousins in no way dampened Jeannette's determination. By rights she should resent them for refusing to aid her in her battle. But they were old and plainly incapable of dealing with that overbearing man, that O'Brien who had them under his big, calloused thumb, right where he wanted them to be.

But he didn't have her.

Somehow she would find a way to curtail his crew's early-morning noisemaking. She need only wait until inspiration struck and then she would have her solution.

But now, almost two weeks later, a satisfactory resolution had still not presented itself, nor had she found any easy means of relieving the tedious monotony of her days.

A bird landed on a tree branch just outside the upstairs drawing room window. She watched him preen his wings for a long moment before he dashed off in a streak of white and brown.

Lord, Jeannette thought, *shoot me now. I am so sick of the idles.*

Wilda sat nearby, a crochet hook and yarn flying through her nimble fingers. Sighing, Jeannette focused once more on the stitchery in her own hands.

Not long after, the daily racket outside abruptly ceased, signaling the end of another workday. Jeannette's spirits perked up. Once the men left for the afternoon, it was her habit to go outside for a stroll, certain she could walk the grounds unmolested by a certain impertinent Irishman and his discourteous hound.

She forced herself to sew for another twenty minutes, then hastily thrust her embroidery into a basket and rose to her feet. "I'm going for a walk before supper, cousin. Would you care to join me?"

Wilda's fingers paused, gentle eyes glancing upward. "Thank you, dear, but no. You go ahead and enjoy your exercise."

Jeannette nodded, walked rapidly from the room.

A few minutes later, she made her way downstairs, an adorable Oatland Village hat with its double curved brim perched jauntily on her head. Almond-hued ribbons streamed downward from where they were tied beneath her chin, the shade a perfect foil for her willow green muslin day dress. On her feet, she wore calfskin slippers, as supple and green as new spring leaves.

Gravel crunched beneath those shoes as she exited the house and set out along one of the paths that led deep into the gardens beyond. A delicate breeze stirred her skirts, the afternoon sun fine and full. Clouds drifted overhead in striated puffs, their underbellies shadowed by the faintest hint of gray, signaling the possibility of rain as late afternoon turned to evening.

But she didn't mind risking a little wet, relieved to be out of the oppressive confinement of the house. She wasn't used to such unrelenting solitude. Hour upon hour with nothing to do but sew and pen letters and share increasingly tiresome rounds of small talk with Wilda.

Her cousin meant well, but mercy, the woman could rattle on about nothing for hours at a time. This afternoon the discussion had focused on the best methods for storing linens, with a thirty-minute oration on the preparation of Wilda's favorite decoction for combating moths.

Gads, why couldn't there be some sort of nearby entertainment? Even a simple country dance would be a welcome relief.

Her footsteps slowed, stopped altogether before a large massing of pink foxglove, a few round black and yellow bees lumbering in and out of the cup-shaped flowers on their quest to collect pollen. Jeannette barely noticed the insects or the flowers, too preoccupied with her imaginings.

She could see the assembly room now, the space ablaze with candlelight and frivolity, laughter floating on the air amidst the mingled fragrance of a dozen different perfumes.

She, of course, looked stunning. Attired in a bravura confection of shot ivory silk with an overskirt of the palest celestial blue, a smattering of forget-me-nots threaded into her silky upswept hair. All the other ladies would watch her, awestruck in their envy, while the men stared, their gazes full of admiration for her exquisite feminine beauty and grace.

The handsomest young gentleman in the room would approach, bow low over her gloved hand, then beg for a dance. She would laugh and flirt, tease him for a breathless moment as if her agreement was uncertain. Then she would, of course, accept, the two of them taking to the floor with all the elegance of royalty.

Oh, it would be quite glorious. Almost as lovely as a London soiree. Her eyelids drifted closed, imagining.

Boot steps crunched on the graveled path behind her.

"You make a picture, lass. What is it that has you dreaming?"

Jeannette startled at the words and the deep, musical voice that glided over her like the stroke of a broad, soothing hand. The tone was warm and rich and full of Irish guile. An invisible shiver rippled through her as though he had actually touched her.

Her eyes popped open. And there he stood, her nemesis, Darragh O'Brien. Today he was dressed in tan trousers, white shirt and lightweight fawn jacket, the cut and quality better, more tailored than some of his other clothing. For him, he looked almost dressed up. A lock of his dark hair curled across his forehead in a way that made her want to reach up and smooth it back. An absurd idea.

Confounded man.

Could she never go anywhere without his appearing? Well, just because he had spoken to her didn't mean she had to offer more than a perfunctory greeting, then continue on her way. After her last two encounters with him, she had no interest in remaining long in his presence, especially if that dog of his was anywhere nearby.

At the thought, she scanned her surroundings, half expecting the enormous creature to dash out from behind a bush and pounce.

"He isn't here," O'Brien said as if he'd read her mind. "Vitruvius is back at the house where I'm staying, though neither he nor the housekeeper were too keen on the idea when I left him there at midday."

"Are you sure you'll have a housekeeper when you return? If she hasn't quit before, a day alone with that great lummox should do the job."

He showed her his white teeth. "Not to worry, Mrs. Ryan is wise to all the lad's tricks, and if he's gotten into her bad graces today, I'll find him tied up in the rear yard, pouting and sad-eyed for the scolding. He'll be wanting an extra half hour's attention at the very least to settle his mood."

Spoiled canine, she thought. No wonder the dog needed obedience training.

"So I haven't seen you out and about in several days." O'Brien tucked his right hand

94

into his trousers' pocket. "Have you been hiding?"

"Not at all," she rushed to assure. "I have been getting acquainted with my cousins and do not generally venture out until late in the afternoon."

"Once my crew has gone home, you mean. Or is it only myself you've been trying to avoid?"

She let out a tinkling laugh. "Now, why would I want to do such a thing? Doing that would require me to think of you, Mr. O'Brien, and I assure you I have far better ways to occupy my time."

Despite her statement, a grin appeared on his mouth, letting her know he knew the truth.

She decided it best to change the subject. "But speaking of your crew, I had hoped that by now you might see reason."

He crossed his arms over his solid chest. "Reason about what?"

"Letting a lady get a little rest in the morning. Your workers begin far too early and make far too much noise."

He shrugged. "So you've already said. The noise can't be helped, I'm afraid, since the building of houses isn't a silent occupation."

"But you could make adjustments if you wished. Another man would understand

and feel some sympathy. He would not be so heartless."

Darragh barked out a laugh. "Another man would soon find himself out of a job if he did as you ask. I've plenty of heart, lass, it's just my head that isn't soft."

"You're right about that. Your head is as hard as they come."

He smiled widely, eyes sparkling blue as the azure sky above.

She drew in a quick breath, her pulse doing a jig. *Blast him,* why did he have to be so handsome? A man of his sort shouldn't have the right. And what was wrong with her? Responding to him, even though her blood boiled at their every encounter. She couldn't remember the last time a man had made her feel so out of sorts.

Deciding her best move was simply to move away, she gave him a clipped nod. "Good day to you, Mr. O'Brien. I have a walk to continue."

But before she took two steps, he reached out and stopped her with a brief touch. "Here now, Lady Jeannette, don't be hurrying off so quickly. I sought you out for more than conversation. I've a gift for you."

A gift? Curiosity rose inside her like an irresistible fever. Helpless to resist, she pivoted to face him. "And what could you possibly be giving me?"

He crossed to a nearby stone bench, picked up the paper-wrapped bundle that lay upon it, plain brown string crisscrossing the square in neat quarters. With it in hand, he strode toward her.

He halted, then made a surprisingly elegant bow before extending the parcel to her. "We've gotten off to a rough start, you and I, and I haven't felt right about what happened when last we met. Vitruvius knocking you over and all. He's a sweet pup, but wayward in his actions. 'Twas a fine frock he ruined. And, of course, there was the other pretty one that day outside the coach. That orangey thing you had on."

Orangey? Why, yes, her beautiful Naccarat traveling dress. She wished he hadn't mentioned it. Since that miserable day, she had done her best to forget the incident. An imperceptible shudder rippled through her, evoked by a fear that she would never completely forget the dreadful sensation of being covered from head to toe in mud.

"And this gift, I take it" — she nodded toward the parcel — "is your way of making amends?"

How singular. How unexpected.

He rubbed a finger along his jaw. "Aye, I am sorry for your trouble. I decided since

Vitruvius is my responsibility, some recompense was in order."

The starch loosened from her spine, her shoulders relaxing without conscious thought. Her fingers itched to take the present, yet she hesitated.

A lady was allowed to accept only certain gifts from a gentleman. Flowers, bonbons, a book of sonnets. Or perhaps if he was especially daring, a pair of gloves or a small bottle of perfume. Anything else was considered scandalously improper.

But then, she reminded herself, Darragh O'Brien was no gentleman and his behavior never in any way proper. So why did the knowledge suddenly make her want his gift even more?

She forced her hands to remain loose at her sides. "What is it?"

Amusement danced in his eyes. "Well now, if I were to tell you that, it would ruin the surprise. You'll have to take it and find out for yourself." He edged the bundle a half inch closer, urging her to take his present.

She swallowed, knowing she should reject the offering, push him and his gift away. Instead she hesitated only a moment more before plucking the gift from his hands.

Light, far lighter than she had expected,

the package rested easily in her grasp. Her interest piqued even further, she nearly raised it to her ear to shake, but stopped herself at the last second. Ladies didn't shake presents — at least not in front of witnesses.

Tall and long-legged, he rocked back on his heels, then up on his toes, his strong hands settled against his lean hips. "So, are you not going to open it, then?"

She shook her head. "I shall do so later."

In case the gift actually was something improper. That way she wouldn't have to pretend to be scandalized. Though what sort of scandalous gift he might have given her she couldn't imagine.

"Well," she said, "evening approaches and I haven't had my walk. If I am to do so in time to change for dinner, then I had better be off. My cousins keep early hours." Very early, she thought, dining at the gauche hour of six o'clock each day, early even by country standards. With a nod, she turned to go.

He stopped her with another light touch upon her arm. "Are you not forgetting something?"

"I cannot think what."

"Can you not? Or don't English ladies thank a man when he gives them a gift?"

A twinge of shame went through her,

abashed that she had forgotten to be polite in her hurry to rush away and open the present.

She tilted her head at an imperious angle to salvage some measure of her pride. "Well then, thank you."

"That didn't sound terribly sincere."

"Nevertheless, you have been thanked."

"Have I now?" He stepped closer and wrapped one large hand around her upper arm.

Her heart beat faster at his touch.

A spark flashed in his eyes. "I think you can do better. Give it a try."

"Release me, sir."

Instead he caught hold of her other arm and closed the distance between them. "I shall, once I've had my satisfaction. Now, shall you thank me nicely, or would you rather show me your gratitude?"

Show him?

Her senses tingled, the scents of plain soap and the clean sweat of an honest day's work filling her nostrils. She wasn't used to such elemental scents. Earthy, powerful, rugged scents that made her stomach quiver, her mouth grow dry.

Her gaze clashed with his. She refused to look away, refused to capitulate by even the smallest measure. His own stubborn determination showed clearly, every inch as resolute as her own.

Just two tiny heartfelt words and he would set her free, she knew he would. Yet her pride refused to let her back down. Her pride and something more, something dangerous and wicked enough to make her pulse points throb in her wrists, to make the air sough in shallow breaths from between her parted lips.

When she said nothing, he drew her to him, the package she held by its slender string all but forgotten in her grasp.

"As you prefer, my lady," he murmured.

Suddenly his lips were upon her own, bold and relentless as he held her steady for his kiss. At first she resisted, but he met her resistance with demand, compelling her to surrender.

She nipped at his lips. He nipped back, snagging her lower lip between his teeth for a quick tug before laving the spot with his tongue in a warm, soothing stroke. She shivered, vulnerable to the blatant masculinity of his touch.

Without warning, he changed tactics, his mouth gentling against her own, turning sultry and seductive and achingly irresistible. Her thoughts grew muzzy. Her resistance weakening like a flower whose petals had been plucked free and left to scatter in the wind.

The man was a pure devil, she mused dreamily, and he kissed like one too. Lucifer couldn't have done better at his most beguiling. Her feet tingled inside her shoes, her body turned lax and liquid.

She whimpered and pressed her breasts against his chest. Opening her mouth, she slid her tongue between his lips.

After a long minute, he broke away. "I see you know what you're about, for all that you're a maiden. You've been well and thoroughly kissed by one man or another."

His statement drove the air from her lungs as if he'd struck her. For an instant, she considered denying his charge, but he would know she was lying. Besides, why not tell the truth? What did she care for his opinion, good or ill?

"You are correct," she flung back. "I have been kissed, and by far better men than you."

His eyes narrowed, their translucent color deepening, ripening like a sky before a storm.

"Is that so?" he murmured. "You ought to be careful in your impressions. They might not always be as accurate as you imagine."

What in the blazes did he mean by that

cryptic comment? she wondered.

"As to the superior quality of those other men, I cannot comment." His gaze lowered to her lips. "As for the kisses, I can safely say you'll never find better than mine."

Reaching down with nimble fingers, he loosened the ribbon beneath her chin and tipped her bonnet so it dangled halfway down her back. Cupping her face in one hand, he angled her chin to his liking and settled his mouth upon her own.

As if bewitched by a spell, she let him take her lips once more. She ought to fight him, she knew. Ought to be struggling against his embrace instead of turning in to it like a tender plant that wanted, even needed, to drink more deeply of the sun.

Her eyes fell shut, the world sliding away as he again proved the truth of his words, the undeniable mastery of his skills.

Curving an arm around her waist, Darragh fit her more snuggly against him as he worked to increase her enjoyment. He knew he should stop. Knew this whole game had begun to spiral wildly out of control.

All he'd intended was a simple kiss. A quick embrace to tease and teach her a lesson for her snobbish ways. Yet he was the one getting the lesson as she brought him a pleasure so intense his head fairly swam with the delight of it.

Ah, good Christ, she tasted like the finest golden honey. Sweet and rich and succulent. Well worth the risk of earning a little sting for his trouble. And trouble she was. Wicked bad trouble, the kind for which he had no earthly use.

How easy it would be to completely lose his head, to lay her down in this fragrant garden and spoil another one of her pretty frocks by staining it green with grass.

He imagined tumbling her gently downward, lying over her while he plundered her moist pink lips as he was doing now, his fingers easing beneath her bodice to cup a lush, full breast. Ah, her flesh would surely feel like a slice of heaven in his grasp. Her legs would shift, passion sparking hot between them as he slid his lips lower to take her nipple in his mouth, his other hand gliding downward over a rounded satiny hip.

Need pounded in his blood like a fever, ached like a wound between his thighs. He took a single step forward, on the verge of succumbing to sheer carnal impulse. A bird screeched in a nearby tree, awakening his rational mind enough for him to remember exactly where it was the pair of them stood.

In plain view of the house.

In eyeshot of the Merriweathers — who,

amiable as they might be, certainly wouldn't appreciate finding him making love to their young cousin. She'd been sent to Ireland as the result of one scandal. He had no wish to find himself at the center of another.

A fair temptress she was and there was no denying it.

Stifling a groan, he forced himself to break off the kiss. If they hadn't been caught already, there was no point in taking further risk.

Jeannette swayed on her feet, blinked twice.

"What is it?" she murmured in a breathy voice that whispered down his spine like a teasing finger.

"Past time you were going inside, that's what it is. If you stay out here much longer, it's for sure you'll be missed. Unless you still mean to take that walk."

"What walk?" she asked.

Doing his best to steady his trembling hands, he lifted her bonnet back into place, retied the drooping bow. His gaze roamed over her, noting the heightened color in her flushed cheeks, the ruddy, glistening lips, which looked well and thoroughly kissed.

He could never send her inside like that. Everyone who saw her would know.

Drawing a deep breath, he pinned a

deliberately arrogant, self-satisfied smile upon his lips. "I must say that was a fine thank-you, Lady Jeannette. Well worth the trouble of getting it."

The look of dazed passion drained from her eyes, color sparking higher in her cheeks. Pain glistening in her gaze, she lifted a hand and slapped him. "There," she said. "Was it still worth the trouble?"

Alarmingly, he realized it was, setting a hand over his stinging cheek and the reddened imprint he assumed she had left behind.

Without waiting for his response, Jeannette gripped the paper-wrapped present he'd given her, whirled and ran.

Visually, he followed her progress as she made her way toward the house. He'd meant to startle her back to her senses, but regretted the necessity as well as the result.

He sighed. 'Twas better she hate him, he supposed. For anything else would surely lead to disappointment and heartache.

CHAPTER FIVE

Jeannette raced into the house and up the stairs as if snarling hellhounds nipped at her feet.

When she reached her bedchamber, she slammed the door shut, then wiped a hand across her mouth in an attempt to rid herself of the kisses that tingled even now upon her passion-swollen lips. Her body still throbbed, flushed with a latent desire she could not seem to control.

Ignoring the sensations, she concentrated on her anger, letting her outrage and affront sweep the other feelings away.

How dare he. To think he'd laid his coarse hands upon her. To think he'd had those crude, Irish-accented lips upon her own, taking her mouth as though he had a right, a claim.

But he had no claim. He was a thief, just as she'd thought him from the start.

Of course, there at the last he'd had her

participation, her agreement as she'd enthusiastically returned his embrace, matching him kiss for kiss, touch for touch. And in those moments she'd been far from a victim.

Appalled by the knowledge, she sank upon the mattress and covered her heated cheeks with her hands.

Gracious, after today she'd never be able to set foot outside the house again for fear of encountering him. And she couldn't complain to her cousins or insist he be dismissed. On what grounds? That he'd kissed her and she'd liked it?

And she *had* liked it, there was no denying the truth.

Did that make her wanton?

Many would say so, considering she'd kissed her fair share of men over the years, starting with a sinfully handsome stable boy when she'd been only sixteen. Yet the dalliance had gone no further than a few innocent pecks, occasional caresses that were more tantalizing than titillating. Until her parents found out and sent the poor boy away. She'd tried to protect him but they would hear none of her words, turning him away without so much as a reference. For long months after, she had felt guilty about it, often wondering what had become of him, and if he had found other acceptable work.

Since then she'd been careful to confine her amorous explorations and curiosity to a select few, who could at least refer to themselves as gentlemen. If one applied oneself, the game of seduction became simple. Stolen moments in the garden. A brief clasp of bare hands behind a conveniently placed pillar or potted palm.

Yet she'd always made sure to keep careful control, making certain nothing went too far. A lady had to protect her virtue and her reputation, after all. Even with Adrian, to whom she'd been engaged, she'd made sure the most they ever shared were a few harmless kisses. Considering he was now her sister's husband, she was relieved. Such a history between them might have proven rather awkward and embarrassing otherwise.

Then there'd been Toddy. She squeezed her eyes tight at the memory of all he had taken. Her love, her pride and so much more.

But no, she told herself, *I will not think of him.* Toddy Markham belonged in her past, and there he would firmly remain. Lowering her hands to her lap, she curled her fingers into loose fists.

How could she have let that Irish rogue

take such advantage of her? How could she have so completely lost her head? If he hadn't broken off their embrace when he had, heaven knows what liberties she might have allowed him to take. There outside in the garden where anyone might have come upon them or spied them through a window.

Gadzooks, she hoped no one *had* seen them. Oh, the shame of it was not to be borne.

A moment later her gaze fell upon the gift O'Brien had given her. When she'd first rushed into the room, she'd tossed it onto the floor. Its utilitarian wrapping appeared quite ordinary lying against the intricate amber and green wool carpeting. Rather out of place inside the delicate, feminine room.

Intrigued despite her best efforts not to be, she crossed and bent to pick it up. Setting the package upon the bed, she untied the rough hemp twine, heavy paper crinkling audibly as she pushed it aside.

Delicate, rose-tinted silk leapt out at her, spilling in a luxurious wash across the light yellow counterpane.

It was a dress, and a lovely one at that, even if the style wasn't quite up to the latest fashion. Unfolding the garment, she held it aloft to inspect it more closely.

With a square, rather low-cut bodice, the

dress had short, straight sleeves decorated along the edges by a narrow pink velvet ribbon. But it was the flounce that caught her attention; the lower quarter of the skirt embroidered with a broad band of exquisitely beautiful flowers, white roses and green leaves in full luxuriant bloom. Like a small garden brought to life. She almost expected to find birds or butterflies hidden among the pattern.

She traced a finger over a single petal, the stitchery smooth beneath her skin.

Magnificent.

And outrageously improper, particularly since it was an evening gown and a rather diaphanous one at that. What sort of man gave an unmarried lady a dress? Most especially a dress like this!

Had he bought it? Or did it belong to some woman he knew?

She felt a sharp frown descend over her face at the idea. Is that where he'd come by the dress? Had he procured it from one of his women? His mistress perhaps or some local widow he'd lately taken to bedding? She was sure he wasn't the type of man to do without female companionship for long, no matter his marital status.

Perhaps she was wealthy, this widow. That would certainly account for the fine quality of the garment. Unless O'Brien made enough as an architect to pay for such a gown. She hadn't the faintest notion what men in such a profession might earn per annum. And if he did earn a reasonable living by middle-class standards, then perhaps the gown didn't belong to his mistress but instead to his wife.

Jeannette drew in a sharp breath. *Was he married?*

She squeezed a handful of the material within her fist, her stomach lurching in a most unpleasant manner. Imagine kissing her half-senseless in the garden, while all the time he had a wife waiting for him at home. For all she knew, he had five children too.

Then again, she didn't know any such thing. She was allowing her thoughts to run amok, to leap to all sorts of wild possibilities and erroneous conclusions. She might be condemning him out of turn. O'Brien might not be married at all and might have no serious amorous ties whatsoever.

Besides, why did she care if he had some other woman?

Because he'd kissed her, that's why!

Striving for calm, she pulled in a pair of slow, deep breaths.

Gazing again at the dress, she reached out

and ran her fingers over the delicate material, tracing a beautifully wrought petal.

It would have to be returned, of course. Propriety permitted no other choice. A great shame really, since the garment was lovely. She pouted for a brief moment before shaking off the emotion.

Suddenly she paused, struck by an interesting notion. True, she had to give back the dress, but perhaps she could turn the situation to her advantage.

Hmm. She would have to think about the possibilities. Indeed, she would.

Darragh ran a set of fingers through his hair and leaned over to consult his drawings.

The last of the north wall was in place, the masons doing a fine job cutting and placing the stone. His crew knew how to put in a full day's work, and if they kept to their present schedule they should be able to complete the wing nearly on time.

He'd hired on a number of local lads, fellows brought in mostly to work the heavy tasks. But many of the others had worked with him on other construction sites in other places. Skilled master craftsmen, they were men who came from all parts of Ireland and beyond. His stucco workers were native Italians, genuine *stuccatori,* who would be traveling all the way from Italy in the next several weeks to finish the intricate interior and exterior plasterwork. And for the cornice work and moldings, he'd commissioned a Prussian woodcrafter whose carvings were nothing short of brilliant. All in all, they were a good lot, his men.

He was too involved in the everyday details, some might say of him, especially for a titled gentleman. As he knew, most architects didn't believe in getting their hands dirty. Many confined themselves to drawing up the elevations, finishing out the plans and renderings, then letting others take them from idea to fact. The actual physical labor would fall to a foreman and a team of laborers and skilled journeymen. But he preferred a more direct approach. That way if problems should arise, he'd be on-site to catch them, to offer a quick solution instead of slowing the work and wasting his clients' money in the waiting.

Others might also condemn him for accepting payment for his talents and services. Many transplanted Anglo-Irish aristocrats looked down upon him for dabbling in trade, as they were wont to call it. They would rather lose their estates from lack of funds than take up a profitable profession.

He saw things differently. The act of saving his family through hard work and ingenuity was preferable to living along the fringes of society as a hanger-on, forcing his siblings and himself to marry for the expediency of money. He refused, believing marriage should be for love, and in no manner related to the making of profit.

So after returning from a long period of study on the Continent, mainly in Italy, he'd put his architectural training to good use. Over the past eight years he'd built quite a reputation for himself, one of which he was justifiably proud. No longer was money in short supply. No longer did he spend his days worrying about the security of his family, about preserving the ancient legacy of his name and his estate.

Squinting up at the sun and the full arc of light just beginning to droop in the sky, he noted 'twas time they were quitting for the day. His crew knew as well, so attuned to the elements none needed watches to judge the hour.

The work site fell quiet as labor slowed then ceased, men climbing down from scaffolding, packing away their tools and starting the walk or wagon ride home.

Darragh had just finished discussing a final item with his chief mason, all the other men having gone home, when a flash of blue caught his attention. Turning his head, he watched Lady Jeannette Brantford saunter into view.

What was the Little Rosebush doing here? She never came to the construction site, avoiding it as if he and his men were a colony of lepers. Yet here she was, looking beautiful as a sunrise over blossoming heather, striding toward him with a gait that set her vivid skirts swaying.

"Good afternoon, Lady Jeannette," he said as she drew to a halt. "What brings you this way?"

"You, Mr. O'Brien, and this."

That's when he noticed the package in her hands and its familiar brown wrapping. Was that the present he'd given her?

She cast a sideways glance at his chief mason, who stood watching them with obvious interest. "Although I had hoped we might have a bit of privacy."

"Oh, aye, of course." He looked across at the older man. "Seamus, what are you still doing here? Go home before the dinner your good wife is cooking for you goes to ruin."

A grin split the mason's face. "Right you are about that. She hates it when I'm late. Good night, then, boss. Miss." Tipping his cap, the other man crossed to gather a few belongings before making his way from the work site.

As soon as he departed, Darragh turned to her. "Now, lass, what's on your mind?"

"This." She thrust the package toward him. "I cannot accept this."

So she *was* returning the gift, he thought, asking his next question aloud. "But why? Was the dress not to your liking?"

"Whether or not I like the dress has nothing to do with the matter. I cannot keep such a gift."

"I thought you'd look a picture in that pink, but if you don't care for the color —"

"It isn't the color."

"The stitchery, then. The dressmaker told me it was done special in Dublin for a lady who failed to . . . well, let's say she ran into financial difficulties and never claimed the garment."

"So the dress isn't your wife's?"

Wife? "What gave you that notion?"

"A gown like this isn't something a single man generally owns."

"I didn't own it, as I just said." He folded his arms over his chest and smiled. *Was she jealous?* He knew he shouldn't, but he discovered he liked the idea. "Is that why you don't want it? You're worried I'm married?"

"Are you?"

He smiled wider, gave a slow shake of his head. "I am not."

An expression that looked vaguely like relief passed over her face. "What about a mistress? Does the dress belong to her?"

His arms dropped to his sides, his lips parting for a long moment before he recovered himself. "And what would a lady like yourself know of such females?"

"Enough to know men keep them. Do you?"

He narrowed his eyes, trying to decide how he should answer, or if he should answer at all. "Not at present, though 'tisn't a proper subject for us to be discussing."

"Which is precisely the problem with this dress. It is not proper." She extended the package again for him to take.

"Why not? 'Tis a beautiful gown."

"Evening gown. And not the kind of gift a man gives a woman, certainly not an unmarried lady."

He felt a frown descend upon his forehead. "I don't see why that matters. Your frocks took harm, so I thought it only logical to find you a new one as a replacement."

"Logical or not, I fear that I cannot accept. Only a loose woman or a wife could do so, however beautiful the dress might be."

Until now, he hadn't considered the issue from her perspective, he'd thought only to buy her something nice. Perhaps she was right, though, and the dress had been ill-considered, no matter how good his intentions.

At least she thought the gown was beautiful.

This time when she pushed the bundle toward him, he accepted. "My apologies, lass. I meant no offense."

She gave a conciliatory nod. "None taken."

Pausing, she gazed over the building site, taking in the stone and wood and metal that would soon be transformed into the new west wing.

"Although," she said, "if you still wish to make amends, there is something I would like."

"And what is that, lass? It would be my pleasure to grant you anything you'd please."

She fixed him with an eager smile before very pointedly gazing again over the building materials. "I believe you know already what it is I would like."

Long seconds passed before he divined

her meaning. The frown settled again on his forehead. "Oh, no, lass, I'll not be giving you that."

"Why not? You said you would be pleased to grant me anything I would like. Well, I would like your men to begin work later in the morning. Nine-thirty, shall we say? It's earlier than I truly prefer, but I don't wish to be unreasonable." She gave him a dazzling, almost coquettish smile.

Oh, she was a crafty one, she was. And if he weren't the one on the other end of her tricks, he'd have admired her skills at maneuvering.

Instead he crossed his arms again and scowled. "Ah, now, lass, you know I can't do that. We've had this conversation before, and of all the things you ask, that's the one I cannot grant. What about a nice bit of jewelry?"

Blue sparks flashed in her eyes. "I don't want jewelry — which, for your information, is every bit as improper as the dress! You know what I want, Mr. O'Brien, now give it to me."

He waited, half expecting her to stomp her feet for good measure. She held steady, her gaze unwavering.

He did the same.

A long minute ticked past, the force of

their impasse almost palpable on the air.

He supposed they could begin a little later, especially since the days would soon begin to shorten, dawn breaking slightly later each morning, creeping upward.

"Seven o'clock," he said.

"Nine."

He shook his head. "Nine is out of the question. Seven. It's the best I can do."

"Seven is barely later at all."

"It's better than you have now. Shall it be seven, then?"

He knew he had her, and she knew he had her too. Her gaze snapped like a lightning storm before she gave a reluctant nod.

"Then we've an agreement. Is there anything else you're after wanting, lass?"

"Yes. Stop calling me lass!" Spinning on her heel, she strode away.

He chuckled and set his hands at his waist, enjoying the way her rounded hips shifted beneath her skirts. "You forgot to say thank you again," he called after her.

Her spine stiffened, her step slowing for just a second before she strode onward. He watched until she disappeared from view. Giving another soft chuckle, he moved to gather his things.

Seven o'clock!

The best he could do was seven o'clock.

Hands curled at her sides, Jeannette strode past a footman as she entered the house. Ignoring the curious look he gave her, she hurried up the stairs to her bedroom.

Well, O'Brien might think she had agreed to his terms, but she hadn't. Not that she'd been foolish enough to pass up the extra half hour's sleep he'd offered. But a mere half hour simply would not do. No, it would not do at all.

She had tried to be reasonable, tried to be amenable to compromise, and look where it had gotten her. Why, he'd barely even budged.

She dropped down into a jade green armchair and gazed unseeing out of the window. She couldn't blithely admit defeat and accept this continued injustice, seemingly grateful for any crumbs he chose to cast her way.

Think, she commanded herself. *Think!*

Knuckles propped beneath her chin, she set herself to the task. Long minutes later, a smile spread like a budding rose across her lips.

Why, yes, she mused, *that just might do. That just might do perfectly.*

CHAPTER SIX

"Rory, did you borrow my plans?"

The head foreman glanced up from his mug of morning tea, then briskly shook his ruddy head. "No, boss. You know I'd never take your drawings, not without telling you first."

Darragh raked frustrated fingers through his hair. "That's what I thought but . . . I've looked everywhere and I can't find them."

"Well now, that doesn't make a bit of sense, does it? Did you put them away as you always do?"

"Aye, rolled them up last night and set them the same place as usual. As you say, it makes no sense. Mayhap one of the carpenters decided to study them first thing and forgot to say."

"Nay, I've seen all the carpenters this morning and not a one of 'em has your plans." Rory took another drink of tea, then set his mug on top of a nearby stack of timber. "Let me ask the lads if they've seen the drawings. I'm sure they'll turn up."

But a full half an hour later, the plans had not been located. Now high and golden overhead, the sun spoke of the maturing hour, negating the necessity of consulting a timepiece. Even so, Darragh snapped open the silver face of his pocket watch, then scowled at the hands.

Blast. Where could they be? Architectural renderings didn't just stand up on their ends, grow feet and walk off.

If the men didn't begin their labor soon, the entire morning would be wasted. Unfortunately most of the men needed his direction in order to progress with their work, and he couldn't give it to them without the bloody plans. Besides, they'd started late to begin with, due to honoring his agreement with Lady Jeannette.

He paused, thinking of her slumbering somewhere inside the house. She wouldn't have taken his drawings, would she? No, 'twas a daft notion, he told himself, brushing the idea aside.

At ten minutes 'til nine, he no longer thought any explanation daft, since the plans were nowhere to be found.

With his usually even temper frayed, he watched in interest as a young maidservant appeared. Crossing the construction site, she paused to speak with one of his men, both of them turning to gaze across at him. Then she began to approach, a small piece of paper clutched tightly in her hand.

Nerves shone in her brown eyes when she drew to a halt before him. "Your pardon, sir. Are you Mr. O'Brien?"

"Aye, I'm O'Brien."

"My lady asked that I give this to you."

He stared down at the note for a long moment before taking the missive from her hand. Opening the page, he began to read.

Dear Mr. O'Brien,

If you are reading this, it must be nearly nine o'clock. I assume by now that you must have noticed that certain papers are missing from your possession. You have only to agree to have your workers commence their day at this same time every morning beginning tomorrow, and I shall immediately return your papers to you.

Yours,
Lady Jeannette Brantford

For a second, Darragh stood utterly mute. A vein throbbed in his forehead, his hand clenching to crumple the note hard inside his fist. He enjoyed the sound as the paper gave a satisfying crackle. Staring at the vellum, he squeezed harder and wadded the note into a snug little ball.

The maid's eyes widened, yet somehow she found the courage to speak. "My lady said I am to . . . to wait for your reply."

He shifted his gaze to her. "Wants a reply, does she? Aye, I'll give her a reply."

What he'd like to do was give her a reply in person. Storm into the house and up to Lady Jeannette's bedroom wherever it might be. Once there, he'd shake her out of her sleep, and after bellowing at her for a minute or two, would soon enough have the stolen plans back in his possession. But he supposed the Merriweathers might not be too keen on the notion of his bursting into their young cousin's bedroom, so a note, he supposed, would have to suffice.

Her crumpled letter lying warm inside his hand, he strode across the yard to his worktable. The worktable where his architectural plans would now be spread out *if he had them!* Jaw tight, he sought out a quill, paper and ink. He settled his knuckles onto one hip and contemplated his response. Moments later, he was scratching out a message.

After sanding the ink dry, he folded the

paper and crossed back to the little, gentle-eyed maid.

He held out the note. "For the lady."

She gave him a faint smile, bobbed a curtsey, then spun to trace her path back around the house.

"What was all that about?" his foreman asked, strolling forward to stop at Darragh's side.

"Nothing but a small delay," Darragh said. "I'll be taking one of the horses and riding home. I've a spare set of plans there, not as complete as the others, but they'll do. In the meanwhile, tell the men to take their dinner break early and be ready to work when I return."

"Aye, boss."

Jeannette stretched against the sheets, slowly opening her eyes as Betsy drew back the bedroom curtains to let in the morning sunshine.

"Hmm," she murmured on a yawn. "What time is it?"

"Ten after nine, my lady."

"Really?" She came fully awake and sat up with a slight bounce. "Did you give my missive to him?"

"Yes, my lady."

"And? Did he give a response?"

Betsy nodded her head and picked up a folded sheet of paper from the vanity top. "Wrote it out while I waited. Here it is, my lady."

Jeannette reached out and accepted the note. "Thank you, Betsy."

"You're welcome. He's a handsome one, if I might be bold enough to say."

"Hmm, if you like that type. I really hadn't noticed," Jeannette lied. Fiddling with the note, she rubbed her thumb across the surface but made no effort to open it. "Betsy, I believe I'll take tea and toast here in my room."

"Oh, of course, my lady. I'll return in a thrice."

Jeannette waited until the maid closed the door behind her before she opened O'Brien's reply.

Bold and rich as the lyrical timber of his voice, his words flowed across the page . . .

Lady Jeannette,

I hope you enjoyed your extra rest this morning. Now that you've had it, return what belongs to me. If you do so immediately, we'll say no more on the matter. If the plans are not in my possession by the end of the day, I promise your days will henceforth begin very early indeed.

Your Servant,
O'Brien

Beast, she thought, crushing the vellum in her hand. Trying to bully her, was he? Well, it wasn't going to work.

Or was it?

She chewed the corner of her lip and thought of the long, thick roll of architectural drawings hidden beneath the armoire. Should she give them back?

Closing her eyes, she listened to the lovely silence outside. How could she give that up? Although when she considered it, she supposed her solution was only a temporary one at best.

Obviously he was quite angry.

But without the plans, what could he do? Besides, his workers must be enjoying the day off. Who was she to deny them their pleasure?

Buoyed by the idea, she smiled. Let them have today and one more morning besides. Tomorrow — after nine — she would have Betsy return the plans.

Until then, she was going to savor the quiet.

Despite her resolve, she decided it might

be wisest to avoid contact with Mr. O'Brien for the next day or so. A journey away from the house, she mused, would be just the thing. Not only would it put her out of trouble's potential path but it would help alleviate the constant boredom from which she suffered here in the Irish wilderness.

With a little coaxing and several encouraging smiles, she jollied Wilda into ordering the carriage so the two of them could drive into Inistioge. Excited just to be out of the house, she entered the village in an optimistic mood. Quaint and charmingly pretty, the little town was settled around a square, many of the buildings quite old, their origin dating all the way back to Norman times, or so Wilda informed her. A shame Violet couldn't see the place; her history-loving twin would have been in raptures.

Yet attractive as the village might be, it was still only a village. Having grown used to the immense array of goods available in London, she found the shops sadly devoid of stock, not even up to the standard of the English villages near Papa's estate in Surrey.

The local millinery sported a miserable selection of ribbons and one of the ugliest groupings of bonnets she had ever seen. She had no better luck at the village dressmakers, where the fashion book the proprietress shuffled out contained patterns nearly two years out of date!

Still, in the end she managed to come away with some beautiful Irish lace, hand-crocheted by the nuns from a nearby convent. She purchased several lengths that she planned to give as little gifts to her sister and several female friends.

Just about the time they were ready to leave for home, Wilda spotted a pair of acquaintances, and Jeannette soon found herself invited to share tea and a strong-tasting local confection, known as porter cake, in the company of her cousin's chatty friends.

Evening was settling over the horizon when the carriage pulled into the main drive at Brambleberry Hall. Due to the advanced hour, dinner needed to be delayed, Wilda sending word to the kitchen about the last-minute change. Cuthbert, as usual, was buried somewhere among his plants and research and would barely notice the change, Wilda assured her with an affectionate sigh. Wilda would send one of the footmen to collect dear Bertie at the appropriate moment.

Upstairs in her bedchamber, Jeannette drew off her bonnet and gloves, then moved to show Betsy her purchases. Her mood indulgent, she decided to give her maid a yard of the lace. "You can use it to trim a new hat or maybe one of your best dresses."

"Oh, thank you ever so much, my lady," Betsy declared, smiling as she admired the delicate workmanship of the lace.

"You are most welcome. Now, if you would please, help me change out of this gown so I am not late for dinner."

"Right away, my lady."

The remainder of the evening passed quietly, Cousin Cuthbert providing a touch of amusement, encouraged to share a few stories about his childhood in England and reminiscences of Jeannette's mother as a girl.

Later that evening, she went to bed content in the knowledge that she would enjoy a second sound night's rest. Though, come morning, she knew, she would have to concede defeat and return Mr. O'Brien's architectural renderings to him, so work on the new wing could continue apace.

As she was settling down to sleep, she wondered where O'Brien was tonight, and what he was doing. Probably sitting in front of a rustic fireplace, stewing over her continued defiance. Well, tomorrow she would give him a delightful surprise. Mayhap she would even deliver the plans to him herself just to witness his expression. This time he'd be the one needing to thank her.

Smiling at the thought, she fell asleep and dreamed of Darragh O'Brien's kisses.

Darragh sipped a small whiskey from a heavy, cut-crystal Waterford tumbler and relaxed into a wide, leather armchair in Lawrence McGarrett's comfortable study. A friend since their days at Trinity College, Lawrence had invited Darragh to stay at his country estate while Darragh "played with his building blocks," as Lawrence liked to call Darragh's architectural pursuits. Presently, Lawrence was away at his townhouse in Dublin, leaving Darragh alone, save for the servants.

Drinking another fiery swallow, he thought about his day, and the fact that sundown had come and gone, and Lady Jeannette hadn't returned the plans.

Stubborn minx.

By rights, she deserved a sound smack on that attractive backside of hers for her childish behavior. Her antics had cost him a half day's work. But the loss hadn't been too damaging. He'd found the spare plans here at the house, and set the men to work through the long afternoon.

He'd half expected her to fly out of the house in surprise at resumption of the construction noise, until he'd learned from one of the Merriweathers' servants that the ladies had taken the carriage and driven into Inistioge. When they still hadn't returned by early evening, he decided to let the lads leave a little beforetimes, an idea percolating in his mind.

Tossing back the last of his whiskey, he grinned and set down his glass. He'd best get to bed, he told himself, for tomorrow promised to be a very interesting day.

CHAPTER SEVEN

Jeannette's eyes shot open to squint into the first frail rays of dawn's light. Groggy and disoriented, she didn't initially understand what had disturbed her. A crash reverberated outside, followed by a pair of bangs. Abruptly, her momentary confusion cleared.

Workers.

Sitting upright in bed, she peered through the gray shadows toward the mantel clock, barely able to make out the hands. One seemed to be pointed straight up, the other straight down. She stared harder.

Six o'clock!

On a weary grumble, she flung back the covers and leapt out of bed, her bare feet moving quickly across the cool, soft wool carpeting. She stared again at the clock, close enough this time to see there was no mistake.

It *was* six o'clock — or six-o-one, to be

precise — and O'Brien and his crew were out there making enough racket to rouse the dead. But how could they be, when she hadn't returned the building plans? Yesterday, the workers had been unable to proceed without them, so how were they managing without the plans this morning? Had O'Brien somehow managed to gain access to her bedchamber and locate his architectural drawings? Surely not. The servants would have noticed if her cousins' architect had barged into the house and conducted a search of her room.

Rushing to the wardrobe just in case the impossible had occurred, she dropped down onto her hands and knees to check beneath the massive piece of furniture. But there they were, the thick roll of papers, exactly where she had left them.

Flummoxed, she sat back on her haunches, flinching as some heavy object crashed to the ground outside. Seconds later, a yawn caught her, moisture welling in her eyes.

Knowing she had to put an end to her misery, she reached an arm under the armoire and dragged out the plans. Climbing to her feet, she took a moment to slip into her dressing gown and silk bedroom slippers before running a brush quickly through her hair and tying her tresses back with a ribbon at her nape.

Acting purely on impulse, she retrieved the plans, opened the door and moved out into the hallway.

" . . . once we're finished here we'll be able to move the scaffolding and start on the last section at the north end," Darragh said, gesturing a hand toward the skeleton of the growing building and the workmen who climbed and clamored over it with the speed and agility of a troop of acrobats.

"The window glass is due to arrive by late week," Rory volunteered. "Had word that the cargo's loaded and on its way."

Darragh nodded. "Good. If the schedule holds, it won't be long before we have need of that glass."

They talked for another couple of minutes before his foreman gave a friendly nod and strode away. Once the other man had gone, Darragh located his mug of strong black Irish tea and raised it to his lips.

"*Psst,* Mr. O'Brien."

Lady Jeannette.

Pausing, he glanced around to locate her, hastily swallowing the hot tea in his mouth to keep it from scalding his tongue.

"Up here," she said in a loud whisper.

Following her voice, he peered through the early-dawn light just breaking over the horizon. His eyes widened when he located her, balanced on her elbows as she leaned out of an open upstairs window. Dressed in some muted color, she appeared as pale and ethereal as a ghost. Only, Jeannette Brantford was much too lovely to be a ghost, and much too alive.

A quick glance over his shoulder verified that none of the other men had noticed her — at least not yet. Setting down his mug, he strode forward.

"What are you about, lass?" he called softly once he stood beneath her window.

She met his gaze. "You know exactly what I'm about. Just as you know what time it is."

He couldn't help but grin. When he'd told the men to start work early this morning, he'd anticipated rousing a reaction from Lady Jeannette. He just hadn't thought he'd spark one quite this quickly. "Wake you up, did we?"

She flicked a look into the distance, toward his crew, failing to answer his rhetorical question. "We can't talk here. Do you know the east garden door?"

"I believe I know the one you're meaning."

"Meet me there in five minutes." Her head disappeared from view, runners above squeaking faintly as she yanked the window closed.

He stood for a moment staring up at the spot where she'd been, a fresh smile playing around his lips. After a quick check to make certain the men were fully occupied, he turned to stroll around the house.

Jeannette was waiting for him when he arrived, the door unlocked and eased open a few inches to give him access to a narrow hallway that ran between one of the servants' staircases and the side garden.

He moved forward to enter. Only as he slid past did he notice her attire. Or rather, her lack of attire. Not that she wasn't properly covered — her flesh concealed from throat to ankle — but she was dressed in nightclothes.

Thin, pink, silky nightclothes that conformed to the luscious shape of her hips and breasts, leaving his imagination to run riot over what delights must lay beneath. Flowing like spun corn silk, her waist-long hair was gathered back, vibrant skeins of pale gold restrained by nothing more than a simple white ribbon.

A quick tug, he mused, and all that glory would spill free, strands cascading into his waiting hands. He could imagine touching her hair, threading his fingers through the tresses to satisfy himself that they were every bit as satiny soft as they appeared. Then he would lean near, breathe in the spring-sweet fragrance he knew would lie there, before turning his attentions to her skin, her lips.

He wouldn't mind enjoying another kiss from her perfect mouth, he thought. Or pulling her into his embrace, pleasuring her until she quivered and sighed and forgot all about the reason she had asked him here.

Instead of doing any of those things, he crossed his arms, tucked his hands tight and took a single, prudent step away.

Plainly unaware of his mental wanderings, Jeannette turned to close the door, then spun back to face him.

He waited while she gathered herself to speak.

On an inhale, she began. "There is no use circling around the subject, since we both know why I asked you here. I concede the point to you this morning, Mr. O'Brien. By awakening me — and everyone else in the household, I might add — you have made your revenge quite apparent."

" 'Twasn't revenge. Just following through on my promise, since you failed to return what you stole from me."

"I stole nothing."

He raised a chastening eyebrow.

"I merely *borrowed* your plans." She reached around and held out a familiar roll of parchment. "I would have returned them to you later this morning, you know, but since you were callous enough to awaken me at this unholy hour, I decided to give them back now."

Restraining his surprise, he accepted the offering.

"Apparently you must not really have needed them," she observed.

"Oh, I have need of them."

A slight frown creased her delicate forehead. "But your men are already working —"

"I had a second set. My thanks for the return of this set, though, since the other plans aren't nearly as detailed."

Her lips parted, ocean-hued eyes enlarging slightly as if she hadn't considered such a possibility. Seconds later, her mouth snapped shut in obvious consternation. He nearly laughed, watching the byplay of emotions flicker like a pantomime across her face. She recovered her composure soon enough, regal as a queen in spite of the intimate nature of her garments.

"Well then," she said, "now that you are

once more in possession of your property, I assume you won't mind telling your workers to cease their labors for an hour or two."

"Want to go back to your bed, do you?"

She nodded, raising a hand to hide a yawn. "It's barely light outside. Were it quiet, I'm sure I could drift off again."

He imagined her upstairs in her bedchamber, pausing to shrug out of her dressing gown and ease between the sheets. How beautiful she would look lying there. Her golden hair spread like honey across the pillows. A sleep-warmed flush rouging her skin, her breasts rising and falling beneath a gossamer drape of thin, pink silk.

Desire curled through him and settled low, a warmth he ought not indulge, heating his bone and blood. Giving himself a hard mental slap, he banished the fantasy.

"The men are working," he stated in a crisp tone that came out rougher than he'd intended. "I can't send them home now."

"Let them have a break, then. I am sure they would enjoy eating a morning meal."

"They've already eaten breakfast, and none of them needs another. They'll stay."

She crossed her arms at her waist and tapped a slippered foot, looking for a moment as if she was going to argue. "Very well. I suppose getting any more rest this morning is a hopeless cause at best. But tomorrow you will begin at the regular time, correct?"

"Half-six, that's right."

Her arms dropped to her sides. "*Half-six?* But that is the old hour, not the one we settled upon. You said seven o'clock, which I might remind you, sir, is still much too early in the day. We had an agreement."

"You dishonored our agreement with your fine bit of thievery. So half-six it'll be."

Darragh didn't know what devil prompted him to tease her. But he had to confess he enjoyed watching her eyes flash, her skin grow flush as she ruffled up in indignation. Besides, she deserved a few minutes' discomfort for all the trouble she'd caused, he decided. Let her stew for a tad, then he would once again agree to their negotiated hour and leave her grateful for the gesture.

"*Ooh,*" she exclaimed, her lower lip protruding in an attractive pout. "That's not fair."

"I can have the men arrive again at six, if half after won't do."

"Don't you dare, you . . . you Irish bully."

He tossed back his head on a laugh. "Seems if you really wanted your sleep, you'd do better trying to persuade me."

"Persuade you? Persuade you how?"

He shrugged. "You tell me. You strike me as the kind of lass who knows how to cajole a lad."

She paused, tipping her head at a slight angle. "I might know how to charm a gentleman on occasion. But then, you, sir, are no gentleman."

"As you take great pains to remind me. Still, any man likes being pleased. If you'll recall, there's an old saying about drawing more flies with sweet than sour."

"So you're craving something sweet, are you?"

Aye, he was, he mused as he swept his eyes over her lush, feminine form, unconsciously letting his gaze linger far longer than he ought. On the next blink, he forced his eyes aside, knowing he needed to call a halt to this dangerous conversation before things spiraled out of hand, much as he was enjoying the game.

Before he opened his mouth, she spoke.

"Very well," she said in a gentle purr that glided over him like a lover's caress. "Mr. O'Brien, would you be a darling and *please* have your men begin work later in the morning? Eight-thirty, shall we say?"

Displaying a set of beautiful, pearly white teeth, she graced him with a smile that could have melted a glacier. It certainly melted him, his heart pumping double time, his loins aching, breath catching like a fist at the base of his throat. He swallowed down the lump and listened to the single word whispering inside his head.

Yes.

Yes? he wondered. Yes to what?

To Jeannette Brantford, that's what.

Gazing at that smile, that voice, those jewel-toned eyes, a man might quickly find himself agreeing to almost anything. 'Twas easy to understand why she led a charmed existence, since he was sure she rarely failed to get her way. All she need do was crook her little finger and flutter those long, pale gold lashes.

But he'd never been a man given to losing his head over a beautiful face, and he wasn't about to succumb now, no matter how agreeable her reception might be.

Smiling back, he leaned nearer, gratified to notice her eyes soften beneath the attention of his gaze. "Prettily done, lass," he said, "and a fair temptation it is to do as you'd like. But the work won't get done by keeping late hours. As I told you before, seven of the clock is the best I can do."

Her smile faded as his meaning sank in, all traces of pleasure wiped clean. "But you haven't budged at all."

145

"I'm granting you an hour. What more do you want?"

"What I want I will not stoop to say. Why, you conniving toad, convincing me to beg."

He linked his hands behind his back. "I don't believe toads know how to connive. And as I recall, I didn't hear any begging. A little cajoling perhaps, but no begging."

"You tricked me."

"Not a bit, lass. All I said was that a man likes to be asked nicely. I never said if you did it I'd agree to your wishes."

"Why, you . . . and to think I returned your plans. I should have burned them instead."

His jovial humor dropped away. "You ought to be glad you didn't, or there would be a heavy reckoning to pay."

"You don't scare me," she declared, tilting her chin upward in defiance.

"Be careful, or I might."

"By doing what, pray tell?"

"Oh, I can think of a few choice things. Such as having the men begin laboring at five."

"But it's dark then. They wouldn't be able to see."

"They'll light lanterns." And complain and moan and grumble about the predawn hour, but he wouldn't tell her that.

"Even my cousins wouldn't like being awakened, not that early."

"I'll explain that it can't be helped if we're to finish on time. The Merriweathers are amiable folk, I'm certain they'll make allowances."

A flood of emotions raced across her expressive features, chief among them annoyance and frustration. To his own annoyance, fresh arousal stirred inside him. He found her more appealing than ever, anger only heightening her vibrant beauty. Prudence made him tighten his hands behind his back, knowing so much as a light touch would be all the impetus he required to reach out and take her in his arms.

"Shall it be seven again, then, lass?" he prodded.

An unladylike growl rumbled in her throat as she came forward and swept past him, the skirts of her dressing gown swirling in a tempest around her ankles.

"I'll take that as a yes," he called toward her retreating back.

Moments later a door slammed, echoing through the house.

In relief, Darragh loosened his hands and smiled.

Upstairs in her room, Jeannette flopped

onto her bed and gave vent to the hurt and anger pouring through her.

O'Brien had played her, and played her well, she thought.

Beast.

Imagine manipulating her that way. Luring her with his charming smile, rakish good looks and clever words. For a minute, she'd actually found herself liking him, enjoying their light flirtation no matter how imprudent it might be. But then he'd shown his true stripes, and made mock of her needs and wishes.

The man had no heart. No compassion.

Couldn't he see she was exhausted? She didn't want much. Just the simple right to slumber a few hours past dawn, as any respectable lady might expect to do. Was that so great a thing to ask?

It wasn't as though she had not made concessions. Before arriving in Ireland, she couldn't remember the last time she had awakened earlier than ten o'clock, and even that hour had proven a hardship some mornings when she had lived in London. Late-night parties, dancing until the wee hours, those were the only times she had come close to seeing the sun rise — when she was climbing *into* bed, not crawling out.

Inurned here in the country as she was,

though, she supposed she could try retiring earlier. Her cousins certainly dozed off betimes, sometimes while sitting in their chairs in the drawing room after dinner — Wilda nodding off over her sewing, Cuthbert rousing at infrequent intervals to the sound of his own snuffling snores as he attempted to read one of his botany books. If she hadn't found being trapped with them so upsetting, their antics would be funny.

But her cousins were old and couldn't help their frail nature. She was young and vibrant and enjoyed late evenings, even if there were no parties and scarcely anything entertaining to do. Besides, she didn't want to give up her Town hours, since it would be the final capitulation to her fate.

Weariness crashed over her, a jaw-popping yawn catching her unawares. Moisture pooled in the corners of her eyes. O'Brien's fault, she grumbled to herself, pulling the pillow over her head. Closing her eyes, she tried to sleep.

But the effort proved futile, the incessant buzz of voices and thuds and thumps raking across her nerves like the pricking of a thousand needles. Uttering an oath that would have made her brother grin in admiration, she flung herself out of bed and across to the bellpull.

Tired and out-of-sorts, she rang for Betsy.

A warm bath and breakfast helped a bit — eggs, ham and a large pot of hot chocolate going a long way toward improving her mood. Afterward, she sat down at a small, satinwood writing desk to pen a letter to her mother. But even as she watched the ink dry on the page, she tore it up, realizing how desperate and lonely she sounded. She would not plead, she vowed. Her parents had banished her here, and they should be the ones to ask her to come home.

Near noon, the house filled with a different sort of noise as Wilda's gray-haired female friends arrived for their bimonthly card party.

"Would you care to join us, dear?" Wilda inquired, raising her voice to be heard over her friends' endless chatter.

"No, thank you, cousin. I believe I shall go outside to take some air."

"All right, dear. Have a nice time."

After exchanging a few pleasantries with the ladies, Jeannette returned upstairs and had Betsy help her change into one of her sturdiest gowns, made of Devonshire brown checkered gingham. Onto her feet, she slipped comfortable dark leather half boots, then perched a pretty but practical straw bonnet on her head.

Deciding she might enjoy more than an ordinary walk, she located her watercolor paper, paints and paintbrushes, and set out for the low, gently rolling hills that lay beyond the house. Once she located the perfect spot, she spread out a lawn blanket, set up her equipment and began to paint.

None of her London friends would have believed their eyes had they seen her. Nor would they have countenanced the fact that she could enjoy a day spent alone, painting the rugged Irish landscape. She could scarcely believe it herself, but by the end of the afternoon she realized she'd passed the first truly happy hours she'd known since arriving in this wild new land.

And she couldn't deny that she was pleased with her painting of a weathered Celtic stone cross standing ancient and lonely in a field. Magenta and purple heather and golden bog grass grew up in clumps around the old gray stone, patches of vibrant green scattered as they ranged off into the distance.

So pleased was she, in fact, that she decided to paint the next afternoon as well, carrying along a light nuncheon she had asked Cook to pack for her.

She was stippling grass-green paint onto her canvas when a movement off to one side caught her attention. Her lips thinned as she recognized the vigorous man striding a few yards distant.

O'Brien.

What was *he* doing here?

True to his word, he'd begun work this morning at precisely seven o'clock, but the extra few minutes' sleep had done nothing to mollify her wounded feelings. On a silent sniff, she pretended not to see him.

Out of the corner of her eye, she saw him slow, then pause as if deciding whether or not he ought to approach her. Mentally, she gave him a push to send him on his way. But he ignored the invisible suggestion and strolled in her direction. Studiously, she applied her paintbrush to the watercolor paper.

When he drew to a halt, his tall form loomed over her in a way that made her breath hitch beneath her breasts despite the respectful distance he'd left between them.

"A fine good day to you, Lady Jeannette," he greeted in a deep cheerful voice, his Irish accent playing a seductive melody.

Determinedly, she continued to paint.

"Don't mind me. I'll just stand here all quiet-like and watch you for a while."

She swished out her sable brush in a jar of water before twirling the ends of it across a small block of brown paint on her palette. "You are in my light."

He took a pair of large sideways steps that brought him closer. "Better?"

"No." Heart beating fast, she steadied her hand, worried she might bobble the next stroke if she was not careful.

" 'Tis a fetching scene you've chosen," he remarked, making no effort to move. "The land hereabouts is enchanting, all fertile and green. Not like my home county in the West, where things are a bit more wild and rough. You'd have a fine time painting there, though, with the scent of the Shannon in your nose and the wind whipping at your skirts."

The pride in his home rang out, along with a faint hint of longing for the land he obviously missed. For a second she wondered what it must look like, his home. But why did she care? she wondered, shaking off her curiosity. After all, it wasn't as though she would ever have an opportunity to see the place.

She shot him a look. "Have you sought me out for a reason, Mr. O'Brien, or are you merely here to gloat?"

"Now, lass, don't take on so about yesterday. I've forgotten all about it."

As well he might, since events had turned

so neatly in his favor.

"I was walking," he continued, "as I sometimes do when I've issues to think through, and there you were. I couldn't help but stop, not after seeing you with your bright blue skirts spread all around, your hair shining golden and pretty as a flower. I'm surprised the bees and butterflies haven't been whizzing about, trying to steal a sip of nectar."

A warm bubble rose in the vicinity of her heart before she could prevent the reaction, her paintbrush drooping in her hand. She caught herself quickly and issued a stern internal rebuke.

It wouldn't do, she warned, to let O'Brien beguile her, not again. She must be careful to guard against him, against any man who might mesmerize her with a debonair smile or the music of a well-turned phrase. Toddy had been such a man, luring her with honeyed words and false promises. Seducing her into believing in a love whose core had been hollow, whose happiness had been built from a lie.

Not that O'Brien was actually trying to seduce her. She knew he was only teasing and playing, like a cat who'd found a lively mouse. Well, she was done being the mouse. From now on, she planned to be the cat.

Dipping her brush into the water and paint, she touched the bristles to the paper.

O'Brien made no comment about her lack of a reply, standing for another long moment before taking a step forward. "I think I'll have a seat, if you don't mind."

Before she could tell him she did mind, he was sinking down into the grass at the edge of the tan blanket she had spread beneath her, lowering his powerful body with a grace uncommon for a man of his height. Relaxing onto an elbow, he reached out and broke off a long green blade.

Casually, he twirled the sliver of grass between his fingers. Elegant fingers, she noticed. Elegant hands. Well shaped and patrician despite the calluses riding their tips.

"You've a gifted touch with the paints," he observed after a time, gesturing toward her watercolor with the grass blade. "Have you done many others?"

"Paintings, you mean?"

"Aye."

"Of course. Painting is a skill all accomplished young ladies must master."

"Well, it strikes me you're better than most. You have a grand talent, a grand talent indeed."

A fresh bubble of warmth rose inside her

chest. "Do you really think so?"

"Aye, I most sincerely do." He smiled then and made her heart spring like a lemming flinging itself into the sea.

More unsettled than she wished, Jeannette swished her brush clean, then dabbed at a new color.

While she did, O'Brien stretched out on his back and linked his hands together behind his head.

"What are you doing?" she squeaked.

"Relaxing, lass."

"But surely you cannot mean to remain here . . . like that?"

"I was, aye. Considering how well we've been getting on, I thought we might attempt a truce. For a few minutes at least."

"We have no need of a truce, Mr. O'Brien. We are not, after all, at war."

"Are we not, lass? I am profoundly glad to hear it. Go on with your painting, then, while I lie here and rest my eyes."

Rest his eyes!

Her own eyes narrowed in speculation, watching him to see if he was watching her. He didn't seem to be, though, his lids remaining firmly closed. What was he up to? He must have some sort of devious plot up his sleeve. Some new scheme he planned to spring.

But as she alternately watched him and tried to paint, the minutes began to pass. First one, then two, then more, without any discernible movement from him other than the even rise and fall of his chest as he breathed. After five minutes, she began to realize he meant what he said.

Unable to restrain the impulse, she let her gaze roam his length, saliva pooling in her mouth at the sight.

She swallowed.

He really was the most absurdly handsome man, she thought. Oh, not in a classical way — he was far too roughly hewn to ever compete with *Adonis* or *David* — but Darragh O'Brien was beautiful all the same. It really was patently unfair that a commoner should possess such splendid looks. Think how dashing he would appear dressed in proper gentleman's attire. She closed her eyes for a moment to imagine it — cutaway coat, waistcoat and tailored pantaloons.

He could make any female swoon, and likely had at that.

Dash it all. What was wrong with her? She should be ignoring him, not ogling him. Neither should her pulse be speeding like a thoroughbred galloping in the final race at Ascot. She didn't like it that he could make her heart do such a thing.

She was the cat, remember?

Some cat, she conceded on a silent exhale.

If he could cause this kind of reaction after so short an acquaintance, just think of the havoc he might wreak after prolonged exposure.

Even more insidious was his undeniable charm, the charisma he exuded like some intoxicating cologne. He might irritate and sometimes anger her all the way down to her toes, but even she had to confess there was more to him than an attractive face and physique.

She'd seen enough of the renovation he was doing for her cousins to realize the depth of his intelligence and talent. He must be educated, she imagined, since architecture required more than an ability to draw and dream. He had to have studied mathematics and physics, as well as history and the arts. She wondered where he had apprenticed, and with whom.

Added to that, he had a glib and clever tongue, even if he was an unprincipled rogue who delighted in plaguing her. Yet he possessed cunning too, and that was a gift she could not help but admire, since ingenuity was something upon which she liked to pride herself. Were he of noble birth, she might well have found herself liking him despite his varied faults. Were he in any way suitable, she might not be trying so very hard to push him away.

Heavens, what a notion! She must have been out here in this field too long and taken too much sun. Clearly, it was making her giddy.

She stared at him through assessing eyes. Was he asleep? She decided to test the matter. "Mr. O'Brien," she called in a soft voice.

Silence.

"Are you awake, Mr. O'Brien?" she whispered.

This time he snuffled slightly and rolled his head, but his eyes stayed firmly closed.

Why, look at that, he *was* asleep.

It absolutely was not fair. *She* was the one being deprived of a proper night's rest, and yet *he* was the one sleeping. And on her lawn blanket, of all things! She ought to give that big, wide shoulder of his a nudge. Or sprinkle a brushful of water droplets across his slumbering face. That would wake him up quickly enough.

But tempting as both notions might be, she couldn't bring herself to do either. He looked far too endearing, almost boyish with a lock of hair fallen across his forehead.

But just because she wasn't going to retaliate did not mean she had forgiven him for hoodwinking her yesterday. Nor did it mean she had given up her quest to get a few extra hours' sleep in the mornings. She was still puzzling over the possibilities, content for now to let him believe she had conceded defeat.

Let him sleep. He just might need the strength for later.

Turning back, she lifted her brush and began to paint.

Blue sky and cottony clouds were beginning to take form on her watercolor paper when a sharp sound pierced the quiet. Barking. Canine barking, carrying to her on the gentle breeze.

She stilled and scanned the fields as the exuberant sound grew louder. O'Brien woke, rubbing a hand over his face as he sat up next to her. Just then, a large animal came into view.

"Vitruvius," she murmured.

"Aye, 'tis the lad back from chasing rabbits in the fields. He adores chasing rabbits." O'Brien sprang to his feet. "Don't worry, though, I'll head him off before he realizes you're here and comes to give you a big, wet kiss."

"Oh, good gracious."

But it was nearly too late as the dog pounded through the meadow grass toward them, his thin tail held high and waving in elation. Sighting Jeannette, he charged faster.

O'Brien, however, stopped him with a shrill whistle and a firm command. Torn as always between his own wants and his need to obey, the dog stood, quivering with pent-up excitement, his eyes locked upon her.

"Have you any meat in that basket of yours?" O'Brien asked.

"What? You mean my nuncheon?"

"Aye."

"Cook packed fried chicken, I believe, but —"

"That'll do splendidly, assuming you don't want mud all over that fine gown of yours. A chicken leg should take his mind off wanting to come over for a pet and a snuggle."

A pet and a snuggle! The great oaf of a dog meant well, she supposed, but he had no regard for a lady's wardrobe. Desperate to protect her gown, she dug into the hamper and withdrew the first piece of poultry she found. A thigh.

"Here." She passed the chicken into O'Brien's waiting hand.

Scenting food, the dog's nose twitched, his tail wagging harder.

"Stay," O'Brien commanded. When Vitruvius remained in place, O'Brien peeled a hunk of meat off the bone and fed it to the animal. "Good lad. Good dog."

Freeing the rest of the thigh meat from the bone, O'Brien tossed it down onto the ground for his pet. Vitruvius gobbled it up in two quick bites, tongue lolling out afterward in happy contentment.

O'Brien strode toward her. "That should settle him for now. I think your skirts are safe from muddy paws."

He raised a finger to his mouth and gave it a lick. "Hmm, good chicken." Stepping closer, he bent forward to inspect the contents of the open wicker hamper. "Looks like the Merriweathers' cook gave you more than a hearty serving. I can't imagine a delicate lass like you will be able to eat all this." Bending down, he set the denuded chicken bone back onto the serving plate. "You don't mind if I help myself to a drumstick, do you now?"

Before she could comment, he took a piece and carried it to his lips, biting deep with obvious enjoyment.

"Oh, please," she drawled sarcastically, "do help yourself."

He swallowed and grinned, then to her astonishment, reached into the hamper to grab another piece, lifting out a big breast this time. "My thanks. 'Tis delicious."

"You, sir, are outrageous."

He winked. "Aye, lass, but you know you love it."

Mouth dropping open, she stared.

"Well," he pronounced, " 'tis time I was off. My appreciation for the excellent company and the delicious food. It's been a rare treat." With a wicked glimmer sparkling in his vivid blue eyes, he grinned, then turned to set off at a brisk pace. A shrill whistle issued from O'Brien's lips, Vitruvius springing up to race after his master.

Crossing her arms, Jeannette watched the procession of man and dog and purloined chicken until the trio disappeared over a rise.

Loved his outrageous behavior indeed, she sniffed, shaking her head. *What rubbish.*

But as she dug a hand into the hamper for her own piece of chicken, she wondered if he might not be right.

CHAPTER EIGHT

"Gather up those as well and be quiet about it," Jeannette whispered, barely able to see her maid in the dark.

"But they're dreadfully heavy, my lady."

"I know, but if we moved the others, we can move these. Now, let's get this done before we're caught."

Jeannette glanced around, left then right, checking to make sure they weren't being observed. One never knew when a footman might sneak out for a late-night stroll and find more than he'd bargained for.

"Follow me." Weighed down, knees near to buckling, she and her maid crossed the lawn, each of them hauling a separate wooden box. "Almost there," she panted to encourage the girl at her back.

A long excruciating minute later, they reached their destination, boxes hurriedly placed onto the ground.

"Well, that wasn't so bad, was it?" she

declared with false exuberance.

Betsy remained silent for a long moment. "You wouldn't have made Jacobs come out here with you in the dead of night."

"What have I said about not mentioning that person's name in my hearing? But you are correct, I could not have trusted Jacobs to aid me tonight. But I can trust you, can't I, Betsy?"

"Yes, ma'am." The other girl smiled.

"Quite right. Now, let's get this finished."

"Are you sure about this, my lady?"

"Of course I'm sure," Jeannette said, squelching any internal doubts. O'Brien would be irritated as a rooster whose tail feathers had been plucked, she knew, but she couldn't imagine her little maneuver bringing anything but smiles to the faces of his workmen. Really, she was giving them all a delightful gift.

"Come, let us finish."

The pair of them worked for nearly an hour, beads of perspiration dampening each of their foreheads by the time their labors were done.

"Well, that's the lot," Jeannette announced. "Now it's off to bed for the pair of us. You may have an extra three hours' personal time in the morning."

"Oh, thank you, my lady."

"In fact, sleep as late as you wish. I know I shall be doing the same."

"I tell you, they've gone missing."

An early-morning chill bit through Darragh's jacket and shirtsleeves, the first full rays of sun just beginning to drive away the cold, grass glistening with a slick coating of dew.

Ignoring the temperature and the damp, Darragh planted his fists at his waist, scowled down at his principle foreman. "Well, they can't have grown feet and walked off on their own. They're tools, for Christ's sake, and who around these parts would want to steal tools? Anyone with half a measure of sense knows they'd never manage to profit from such a deal even if they could locate an idiot foolish enough to trade in stolen goods. The bother alone of hauling them would be discouragement enough."

Rory shrugged a pair of burly shoulders. "If the tools weren't pinched, then where'd they go? I've asked all the men and none of them knows a blessed thing. Packed up yestereve, same as they always do, before they leave for the night."

Darragh released a sigh, aware his foreman was right. He'd checked the work site himself last night, making certain it was tidy and secure before he'd headed off for his lodgings. The toolboxes had been exactly where they should be, he distinctly recalled, stacked neatly inside the ground-level mudroom.

Yet this morning when he'd arrived, the first thing he'd heard was talk about the missing equipment. Without tools, no work could be done. Without tools, his men would stand idle, the job delayed, perhaps seriously. And if the tools remained missing, they would have to be replaced at great trouble and expense by a trip to Dublin.

The most obvious culprit had to be one of his workers, but that Darragh refused to believe. None of his men could be responsible. His people were honest, even the local boys hired on for this one specific job. There must be another answer, another explanation.

Turning the knob, he studied the lock to the mudroom. "The door doesn't appear to have been tampered with. There'd be some sign if thieves had picked the lock or forced the door."

The foreman nodded. "Odd, it is. Almost as if somebody from inside did the deed. But there's no sense to that. Who in the house would have cause to do such a thing?"

Darragh paused, the other's man's statement coming as a revelation.

Someone in the house? Someone who had reason to be pleased at any interruption to his work? Someone who had a premeditated agenda, such as sleeping late. Only one person, to his way of thinking, who fit all three of those descriptions.

Lady Jeannette Brantford.

Still, as dead certain as he was that she must be behind the theft, how had she managed to move all those tools? They were brutally heavy, those boxes of tools. Too heavy to be wrangled by a mere woman. Yet the Little Rosebush was no ordinary woman. It was certain that whatever she lacked in strength, she more than made up for in determination. But if she was behind the mysterious disappearance of his tools, where would she have hidden them?

"Search the grounds," he instructed Rory. "Set all the lads to the task."

The other man's eyebrows lifted in apparent surprise. "You think the tools are still here on the estate?"

"There's a high probability of it, aye." He scrubbed his hands together. "Let's get to it, then, shall we?"

Jeannette snuggled against the soft sheets, eyes closed as she luxuriated in a last few moments of sleep.

Pure heaven, she mused as she let herself slowly drift awake. So quiet. As though the house slumbered too, filled with blissful peace and harmonious silence. A smile spread over her mouth as she stretched her arms above her head and wiggled her fingers, reveling in the marvelous sensation of feeling well rested for the first time in weeks. Full sunlight peeped from beneath the curtains, a glance at the mantel clock displaying the hour at just shy of eleven.

Giggling like a naughty child, she sat up, bounced against the feather mattress. Her plan had obviously worked to perfection. How delicious. Somewhere on the property, O'Brien must be dragging his fingers through his hair in confused frustration. Likely he would think the missing tools had been stolen, forcing him to send for more, hopefully all the way to Dublin. Just imagine the days such a task would take. Day after day of luxurious quiet. Day after day of sleeping in.

Energized, she sprang from the bed and tugged the bellpull for Betsy. Because of the late hour, she ate breakfast in her room, sending word to Wilda that she was well and would see her later that afternoon. She bathed and dressed at a leisurely pace, donning her favorite Nicholas blue poplin for today's painting expedition.

Whistling a jaunty tune under her breath, she made her way through the house toward the east door, where, only a couple days ago, she and O'Brien had conducted their early-morning encounter over the plans. She knew he was probably too busy reporting the "theft" of the tools to the local constabulary to give her any thought. Even so, making herself scarce for the remainder of the day didn't sound like a bad idea.

The instant she stepped from the house, she realized she was already too late.

Before she could retreat, O'Brien saw her. Peeling away from the side of the house where he'd been leaning, he stalked toward her, his steps as powerful and hungry as those of a hunting cat. A large, fearsome cat who'd been anticipating the capture of its prey for some long while.

"About time you put in an appearance," he said, drawing to a halt in front of her.

"Ah, good day to you, Mr. O'Brien." She tossed him a look of utter innocence. "What brings you here to the garden?"

Standing squarely before her, he blocked her path. "You know exactly what, you wily minx. I was beginning to think I'd have to concoct some fib so I could come inside the house and roust you out, but here you finally are."

As if he would dare, she thought. "My pardon, but I cannot imagine why you would be searching for me."

"Can you not?"

"No," she said, still hoping she could bluster her way past him. "Now, if that is all, I would like to continue on." For emphasis, she raised the art supplies and nuncheon basket she held in her hands.

"You can set those down, since you won't be doing any painting this afternoon. You have other chores that will be occupying your time."

"Chores?" She tossed back her head on a light laugh. "How quaint. I am a lady, and as such take part in activities. I do not do chores."

"Do them or not, you'll be trying your hand at a few this afternoon. My men and I found most of the tools, by the way. You'll be helping me locate the rest."

Fiddlesticks. How could they have discovered them so quickly? And to think of all the effort she and Betsy had gone to last night to hide the pesky things.

"You have me at a loss." She shrugged. "I know nothing about any tools. Are some missing?"

He delivered a loud, disbelieving snort. "You're a corker, girl, you surely are, and slick as a selkie with the lies. Go on now and set those belongings of yours inside the house, then we'll be off."

She straightened. "I am on my way to the fields to practice my watercolors. If you have misplaced some tools, I wish you luck in finding them."

"If we'd had luck, I wouldn't need you to point out their location. So you'll be accompanying me."

"How would I know where to find them?"

He fixed her with a long, hard stare that nearly made her squirm. She held out for a full minute. "All right, all right, perhaps I have some idea where they might be. But I fail to see why you're so upset. If you really consider the matter, I did everyone a favor."

His brows shot high. "And how do you figure that, lass?"

"By giving your men a day of rest."

"Is that what you believe? That they've been idle? Quite the opposite, they've been searching under every bush and rock and tree on the estate, hunting for the tools. They haven't had a day off, they've had a wasted day. And for what? So you could get a few extra hours' sleep."

"It wasn't only for me."

"Of course it was. No one else of my acquaintance has been complaining about the time except you."

"That's because they are used to early hours. And because you keep them under your thumb. Your dictatorial thumb."

"If I were that, lass, you wouldn't have gotten so much as an inch out of me. My only fault is that I refuse to let you take a mile. Enough now, you've got tools to find."

"Mr. O'Brien, surely you cannot be serious about having me accompany you to search the grounds?"

"Why not? You didn't have any trouble traipsing about last night in the dark. This time you'll have plenty of sunshine to light your way."

Lower lip puffed out, she crossed her arms. "But I am going painting."

"You can paint later. After we've found the tools."

"No."

"Yes."

She shook her head. "You have no right to insist I do anything."

"Your antics have given me the right. Enough talk, we've work to do."

Before she could prevent it, he reached out and grabbed the hamper and paints from her hands. She made a desperate attempt to fend him off, but lost her parasol as well for the effort.

Turning, he placed all her painting paraphernalia inside the house, then closed the door with a light *bang.*

"You are a brute."

"And you're spoiled and selfish."

Her lips quivered. "I am not selfish."

"Come along, then," he said, taking hold of her elbow, "and prove it."

Burning with silent indignation, she allowed him to lead her forward. Knowing there was no point in further protest, she fell into step at his side.

The construction site lay in quiet stillness when they arrived, the usual busy hive of workers absent from the grounds.

"Where are your men?" she asked. "I thought you said they were still working."

"With all of today's unexpected disruptions, I sent them home."

Darragh paused, thinking back upon the morning. Once he'd made the decision to waylay Jeannette and make her pay recompense by ferreting out the equipment she had hidden, he also decided it might be best to do so with a measure of privacy. So he'd sent the men home, telling them to arrive at the site early on the morrow. Luckily, Jeannette's cousins wouldn't be looking for her, since he knew Mr. Merriweather spent his afternoons locked inside his laboratory and Mrs. Merriweather usually puttered around in her rose garden on the opposite side of the house.

Jeannette smiled in triumph. "So, the men did benefit from my actions, after all."

"Not really, since they don't get paid if they don't work."

"They do not receive a salary?" She frowned as if such an idea had never occurred to her.

"Journeymen and laborers are paid for the work they perform. They aren't house servants, who earn a wage no matter how many or few hours they toil."

"Oh."

She looked so chastened that he almost told her not to worry — he was paying the men for the whole day despite the loss. But regardless of the twinge of guilt that crept through him, he remained silent.

Crossing to the small wooden table that held his papers and plans, he leaned over and retrieved an inventory list written out in a neat hand. "This will tell us what we've yet to find."

He picked up an empty wooden toolbox and a pencil before stalking her way. Gently, he urged her forward.

"Lead on, MacDuff."

"Mac who?"

"MacDuff. It's Shakespeare. Even a *common* fellow like me knows that. Now take me to those tools."

Jeannette huffed out a breath as she walked, O'Brien looming at her back. She did her best to ignore him as she strolled across the verdant lawn, late-summer grass plush beneath her slippers.

"Where do you expect me to begin?" she asked.

"Where did you start last night?"

She scanned the grounds. "I can't recall for sure. Even with the moon it was rather dark, it being night and all. But I believe I began at that shrub over there." She pointed toward a large mulberry bush. "Did your men search beneath?"

O'Brien shrugged. "I can't say, since we spread out to cover as much ground as possible. Appears the best method will be to start the process anew."

She met his complacent expression with an alarmed one of her own. "Surely you are not suggesting we search under every shrubbery and rock and bit of tall grass in the place?"

"Aye, if you think there's a chance we'll find some tools hidden there." He tapped a finger against his list. "Until everything on here is located, we'll keep up the search."

"But . . . but that could take *hours.*"

"You're right, it could. So we'd best be on about it, hadn't we now?"

Dismay poured through her, together with the urge to tell him to go to the devil. She quashed the feeling and waggled an imperious set of fingers toward the bush. "Very well, look beneath and see if you find anything."

Instead of obeying, O'Brien shifted his stance and crossed his arms.

"Well, what are you waiting for?" she questioned.

"For you, my lady. Under the circumstances, it seems only right to me you should be the one doing the searching."

"You expect me to crawl under bushes? But my clothes . . ." she protested.

"You didn't worry about your clothes last night. You'll be fine. Now, you'd best get a move on."

"But —"

"Don't fret. I'll be here to keep tally of whatever you find, and I'll carry the toolbox as well. I wouldn't want a delicate lass like yourself taking an injury, after all."

"You'll carry the toolbox?" she exclaimed, hearing her voice rise to a high pitch. "Why

. . . you . . . you . . ."

Breaking off, she felt herself quiver with indignation. Tears rose up behind her lids but she blinked them away. She would not let him see her cry, nor would she run. It wasn't that she didn't want to run, she did, but knowing him, he would give chase, catch her and bring her back to finish the task!

His blue eyes infinitely patient, he waited for her to proceed. Aware he had her neatly boxed in, she mumbled an unintelligible curse, then paced to the bush, pushed the foliage aside and bent at the waist to search underneath.

And so it went, the pair of them moving from one location to the next, Jeannette locating tools here and there for O'Brien to check off his infernal list and place into the toolbox.

The sun was past its zenith, hot perspiration dampening Jeannette's face and dotting the fabric of her gown by the time she flung a final tool into the box.

Back aching, she straightened, then pressed a forearm to her moist brow. "There, that is all of them."

O'Brien perused his list. "Says there's one last wrench yet to be found."

This time she didn't want to cry, she

wanted to kill. She restricted herself to a glare. "If you want that wrench found, find it yourself. I've looked under my last shrub and I'm not looking further."

Darragh hid a grin, realizing he'd pushed her as far as she could possibly be pushed. To give her credit, she'd held up better than he'd ever expected, throwing herself into the task with a martyred determination worthy of a saint. Looking at her now, drooping and bedraggled, he imagined she had more than learned her lesson. He seriously doubted she would ever hide another tool in her life, even if she lived to be a hundred.

Bowed but clearly unbent, she thrust her chin in the air. "If you are done torturing me, I should like to leave now."

"Aye, you should be going on inside before you're missed. But first you ought to tidy up a bit. You've mud on your cheek."

Without considering the streaks of dirt on her hands, she wiped at the spot.

He hid a smile. "Now you have more."

Setting down the toolbox, he reached inside his pocket and withdrew a linen handkerchief. "Here now, let me see to that for you."

He rubbed the cloth against her skin, and although it cleaned away some of the dirt, it didn't remove it all. Glancing at the orna-mental pond only feet away, he urged her across with him, then bent down to wet the handkerchief.

"Let's try this again."

Jeannette knew she should have taken the cloth from him and wiped her own face clean. Instead she stood quiescent and let him do the work, vividly aware of his strong yet gentle fingers as they stroked the linen across her skin. She held steady and fought the urge to tremble, assuring herself the need came from weariness and nothing more. After everything he'd put her through today, how could she feel anything except outrage?

Yet she did not pull away when he finished cleaning her cheek. Nor when his hand stilled, his eyelids drooping as a lambent gleam of desire caught fire in his vibrant eyes.

Time slowed, the world narrowing until it seemed nothing existed save the two of them.

Then his mouth was upon her own, his lips taking hers in a series of gentle seduc-tive kisses that left her unable to catch a satisfactory breath. A tiny voice in her brain whispered against him, warned her to resist and pull away. But he tasted too delicious.

Smelled too good, the warm, earthy, masculine scent of him muddling her judgment and devastating her senses.

There ought to be a law against such pleasure, she mused in a dreamy haze. No man should have the right to turn a woman as gooey and pliant as melted chocolate with nothing more substantial than a touch. Certainly not a man like Darragh O'Brien. A rogue and scoundrel who seemed to delight in tormenting and teasing her. A man who only minutes before had been marching her around her cousins' estate like some prisoner, forcing her to labor in ways no lady ought to be forced to endure.

Yet here she was, letting him kiss her, and enjoying it to boot! Suddenly her thoughts pierced through the haze of pleasure ensnaring her, brutally reminding her where she was and precisely what it was she was doing.

"No!" She panted, mustering the strength to wrench her lips from his.

He stared down at her, his features sharp and hungry with passion. Eyelids lowering once more to half staff, he bent to feast yet again upon her mouth.

She forestalled him with a hand. "No."

He paused. "Why not, when I can tell you're as keen for it as I am?"

She stiffened. "I am not *keen* for it," she lied, deliberately wiping a hand across her lips. "I didn't like it at all. It's just . . . just that you took me by surprise."

"If you'd been surprised, you'd have let out a protest at the start. Or are you in the habit of letting a man kiss you senseless before deciding to push him aside like a tease?"

Her hand flashed upward to strike but he caught her wrist before she could land a blow.

"There'll be none of that now," he chastened. "Admit the truth, since both of us know you like my kisses."

She twisted in his hold.

He held her steady. "Come on, lass, just say the words. I'm waiting."

"And you'll go on waiting. For an eternity would be my guess."

"I see I'll have to wring a confession from you, then."

Before she could utter a sound, he swooped, taking her mouth in a lush, fevered claiming that held nothing back. Crushing her against his rugged body, he plundered her lips with dizzying skill and a determination that sent her reeling out of control.

Jeannette tried her best not to respond this time, holding her body stiff and uncompromising within his arms. She would not give in to his kisses, she told herself. She would not yield, no matter how infinitely sweet his touch. But merciful heavens, he had a way about him that was all but impossible to resist. He was the very devil sent to earth to plague and beguile her.

So despite the cool dictates of her mind, her body began to burn, quickening with an ardor that turned her knees to jelly, her blood to molten lava sizzling through her veins.

She made one last muffled murmur of protest before her mind melted too, whimpering when he swept his nimble tongue between her lips to stroke her teeth and tongue, to caress the sensitive flesh of her smooth, inner cheeks. She quivered and went under like a storm-tossed ship at sea.

Abandoned to the power and pleasure of his embrace, she moaned and arched against him, sliding her hands up to cling tighter to his wide, resilient shoulders. She kissed him back for all she was worth, seeking his tongue as it retreated from her touch, wanting to play with him the way he was playing with her. Their kiss went on for a breathless, impossible span of time before he set her from him, breaking the kiss with a startling, shattering abruptness.

Winded and weak, she peered up into his face, her passion-dazed senses clearing abruptly when she read the mocking I-told-you-so in his expression, the gleam of undisguised satisfaction for a lesson well taught.

Too late she understood. Too late she realized just how splendidly she had been baited into his trap. How, all the while she had been melting against him, he had been in full control and command. How, like a bee lured into a bottle of sugar water, she had been neatly caught. Her stomach somersaulted but not from desire this time, reawakened hurt curdling like sour milk in her belly.

Yet she knew he wasn't immune to her touch either, not immune by a long shot. His pupils were dilated, large and black as a moonless night, surrounded by narrow rings of bright, bright blue. His color was high in his fair cheeks, his breath ragged.

"Well now, still claiming you don't care for my touch?" he taunted. "Or will you be needing a few more kisses to prove the point?"

She wished she had the time and the place to turn the tables. Wished she could teach him the lesson he so rightly deserved. If she applied herself, she knew she could make him beg for her kisses, despite her propensity to lose her head at his touch. But that sort of revenge would have to wait for another day. Right now she would have to settle for other means of wiping the impudent self-satisfaction off his face.

"Maybe I'd like a few more kisses and maybe I wouldn't," she purred in a silky tone that made his eyes light in surprise. Stepping forward, she subtly encouraged him to take a step back.

She raked the tip of one manicured fingernail down his chest. "But I do know one thing I would love for sure."

He quirked a skeptical, yet nevertheless amused brow, letting her coax him back yet another step. "And what would that be, lass?"

"This!"

Using the flat of her hands, she shoved at his chest with every ounce of strength she possessed. Normally she'd have been no match for him, but offended pride and the element of surprise worked in her favor. Back he went, his boot heels sinking into the soft soil around the pond's edge.

Leaping out of reach as he careened backward, she watched him frantically try to catch his balance. He flailed his long arms in wide arcs, feet shuffling, a comical look of shock decorating his bold features as he tried desperately to save himself. Seconds later he hit the water, a loud, messy splash arcing upward before he sank beneath the murky surface.

He came up sputtering, spitting out water and a stream of Gaelic curses she didn't understand but got the gist of well enough. Wiping his wet face, he shot her a fulminating glower, then slicked his hands over his dripping hair.

She chuckled when he discovered a clump of slimy pond weeds sticking to his forehead. He plucked them off and cast the plants back into the pond with total disgust. Seated chest deep in the water, he paused suddenly before shifting from hip to hip. Dipping in a hand, he yanked out a wrench.

At the sight, she doubled over and giggled with unrestrained hilarity. "Why, you've found the missing wrench. How lucky. Shall I retrieve your list and check it off?"

He shot her a glare. "I've a better idea. Come over here so you can give me a hand out."

She shook her head. "You mean a hand *in,* don't you? I'm on to you this time, Darragh O'Brien, so keep your distance."

"And what if I don't?" he growled, rising slowly to his feet, water sluicing like a falls along his impressive frame.

Deciding she had better escape while the opportunity still availed itself, she hurried toward the house.

"That's right, girl," he called. "You'd better run, else I catch you and carry you back."

Jeannette laughed again and raced on, knowing it wouldn't take much to encourage him to come after her, half worried she might not really mind.

"What in the world happened to you? Did you decide to take a swim in your clothes and boots?"

Chilled and miserable, Darragh looked daggers at his friend Lawrence McGarrett. In Gaelic, he made a short but crude suggestion about where Lawrence could put his questions, then stomped toward the staircase.

Lawrence laughed and shook his carroty head. " 'Tis the truth and nothing but that I'll be having out of you later, my lad," he called after Darragh. "Don't imagine I won't."

And Lawrence did, slowly prodding the tale out of Darragh over a delicious supper of succulent roast lamb, buttery mashed potatoes and tender braised leeks.

"Tossed you in the pond, did she?" Lawrence chuckled, motioned for the footman to clear away their empty plates.

Relaxed and pleasantly warm again thanks to a dry suit of clothes and the healthy fire that crackled in the dining room fireplace, Darragh leaned back in a comfortable Chippendale chair. He downed a last swallow of wine, then placed the fine, Waterford crystal goblet on the elegant linen-clad table.

"She sounds a wildcat, that one," Lawrence said.

Darragh hadn't told his friend everything, but enough. More than enough. "She's spirited, I'll grant you that."

"Well, 'tis to be expected from an Irishwoman. I'd enjoy meeting her, this firebreather of yours. Tell me now, is she redheaded?" Lawrence grimaced, stuck a finger toward his head. "Cursed with the same flaming thatch as myself?"

Darragh reached for the crystal decanter in the center of the table and poured himself another draught of wine. Setting the stopper back in with a light *clink,* he raised his goblet and drank.

At length, he returned his glass to the table. "She's blond. Pale, golden blond and pretty as the first rays of a new sun. But she isn't Irish. 'Tis English, she is."

Lawrence frowned, his eyebrows meeting like a pair of bright flags in the middle of his forehead. "Oh."

"What's that supposed to mean, oh?"

"You know very well what it means. English girls are nothing but trouble, especially the aristocratic ones. I assume she is an aristocrat."

Darragh thought of Lady Jeannette and her pampered, self-indulgent ways. "Oh, aye, she's as aristocratic as they come. Merriweather's cousin and the daughter of an English earl. Some Society scandal back home brought her here, so I understand."

"Even more reason, then, to put an end to these games the pair of you have been playing. Why didn't you tell me from the first she was Merriweather's cousin? Are you knocked in the head, boy-o? You know how *na Sasanaigh* feel about Irish lads, even ones with good money and fine old titles."

"Well, I don't see the problem. It's not as if I'm in any danger of turning sweet on the girl."

Lawrence snorted and reached for the decanter. "Are you not? She's all you've talked about the whole evening long."

"At your insistence."

"And then there's that look in your eyes."

"What look?"

"*That* look. The one you get when you're halfway to falling in love with a lass. It's there staring back at me even as we speak."

Darragh bristled, jaw tightening to the consistency of rock. "There is no look, only the gleam from one too many glasses of wine." He raised his goblet, downed what remained. "And if you're suggesting I'm in love with the girl, you're crazy as old man Maguire, who says he takes tea every Sunday evening with the little people. She's a beautiful lass, but love . . ." He broke off, gave a dismissive grunt. "I've no love for that one. Most days she's naught but a thorn in my side."

Lawrence looked plainly unconvinced. "If you say so. I just don't want to see you lured in then left with a shattered heart. Marry a good Irish girl as your mam told you to and leave that one alone."

"Not to worry, Lawrence, my lad. I'm heart whole and there's nothing over which you need be worried. Work will start again as usual tomorrow, and the boys'll move along at a grand pace. We'll be done and gone before the first flakes of snow hit the ground. And she'll be gone back to England."

An odd melancholy he refused to consider settled over him. Inevitable, he realized, that one of these days Jeannette Rose Brantford would be traveling back home, setting not only a country but an entire sea betwixt them.

Gratefully, he let Lawrence change the subject. The two of them talked of sport and horses over bites of cheese and fruit, savoring robust, ruby-hued port out of small glasses until sleep could no longer be avoided.

Yet Darragh didn't sleep, lying awake in his bed long after he should have found himself lost deep in the world of dreams.

All he could think of was Jeannette.

Lawrence's fault, he decided as he punched an irritated fist into his feather pillow and rolled over onto his side.

Love Jeannette?

Impossible.

Yet he couldn't stop thinking about her, especially the kisses they had shared earlier today. Like the creamiest spun honey, they were, those kisses, sweet and warm and rich. If he was honest with himself, he had to confess he'd never known finer. She might be flighty and willful, but damn if she didn't know how to make a man's head reel.

And her mouth. Sweet Mary, she had some of the softest lips he'd ever touched. Pink and silky smooth as tender young rose

191

petals, her skin every bit as fragrant. He could spend all the day long with his nose pressed to that skin, drinking in her luscious feminine scent.

He closed his eyes and could nearly smell her, taste her, feel her again pressed close inside his arms. Desire pumped through him, blood rushing to all sorts of parts best left dormant. Especially considering the fact that kisses were the best he could honorably expect to enjoy from Lady Jeannette unless he wished to offer her a wedding ring. And he had absolutely no intention of doing any such thing.

Up until now, he hadn't had the time nor the inclination to consider taking a wife — he'd been far too busy studying and traveling and concentrating on doing what was necessary to rebuild his family fortune. Not that he'd been bereft of feminine company over the years. No indeed, far from it. But the kind of women he dallied with knew what she was about and didn't expect promises of undying love and commitment.

When he did marry, it certainly wouldn't be to a coddled English beauty who thought herself better than most of humanity. Instead he wanted a gentle lass, sweet-tempered and caring, simple in spirit and expectation, who would fill his life with happiness and love. Not some wild-willed vixen who would see to it he never knew another moment's peace for all the rest of his days.

Still, he had to admit a life spent with Lady Jeannette would never be dull or boring. Excitement and surprise would lie around each corner while passion smoldered hot beneath the surface, ready to burst into flames at any time of the day or night. He groaned at the explicit images that flashed through his mind, shifting restlessly against the sheets as his body responded in unsatisfied demand.

Lord, what if Lawrence was right? What if he was getting in too deep and this hunger he felt was more than a case of simple lust? What if these games he and the Little Rosebush were playing amounted to more than juvenile tricks and pranks? What if, heaven forbid, they were part of some sort of elaborate mating ritual?

He climbed out of bed and paced across his bedroom to the window, open to let in the night breeze. He stared out, barely aware of the moonlight spread like a shimmering river over the night-blackened lawn. An owl hooted somewhere in the distance.

Mad, he was, crazy mad to be entertaining such nonsensical delusions. Lady Jeannette delighted in testing and challenging him. And he did a fine job reestablishing the limits. Even now he could cheerfully strangle her for all the trouble she'd caused him today with the missing workmen's tools, not to mention the unexpected swim she'd sent him on in the Merriweathers' pond.

He growled beneath his breath, then had to smile and shake his head at her outrageous antics.

Yet Lawrence made a good point. Playing these games with a girl like her was akin to striking a flint near a pile of oil-soaked tinder. If he kept it up long enough, wasn't he sure to end up burned? Better to withdraw before it became too late.

He gazed sightlessly out into the night for several more long minutes. By the time he returned to his bed, he was resolved to focus on the task before him, finish his work and push a certain fiery young miss from his mind.

After the job was done, he would leave and make sure he didn't let himself look back.

CHAPTER NINE

Jeannette tread cautiously over the next couple days, remaining indoors rather than risking a fresh encounter with O'Brien. He'd looked none too happy about his impromptu swim the other afternoon. It had been worth it, though, to see his look of stunned panic seconds before he'd splashed like a floundering trout into the pond. Too bad she hadn't been able to share the humorous tale with her cousins, but Bertie and Wilda simply would not understand.

Nor did they fully understand the tale of the "missing" tools, wondering aloud how such a strange circumstance could have occurred. Amid much puzzlement and speculation at the dinner table, Jeannette listened to her cousins discuss the matter.

Cousin Bertie recounted that when he questioned O'Brien, the architect had apparently shrugged and claimed to be at a complete loss.

"Makes no sense at all, does it now?" O'Brien had remarked. "No accounting for the odd peculiarities of people, particularly thieves and pranksters. 'Course, it could be the work of faeries, as the men say. Crafty, mischievous imps, faeries are. Any way you look on it, 'tis a pure mystery."

Faeries indeed, she had marveled with an amused half smile. Much as it galled her, she admitted a reluctant admiration for O'Brien and his highly inventive explanations. He'd certainly managed to get her cousins to consider the possibility of faerie folk as tool thieves, despite the fact that Bertie prided himself on being a man of science.

Far more superstitious, Wilda had discussed the event with her housekeeper, Mrs. Ivory, a forthright, energetic Irishwoman, who'd convinced her to have the servants set out a glass of milk and a small plate of victuals each night. The offering, the housekeeper maintained, was a wellknown way to appease the Good People or any other restless spirits that might be roaming the land.

Now, days later, Jeannette snorted at such nonsense, shaking her head as she moved her drawing pencil over the piece of sketch paper balanced against her updrawn knees. With the fields wet from a steady morning rain, now thankfully ceased, she'd decided to stay inside again.

Tucked into a window seat in one of the guest bedrooms, she sat snug and comfortable, enjoying a stellar view of the construction site below. The workers were again hard at their labors, their rhythm reestablished as though the interruption over the missing tools had never occurred at all.

She had feared after that first morning that O'Brien would retaliate by having his men begin work extra early. But she'd awakened to the sound of their toil at seven, realizing to her chagrin that she'd been dreaming of O'Brien's kisses.

Her pencil slowed, her skin tingling anew at the memory before she shook off the phantom sensations. No, she admonished herself, she was not going to spend the afternoon dwelling upon Darragh O'Brien's kisses. His delectable, delicious, pulse-pounding kisses that occupied her thoughts in daylight and plagued her dreams at night.

Despite every attempt, she could not contain those dreams, amorous fancies that left her restless and edgy, longing for a male touch that was not there. Any other unmarried lady of her class would have cringed in mortification to wake and find the sheets twisted around her limbs, heat burning high in her cheeks and low in her belly. Yet secretly she couldn't deny a certain pleasure, her nocturnal wanderings rousing her passions in ways she had never thought to explore. Still, what she craved at night had to be held strictly at bay in her waking life. To succumb in a dream was one thing. To do so in reality was something else altogether.

Through the window, O'Brien passed into view below. His pantherlike stride catching her eye, hints of auburn glinting in his dark chestnut hair like bits of copper in the sun.

Catching her lower lip between her teeth, she followed his progress across the lawn to the high, thin table where he spread out a long, familiar-looking sheath of parchment. His plans.

He consulted something on one of the pages before glancing up to call an order across to a pair of his men.

As usual, he was dressed in ordinary attire. Leather boots, plain brown trousers, a simple green cotton waistcoat, white neckerchief and shirt that he scandalously left unbuttoned at the throat and sleeves. He'd rolled them up again, those sleeves, revealing the solid muscles of his forearms, the intriguing sprinkle of dark, masculine hair on their length.

She wet her lips and sighed, then caught herself in the act.

Irritated, she pulled out a fresh sheet of paper and set her pencil in motion. Slowly over the next half hour, O'Brien's likeness came to life. Starting as simple lines and dots and flourishes, the picture evolved into what she decided was a very competent sketch of the man in her sight.

The seductive devil in her sight.

Yes, exactly, she judged, an impish quirk spreading over her lips.

The expressions on his men's faces should have warned him. That and the laughter trailing him the next morning as Darragh walked onto the construction site.

He called out the usual round of good mornings and got smirks along with their replies. Smirks and stares. Long expectant stares, as though the men were watching and waiting for an explosion of some kind to occur. Perplexed, he glanced around, found nothing at all out of the norm.

He was striding along the new north wall a minute later when he saw it, propped atop the first level of scaffolding like some rude crimson smear.

Now it was his turn to stare.

Hell's teeth. Lady Jeannette had painted

him as Satan, and done a damned fine job of it too. Putting her artistic skills to work, she had accurately captured his likeness, leaving no room to mistake his identity. His eyes she'd turned from blue to red, back-lighting his dark hair and the horns above with an evil golden glow that gave the effect of smoldering fire. She'd colored the rest of the paper in shades of red and black so he looked as if he'd just ascended from the furnace pits of Hades itself. Humorously, though, she'd tucked a pencil behind one horn and set his architectural plans afire, leaving him to use his forked tail and clawed hands to tamp out the flames.

Minx. What did she think she was about? Was she deliberately trying to anger him? Or was this merely a new salvo, her way of gaining his attention in their unfettered game of give-and-take.

He suspected it was a little bit of both.

But would he take the bait?

Suddenly he noticed the hush, almost deafening in its volume as every one of his men waited to see what he would do.

Striding toward the picture, he plucked it down off its lofty perch and studied it. Suddenly the absurdity of the piece struck him and he astonished them all — including himself — by tossing back his head on a long, hearty laugh.

"A fair likeness, wouldn't you say?" he called out as he turned. "Especially the tail and the horns. Fair warning, though, that I'll use them on the pack of you, together with the pitchfork, if you don't get straight back to work."

Laughter rumbled in a wave from man to man. Rory approached and gave him a good-natured slap on the shoulder before consulting with him about more serious matters.

Once done, Darragh crossed to the small wooden table where he kept his architectural renderings and plans. Setting down the painting, he covered it with a large rectangle of paper, then did his best to forget about its exasperatingly lovely creator.

In a sad funk, Jeannette sat in a chair and watched a trio of raindrops chase one another across her bedroom window. She sighed against her boredom, this afternoon as dull as many of the others she had endured over the past four weeks, with nothing but her cousins and her own solitary pursuits to entertain her.

Because of the rain, the building crew had gone home for the afternoon, the house silent except for the drum of droplets on the roof, and the drip and gush of water flowing through the gutters.

Of Darragh O'Brien, she saw virtually nothing these days. Not that she wished to see him, she strove to assure herself. She was relieved he had chosen to voluntarily absent himself from her life, really she was. But her encounters with the man had helped to pass the time and his unexplained withdrawal had left a noticeable void.

She remembered back to the morning when she left her painting of *Darragh, the Devil* for his workers to see. Awakening early, she had rushed to one of the guest bedroom windows, where she would have a bird's-eye view of his reaction. At first, she had laughed along with his men as each one of them came forward in turn to view the caricature. Brimming with mischievous delight, she had waited for O'Brien to arrive, glimpse her latest handiwork and explode.

But beyond an initial burst of laughter and a few teasing comments, he'd shown little reaction. Perhaps, she had thought at the time, he was saving up his true feelings for a tête-à-tête with her later that day or the next.

So she had waited, expecting him to seek her out. Only he had not, leaving her to grow increasingly annoyed and deflated as each day drifted monotonously one into the other. He hadn't even let Vitruvius run loose, keeping the dog on a lead so the half-grown, house-sized lummox couldn't molest her in the gardens or in the fields as she came and went during her afternoon painting sessions. Not that she wished to see the canine monster, since she'd been slobbered over and ravaged by enough dirty paw prints to last a lifetime.

But master and dog kept well away.

She could have sought O'Brien out, but what excuse would she have used? After the afternoon of misery to which he'd subjected her as punishment for hiding his tools, she had decided the prudent choice would be to withdraw from that particular fight. Much as it galled her to have the construction racket begin so early, she realized the impossibility of ever getting her way.

That alone should have sparked a visit from him, if for no other reason than to gloat. But as the days progressed, one week flowing into two, and two into three, she realized he had lost interest. In their sparring and in her, it would seem.

Lowering as it was to admit, she ventured on occasion into the far guest room to watch for a glimpse of him. But she never lingered long, telling herself it was only tedium and curiosity that drove her there.

It wasn't as though she harbored tender feelings for the man. How could she, considering the two of them came from completely separate worlds? She was an English lady of good breeding and fine family. He was an ordinary, middle-class Irishman with nothing to recommend him, in spite of his obvious skills as an architect.

Yet none of that really mattered, since she had no interest in encouraging a flirtation. Once she returned to England, she would marry and marry well. So really, O'Brien was doing her a favor removing himself from her sphere.

He was too busy with his work, likely that was the reason she no longer encountered him, the new edifice demanding a full measure of his time and talent. And he did possess talent. Even she, who had little interest in such matters, could appreciate the beauty of what he was creating, the magnificent wing daily taking shape before her eyes.

Outwardly designed to remain in harmony with the rest of the structure, the recently finished exterior retained the classical lines of the Palladian style, creating an unbroken transition from old to new. To anyone unaware of the fire, Brambleberry Hall would appear as if it had stood unscathed through all the years of its existence.

The interior, over which the workmen were now busy laboring, was to employ a more modern design, with an emphasis on functionality and comfort. O'Brien had laid out each new room for a specific use, made to suit the lives of its owners while still maintaining an atmosphere of quiet country elegance.

Then there was the elaborate glass-walled conservatory that each day rose steadily toward the sky like a glittering cathedral. And Bertie's laboratory, a small square stone house placed well away from the main residence in case of future calamity.

Once completed, the renovation would be stunning, and worthy of genuine praise.

All that aside, her days had grown dull as proverbial dishwater. Sweet and well meaning as they might be, her cousins had proven themselves to be two of the most thoroughly eccentric, reclusive people she'd ever met. Except for church on Sundays and Wilda's small card parties, Wilda and Bertie never did anything even remotely social.

Bertie occupied himself with his books and plants and experiments. Wilda with her sewing, reading and gardening. To her horror, Jeannette had discovered that Wilda did most of the work in the garden herself. Her cousin had even suggested last week that Jeannette join her in trimming back the rosebushes and preparing some of the flower beds for fall. Worst of all, she'd been so bored she'd actually agreed!

Jeannette shuddered anew at the memory, then pushed it aside.

She sighed, her shoulders falling into a mournful slump. Chilly raindrops continued to patter on the windowpanes while she slouched in her chair.

A gentle knock sounded at the door.

"Come," she said, sitting up straight.

One of the housemaids entered, bearing a letter on a silver salver. The girl curtseyed. " 'Tis just now arrived for you, me lady. The housekeeper asked me to carry it up to you."

Jeannette smiled and waved her over. "How delightful." She picked up the letter, but made no effort to open it, not in front of the servant.

The girl hovered, obviously unsure of herself.

Jeannette nodded. "Thank you. You may go now."

The maid bobbed another curtsey and retreated from the room, closing the door behind her.

Jeannette glanced at the envelope, recognizing Raeburn's frank wax seal. The missive must be from Violet, since nothing short of a gun to his head would prompt Adrian to write to her these days. She smiled, her mood elevating a bit. Settling back into her seat, she used a silver opener to reveal Violet's words.

Dear sister,

I hope this missive finds you well, or as well as can be expected considering your current privation. As promised, I will try to speak to Mama again on your behalf when she and I next meet. However, I do not hold out a great deal of hope that she will be amenable to listening. Not long ago, she attended Lady Symmerson's annual country musicale and she says she could barely force herself to remain for all the whispering about her and the scandal we caused. Afterward, she suffered another one of her nervous attacks and remained abed for a week entire. She corresponds with me quite regularly, though I confess to still feeling the sharp side of her tongue even in her letters. If not for my being with child, I fear she would cease to speak to me at all.

Jeannette snorted, knowing how that felt. Until the scandal, Mama had never been cross with her, not even when she'd deserved it. Since her exile, her mother had written only twice. Once to confirm she'd arrived. The second time to lecture her for her misdeeds and to castigate her for all the shame she'd brought into her parents' lives. Jeannette read on.

Speaking of such matters, I have the most astonishing news. As I told you before, I was convinced the baby must be an elephant, I am so horribly large. Dear Adrian called Doctor Montgomery to examine me. He listened to my belly with a very odd little device and said he heard two distinct heartbeats. He believes I am carrying twins! Adrian turned quite ashen with worry for my health but he has since recovered, being assured by the doctor that my delivery should pose no undue difficulties. Imagine, Jeannette, twins. Do you think they shall be identical like us?

Jeannette lowered the letter to her lap, abruptly homesick. Despite their past difficulties, she wished she could be there to help her sister through this trying but excit- ing time. Brave as her words might be, Violet had to be nervous, especially knowing she carried two babies instead of one. Jeannette hoped she didn't someday suffer the same fate as her sister. One child at a time would be more than sufficient for her.

Besides, she pouted, she was missing all the fun. If her parents didn't relent soon and tell her she could come home, she wouldn't have a chance to see Violet waddle around. Nor would she be there for the birth and christening this winter.

She considered penning a reply to her twin, but a glance at the clock showed her it was past time she dressed for supper. Folding up the letter, she rang for Betsy.

". . . he says that in spite of the earlier unfortunate delays, the work is now moving along splendidly," Bertie announced in between bites of poached salmon in caper sauce and buttered roast potatoes. "Our new wing should be finished in no more than another month complete." He and Wilda shared pleased smiles while Jeannette looked on.

She swallowed against an odd constriction in her throat and reached for her glass of wine. Another month and all the workmen would be gone, Mr. O'Brien with them. Well, *huzzah,* since that would turn the mornings deliciously quiet and leave her free to sleep as late as she wished.

She should be ecstatic over the news.

She was ecstatic. Of course she was.

Frowning, she picked at her fish with her fork, an odd melancholy rolling through her. She just needed a bit of cheering up, that was all. Relief from the endless daily monotony of her current existence. If she were at home, her answer would be to throw a party.

She paused and drank another sip of wine.

Why hadn't she thought of it before?

Setting her fork aside, she patted her lips dry with her napkin. "I have the most wonderful idea. We must host a ball."

Wilda's eyebrows bobbed upward like a pair of corks, while Cousin Cuthbert's forehead scrunched into a mass of wrinkled lines.

"Oh, dear, I don't believe we have ever had a ball," Wilda said in a faint voice. "No, no, nothing larger than a holiday luncheon for some visiting friends and relations several years ago."

Only pure willpower kept Jeannette from rolling her eyes. "Then it is well past time you entertained. And what better reason than the completion of your new renovation? Clearly a time for celebration."

Bertie grunted. "Being able to use the new wing and my laboratory shall be celebration enough. No need to invite a bunch of people over to crowd up the house."

"But what about the conservatory?" Jeannette persisted. "Surely you would like to show off your amazing display of plants. You must have colleagues who would be delighted by a firsthand view."

Bertie paused, clearly caught up by the idea. "Well, there are my fellows in the Royal Horticultural Society. Many of them would have to travel from Dublin and beyond, but I daresay they'd be agreeable, considering the requests I've received to view my *Epidendrum nocturnum.* I suppose it might be an excellent occasion, as you say, to display my collection."

"Just so," she agreed with extravagant enthusiasm. "And Cousin Wilda, surely you would love to set up several tables of cards in your new card room. Just think of the exciting games you could initiate."

A soft smile curved over the older woman's lips. "Oh, I had not considered that. We could have cards, could we not?"

"Why, of course. It wouldn't be a successful ball without offering cards for those who do not care for dancing. In addition to the ladies with whom you regularly play whist, there must be others of good breeding in the area who would be eager to accept such an invitation."

"Yes, there are a few families who might be willing to come." Wilda raised an anxious hand to her chest. "But dear me, I'm not sure I would feel comfortable organizing such a large undertaking."

Jeannette waved a hand. "Leave all the details to me. I thrive on arranging parties and gatherings. There's only a month to prepare but I am certain we can put together a spectacular event in that amount of time. I assure you, once I'm done no one will talk of anything else for months to come. Perhaps years. Why, even your colleagues from Dublin will have nothing but compliments, flattered to have received an invitation to such an illustrious function. Envious they did not host it themselves."

Jeannette clapped her hands in excitement. "So, is it settled? Shall we have a ball?"

Bertie and Wilda exchanged bemused glances, then nodded their heads in unison.

"Yes, dear, let us proceed," Wilda declared.

CHAPTER TEN

The next month passed more rapidly than the two that had come before, as Jeannette oversaw the plans for the Merriweathers' ball.

On the morning of the event, she stood, gesturing around the ballroom with a hand, the space overlain by the clean scents of polish wax and fresh flowers. "No, no, the pink and white hollyhocks in the epergne are to go on the sideboard over there. While the chrysanthemums and accompanying greenery should be placed in the large pedestal vases near the musicians' stand."

Mrs. Ivory, the housekeeper, nodded and instructed the pair of footmen hovering nearby to begin making the necessary changes.

"What about the lobster patties, my lady? The fishmonger arrived at half-six this morning and the order was short of lobsters by nearly a full crate." The woman clucked in obvious disapproval. "Cook gave him a fine scolding, she did, but what's to do about it now?"

Jeannette tapped a considering finger against her hip. "There are plenty of prawns, are there not?"

"Yes, my lady. More than sufficient."

"Then instruct Cook to create a new dish using prawns, and perhaps serve more oysters as well, to make up for the deficiency of lobster. That should resolve the problem while still leaving a proper selection of seafood for the buffet."

"Very good, my lady."

"Anything further?"

"No, my lady, not at present. The silver and crystal are being cleaned and polished. The chandeliers have been dusted and fresh candles set in. And the last of the rooms are being readied for the guests expected to stay overnight, arrangements made among staff to accommodate the visiting servants as well."

"Excellent. It sounds as though plans are proceeding apace."

Mrs. Ivory nodded, then curtseyed as she prepared to withdraw.

"Before you go," Jeannette said, stopping the older woman, "I would like to tell you on behalf of my cousins and myself what a fine job you and the staff are doing, and have done over the past few weeks. Even my parents' staff in Surrey would not have done a better job." Jeannette folded her arms at her waist. "Assuming nothing essential goes awry, tonight's festivities are sure to be a splendid success. Please thank everyone on my behalf."

Pleasure moved over the housekeeper's plump features, a wide, toothy smile spreading across her lips. "Yes, my lady. Thank you, my lady. It's that much harder we'll work tonight to make certain nothing goes amiss. If you'll excuse me now, Lady Jeannette, I'll be off to have a talk with Cook about those shrimps." Murmuring more words of gratitude, the servant curtseyed again and hurried away.

With satisfaction, Jeannette watched the woman depart.

During the past four weeks, she had truly been in her element. She loved many things, but nothing compared to the thrill of a party, whether planning one or simply being in attendance.

At first, poor sweet Cousin Wilda had done her best to help, but unaccustomed to lavish gatherings, she had soon found herself overwhelmed by the preparations. Jeannette gladly stepped into the lead, taking command like a seasoned general assuming control on the eve of a great battle. Rallying her troops in a way that would have made Wellington proud, she had orchestrated the entire affair, from penning invitations in an elegant hand to deciding upon the food and wine that would be served.

The one area she had left entirely up to Wilda was the flowers, a responsibility her cousin had been delighted to accept. As for Cousin Cuthbert, once he'd presented his list of friends and colleagues to invite, he'd hidden himself away in his makeshift laboratory and hadn't been seen since — except, of course, for meals.

A pair of footmen stepped out of the room, leaving Jeannette momentarily alone. She turned a slow circle, admiring the decor. The floor-length maroon velvet curtains, the flocked Chinese print wallpaper painted in shades of red and gold, the gleaming wooden floors and double-hung sash windows that opened to let in the light and air. She drew in a breath, enjoying the hint of fall-blooming jasmine that teased her nostrils.

For once the house was silent. Free at last of the constant racket made by O'Brien's crew of pesky carpenters and craftsmen. Finishing the renovation had been a close thing, work on the new addition concluding only three days prior. She had experienced a few moments of panic when the week began and O'Brien and his men were still setting the last touches into place. But they had since finished their work as promised, packed up their tools and supplies and then been on their way. Leaving just enough time for the servants to give the new rooms a thorough cleaning then carry in and arrange the permanent furnishings. They had also labored under Cuthbert's terse, worried directions to transfer his extensive collection of exotic plants to the conservatory.

O'Brien had not stopped to say good-bye.

More wounded than she'd wanted to admit, Jeannette refused to give in to the desire to seek him out one final time. If he did not wish to see her, then she certainly had no interest in seeing him. Anyway, what would they say to each other? Likely they might exchange a few words of meaningless small talk, mentioning nothing of their sparring and wrangling. Their teasing and flirtation. Their kisses.

Her eyes slid shut as memories assailed her. Memories of the way his lips had felt pressed to hers, intense and passionate and impossible to resist. The heady male scent of him heating her blood, swimming inside her brain. His tantalizing flavor lingering wicked as sin on her tongue. And his body, his tall, sinewy, powerful body holding her to him as if he never again wanted to let her go.

Shivering, she curled a fist against her chest where her heart raced, unnerved by the fierceness of her reaction, and disturbed by the dejection that swept over her like an icy wind. Why should she care if she never saw him again? What did Darragh O'Brien matter to her?

Nothing, she assured herself. Nothing whatsoever.

Opening her eyes, she gazed around the room, forcibly reminding herself of the exciting evening ahead. She had much to celebrate, after all. Tonight was the night of her ball, the first she would enjoy in many long months. Perhaps Inistioge wasn't London. Perhaps many of the Merriweathers' friends and neighbors were a group of provincials. But tonight she had every intention of enjoying herself. She'd done her best to imbue the festivities with equal measures of elegance and animation. Every single person attending tonight would have fun, or she would want to know the reason why.

And that went double for her.

Yet not all the company were locals.

Included on the guest list were several Englishmen, a couple of them titled gentlemen who had decided to travel all the way from London to see Cousin Cuthbert's latest botanical acquisitions. Who knows, mayhap she'd meet someone new. Someone special. Someone simply dripping with titled good looks and money who would erase Darragh O'Brien from her mind, as though he'd never existed at all.

Footsteps rang in soft percussion against the wooden floor as one of the footmen crossed to her. "Excuse me, my lady, visitors have arrived."

"Already? The first guests aren't expected until later this afternoon. Well, there's nothing for it. Please inform Mrs. Merriweather we have company."

"Certainly, my lady. But the guests asked specifically for you. I took the liberty of putting them in the yellow drawing room."

Guests asking for her? How curious. She couldn't imagine who it might be since she was not personally acquainted with any of the people arriving for tonight's ball. True, she had organized the guest list and written out the invitations herself, but surely they would have asked for Wilda and not her.

Obviously the footman must be in error.

Well, it would be impolite to leave guests

waiting on their own. She would see to their comfort and amusement until her cousin arrived.

Nodding her thanks to the footman, who stepped aside after a bow, she exited the ballroom. When she reached the closed drawing room doors, she paused and checked to make certain her gown of spotted peach muslin appeared exactly as it ought. Shoulders straight, she entered the room and felt her eyes turn round and wide. She hung in the doorway, brass knob gripped in her hand as four familiar faces turned her way.

"Violet!" she exclaimed, her voice pitching high in happy astonishment. A giddy laugh escaped her as she hurried forward into the room. "Dear heavens, is it really you? All of you. Here!"

From her spot on the cream damask sofa, her twin met her look with a blue-green gaze, identical to her own except for the fact that Violet's eyes were half hidden behind a pair of gold, wire-rimmed spectacles.

"Yes, it's true. We are all of us really here." Violet grinned widely and laid a pair of hands over her pregnant stomach. "Including these two, who had absolutely no say in the matter."

Shifting forward, Violet started to rise. She made it a bare few inches upward before she lost her balance and plopped ignominiously back down onto the sofa cushions. Momentarily floundering, Adrian rushed forward to steady his wife and help her to her feet.

Jeannette looked shocked. Violet had warned her she was large with child, but Jeannette hadn't realized exactly how large. Violet's belly protruded, round and ripe as a prized melon ready for exhibit at a country fair. To the casual observer, her twin looked on the verge of giving birth, but Jeannette knew she had another three months to go.

At least carrying twins hadn't caused Violet to retreat into her old unfashionable habits, Jeannette noticed. Violet's carmine traveling dress was very becoming, making her plump cheeks glow with radiance and beauty. On second thought, perhaps pregnancy was responsible. And a happy marriage, Jeannette concluded, watching Violet trade a warm look of intimacy with Adrian as he fussed over her.

"Whatever are you doing here?" Jeannette chirped. "I had no idea you were coming."

"Did you not receive my letter? Well, clearly you did not or you would not be so surprised."

"I am surprised, delightfully so. Here, let me give you a hug." Jeannette wrapped her arms around her twin, the both of them laughing when her embrace barely fit around Violet's immense girth.

"Don't worry," Violet said as they pulled apart. "Even Adrian can't quite get his arms around me these days."

Jeannette's smile sobered slightly as she turned to her brother-in-law.

Tall, raven-haired and undeniably handsome, Adrian Winter, Sixth Duke of Raeburn, bore upon his broad shoulders with instinctive ease the responsibility of his position as one of the richest, most powerful men in England. A forceful presence, Adrian commanded any room he entered. Yet his true nature was one of quiet intelligence and shrewd regard, and many of his interests were far too cerebral for a young lady of Jeannette's tastes. Amazing to consider then, Jeannette mused, that she had once been his fiancée. And were it not for her decision to back out of the marriage at the last possible second, she would still now be his wife.

She breathed in, relieved that she was not his bride, despite her ridiculous attempt last spring to get him back. She cringed inwardly to think of her behavior then, excusable only in light of her despondency over being jilted by that scoundrel Toddy.

But wisely, Violet had fought her for Adrian and won, correct when she'd pointed out that Jeannette had wanted him only for what he possessed, not for the man he was.

And as irony and fate would have it, Adrian and her quiet, scholarly sister had truly fallen in love, suiting each other to perfection. How lovely to see them so vastly contented, so thoroughly enriched by their union. After all, Jeannette realized now, Violet was deserving of all the happiness she could possibly hold.

"Raeburn." Jeannette extended her hand, knowing better than to attempt a hug, with which neither one of them would have been comfortable.

He made an elegant bow over her hand. As he straightened, he made a point of meeting her gaze. Lingering long enough to let her see the glint in his brown eyes, along with the silent warning that there were to be no tricks.

She pulled her palm from his, shoulder muscles tight. What tricks could there be? Jeannette wondered, with her sister so hugely pregnant. Even if she still harbored an interest in exchanging places with her twin — which she no longer did, having learned her lesson quite thoroughly last spring — the deception would never have worked.

If — and it was a great if — she somehow managed to tuck a large feather pillow under her dress, she still wouldn't be able to add the two or three stone of weight her sister had clearly gained. It showed in Violet's face and, most particularly, in her breasts, already swollen to an impressive size to accommodate the babies' arrival.

With deliberate forbearance, she forced her affront aside, far too happy to be among close family once again.

Striving to remain pleasant, she turned to Adrian's younger brother. "Lord Christopher."

A younger, sparer version of his brother, twenty-three-year-old Kit Winter was darkly handsome. His looks would have been dangerously appealing if not for the imp that winked back at her out of his irrepressible green-gold eyes.

"Lady Jeannette," he said on a nod.

To a casual observer the greeting would have sounded fine, but she could detect the mocking undertone beneath. *Whelp,* she thought, remembering his overbearing treatment of her at last spring's ball, a slight for which she had still not entirely forgiven him.

She bit down the remark that rose to her lips and turned instead to acknowledge the last occupant of the room, a girl so ordinary and shy as to be nearly invisible.

Eliza Hammond, her sister's longtime friend. She was dressed, as usual, in an appallingly unattractive gown. Today's shade — mud brown — was a ghastly foil for her mousey brown hair, gray eyes and pale, nearly colorless white skin.

"Miss Hammond. How do you do?"

Eliza cast a quick, almost startled glance upward and bobbed her head. "F-fine, Lady Jeannette. Thank you for inquiring. And yourself?"

"I am tolerably well. Even better, I must say, now that all of you are here."

Jeannette paused, waiting to see if the other girl would offer further comment. But she did not, Eliza's eyes cast downward to the fingers she had linked together in her lap.

Deciding it easiest to simply move on rather than attempt to draw Miss Hammond out any further, Jeannette turned her attention back to her sister. "So, you haven't told me. What are you doing here? Why have you come? Especially in your delicate condition."

The small frown on Violet's face eased as

she gazed away from her friend. She opened her mouth to speak, but Adrian stepped in first.

"Yes, her condition is delicate," he scolded in a soft tone. "The exact reason I tried to dissuade her from making this long journey."

"It wasn't that long, particularly not since we came on your yacht," Violet said. "An extremely comfortable craft that is rather like being inside a floating country house."

"Floating country house indeed," he said, lips twisting with wry humor. "And what of the coach rides?"

"Your coaches are exceptionally well sprung, daring the roads to do their worst. Besides, I wasn't about to let you leave me behind, nor Kit and Eliza either, both of whom were longing for an interesting change of scenery. It was my last chance to go anywhere since I'll barely be able to waddle by this time next month, forced to remain inside our estate with your mother until the babies arrive."

"I thought you liked my mother."

"I've come to love your mother, you know that. But before my confinement begins, I wanted one last adventure."

"Ireland," Jeannette declared in a lowering tone, "is no adventure."

"Oh, but it is," Violet said, turning again toward Jeannette. "The drive here from Waterford was lovely, so green and verdant despite the season. But then, I have always enjoyed the country. Just as it has always been the city for you, which is precisely the reason we've come."

"What do you mean?"

Violet grinned, barely contained excitement sparkling in her gaze. "Only ten days past, I had a visit from Mama and Papa. The three of us had a long talk, and after a while I was able to convince them how sorry you are for the embarrassment you caused —"

A loud, derisive snort rang out from Kit's direction.

Violet shot him a quelling look to which he shrugged, clearly unrepentant. "As I was saying, the embarrassment and shame we *both* caused others with our imprudent, hurtful deception. Although I cannot pretend to be entirely repentant, considering the ultimate outcome."

She took Adrian's hand in hers and gave it a squeeze, exchanging a long, tender look with him that spoke volumes.

Violet resumed her story. "I know I hadn't your permission, but I showed our parents a few of your letters to me to let them see what a quiet life you are leading now and how contrite you have become. Without too much more argument, I managed to persuade them to relent."

Jeannette clasped her hands between her breasts in sudden, hopeful anticipation. "Yes? And?"

"And I have come — we have come — bearing the most wonderful news. You have been forgiven and may return home. We are here to take you back to England!"

A bolt of delight surged through Jeannette, setting her entire frame atingle. Clapping her hands, she squealed and stamped her feet in a rapid dance against the carpeted floor, uncaring whether or not the reaction appeared ladylike.

Racing for her twin, she enveloped Violet in a rapturous hug, squeezing her tight despite her sister's bulk. "You mean I'm reprieved? No more prison? No more exile? No more Ireland?"

"Well," Violet said, "I would never call this lovely house a prison, but yes, you are free."

She released Violet. "Hooray, hooray and huzzah. Oh, you are the dearest, kindest, most wonderful sister anyone could have. I take back every cross word I've ever said about you and promise never to utter another to you again."

Violet laughed. "I shall hold you to that next time I turn up in your black books."

Jeannette waved a hand. "For this, you never shall again." She did another improvised jig. "Thank you, thank you, thank you."

Home, she sang to herself. *I am going home.* Back to England, to civilization, where everything would once again be just as it ought. Where she would see her friends again, resume her place as a trendsetter among the young set. Oh, the parties and soirees and fêtes she would attend. A round of country visits this winter perhaps, then off to London for the Season in the spring. The very idea made quivers of glee race up and down her spine. She could scarcely wait, already envisioning how best to accomplish what was certain to be her triumphant return to Society.

"Now that's settled," Kit said, "do you suppose someone could ring for tea? I, for one, am famished."

"Nuncheon is due to be served in a little over an hour." Still floating aloft on a cloud of happiness, Jeannette launched into another series of questions for her sister. "So what exactly did Mama say? Does she seem eager to have me home again? And what of

London? Did she mention a trip to London?"

Violet smiled and with good grace began to answer.

"But I am hungry now," Kit complained after a minute.

Jeannette tossed him a glance. "Then you'll enjoy the meal that much more. Tea now will only spoil your appetite."

"It won't spoil *my* appetite. The ham and eggs I ate this morning wore away hours ago. Not to worry, I shall be fully able to do justice to two meals."

Violet joined the discussion. "Actually, I could do with a light snack before nuncheon as well." She laid a hand over her belly. "I seem to share Kit's affliction these days and am forever hungry. The babies give me such cravings. I've quite driven our chef at Winterlea mad with all my requests. Lately, I've developed an alarming penchant for fresh fig pudding and pickled beets."

"Eaten together, if you can believe," Kit interjected before making a humorously disgusted face.

"They are delicious," Violet defended. "Oh, and I cannot get enough steamed artichokes and lemons and bananas too. All of which are frightfully expensive and very difficult to obtain this time of year. Poor

François. And poor, dearest Adrian, whom I awaken at all hours of the night."

"I don't mind, my dear," Adrian soothed. "The interrupted sleep or the increased appetite."

"What about the added pounds?" Violet questioned.

"Just more of you to love, sweetheart. I believe I once told you a bit of weight would not bother me in the least." Adrian slipped an arm around Violet's back, drawing her close against his side.

They gazed deeply into each other's eyes.

For an alarming instant, Jeannette feared Violet and Adrian were about to fall into a passionate embrace and start kissing right there in front of everyone. At the last second, the couple came to their senses and reluctantly broke apart.

Adrian cleared his throat. "If we are to take tea, then you ought to be seated. Too much standing will only make your ankles swell."

"You never cared about your sister Sylvia's swollen ankles," Violet said.

"That's because I am not married to Sylvia. Besides, her ankles are not nearly so lovely as yours."

A solicitous hand tucked beneath her

elbow, Adrian helped Violet return to the sofa.

Kit crossed his arms, an expression of satisfaction on his face. "So? Shall you ring or shall I?"

"Already done, my lord," Eliza Hammond said in a soft, faintly breathless voice. "While you were conversing, I took the liberty." She glanced quickly at Jeannette. "I hope you do not mind, my lady?"

Jeannette blinked in surprise at the other girl, whom, to be quite honest, she'd forgotten was even in the room. She certainly hadn't noticed Eliza move from her chair and cross to the far side of the room. Then again, she didn't think anyone else had noticed either. Considering how timid the little thing was, Eliza's independent actions seemed rather amazing.

"No, not at all."

Kit turned a wide, beguiling smile upon her sister's friend. "My thanks as well, Miss Hammond, for your gracious generosity." He placed a dramatic hand across his chest, made her an elegant half bow. "If not for your quick-thinking actions, I would no doubt have soon grown faint from starvation. You have my undying and eternal gratitude."

Hot color washed into Eliza's cheeks,

causing her skin to glow, a tremulous smile limning her lips. In that moment, she actually looked pretty, her eyes alight in a way Jeannette had never seen before.

"You are very welcome, my lord," Eliza replied on a near whisper.

But Kit's attention had already moved away, focused on the conversation his brother and Violet were having.

Eliza's gaze lowered, the attractive color fading from her cheeks, as if they had been washed with snow.

So that's the way the wind blew, was it? Jeannette mused. Poor Miss Hammond. In love with a young man, who was nearly oblivious to her existence. Who was used to drawing the gaze of all the most beautiful, accomplished, eligible young ladies of the Ton. A man who would likely never see ordinary Eliza Hammond as anything but the shy, dependable, bookish friend of his sister-in-law.

An unexpected curl of sympathy settled inside Jeannette and for the first time she felt honest sorrow for the girl.

Ah, love, how cruel an affliction.

A knock came at the door, one of the parlor maids entering the room. The girl curtseyed and bobbed her head, eyes going wide at the sight of such elegant company.

Her eyes grew wider as they landed upon Violet, the maid's lips parting as she looked between Jeannette and her twin. Then she fixed her sights on Jeannette. "Is there something you'd be needing, my lady?"

"Yes. Please ask Cook to send up the tea tray as soon as may be. Pray also inform the housekeeper that extra rooms will be required. My sister and her husband have arrived, along with his brother and my sister's friend. They shall need accommodations."

"Sure and it please you, your ladyship, but what's to do? Nearly all the rooms have been taken for the other guests."

"More shall simply have to be found. I am sure Mrs. Ivory will know how to remedy the situation. The tea, please, Janey, if you would."

The maid bobbed again and hurried from the room.

"What's this about guests?" Violet inquired.

Jeannette turned. "Our cousins are hosting an entertainment this evening. A ball. In all the excitement, it very nearly slipped my mind."

"Our cousins hosting a ball, hmm? And here I thought you were withering away from loneliness and boredom in the so-called wilderness."

"I was. I am," Jeannette defended. "To-night will be the first bit of Society I have enjoyed since my arrival."

"Leave it to you, Jeannette," Adrian said, "to put together a party at someone else's house while you are supposedly in exile."

"I *am* in exile and it's been dreadful."

A small noise came from the doorway. Jeannette heard it, turned her head to find Cousin Wilda hovering there. She saw the look of hurt on the older woman's face and cringed.

Oh, dear.

"Cousin," Jeannette said, jumping in to cover the awkward moment. "Only look who has arrived. Come in, pray, and allow me to make them known to you." Rushing forward, she drew Wilda's arm through her own, lowering her voice to a murmur. "And please forgive my thoughtless comment of a moment ago. You surely know I wasn't refer-ring to you or Cousin Cuthbert. You're both a delight, and I have so enjoyed my time here with the two of you."

"But we are not young and exciting, are we?"

Jeannette stared, not knowing how to reply without worsening matters.

Wilda unbent and patted her hand. "I understand, dear. Don't trouble yourself over it. Now, please make me known to your friends, if you would."

"Of course, and they are not friends, they are family."

Relieved to have been so easily forgiven, she led Wilda forward and began the introductions. The others offered a warm round of greetings, quickly setting the older woman at her ease.

"Pardon me for not being here earlier to welcome you," Wilda said, fingers plucking at the folds of her skirts. "We weren't expecting anyone to arrive for a few hours more."

"Do not worry yourself, madam," Adrian said. "The fault is entirely ours for not giving you better notice of our arrival. Come now, as Jeannette said, we are all family. There is no need to stand upon strict formality."

Wilda visibly relaxed, a wide smile tilting her lips. "No indeed, your Grace."

"Adrian, please. Or Raeburn, if you would prefer."

"Thank you, your Gr— I mean Adrian." She gave an amazingly girlish titter, briefly covering her mouth with a hand. "And you must call me Wilda."

"With pleasure."

Wilda paused and cast an animated gaze

over the group, as if a wonderful thought had just occurred to her. "Do any of you by chance care for whist?"

CHAPTER ELEVEN

"La, what fun." Jeannette dropped down into a chair next to her sister and Eliza. "Thank heavens for the interval between sets or I fear my feet might fall off from all the dancing."

She opened her fan to cool her warm cheeks. White, the fan had been chosen especially to match her ball gown of equally white watered silk with an overdress of beaded tiffany and blond Bruges lace. White silk slippers, long white gloves and a strand of simple, yet elegant pearls completed her ensemble.

"The evening is progressing splendidly, do you not agree?" she commented.

"Very splendidly. You have outdone yourself as usual," Violet said, raising a glass of punch to her lips.

Jeannette smiled, gratified by the compliment. She was gratified as well to see her sister dressed in another modish gown tonight, an utterly glorious confection of sapphire-shot silk with lines that complemented Violet's ripened figure in a very tasteful way.

Apparently exchanging places with each other for a few months last year had left behind some beneficial results, such as a much improved sense of style on her twin's part. For years she had harangued Violet to take a more active interest in her wardrobe. The needs of their deception, and a continued desire to be an asset to her husband, must have finally convinced Violet to mend her unfashionable ways.

Now, if only her sister could work the same miracle upon her friend Eliza. The young woman looked like an utter drab in her gown of filemot-colored taffeta. And if the shade weren't gruesome enough, the six-inch flounce around the hem turned the dress into an utter fright. Perhaps Miss Hammond's mantua-maker was blind, Jeannette mused. What other excuse could there be for such unapologetic ugliness?

No surprise that the men were staying well away. So far Adrian and Kit were the only gentlemen to take pity upon Eliza, offering a single duty dance each at the beginning of the evening. Their visible attentions had not been enough, however, to persuade the other men to follow suit. Not even the provincials, it seems, would stand up with timid, unfashionable Eliza Hammond.

At least Miss Hammond had Violet. Society being what it was, most people would have dropped the girl by now, but Violet had never allowed others to dictate her choice of companion. Violet's decision might not be the wisest one, but Jeannette could not condemn her sister's loyalty. Violet was a most excellent and steadfast friend — kind-hearted, thoughtful and generous to a fault.

Jeannette's gaze lowered to the visible evidence of her twin's pregnancy. What a fine mother she was going to make, Jeannette thought. Violet's children, whether they be boys or girls, would be very lucky indeed.

"How are you feeling?" she asked.

Violet raised a brow, as if mildly surprised but pleased by the inquiry. Resting a palm over her belly, her lips curved in a placid smile. "Perfectly well, all in all. The babies apparently realize something special is occurring this evening and are on their best behavior — only a single set of kicks thus far. I must confess I am no longer much used to late nights, though. At Winterlea I would be slipping into bed about now. But thankfully the nap I took after our nuncheon has proved very refreshing. So long as I can make it until supper, I should be fine. At midnight, you say?"

Jeannette nodded. "Among other things, we're serving lobster patties and prawns."

"Oh, I adore prawns," Eliza murmured from her seat on the opposite side of Violet. As if only then realizing she'd spoken aloud, she cast her eyes toward the floor.

Jeannette waited a second to make sure Eliza had nothing further to add, then changed the subject. "So, when do we return to London? I suppose tomorrow would be too soon."

"Rather," Violet said in a mildly ironic tone. "We ought to remain a few days at least. And I, for one, would like to become better acquainted with our cousins, dears that they are. I should also like to visit a few of the local sites while I am here. I understand there are some very fine Cistercian ruins at Jerpoint Abbey only a few miles distant. And then there is the Browne's Hill Dolmen not far in the other direction." She clasped her hands, warming to her subject. "Though we didn't have time to dawdle, it was intriguing to land in Waterford, where Strongbow, the first Norman king of Ireland, led his men ashore and conquered the country in 1169." She tapped a gloved finger against her lower lip. "Or was it 1170?"

"Seventy, I believe," Eliza piped up. "I distinctly remember reading about it in the guidebook. Though to be exact, I believe, his men came ashore at Bannow Bay."

While Violet and Eliza continued to debate the finer points of Irish history, Jeannette's thoughts winged unexpectedly to O'Brien. What would he make of it, had he been privy to the discussion? One thing of which she felt certain, he wouldn't be speaking of the invasion and conquest of Ireland with impartial detachment, regardless of the fact that the events had transpired over six hundred years ago.

"Wherever or whenever the Normans came ashore," Jeannette said, "I don't imagine the native Irish had much liking for it."

Violet and Eliza stopping talking, turned their heads to stare.

Jeannette stared back, nearly as surprised as they by the challenging remark that had slid so glibly off her tongue. Never before in her life had she uttered so patently philosophical a thought — at least not aloud and certainly never in public. Obviously, living in Ireland and associating with Irishmen, such as O'Brien, was having an alarming effect upon her. In London, she would not have bothered to listen to such talk, let alone taken the time or trouble to comment upon it.

A good thing she would soon be leaving for home.

A little V formed over the bridge of Violet's nose as she responded to Jeannette's remark. "No, I suspect you are entirely correct, particularly given the brutality I understand was used to capture the city and surrounding territories. To solidify his power, Strongbow subsequently married the daughter of one of the old Irish kings. But he remained with her and their offspring in the country afterward, even learning the Gaelic language. So one can't claim he reviled the natives. Not like later men, such as Oliver Cromwell."

Knowing she'd expressed far too much interest already, Jeannette hurried to re-establish her trademark air of disinterest. It wouldn't do for anyone, not even her sister, to suspect she was turning intellectual. "Enough, I beg you, or my poor brain may suffer a seizure. I suppose you can't help it, though, used as you are to regaling Raeburn with such talk while you are dragging him around from one moldy old place to another."

"Adrian enjoys such conversations and visiting ruins and other historical sites. He's a man of very diverse interests. In fact, he's off in Cousin Cuthbert's study right now, enjoying a lecture on exotic flora given by several members of the Royal Horticultural Society. He has hopes of convincing our cousin to give him a few cuttings to take back for propagation in our conservatory at home."

"And why aren't you in there listening? Such tedium sounds exactly the sort of thing you'd enjoy," Jeannette teased.

"I would have joined them, but apparently the lecture is for gentlemen only. I considered protesting, until I discovered they are smoking cigars, and smoke these days quite literally turns my stomach." Violet rubbed a hand over her rounded middle as if fighting queasiness at the thought. "Adrian is listening for me."

"How considerate of him." *How dull*, Jeannette thought.

"Cousin Wilda invited Eliza and me to play cards in her new card room, but I declined, fearing I wouldn't be able to sit close enough to the table to play." Violet gave a self-deprecating grin. "Not with this belly of mine. I was trying to convince Eliza to go and join the game only moments before you came off the dance floor."

"Oh, but I cannot leave you alone," Eliza protested. "You cannot dance and it would not be right to desert you."

"You wouldn't be deserting me," Violet said. "Honestly, I will be fine here in my chair, enjoying the music, watching the dancers."

"Raeburn would surely not approve of my abandoning you . . ."

Jeannette surveyed the room, listening with half an ear as her sister and Eliza continued to thrash out the issue. Guests congregated in groups of varying size around the attractively appointed room, chatting and gossiping and flirting while they sipped champagne from elegant crystal flutes or punch from delicate china cups. Others strolled at a leisurely pace around the periphery, a few taking advantage of an unlocked door to disappear into the gardens beyond despite the chilly air. If she wasn't mistaken, she had seen Kit Winter do that very thing not too many minutes past, a lithesome young redhead giggling on his arm.

A movement near the ballroom's large double doors caught her attention, her gaze drawn to a new figure standing in the entrance.

Dark and tall, he surveyed the room with a commanding gaze, his broad shoulders square beneath his exceptionally well-cut coat. He wore breeches of black superfine, a pure white shirt and an equally snowy Marcella waistcoat. His crisp linen cravat, also white, was tied around his neck in a fashionably precise Mathematical that would have satisfied even London Society's highest sticklers of style. White stockings molded a pair of attractively firm masculine calves, black dress pumps graced his feet.

Who is this now? she wondered, unable to place such a gentleman on the guest list. Obviously the man was late arriving, since he had not been introduced at the start of the evening as part of the receiving line. Might he be one of her cousin's colleagues visiting from London? But no, all those gentleman had arrived earlier, and surely no man of science would ever present a figure of such sartorial splendor.

So who was he?

Her breath caught in her throat, pulse quickening with interest as he strode into the room. He turned his head and she stopped breathing altogether, noting the unusual, vibrant color of his eyes.

Deep gentian blue. A shade she'd encountered only once before. A shade that belonged to one very specific, very Irish man.

Blood drained from her head then flooded back in a dizzying rush, making her glad for the support of the chair beneath her. Her thoughts scattered like so much dandelion fluff as the full weight of the truth settled upon her.

No, she denied, that gentleman could not be Darragh O'Brien.

Yet with every step that led him deeper into the ballroom, she became more certain that it was O'Brien, from the crown of his neatly brushed chestnut hair to the soles of his expensive shoes.

And where, she wanted to know, had he come by those shoes? Not to mention the clothing? To any casual observer he looked the part of a gentleman. Only, she knew better.

Her lips tightened. She had not seen him in weeks, had not exchanged so much as a word with the man in longer than that, yet here he stood, barging uninvited into her cousins' party. *Her* party, if truth be told; a fact of which he was very likely aware.

What was he doing here? And why? All her confusion and hurt over the way he had so thoroughly dismissed and ignored her returned with a vengeance.

"Well, whatever it is he wants, he can just do without," she muttered.

"Who can do without?" her twin inquired. "Of whom are you speaking?"

"What?" Jeannette blinked, found both Violet and Eliza watching her with curious interest. "No one, nothing, I . . . it is of no import." She raked her mind for an excuse. "I . . . um . . . only just remembered there is a matter I must check on before supper. With the dancing to resume shortly, I'd best not tarry."

That said, she leapt to her feet. With Darragh O'Brien firmly in her sights, she plowed forward like a mighty ship through deep seas. Her hope was to reach him before he made contact with any of the other guests. But seconds later she saw her hopes dashed as he engaged a couple in conversation. The Gordons, if she was not mistaken, cousins to Viscount Gordon himself. She increased her speed, determined to separate him from such illustrious personages before he did any irreparable damage.

Forcing her step to slow as she converged upon them, she barely restrained the unladylike urge to lock a hand around O'Brien's arm and physically yank him aside. She affixed a pleasant smile to her lips instead and murmured a greeting.

O'Brien turned, executed a precise bow. He met her gaze, eyes twinkling despite the polite expression on his handsome, clean-shaven face.

"How are you enjoying the evening thus far?" she asked the Gordons. "I couldn't help but notice what a striking couple you made earlier out on the dance floor."

"Thank you, Lady Jeannette," Mr. Gordon said. "We are indeed having a most excellent time. Mrs. Gordon and I always enjoy an opportunity to dance and make merry, especially when the musicians are as talented as those playing tonight."

Jeannette inclined her head. "They came all the way from Dublin . . ."

They spoke of music for a full two minutes before moving on to the weather, which of late had been turning brisk at night. Mrs. Gordon offered a story about one of her sons getting caught out in the rain and catching a terrible head cold, a tale Jeannette soon despaired might never come to an end.

Over the course of the conversation, O'Brien said little, offering only the occasional comment as he listened with apparent interest.

Finally, politeness dictated the four of

them separate to mingle with others. Jeannette curtseyed then seized the opportunity to maneuver O'Brien aside on the pretext of having him accompany her to the refreshment table for a glass of punch.

"Mr. O'Brien, whatever brings you here this evening?" she asked the instant they were out of earshot. She steeled herself against the dark, delicious scent of him that lightly teased her senses. Not cologne, she realized, but man.

All man.

Aware of her unwanted response, her discontent peaked higher.

"The festivities, of course." He nodded toward the ballroom full of guests. "You've put together a lively entertainment."

"Thank you. Though I must admit to a certain puzzlement at your attendance. Perhaps you are not aware, but this ball is for invited guests only."

One corner of his mouth curved upward. "So it is, but who says I wasn't invited?"

"I do, since I prepared the guest list myself. I know every name, and yours was not one of them."

"Obviously an oversight. Your cousin asked me a few days past. Did Merriweather say nothing of it to you?"

She frowned and refrained from rolling

her eyes. Leave it to Cousin Cuthbert to go around handing out impromptu invitations — and to his architect, no less.

"Yes, he did forget to mention it. And I must say I am surprised to see you here, since it was my understanding you had already departed, what with your work now complete."

"I was ready to travel home but changed my mind. After all, how could I leave without saying good-bye to you?"

His comment struck a nerve. "Quite easily, I should think, since you and I have had nothing to say to each other for months now."

There, she thought, that should set him on his ear.

His eyes gleamed, blue as gemstones. "Missed me, have you?"

Her heart jolted. "No, not a bit," she denied hastily. "Why, I have been so busy, I scarcely took notice of your absence."

"Ah." He grinned.

She didn't care for his grin, gorgeous as it might be. Nor for his cryptic exhalation.

"Just so," she continued. "Preparations for tonight's ball have kept me occupied from dawn to dusk, so I have scarce had time for aught else, not even my painting."

" 'Tis a shame to hear you've been neglecting your artwork."

She paused, wondering if he might finally mention her last infamous bit of artwork — her depiction of him as the devil. But other than a twinkle in his beautiful eyes, he said nothing further.

The devil.

"Yes, well," she said, absently watching the line of couples as they danced to the music. "Now that you've seen the ball, you'll probably want to be going."

"Going? But I only just arrived."

"Exactly. I am sure you'll be bored in no time at all."

"I find that unlikely, not with this crowd."

"But that is precisely the reason. Let us be honest, Mr. O'Brien, and admit this isn't exactly your usual sort of event."

Something hard flickered through his gaze. "A fancy ball, are you meaning, lass?" he said, his brogue growing audibly thicker. "Your dance isn't a ceili, I'm after admitting, but it'll do for now."

"What is a ceili?" she said, unable to keep herself from asking.

"A fine Irish shindig with drink and dance and all the trimmings. Like this but more boisterous. That said, you can't claim I'm not dressed for your fancy doings tonight."

She swept a glance over his unmistakably

elegant attire. "Hmm, where did you happen by those clothes?"

"Got them from a tailor, the last time I was in London."

"You were in London?"

"Aye. We architects kick the ol' sod off our feet every now and again. I've traveled to many of the best cities in the world."

"Really? Which ones?" she questioned, her attention caught.

"Paris, for one, not long after Bonaparte took his second beating at Waterloo. Then there was Brussels and Vienna and Geneva, to mention a few more."

"What of Rome? Have you been to Rome?"

"Aye, I've been there a time or two. What of you? Where have you been?"

"Italy. I traveled quite extensively through the country with my great-aunt last year. We took in Rome's sights before moving on to Venice, Florence and Naples."

"What about Greece? 'Tis a grand country. You haven't completely lived, in my opinion, until you've seen the Parthenon at sunset. Or stood at the foot of the Acropolis while the afternoon heat ripples around you, the air so hot you can actually see it move. Then there's the ouzo and the olives. A fine delight, sipping a glass and eating at your leisure while you relax beneath an outcropping of shade."

For a brief instant, Jeannette's imagination took flight and she was there, basking in the heat, the briny tang of olives sharp against her tongue. O'Brien was there too, teasing her to indulge in a taste of the clear, potent brew she'd heard tell rushed straight and dizzying to a person's head.

Her gaze collided with his, a tingle of awareness streaking down her spine as if he had skimmed a finger over her flesh. Suddenly, she stiffened, returning to herself and her surroundings. She would not be drawn in by him, she thought, not again.

"No," she said, "I have not been to Greece nor the other places you mentioned."

He smiled teasingly. "Well, I won't hold it against you, lass. And you needn't worry I'll be bored this evening. I have a knack for fitting in wherever I may roam. Fact is . . ." His words trailed off as he stared across the room. "Did you know there's a woman across the way who looks precisely like you? Assuming you were to put on a pair of spectacles and find yourself in the family way, that is."

She flicked a glance across the ballroom to Violet. "Of course. That lady is my twin sister."

"Your twin? Saints be praised. God truly does work in mysterious ways to make two such magnificent creations as the pair of you."

He showed his teeth in a heart-stopping smile, the force of his magnetism enveloping her like a warm pair of arms. For a moment, she felt herself respond and lean into the invisible embrace.

Abruptly, she shook herself free. *This will not do,* she thought. *No, this will not do at all.* She was supposed to be annoyed with him, not on the verge of melting from a simple turn of phrase and a smile.

There was only one solution.

Darragh O'Brien must leave.

"My sister is a duchess."

"Is she, now?"

"Which should be explanation enough for why you would be more comfortable in other company. Surely you must see that you and the other guests here tonight move in different circles."

He folded his arms across his chest. "Do they, now?"

She shifted, discomfited by the amused derision that flared in his gaze. Dismissing it, she plunged onward.

"I am only trying to be honest. Cousin Cuthbert means well but he ought not to have invited you tonight. The people here are of good Society, even if most are little more than country Society."

The light in his eyes froze over, cold as an icy pond. "Don't forget the Irish in your statement."

"What?"

"The Irish, as in Irish country Society, or have you forgotten what nation you're in? I wonder how the rest of your guests would feel if they knew what you really thought of them, being no better than country folk and all."

"I never said —"

"You didn't have need to, your tone says it all. You may be a lady, Lady Jeannette, but you're also a blatant snob. Your high manners may serve you well in London, but they won't serve you here. As unfit as you may think me, I know more about the people here in this room tonight than you. Now, I'm going to ask one of the other young ladies to dance. Hopefully she won't find it too much of an offense."

He gave a crisp bow, strode away.

Dear heavens, that had not gone well at all. Not only had she insulted him and made him angry, but he wasn't leaving. And really, despite the severity of her words, that did not diminish their truth. He was an architect and middle-class — and in her world, middle-class architects did not rub elbows with lords and ladies, dukes and duchesses; not socially, at least.

And she wasn't a snob, she thought, no more so than any lady of her class. How dare he accuse her of such. Just because she came from noble bloodlines and moved in elite circles did not make her a snob. If she were, she would never have planned tonight's entertainment at all. By the standards of the Haut Ton, a mere handful of the guests present this evening would be tolerated by her usual group of peers in London. Governed by such strictures, even a dinner party would have been out of the question.

She drew in a shaky lungful of air and forced the tight muscles between her shoulder blades to relax. Opening her fan, she waved it quickly across her flushed face.

The musicians resumed their seats and took up their instruments. Playing a few practice notes, they signaled the guests that a new dance was about to begin. Eagerly, couples started to assemble on the floor.

A sandy-haired man several years her senior, a widower whose name she could not clearly recall, arrived to collect the dance she had promised him earlier in the evening. He bowed and extended an arm. She placed her hand upon his sleeve as manners required, allowing him to lead her onto the floor for the next set.

Two lines of dancers stood at the ready, men on one side, women on the other. A sprightly tune soon filled the room. Knowing the steps by heart, Jeannette found it an easy task to exchange polite, meaningless snippets of small talk with her partner as the movements of the dance brought them together then drew them apart again. Yet even as she danced and conversed, her thoughts were elsewhere, centered upon the tall, strikingly masculine figure of Darragh O'Brien as he moved only a few feet distant.

She did her best to ignore him, but felt her gaze drift toward him time and time again. He danced beautifully, moving with a smooth sophistication and skill that was nothing short of mesmerizing. It wasn't fair he should dance so well. Why couldn't he be some oaf, bumbling the complex steps of the country dance and crushing the poor toes of his partner? Instead, the girl was grinning ear to ear in rapt delight.

He ought to look out of place despite his urbane attire, his common manners revealing him for the rube he was. But his manners appeared anything but unrefined now as he moved among the company, looking as if he did indeed belong. Quite without trying he dominated the room, eclipsing every other man in attendance. And then he stood before her, his large hand enveloping her own much smaller one as the movements of the dance brought them together. For a few seconds, time slowed as their gazes collided, the impact sending a lightning bolt of sensation all the way to her toes. Her lips parted on a long breathless inhalation. Then he was gone, torn from her by the requirements of the dance.

Her body throbbed as though he'd done far more than simply touch her gloved hand. She made a misstep and nearly disgraced herself but managed somehow to regain her composure.

Only strict training saw her safely through the remainder of the set. Relief swept through her as the music finally fell silent. Her partner escorted her off the dance floor, but rather than go back to Violet and Eliza, she asked him to take her to the refreshment table. After politely ridding herself of the man, she waited, wondering if O'Brien would approach her. Whether he might ask her for the next dance despite their earlier words with each other.

Instead he stayed across the room, talking

with the dark-haired chit with whom he'd shared the last dance. He laughed, the sound of his merriment raking over Jeannette's spine like a sharp set of nails. The girl giggled and nodded her head, stars sparkling in her pert green eyes.

What was so amusing anyway? Jeannette ground her teeth as she watched them. Spinning on her heel, she forced herself to turn her back and remove Darragh O'Brien from her sight.

Why did she care if he danced and flirted with another young lady? Let him cavort with all the girls he wanted, it would not matter to her.

No more ridiculous moping, she rallied. This was her party and she was going to enjoy herself, even if it killed her.

Glancing up, she noticed a young man not much older than she gazing at her from across the room. He smiled at her, and against her better judgment she smiled back.

Encouraged, he gave a tug to his puce waistcoat and black coat sleeves then strode forward like a man prepared for battle. He bowed, a lock of his blond hair drooping over his forehead. "Good evening, Lady Jeannette. Neil Kirby. We met earlier in the receiving line."

"Of course, Mr. Kirby. A pleasure for the second time this evening," she said, smiling.

He smiled back, displaying a set of mostly straight teeth. "Ahem, I was wondering if you would do me the honor of standing up with me for the next dance?"

The next dance was the supper dance. Which meant she would not only have to take to the floor with him but would have to remain in his company during the midnight buffet set up in the adjoining dining room.

Manners dictated she accept. Personal inclination urged her to refuse. But she had no convenient excuse to offer, even her hostessing duties were merely a formality at this point. Looking into Neil Kirby's earnest brown eyes and boyishly appealing face, she decided to take pity. He appeared a pleasant enough young man, easily managed and effortlessly entertained, a new supplicant literally begging to worship at her feet. Just the sort of balm she needed to soothe her ragged emotions.

Let O'Brien ignore her. She had no need of his attentions.

Turning her most dazzling smile on the hapless youth before her, she watched him stare as though momentarily stunned by an intense flash of light.

"Thank you, sir," she said, "I should be delighted."

He ought not to have come to the ball, Darragh berated himself, knowing he was the world's grandest fool.

He nearly hadn't attended, changing his mind at least a dozen times after going downstairs to Lawrence's study earlier this evening. Over a draft of Irish whiskey whose bite had been sharp enough to scald the first layer of skin from his throat, he'd worried and debated, all but pacing a hole in his friend's fine Persian carpet while he dithered over the matter.

Last week, when Merriweather had issued the invitation, a refusal had come readily to Darragh's lips. Not out of pique but from pride. The invitations might say Mr. and Mrs. Merriweather on them, but the party was *her* doing. Formal written invitations, not a one of which had been addressed to him. An oversight, Merriweather had said, flustered when he'd realized Darragh's name had been omitted from the guest list.

Everyone who was anyone for fifty miles around had been invited. Even Lawrence had received one of her cards, his friend's name scripted out in her delicate, flowing hand. But Lawrence was away in Dublin on business these three weeks past. He didn't know a thing about the ball. If Lawrence had known, his friend would surely have warned him off, congratulating Darragh for resisting the charms of Lady Jeannette these many weeks.

"Why tempt fate, lad?" Lawrence would have said, when Darragh was all but free.

Yes, why tempt fate?

He'd been prepared to be on the road by now, traveling home to his siblings in the west country. In the midst of packing his bags, he'd gone downstairs to purloin a piece of notepaper and seen the invitation lying on Lawrence's desk. That's when he'd reconsidered Merriweather's offer.

But now that he was here, he knew he should have stayed away. Just seeing her again brought back all the old urges, Jeannette Rose Brantford drawing him in a way no other woman ever had. He didn't even have to glance in her direction for her beauty to beckon him, mad and alluring as a siren's song.

Pure Irish pride was the only thing that had kept him on the dance floor, kept him dancing with other women when there was only one he really wanted in his arms.

Afterward, he'd watched her promenade into the dining room on the arm of some sophomoric youth, the lad clearly besotted and utterly out of his league. Since then Darragh'd done his best to focus his attention on the young lady he'd taken in to supper, as well as the other trio of couples at their table. In between bites of succulent roast beef and buttery lobster, conversation buzzing at a leisurely pace in his ears, his gaze drifted far too frequently across the room to her.

Jeannette.

Her name whispered like an illicit murmur through his mind, its rhythm sending his blood pumping harder and hotter through his veins. The sight of her enough to make him ache in places best not acknowledged in mixed company. He was glad he hadn't worn the skintight breeches some gentlemen favored, else he would have found himself hastening to hide the evidence of his semi-aroused state. He shifted in his chair and warred against the baser side of his longings.

She'd galled him tonight with her arrogant talk and her narrow-minded assumptions. If only she knew the truth about his real circumstances, and especially his title, only imagine what she would say and do?

But for all the irritation she sometimes caused him, she entranced him even more.

He missed their verbal jousts and gentle sparing. He missed their flirtatious banter. Most especially, he missed their kisses — those dangerous, delicious, forbidden kisses that were worth every second of risk.

He shook his head against such thoughts. A glutton for punishment, that's what he was. Yet hard as he'd tried to erase her from his mind over the past two months, he'd failed miserably.

'Twas true he had forced himself to stay away from her, but in his head he'd been with her every day. Watching while he worked, a part of him always alert and hoping to catch a glimpse of her as she went about her day. Listening for the unexpected murmur of her velvet-soft voice. Closing his eyes if he happened to catch the sound of her words drifting through an open window or along a corridor. Savoring the sensation with the care of a man holding a rare, precious butterfly in his palm.

When he'd left Lawrence's house tonight he'd told himself he was going to the party to prove he could walk away from her and never look back in regret. That he'd built up the memory of her in his mind and when he saw her again the spark would be well and truly extinguished.

Well, all he'd proven was what a colossal

idiot he was — the flame a long way from extinguished, on both sides. Aye, she might profess to care nothing for him, but it was clear she felt more than she let on, else his withdrawal from her life would not have bruised her feelings. And the spark between them leapt like electricity arcing through the air ahead of a fierce storm. He could feel the power of it even now, as if there were some invisible tether stretched between them, tugging them toward temptation.

What did she think she was doing with that boy sharing her table? Surely she couldn't be interested in the stripling?

He watched Jeannette nod and smile at something the youth said moments before she raised her glass to drink a sip of champagne. Darragh nearly groaned aloud at the sight of her lips, left moist and glistening from the taste of cool wine.

She was glorious, regal. Glowing moonbeam pretty in her white finery, her pale golden hair caught in a delicate upsweep that curled becomingly around her ears. He'd like to see that hair down. See it loose and brushed, flowing like spun silk around her bare shoulders.

His fist tightened where it rested on his thigh. Likely he wasn't the only male feeling her effect, that poor stupid boy obviously bespelled and having no notion of the pain she'd leave in his heart when she cast him aside.

Darragh's own heart gave a painful, mocking squeeze, warning him afresh of the hazard.

If he had any sense, he'd stand up this instant, make some feeble excuse to the others and walk out. Sever the connection. End this senseless, hopeless attraction once and for all. Then in the morning he'd be off as planned, riding hard and fast to put nearly the whole of Ireland between them.

Instead he sat. He ate. He talked, doing his best not to glance in her direction, at least not more than once or twice a minute.

At length, supper finally came to an end. Everyone returned to the ballroom. Once there, Darragh bowed and thanked the young lady with whom he'd shared the meal, ashamed he couldn't so much as recall her name.

Duty done, he scanned the room for Jeannette, but she wasn't there. And neither, as he made a further visual survey, was the stripling lad.

Chapter Twelve

Young Mr. Kirby was foxed.

Jeannette had known he was foxed — how could he be otherwise after imbibing five glasses of champagne at supper! But despite the drink, he seemed harmless enough. So harmless, she had thought nothing of accompanying him on a tour of the new wing when he'd suggested the expedition, thinking the exercise might help him walk off the worst of his drunk.

Her family had all but deserted the festivities. Supper done, Violet had quietly murmured into Jeannette's ear her intention to retire upstairs to bed for the night. Eliza decided to go up as well, eager to escape what had clearly been another disappointing evening for her. As for the gentlemen, Adrian said he planned to see his wife safely tucked into bed then return downstairs to hear one last lecture on horticulture. While Kit made merry on the dance floor with yet another winsome brunette.

Jeannette would be there now as well, dancing her feet numb, had it not been for the continued presence of Darragh O'Brien. Contrary to her fears, the other guests seemed to find him scintillating, particularly the female guests. After hours watching him flirt and flatter his way around the room, she'd had enough and needed to get away.

The man was an unrepentant wolf and shameless about it to boot. He'd certainly smiled often enough at whatever that willowy redhead he'd escorted into dinner had been saying. In between listening with half an ear to Kirby's ever more rambling diatribes about horse racing and golf — as though she could possibly care a whit about either topic — she had kept a surreptitious eye on O'Brien during the intolerably long meal.

How dare O'Brien come here tonight and disrupt her entertainment. How dare he sit barely four yards away and act as if she didn't even exist!

Well, in a couple more hours he would be gone. Gone for good, and she, for one, would be glad.

Wouldn't she?

Suppressing a desolate sigh, she gazed around the dimly lighted conservatory. The space was warm and humid, the cool night air outside pressing against the glass-paned room like the hug of an insistent lover. Vegetation thrived thick and green within, spilling up and out and over from every possible direction.

She turned to Kirby to ask him to escort her back to the ballroom. But before she could even form the words, he yanked her hard against him and fastened his mouth to hers.

On a yelp, she shoved against him, twisting her head to avoid the sloppy, drunken kisses he was intent upon taking. His breath wafted over her face like a stiff, wine-scented breeze. Wrinkling her nose, she redoubled her efforts to push him away.

"Mr. Kirby, stop that this instant," she admonished.

He ignored her, enthusiastic hands roaming to places he had no right to touch. *Good gracious,* she thought as she squirmed to get away. She'd heard about octopi and their eight long tentacles, but she'd never before found herself in the clutches of such a creature. Apparently alcohol had helped Kirby grow far too many arms along with a sudden burst of daring.

"Mr. Kirby, did you hear me? I said *let me go!*"

She shuddered as his moist lips grazed her cheek, then thrust her arms between them and gave a mighty shove. When the move once more failed to set her free, she lifted her foot and stomped down hard, grinding her heel into his instep with as much force as she could muster.

This time he was the one to yelp, sounding like a hurt puppy. As quickly as he'd grabbed her, he set her free, stumbling backward in a trio of unsteady steps. Fighting for balance, he reached out and grabbed on to a nearby bush, tearing off a large handful of leaves.

Swaying, but on his feet, he shot her a wounded look. "What'd you do that for?"

"To get you off me, you idiot." Disgusted, she wiped a hand over her damp cheek. "Don't ever do that again."

He blinked, confusion clear on his face. "But you wanted me to kiss you."

"I most certainly did not."

"Yes you did. Why else did you come here with me?"

"To take a stroll, not so you could grope me like some slippery ten-armed eel. You, Mr. Kirby, are obnoxiously drunk and not in your right senses. Since you are, I will excuse your ungentlemanly behavior. Now, go back to the party."

He thrust out his lower lip. "But I don't want to go back to the party." He paused, gave her a leering grin. "Not without you."

"Go, sir. This instant." She pointed an imperious finger toward the doorway.

He grumbled something unintelligible under his breath before swinging around like a petulant child to do as he'd been told. He took two steps then stopped and clutched his stomach. "Don't feel well."

"I am scarcely surprised," she scolded. "It's what comes from overindulging."

He puffed out his cheeks. "I mean I really don't feel well. I think I may be sick."

She took a closer look at him, noting his sudden pallor and the perspiration beading on his forehead. She'd seen her brother, Darrin, look just like that the last time he'd been too deep in his cups. The results had not been pretty.

"Good heavens, don't you dare cast up your accounts in here."

Losing no time, she grabbed him by the elbow and hurried him toward a small glass side door. Twisting the handle, she flung it open and ruthlessly shoved Kirby outside. He stumbled a few steps then caught himself. Seconds later, he broke into an indelicate run toward a hedge of low bushes that grew a few yards distant.

Grimacing in disgust, she closed the door behind her, turning the lock with a decisive *click. Nodcock,* she thought, catching sight of him bent double, heaving violently before she could manage to look away. She swung around, relieved to note that the thick glass around her muffled the worst sounds of his distress.

Not long afterward, she saw him slink away, hopefully in search of his coach and the long ride home.

Grass-green fool, she thought, relieved to be rid of him.

But to be fair, he wasn't the only fool tonight. She'd been stupid to come here with Kirby in the first place, especially since she'd thought him far too young and no more than passably interesting even at the start. Obviously all this rural air was muddling her judgment.

Releasing an audible sigh, she decided she ought to return to the ballroom. It would not do to be missed. Glancing down, she checked her dress to make sure nothing was askew after Kirby's crass, drunken attempt to kiss her. Noticing a ruffled bit of lace, she brushed her fingers over the material to smooth it back into place.

"Concealing the evidence, are you now?" a deep male voice challenged from the shadows, the tone one of velvet over steel despite its outwardly musical lilt.

Even if there had been no accent, she would have recognized the speaker anywhere. Her head snapped up, gaze colliding with Darragh O'Brien's as he stepped forward out of the muted darkness.

She straightened, her heart skipping a single hard beat beneath her breast. "What are you doing here? And how long have you been standing over there, lurking in the vegetation?"

His lips quirked into a humorless half smile. "Not long. Actually, I only just arrived. But you haven't yet answered my question."

"Was that a question? It sounded more like an accusation to me."

He turned his head, scanned the area with an inquiring gaze. "Question or accusation makes little difference. Where is he, then?"

Whether from temper or conceit, she decided to play dumb. "He who?"

"You know who. That pale-haired stripling whose arm you were hanging on when you came in here to tryst. Lost his nerve, did he, and ran away? Or was it a case of his kisses being so dreadful you had to throw him out entirely?"

Jeannette bristled, annoyed that O'Brien's

suspicions were so close to the mark. "I did not come here to tryst. But even if I had, it is no concern of yours."

He set his palms on his narrow hips. "Ah, so his kisses were that bad, then. Still, considering he's no more than a wet-behind-the-ears lad, you've little right to be surprised or disappointed. If you had a craving to indulge in such forbidden temptations, you oughtn't to have settled for a boy. You should have come to a man."

She barked out a laugh. "A man like you, I suppose."

He stepped closer, looming over her, dark and magnetic and powerfully appealing. "I haven't caught sight of any other man worthy of you inside that ballroom tonight."

The bottoms of her feet tingled inside her slippers, nerve endings humming as if electrified. For the first time in months, since the last time she'd stood with him toe to toe in confrontation, she felt vibrantly, intensely alive.

She held her ground, outwardly calm despite the frenzied pounding of her heart. "Lowering as it may be to hear, you aren't that man either. Until you arrived tonight, I'd quite forgotten you existed."

His eyes snapped hot. "Did you now, lass?"

He took a menacing step forward, measuring as he held her captive within his gaze. "Or are you lying? Lying to hide the fact that you haven't been able to forget me no matter how hard you've tried. Lying when the truth is you've thought of me and dreamed of me and missed me so, it shames you to admit it even to yourself."

The air rushed from her lungs, her knees growing dangerously weak. "Don't be absurd. You've never been anything but a thorn in my side. A very large, very aggravating, thoroughly annoying thorn of which I cannot wait to be rid."

He moved until a bare inch remained between them, so close his clean male scent filled her nostrils, heat and strength rippling off him like the force of an indomitable tide.

"A thorn, am I?" he said. "Well, to my knowledge thorns are known to sting and prick and be devilish difficult to remove. I'm a man given to taking on the occasional bet and I'd wager I'm one thorn you've yet to work free."

His voice lowered to a whisper, husky and seductive. His gaze roved over her face, skimmed and lingered upon her lips. "Am I, Lady Jeannette? Am I out from under your skin? Or am I burrowed in there even now, making you ache in places no proper lady should confess to feeling?"

She gasped, nearly choking on the warm humid air that made it all but impossible to draw a satisfactory breath. Air that left her dizzy and half-suffocated. But for what? Him or her next breath? And why did both suddenly seem vital to her continued existence?

"Why are you here?" she murmured. "Why did you seek me out when it's been ages since we last met. Mayhap you are the one who hasn't been able to forget. Who has found it impossible to get me out from under your skin. Is that the real truth? That you're besotted and can't get me out of your mind?"

His jaw tightened, their eyes locking, neither of them able to look away.

Her lips parted.

His eyelids drooped.

And then without any conscious awareness they came together. She whimpered as he took her mouth with savage purpose, his arms crushing her, cradling her as passion exploded between them like a smoldering conflagration.

Desire tore through her, rocket hot, every thought and caution melting beneath the need to touch him, taste him and have him do the same to her. She raised her arms, slid her questing fingers into the thick wavy silk of his hair. He groaned as she tugged his head closer and opened her mouth to invite his tongue inside.

He played upon her, waging a passionate battle of tempt and delight. Then he let her do the same to him. Let her trace the shape of his teeth. Glide the tip of her tongue over the ultrasmooth skin of his inner cheeks. Lose herself in the perilous thrill of exploring every dark, wet, delicious taste and texture, each wonderful sensation that rippled like a wicked breeze over her entire body.

If she'd thought her memory of his kisses had been exaggerated and overblown, she quickly discovered her error, dazed and dazzled by his undeniable skill in matters of the flesh.

But all too soon kisses weren't enough for either one of them, merely a prelude to a far grander symphony of carnal gratification that could yet be had. Unlike with Kirby, whose touch she'd found distasteful, she welcomed each stroke and caress of Darragh's broad, capable hands roving over her body. They glided, those hands, along her neck, down her back, across her hips. Over the delicate base of her spine, lingering with a gentle kneading motion that left her half-mad and thoroughly tormented.

She arched and purred low in her throat, striving to get closer. He bent to assist, planting his palms over her buttocks to raise her upward, settling her pelvis against the arousal that strained iron hard beneath his breeches.

Darragh groaned and shuddered with need, knowing he'd made a monumental mistake. He drew a ragged breath, unable to keep himself from pressing her tighter. He rocked ever so slightly, letting her feel his erection, his ravenous, poorly leashed hunger, wondering if such a blatantly sexual move would shock her, repel her.

Instead she clung, continued to kiss him as if he were a delicious feast and she was starving after months without food.

He'd better put an end to this, he thought, barely coherent. Set her safely away from him before things got completely, disastrously out of hand. But Blessed Mary, how he wanted her. Wanted to throw up her skirts and feel her firm legs lock around his waist. Wanted to tear open his breeches so he could drive into her over and over and over again until the bliss shook them both.

He waited, the sensible part of him praying she would put an end to the insanity and make him release her. The wicked part urged him on, coaxed him to cup one of her sweet pliant breasts in his hand, to tease the nipple until it peaked against his palm.

Shaking, he fought his inner demons and prepared to let her go. Then she moaned, a sound that shot straight to his loins, making him throb and ache. Her arms looped around his neck and she clung, biting at his mouth, sucking at his tongue in a way that made his head spin, that scorched every last rational thought from his mind like fire set loose in a patch of dry forest.

Driven by instinct, he carried her across to a nearby wooden potting table, knocking over a pair of empty clay containers that rolled toward the edge. The sound of their shattering onto the slate floor scarcely registered as he set her down, pushed up her skirts so he could spread her legs and settle himself in between. Reaching out, he loosened her bodice, nearly ripping the delicate material in his haste to expose her breasts to his touch.

She murmured, stiffening slightly as if in confusion. He kissed her again, a wet, open-mouthed mating that literally stole his breath. And obviously hers, since whatever inhibitions might have remained seemed to die a quick, febrile death. He gave one last tug to her bodice, releasing her glorious rounded breasts into his waiting hands. He stroked her for a long intense minute, then replaced his hands with his mouth.

Her nipple was tight, puckering into a bead beneath his greedy, wandering tongue. He toyed with her flesh, making her shift in seemingly restless, unsatisfied want while he suckled deeply upon her. She lifted one hand, massaged his scalp, sifting her fingers through his hair, soughing with unmistakable pleasure as he moved to lavish attention upon her other breast.

Jeannette stroked his cheek, utterly abandoned as he drew upon her, his jaw working beneath her encouraging hand. His mouth was pure magic against her flesh. Her head buzzed, lost in a fervid haze she didn't fully comprehend or have the will to question.

She wasn't an innocent, she had been touched before. But never like this, never in a way that made her blood rush quick and burning through her veins, that sent her heart caroming so hard and fast she feared it might beat from her chest.

She trembled, surrendering herself to his every caress, each faint wish and whim that somehow became her own only moments after he suggested it with a fresh, inventive touch. Her eyes closed, head lolling back, her neck weak as a wilted flower stem.

Still feeding upon her breast, one sturdy arm at her back to support her, his free hand skimmed over her calf and knee before slipping upward beneath her rumpled gown. He continued onward, sliding his palm in a long, smooth stroke over one bare thigh. Her muscles quivered, completely at his mercy as his fingers traveled higher.

Her head came up and her eyes flew open as he parted her most vulnerable flesh and slid a finger inside where her body wept with desire. She gasped as he stroked within her, as he added another finger to stretch her wide.

And the world narrowed down to his hand, to his mouth, to his least touch and command. He moved his thumb and brushed her in the most sensitive of spots, then gently bit her nipple.

She cried out, shuddered violently. Pleasure, more amazing than anything she'd ever experienced, flooded inside her. She felt herself dampen his hand, slightly embarrassed when he withdrew his fingers moments later.

But she needn't have worried that she was in any danger of being abandoned. Pulling her closer to the edge of the table on which she sat, he straightened and reached toward his breeches' buttons. He opened one, nearly fumbling it in his haste. He was opening the second when a voice spoke, the sound of footfalls echoing against the conservatory pavers.

"Let me assure you, gentlemen, the scent of the *Epidendrum nocturnum* is well worth the trouble of viewing it so late in the eventide."

Dimly in some remote recess of her brain, Jeannette heard the words, recognized her cousin's voice.

Darragh must have heard it too, since he froze suddenly against her. But even as their dazed, horrified gazes collided, she knew it was already far, far too late.

"Right this way. I think you'll find this most intrig— Dear saints in heaven, preserve us!" Bertie's exclamation reverberated like the crack of a pistol shot through the conservatory, he and the group of gentlemen behind him coming to a sudden halt.

Over Darragh's shoulder Jeannette encountered the stare of a dozen pairs of eyes. Even in the low light she could read a range of expressions, from shock and disapproval to amusement and even lust.

Among them were three far too familiar faces. Cousin Cuthbert, his mouth working like an out-of-water trout, cheeks stained red as currants. Kit Winter, eyes wide with a mixture of surprise and amazement. And Adrian, tall and forbidding, his features stiff with a condemning displeasure that would have set a hardened battlefield veteran atremble.

She tried to move, wishing desperately she had the power to simply vanish. But her body refused to obey, as though her limbs had hardened to stone. On a whimper, she buried her face against Darragh's shoulder.

In response, he sprang into action and lifted her from the table. Deft and efficient, he tugged her skirts downward to discreetly cover her legs, then angled his body to shield her from view. In a final protective gesture, he opened his evening coat and tugged her close, providing her an opportunity to adjust her bodice into its proper place.

A pronounced silence settled over the room.

"Well, Merriweather, you promised us a superlative display and I must say you did not disappoint," one of the gentlemen quipped. "Though I fear your orchids may pale in comparison."

Several of the men chuckled, while others coughed behind their gloved hands to cover their embarrassment.

"Speaking of orchids, cousin," Adrian

interceded in a soft but implacable tone, "why don't you proceed on with the tour. There is nothing further to see here."

Cuthbert cleared his throat and shuffled his feet as if awakening from a fugue state. "Yes, yes, quite right, quite right. Um, straight ahead, gentlemen. The . . . the orchids are just through here."

Cuthbert motioned his fellow members of the Royal Horticultural Society forward, spreading his arms wide to herd forward a couple stragglers who would obviously have preferred to linger. The sound of their footsteps echoed against the stone flooring, along with their murmuring whispers, before both gradually receded.

Only when they'd gone did Adrian turn.

Jeannette stole a peek and swallowed hard at the expression on her brother-in-law's face. Gathering the shreds of her courage, she tried to step out of Darragh's sheltering embrace. But he wouldn't let her, at least not entirely, keeping his hand linked with hers as he turned to face forward beside her.

"And here you were worried about me courting scandal with too much indiscriminate flirting," Kit remarked to Adrian. "Guess I'm looking pretty wholesome now, hmm?"

Adrian turned his head to glare at his younger brother. "What are you still doing here? Why didn't you go with the others?"

Kit shot him a beleaguered look. "To view a bunch of flowers I didn't want to see in the first place? Thank you, but no thank you. If you'll recall, you're the one who near twisted my arm off to get me out here."

"A lamentable necessity considering the fact that you were on the verge of being hunted down by an irate father."

Kit shrugged, his expression one of utter innocence. "Lydia's father was overreacting. I only took her outside for a bit of fresh air, since she said she was warm."

"So warm it took her a half an hour to cool off?"

"Some women have hot-blooded constitutions."

Adrian closed his eyes as though pained. "Enough. Now go."

"All right, but you're a fair way to becoming a curmudgeon, do you know? Must remember to have a talk about it with Vi, when she's a little less in the family way."

"Leave Violet alone and go to bed."

"Like I said. Curmudgeon." Tossing a last sympathetic glance toward Jeannette and Darragh, Kit turned and walked away.

Jeannette swallowed, her throat tight as

though she were about to face the Spanish Inquisition. Instead she had to face Adrian, mortifying under any circumstances. Doubly so considering their history with each other.

He waited, arms crossed reproachfully over his chest. "So, have you nothing to say? You haven't even made it back to England and already you've landed in the scandal broth again."

She opened her mouth, but no words emerged. What could she say? There were no explanations to justify being caught in an act she could barely justify to herself. She'd lost her head utterly and completely in a way she never imagined she could, so given to passion she'd forgotten any sense of place or propriety. Worse, she'd been discovered in the most humiliating manner, leaving her without any hope of redemption. She didn't even want to contemplate what this would mean to her reputation or her future. The possibilities made her shiver.

When she said nothing, Adrian pinned Darragh with a grim look. "And what of you, sir? Do you have a voice or are you conveniently mute as well?"

"Aye, I've a voice, and a name as well. Darragh O'Brien." He thrust out a hand. "And you are?"

Adrian made no effort to accept Darragh's proffered hand. "Raeburn. The Duke of Raeburn. The lady's brother."

"Brother-in-law," she corrected, breaking her silence.

Adrian inclined his head. "Quite right, brother-in-law. And as your brother-in-law and the most immediate male member of your family present, I believe it is my duty to oversee this matter."

Jeannette scuttled her brow. "What do you mean, oversee?"

"You've been compromised, Jeannette. Thoroughly and very publicly compromised. Steps must be taken without delay to set this situation aright. Or as right as it may reasonably be put under the circumstances."

Jeannette watched Adrian glower at Darragh, the two men's eyes virtually on the same level. Tall and sturdy, they were nearly a match for each other in terms of height and power. Darragh's build was leaner and looser, more acrobatic. Adrian's shoulders wider, his chest heavier. But in a fight, she suspected they'd both give as good as they got. The winner would be anyone's guess.

However, Adrian was far too civilized to engage in a brawl. At least she assumed he was, aware that he regularly sparred and won at Gentleman Jackson's Boxing Salon when in London. She knew instinctively that Darragh wouldn't be nearly so refined. Over the years he'd probably fought in the streets, relying upon bare knuckles and sheer Irish stamina. She tightened her hand in his as if to restrain him. But she needn't have worried, both men seemingly satisfied at the moment to duel merely with their eyes.

Adrian thrust out his chin. "I shall expect you tomorrow. Promptly at nine, shall we say?"

Darragh nodded. "Nine it is."

"Nine? What happens at nine?" she asked. "I won't have the two of you fighting."

Adrian met her gaze. "Don't worry. There will be no fighting. At least not so long as he agrees to the terms."

A sense of impending doom settled like a lead sinker in her chest. "What terms?"

"Of your marriage settlement, of course."

"M-marriage!" she exclaimed. "You mean to O'Brien? But I cannot marry him."

Becoming violently aware of her palm nestled inside Darragh's clasp, she dropped his hand as if it had turned red hot. Then for good measure, she put several more inches between them by taking a single, dramatic step sideways.

Darragh quirked a rueful eyebrow but made no comment.

"I am afraid, Jeannette," Adrian said, "that you have little choice in the matter. Your fate, as it were, was sealed the moment you chose to go beyond the bounds of propriety and do what you did with this man."

"From the sound of it, Lord Christopher went beyond the bounds of propriety to-night too."

"Perhaps. But the difference is, he didn't get caught."

She gulped, a sick wash sliding through her middle. "But I can't marry O'Brien. He isn't even a gentleman. He's an *architect*."

Darragh drew a deep breath and straightened his shoulders. "As fact would actually have it, I'm also an ea—"

"If I marry him, it will ruin everything," she wailed, drowning out the end of Darragh's statement. "I am supposed to return to London. I am supposed to regain my place in Society. I am supposed to marry a duke."

Adrian shook his head, plainly incredulous. "Well, it would appear you have once more put paid to your chance of that event ever happening. No man, duke or otherwise, will have you now. Mr. O'Brien is your only hope." He sighed, his tone softening slightly.

"Heavens, Jeannette, surely even you must recognize that fact."

"But —"

"There are no buts." Adrian gave her a firm stare, then turned to O'Brien. "Now, sir, you were saying?"

Darragh crossed his arms, his lean-hipped stance set at an almost pugnacious angle. "Nothing. Nothing at all. I believe everything that has need of saying has already been said."

Jeannette tossed him a glance, noticed the inflexible tilt to his jawline. Was he angry because she'd said she didn't want to marry him? Surely he couldn't wish to marry her either. Yet it would seem they had few options, both of them trapped like a pair of cats in a cage.

Unless Darragh reneged.

Perhaps if she could find a moment alone with him she might be able to convince him not to meet with Adrian tomorrow. Perhaps he could leave for his home, as relieved as she by his narrow escape from the parson's noose. But if she convinced him to flee, where would that leave her?

Ruined, that's where.

The gentlemen of the Royal Horticultural Society would flap their mouths like mynah birds, repeating every titillating detail of the debacle to anyone who cared to listen. The story would race through the Ton faster than a Derby-winning horse crossing the finish line.

If she accepted her fate and married him, the tale would soon enough die away. But if she did, she would be irrevocably wed to Darragh.

Why had she let him kiss her? Touch her? What insanity had possessed her to do the same back?

Desire.

The word slid over her senses like a caress, reminding her of embers that lay barely tamped even now. Her gaze roved over his face, recalling the faintly rough texture of his cheeks gently abrading her own, the hot, velvety interior of his mouth as he captured kiss after delicious kiss.

Yet there had to be more than physical need to make a marriage last. With another man she would have been prepared to let money and a title compensate for a lack of affection. But with Darragh, neither wealth nor social position would be forthcoming.

So what, then, of affection? What indeed of love?

Could she love him? She greatly feared she could, deeply and enduringly, if she allowed herself to succumb to such feelings.

Did she wish to love him? Most decidedly not.

She had been betrayed once by that tender emotion. She had no intention of being betrayed again. Which left her only one path — finding a way out of this marriage without completely closing herself off to the possibility of someday making another, more advantageous match.

She would take the easiest route to start. She would speak to Darragh and convince him not to agree to a wedding. After all, he wasn't a gentleman, bound through birth to abide by the rules of duty and honor.

"I don't believe everything has yet been said," she began, responding to Darragh's last remark. "If you don't mind, Raeburn, I should like a chance to converse with Mr. O'Brien. Alone. He and I have matters to discuss."

Adrian scowled, glancing back and forth between her and Darragh. "Whatever these so-called matters are, you can discuss them tomorrow, *after* arrangements have been settled concerning your marriage. Until then, I believe the two of you have spent more than enough time alone without the benefit of chaperone."

Jeannette bristled. "I haven't had an actual

chaperone since the first year of my come-out."

"Perhaps that is the problem. Come along, Jeannette. I'll escort you along the servants' stairs to your room, since I very much doubt you'll be desirous of returning to the ball."

She felt her skin pale, aware of the rumors that must already be spreading among the guests like a plague. Yes, mayhap it would be best to simply sneak upstairs. If she couldn't speak with Darragh tonight, she could catch him early tomorrow before he met with Adrian.

With a defiant set to her shoulders, she turned to Darragh. Leaning up, she lowered her voice to a whisper. "Don't agree to anything until after we've talked."

Darragh gave her an enigmatic look before some of the harsh lines slowly eased from his face. He reached for her hand, bowed over it before dropping a light kiss on top. "Don't fret, *a stóirín.* It'll all come right in the end."

She gazed into eyes blue as a summer sky, even in the tenebrous evening light, and prayed with all her soul that he was right.

CHAPTER THIRTEEN

Darragh presented himself promptly at nine the following morning.

To his surprise the duke had left instructions with a footman to have him shown immediately to a small study in the rear of the house. The room radiated masculinity, done in warm walnut with pieces of heavy, old-fashioned furniture and prints of birds and game on the walls. The fireplace grate stood unlighted, the odors of cold ashes, leather and ancient pipe smoke lingering in the air.

Of Jeannette he'd seen nothing on his way to the room, despite her whispered admonition that he not talk to her brother-in-law until after she had spoken to him.

But what was there for them to discuss? They'd been caught, discovered in the most compromising situation possible. Mother Mary, he'd been standing between her legs, tugging at his breeches' buttons when the whole crowd of them had shuffled in. He could only imagine the bawdy sight he and Jeannette must have made, putting on a show fit only for a house of sin.

And whether or not they'd actually completed the act made no matter, especially considering all they'd done beforehand. Jeannette was officially soiled goods and he was the ruin of her. Willing or no, they had to marry to set matters aright. He'd be a black fellow indeed to think of doing otherwise. And truth be told he had no real wish to do aught else.

Last night, after all was done and he'd lain in his bed with her fresh upon his mind, he'd waited for the panic to set in. Waited for the terror to sink deep and turn his bowels soft and liquid at the idea of being shackled to her for life.

But the feeling never came.

Instead he'd felt a kind of odd satisfaction, even anticipation at the knowledge that she would soon be irrevocably his own. His wife, to protect and keep, to delight and bedevil and cherish for all the rest of his days.

And with his ring upon her hand, he would be able to satisfy the lusty cravings that plagued him as if he were a brash lad sowing his first field of wild oats instead of a mature man full grown. He still couldn't fathom how he'd lost all control last night, so intent upon having her that every last shred of common sense had flown straight out of his head.

Perhaps a part of him hadn't cared, willing to face the risk, whatever it might be, in order to burn for a time within the fire of her touch.

And burn he had — and did still.

He had plans for a lengthy honeymoon, where they could lie abed and indulge in every explicit sexual act the two of them had a mind to try. Assuming he could coax her to the altar. She might have no choice in the matter, but that didn't mean she'd give in without a murmur.

But say her vows she would. Later, he would find a way to chase away her reservations and soothe her doubts.

Turning, he began to study the titles of several books lined up on a shelf. Not long after, the door opened.

Raeburn entered, looking every inch the English gentleman in conservatively cut biscuit pantaloons, pristine white linen and a Spanish blue morning coat. The tailoring was exceptional — Weston, if Darragh were of a mind to wager.

He'd taken some pains with his own attire

today as well, wearing well-made buff trousers, gold waistcoat, white shirt and a coat of fine brown woolen broadcloth. Unlike the duke, he'd eschewed a cravat, unwilling to endure the restrictive feel of one around his neck two days in a row. He detested the things, and wore them only on the most formal of occasions, such as the evening just past. Instead he'd chosen a white neckerchief for today, tied in a neat square knot at the base of his throat.

Raeburn crossed farther into the room, once again failing to extend his hand. Darragh didn't make the mistake of offering his own again, leaving his fists loose and free at his sides.

Jeannette's brother-in-law had a dour cast to his dark, clean-shaven features. Deadly serious and reserved.

"I am relieved to see you decided to keep our interview," Raeburn began. "Knowing nothing of the sort of man you are, I could not be certain you would put in an appearance this morning."

Darragh's shoulders tensed and squared. "I'm a man who understands the meaning of honor. And since I do not yet know what kind of man you are, I'll make an exception and agree not to take offense. This time at least."

A subtle gleam of respect crept into Raeburn's dark eyes. "We're both aware why you are here, a reiteration of the details are unnecessary and frankly unwanted under the circumstances. Suffice it to say, what I came upon last night leaves an image in my mind I should as soon wipe clean if only that were possible."

The duke moved toward the large rectangular desk that stood at the north end of the room. Leaning a hip against the edge, he reached out, picked up a clear glass paperweight from the desk's top. "So, I assume you are willing to do the proper thing and offer for my sister-in-law?"

"Aye, I'm willing."

With a kind of absent grace, Raeburn played with the paperweight, slowly shifting the globe from palm to palm. "Despite her less than suitable behavior last night, she is a lady of quality."

Darragh's lips parted in an ironic grin. "A fact she has pointed out more than once since first we met."

"How did the two of you meet? I assume it was here at the estate. You are the Merriweathers' architect, I am given to understand. Just finished building their new wing — with admirable results, I must say."

Darragh accepted the compliment with a

nod. "Aye, the new construction is mine. As for telling you the particulars of my relationship with Lady Jeannette, I can't oblige you. Those are private matters between the lady and myself and no other, not even you, your Grace."

The globe stilled in Raeburn's hand. "They weren't private last night, the pair of you saw to that quite nicely. Which leaves us all in our current deplorable situation. So how is it exactly that you plan to provide for my sister-in-law?"

Darragh met the duke's challenging stare with an unflinching one of his own. "She won't want for the necessities of life, so you can set your mind at ease on that score."

"It isn't the necessities per se that concern me. Jeannette is not a female accustomed to doing without. She was born into luxury and privilege as befits her station, and she has rightly known nothing else. That said, the dowry provided by her father will be negligible at best, a disappointment if you were perhaps counting on it being otherwise. Wightbridge is a gentleman through and through, but he enjoys spending his money perhaps a bit too freely, if you take my meaning."

"Frequents the racetracks and dice tables, does he?"

"Among other leisure pursuits that have a nasty habit of draining a man's pockets." Raeburn sighed, set the paperweight onto the desk with an audible *thump.* "Which is why I have decided to settle a sum upon Lady Jeannette that will guarantee her a comfortable, if not extravagant, way of life in the future."

The duke rattled off a sum that made Darragh's eyes go wide, leaving him to wonder precisely how wealthy the duke was. Extremely wealthy, from the sound of it. Wealthier mayhap than even the royals, if that were possible.

"The sum I mentioned, however, does come with some caveats," Raeburn continued. "The money will be apportioned in a semi-annual stipend over which you will exercise only the appearance of control. In addition, should you have need of a suitable dwelling here or in England, funds will be forthcoming for its purchase or construction. The deed to remain in the lady's name and my own, of course."

"Of course," Darragh said between clenched teeth, bristling at the implication that he was the sort of man who would squander a fortune for his own gain. Yet there were many such men in the world, including apparently Jeannette's own father.

He forced himself to relax, aware the duke knew little of him. Raeburn was simply attempting to provide for his sister-in-law in the soundest and safest manner possible. Had their places been reversed, he might well have done the same.

"As her husband," the duke continued, "you will by association benefit from the arrangement in terms of both your living situation and your elevated social standing. I have many connections that may prove beneficial to you in the future, though for appearance sake you likely ought to cease accepting remuneration for your work as an architect. And so long as Lady Jeannette is well treated and the marriage sound, a minor title may be in the offing as the years go by. A knighthood or even baronetcy is certainly within reach."

Darragh rocked back on his heels, affront now burning a hole in his gut. " 'Tis quite a bribe you offer, your Grace, though a rank insult to any man with a thumbnail's speck of pride left in his body. Were I the kind of base villain willing to take on such a bargain, Lady Jeannette would surely find herself saddled with a sad bastard of a husband. A man not worthy of her hand at all. So it is a good thing I've no need of taking you up on the deal."

Raeburn lifted an imperious brow. "No need? Perhaps you see insult in my offer, but I see practicality and an interest in ensuring beyond any doubt that Jeannette will be well looked after. Legally, women are chattel, all of their assets their husband's under the law from the instant the marriage vows are taken. I seek only to ensure that she, and any offspring that should arise from your union, will be protected and maintained in a manner befitting her status as a lady born."

" 'Tis my wish as well. Believe me when I say I have more than adequate means with which to provide for her as my wife, and for our children, should God grant us the blessing of them. But perhaps I ought to be begging your pardon for not introducing myself properly from the start of this interview."

Darragh walked two paces forward. "Let us start afresh, shall we, your Grace? My name is Darragh Roderick O'Brien and I am the present Earl of Mulholland. The eleventh of us, if you're interested in keeping count. My family comes from a fine lineage of brave men and women that stretches all the way back to our greatest Irish king, Brian Boru himself. I've holdings in County Clare with a grand house and fine land not far from the sea, held by my family longer than that of your own ancestors, I suspect."

He held Raeburn's gaze. "I've spent the past decade rebuilding my family's fortunes, actions for which I take no shame. I've plenty of money, more than enough to keep Lady Jeannette in expensive dresses and silken sheets for the rest of her days. I can't tell you what kind of husband I'll make since I've never been one before. But I can say I come to this marriage with a willing heart, and I think with a bit of time the lady will come to it that way as well."

"If this is true," Raeburn said, "then why the deception? Why let us all believe you're a commoner whose only distinction is his gift at designing and constructing buildings?"

Darragh rubbed a sheepish finger over his jaw. "Well now, that would be Jeannette's doing. I've tried more than once to tell her who I am, but she always seems to be interrupting before I can get the words out of my mouth. She did it again last night. She's a stubborn lass and chooses to think what she will, so I've been letting her."

A smile started off slow, then spread over Raeburn's face like a rising sun. He barked out a laugh, then a second.

"You're not angry, then?" Darragh asked.

"Not a bit. Serves her right, the vixen. Won't she be surprised and relieved when she realizes the truth?"

Darragh rubbed his jaw a second time. "About that. I'd rather you not tell her for a while yet, if you'd be willing to keep it a secret. Perhaps it's a frightful conceit on my part, but I'm convinced she has a measure of love for me despite what she believes to be my meager circumstances. I'd like the chance to prove that love to both of us before she learns she will be a countess, and a wealthy one at that. A few weeks alone as newlyweds should give me enough time to work the trick. Once she admits she has tender feelings for me, I'll put her mind at ease about the other."

The duke's eyebrows went high. "That's a dangerous game you're choosing to play. What if you are wrong?"

What if he *was* wrong? Darragh considered. He had naught but his gut to persuade him Jeannette felt more for him than simple passion. Yet surely she *must* feel more. What other than burgeoning love could have lured her to risk everything last night — especially her precious reputation — in order to tryst in complete abandon inside his arms?

Mayhap her actions did stem from nothing more complex than physical desire, but he didn't think so. He couldn't believe a woman with her social panache would ever be so foolish as to jeopardize her future unless her heart was engaged, at least a bit. Finding out how much she felt for him was now the gamble he must take.

Aye, he assured himself, casting aside his doubts, she loved him. He had only to make her confess it — to herself, as well as to him.

"Nay, I am not mistaken," he told Raeburn with more confidence than he actually felt. "So, have I your agreement to keep quiet and let me tell her the truth in my own way and time?"

The grin widened on the duke's face, brown eyes twinkling with an irrepressible gleam. "Deceive Jeannette? What a perfect turning of the tables. Yes indeed, you have my word and my permission to wed her, assuming you haven't decided to run, after all."

"Not a bit. Circumstances may have forced my hand, but fate has a curious way of working miracles. Even if we had no need to marry, I'd still want her for my bride."

"In that case," Raeburn said, extending his hand, "let me welcome you to the family, Lord Mulholland."

"Darragh, your Grace. Darragh will do fine."

CHAPTER FOURTEEN

"You look beautiful."

Jeannette didn't respond to her sister's declaration, barely slowing as she paced from one end of the church's narrow antechamber to the other. She gazed down at the dress, a garment that in its own way had played a part in leading her to this alarming turning point in her life.

It was the gown Darragh had given her all those weeks ago, the one she had once returned.

A few days ago, Darragh had presented the dress to her again, this time as a wedding gift, asking her with sincerity shining in his eyes if she would consent to wear it for the ceremony.

Caught in a moment of unexpected vulnerability — an emotion from which she seemed to suffer a lot lately — she had found herself murmuring "Yes."

And it did make a charming wedding

gown, as lovely as the instant she'd first glimpsed it, the delicate rose-tinted silk fitting her body as if the gown had been crafted exclusively for her, the band of embroidered white roses and green leaves that trailed across the skirt lending the garment an unmistakably romantic grace.

If only today's ceremony was truly a joyous one.

Quivering at the realization, she fluttered her hands in a flurry of nerves. "Oh, what am I to do?"

Violet reached out, stilled Jeannette's restless hands inside her own. "You are to do what the situation requires. Walk down the aisle in a few minutes and marry Mr. O'Brien. That is all you can do and what you must do. There are no other options."

No other options.

The words tolled between her ears like a funeral dirge. In the five days since she and Darragh had been caught together in the conservatory, she had tried desperately to conceive of a way out of proceeding with this marriage. Yet as the days flew past, one by one, nothing had come to mind, her panic increasing with the rising of each morning sun.

Her family was of no help whatsoever.

After the initial meeting in the study that

first morning, Darragh and Adrian had emerged from the room grinning and talking like best friends. She'd been dismayed at first, then irritated. How could they be so cozy together so quickly? Did Adrian care nothing for Darragh's lack of proper lineage? Surely he could not be eager to welcome the Merriweathers' architect into the family?

But apparently he could.

Violet, Kit and Eliza Hammond were introduced to Darragh next, and after an initial spate of awkwardness, quickly fell prey to his charm as well. By the end of the first afternoon, it was as if she and Darragh were engaged by choice rather than necessity. Only she and her cousins seemed less than enthused.

The Merriweathers, in fact, could barely stand to look at her, particularly Cousin Cuthbert, who grew red-cheeked and flustered every time she came near. Wilda did her best to be polite, but the usual warmth she had always shown to Jeannette was gone.

And really, how could she blame either of them? She had embarrassed her relations in the most mortifying of ways. And despite the fact that her reputation would be restored upon her nuptials, the delicious details of the scandal would linger on.

Likely for quite some while, since, unlike in London, scandals of this magnitude didn't happen in the country all that often.

As for herself and Darragh, the two of them barely had time to exchange more than a few words. Her plan to waylay him prior to his conversation with Adrian had gone completely awry because Betsy had, of all things, let her oversleep! By the time she'd dressed and hurried down the stairs it had been too late, the men already behind closed doors.

Afterward she'd waited, expecting Darragh to seek her out for a private conversation. Instead he'd come to her when she was with company, her sister and Eliza in the room looking on.

"So we shall be wed, then," he'd said as though it was a foregone conclusion and there was nothing else to discuss. She had wanted to argue but felt reluctant to do so in front of the others. Before she had a chance to shoo them out, Darragh had announced that he would be leaving immediately for Dublin, where he could obtain a special license. As soon as he returned, he declared, they would be married.

She'd balked at the notion of being married in such haste, but everyone else had chimed in, agreeing that she and Darragh must be wed without delay. To do otherwise would only prolong the scandal, inviting even more gossip, censure and disgrace.

So here she stood in her wedding dress that was not a wedding dress, waiting to be irrevocably joined in matrimony to a man she had never intended to wed. Even if said man did happen to make her pulse jitter and her knees turn to the consistency of pudding every time he touched her. Even if he had the power to make her emotions zing and zip from one end of the spectrum to the other, turning her madder than a yellow jacket one minute then teasing a hearty laugh out of her the next. A life spent with him would never be easy, she realized. Then again, it would also never be dull.

Violet gave her a knowing look as if she could read Jeannette's thoughts — which perhaps she nearly could, considering they were twins. "It is obvious you have feelings for Mr. O'Brien, considering the cause of today's hasty nuptials. And in spite of the unenviable circumstances, he seems a good man. Adrian told me he was most favorably impressed with him."

"Mayhap Adrian is, but he isn't the one being wed to the man. He isn't the one being asked to give up her family and friends, being expected to move into the frontier."

"Ireland has a frontier?" Violet queried, a skeptically amused gleam in her eyes.

"It does compared to England! O'Brien plans to take me to his home in the western wilds for our honeymoon. Even Cousin Wilda says she's heard it is a rough, untamed land where half the populace doesn't even speak *English*. I was supposed to be going back home to Surrey with you."

Her twin gave her a sorrowful look.

"Oh, Violet, I can't go through with the wedding," Jeannette said, letting her trepidation show in her eyes, ring in her voice. "You have to help me. We must find a way to delay the vows long enough to send word to Mama and Papa. Surely once they learn what is happening, they will wish to aid me. Find some other, less irrevocable means of remedying the situation."

She gazed down, studying one snowy satin pump. "I know I've brought disgrace upon them yet again, upon us all, but it isn't entirely my fault. Darragh seduced me. I . . . didn't realize how far a simple kiss might go until it was far, far too late."

Her sister rested a hand atop her protruding belly. "So you're saying he's a rake?"

"No, I'm saying he's . . ." She trailed off, trying to decide exactly what it was she was attempting to say. Swallowing against the tightness lodged in her throat, she continued. "He has a way about him that quite makes a girl lose her head. *He* approached me in the conservatory. I fail to see why I should be forced to accept all of the blame."

"Women are always the ones forced to accept the blame when it comes to matters of virtue and modesty. Be glad, Jeannette, that he is honorable enough to wed you and restore what he can of your reputation." Violet hesitated, a mild frown wrinkling her forehead. "Unless when you say *seduced* you actually mean *forced*. He didn't force you, did he?"

This was her out, Jeannette realized, her way to gain her twin's complete sympathy and support — and thus, her freedom. If Violet believed Darragh had tried to violate her, not even the ensuing uproar would keep her sister from rallying to her side and preventing the wedding.

Yet even as she opened her lips to utter the falsehood, she hesitated, the words refusing to come. Whatever Darragh O'Brien's faults, however obstinate and outrageous, brash and, on occasion, bossy he might be, he wasn't the sort of man who would ever resort to forcing his attentions upon a woman.

For one thing, he didn't need to. Men like

O'Brien attracted women the way flowers lured bees. She suspected he could stand silent in a field and some winsome girl would find him, an encouraging smile on her lips.

For another, he was too innately decent a man to ever cause harm to something smaller or weaker than himself, be that something a woman, child or animal.

He would be hurt, she thought, imagining his shock and disillusionment should she lie and cry rape. If she perpetrated such a horrible deceit, her conscience would haunt her for the rest of her days. So, no matter her misgivings over their pending union, she would not resort to using such a low method of escape.

Her shoulders sagged. "No, he did not force me. I returned his attentions of my own free will."

"Then I am afraid there is nothing for it," Violet said. "The two of you must be married. Now, if you are ready, I imagine we should be getting on with the ceremony."

"But what about Mama and Papa? It only seems right they should be consulted before I take such a monumental step. Instead of proceeding with the wedding today, we could postpone it and return to England exactly as planned. Once there I shall plead my case. You could help me. They listened to you once. I am sure they would do so again."

An expression of regretful resignation settled over Violet's face. "Unfortunately, I am sure they would not. You have no notion of the lengths I went to in order to convince them to let you come home in the first place. And now with this new scandal . . . Oh, Jeannette, it's just no use. And if you were to return home unwed . . . well, I hesitate to say this, but our parents might very well disown you."

Jeannette drew in a harsh inhalation, then waved off her shock an instant later. "They would not, do not be absurd. Mama and Papa have always doted on me, you know that better than anyone. You are being extreme, that is all."

"I am not. Papa grumbles and growls about everything, so I cannot comment upon his true feelings. But as for Mama, well, I have never seen her so thoroughly distressed as she was after learning the truth about what we did. She has been quite beside herself ever since. Breaking the news to her that you have made an impecunious marriage will be difficult enough. Telling her you are ruined with no wish to marry the man responsible —"

Violet broke off, shivered delicately. "I am sorry, but you must marry Mr. O'Brien and make the best of whatever is to come. Even if I were willing, there can be no trading places this time, no last-minute possibilities of flight. If you do not marry him you will bring irreparable disgrace upon our families. A disgrace from which neither Adrian nor I could ever hope to shield you, especially considering we have had our own difficulties of late in that regard.

"Should you be cast out," Violet continued, "I don't know what would become of you. You could live with us, I suppose, if Adrian would permit it. Otherwise, you would be on your own, and I fear for you should that happen. No one would have you as a governess —"

Jeannette gave a delicate snort. "I wouldn't want them to."

"— which would leave you with no reputable options. You might even have to become . . ." Violet broke off, clearly distraught.

"Some man's mistress, is that what you were going to say?"

Her twin met her gaze, Violet's sad but serious. "Accept your fate, Jeannette, and do your best to be happy. Once you are husband and wife, I think you may be surprised how well you and Mr. O'Brien get on."

"What if we don't?" Jeannette's insides squeezed uncomfortably at the prospect. Truly, she and Darragh knew little about each other and had even less in common. What if those differences grew more pronounced instead of less once they found themselves shackled together for a lifetime?

She repeated her qualms aloud to her sister.

A gentle smile curved Violet's lips. "Ah, but you have genuine passion between you, something of which a great many couples cannot boast, especially those of our class. And there is the way he looks at you, when he thinks you do not notice."

"And how is that?" Jeannette asked, unable to resist the inquiry.

"With the longing and intensity of a man gazing upon a rare and cherished prize. Perhaps he isn't who you would have chosen, but he is the man you will have. Give him a chance. Give your union a chance and let him make you happy."

"Likely Darragh and I shall drive each other to distraction, and I shall find myself more miserable than I have ever been in my whole life."

Violet sighed. "I pray you will find otherwise. But if, after a time, you discover yourself desolate beyond all hope, know that you may always come to me. We have had hard words and bad feelings between us in the past, but you are my sister. I care, even if you do make me want to throttle you sometimes."

Jeannette met her twin's gaze with an identical one of her own, deeply touched. Giving in to impulse, she hugged Violet to her and dusted a quick kiss over her twin's cheek, something she hadn't done since they were children.

In obvious surprise, Violet hesitated for a scant second before returning her embrace, rounded belly and all.

The moment soon over, they parted.

Violet smoothed a hand over her full green skirt. "Shall I go out and let everyone know you are ready? Five minutes, shall we say?"

A new lump of nerves formed in Jeannette's chest. Doing her best to breathe past it, she gave a nod.

Violet nodded back, then quietly crossed to let herself out the door.

Standing motionless, Jeannette became aware of her pulse thundering unsteadily as her panic spiked higher. Five minutes and the ceremony would begin. Fifteen minutes and she would be Mrs. Darragh O'Brien.

To have and to hold, to love, honor, cherish and obey until death do them part.

She pressed a palm flat against her chest and tried to calm her raging nerves. Marriage to O'Brien wouldn't be so bad. At least he was handsome and would presumably bring her pleasure in bed.

What did it matter if he came from a different world, a separate social sphere than her own? Why worry that he would be carrying her off into the wilds of Ireland, away from everyone and everything she'd ever known? Or be upset that she might never see London again, and that if she did, her friends might shun her for no longer rightfully belonging inside their circle?

She'd planned to marry a rich, titled man. Had been willing to forgo love in exchange for security and the other pleasures great wealth would afford her. But Darragh could offer her none of those things.

What if he couldn't even offer her love?

A chill swept through her.

What if, heaven forbid, she fell in love with him and in the end wound up with nothing, not even his affection? She'd been betrayed by one man. What was to say she might not be betrayed by another? By Darragh?

Her breath shallow in her lungs, she hurried into action. Crossing the room, she closed and locked the door, knowing there wasn't an instant to lose.

Rigged out for the occasion of his marriage in a formal dark blue tailcoat and pale gray breeches that buttoned with noticeable snugness just below his knees, Darragh stood at the altar and waited for his bride.

His friend Lawrence McGarrett was at his side. Just returned from Dublin, Lawrence had agreed to act as best man — after he'd recovered from his shock at the unexpected news.

"Better hope she's not like one of those insects that chews off the head of her mate during intercourse," Lawrence had outrageously advised. "Or you'll soon be losing yours, and to an English assassin at that."

Darragh had laughed, clapped his friend on the back and told him not to worry. Still, as he stood here now, he couldn't help but feel a bit of nervous trepidation. Not at the thought of marrying Jeannette, but in wondering if she would have a last-minute change of heart.

A movement in the vestibule drew his eye. He watched as Jeannette's twin sister made her way at a measured waddle up the aisle, the picture of Mother Earth in her vivid green maternity dress. The duchess paused long enough to relay word that Jeannette would be ready to proceed any minute. Announcement made, she allowed her husband to help her take a seat on the wooden front pew — her brother-in-law Lord Christopher and her friend Eliza Hammond on either side.

As matron of honor, Violet would be required to rise to her feet again once the bride appeared, ready to act as Jeannette's attendant. Raeburn, on the other hand, had agreed to serve as father of the bride in the absence of Jeannette's real father. Darragh understood the duke had been reluctant at first to perform the duty, some mention as to how it might seem awkward after his and Jeannette's previous association.

Darragh had been stunned, then annoyed, then accepting, when he'd finally learned the details of the scandal that had sent Jeannette here to Ireland. The story had come pouring out of Kit Winter last night over a late glass of fine Irish whiskey.

A nasty twinge of jealousy had risen within Darragh and burned there for a solid five minutes before he'd had the sense to realize what a fool he was acting. 'Twas plain Raeburn doted on his wife, his eyes for her and her alone. Plain as well that Jeannette felt no romantic love for the duke. Particularly considering she'd jilted him at the altar, deceiving everyone by convincing her twin to act as Raeburn's substitute wife.

Question was, what was Jeannette thinking today?

He wished his family were here to share the day, his three brothers and three sisters. Mary Margaret, two years his junior at six and twenty and the eldest of his sisters, was herself wed and the mother of four. She, above them all, would be particularly hurt to have not been included in the ceremony, since she put great stock in the trappings of ritual and tradition. Well, 'twould give her added reason to throw a ceili once she got over her bruised feelings, a big, noisy Irish party just the thing to set matters right.

Yet even had he been able to get word to them in time, he couldn't have afforded the risk of having them here. Bad enough depending upon the duke not to reveal his identity without having to worry over one of his six siblings spilling the beans out of the bag — assuming they would have agreed to keep their lips sealed from the first.

He glanced at the Merriweathers, seated straight-backed and slightly disapproving in the pew behind their relations. They were the only others who concerned him, but he didn't think they realized he had a title, or else Jeannette would likely have known too. When he'd hired on, neither Cuthbert nor his wife had asked about such matters. And since his being an earl had naught to do with his work, the thought had never come to his mind to mention his lineage. To his knowledge, the only thing the Merriweathers knew was that he came from a good family in the West, but not much else. He was glad now that he'd never taken the time to fill in all the details.

He would be teaching his new bride a lesson or two. Lessons she wouldn't learn living life as the pampered bride of a wealthy earl — at least not immediately.

That would come later.

He tugged at his waistcoat to keep it neat and watched Raeburn disappear into the vestibule to retrieve his sister-in-law and escort her forward. Only a minute or two now and he and Jeannette would begin to speak their vows before the Anglican minister hired to perform the ceremony.

A warm prickle tingled suddenly against the back of Darragh's neck beneath his cravat, spreading over his skin like some peculiar rash. It was a vaguely familiar feeling, one he got every now and again when something untoward was about to occur.

The first time he experienced the sensation had been as a boy just before his younger brother Michael had fallen out a yew tree and broken his left arm in two places. Then another time years later while walking a lonely night street in Dublin. As he'd rounded a corner, he'd found himself set upon by thieves, the prickle issuing a warning only seconds before the attack. An alert that in hindsight had saved him from taking the sharp end of a shiv between his ribs.

So why get the itch now? he wondered. Clearly no one in the church was about to set upon him nor was anyone in danger of falling out of a tree.

He gazed down the aisle toward the wide wooden entrance doors and the stone vestibule beyond. He thought of the antechamber where Jeannette was readying herself, his neck tingling like mad.

A second later Raeburn reappeared at the far end of the aisle, a scowl on his dark patrician brow, Jeannette quite noticeably *not* on his arm. Moving on instinct, Darragh strode forward, long legs rapidly covering the distance between him and the duke.

All eyes trailed after him.

"What is it?" he demanded the instant he reached Raeburn.

"She's locked the door and will not come

out. I tried to talk to her."

"And?"

"And she told me to go away. Says she'll come out when she is ready and not a moment before."

"Perhaps I ought to have a word with her."

"It might be better to summon my wife again. Goes against my grain to let those two put their heads together in such a situation, but what harm can come of it? Even if I didn't have Violet's promise, it isn't as if they're going to concoct any more insane schemes. Violet may be able to make her see reason. Besides, Jeannette will have to emerge from the room eventually. There is only one way out."

Or was there? Darragh wondered.

The prickle on his neck intensified.

His feet moved before he was aware he was walking, Raeburn left to stare open-mouthed in his wake. But rather than heading toward the antechamber where Jeannette had locked herself, he hurried outside. Taking the stone church steps at a quick clip, he stalked out across the grounds. Moist green spears of grass flattened beneath his dress pumps as he let instinct dictate his direction.

Jeannette hung by her waist over the windowsill, slippered feet dangling well above the ground. When she'd climbed out here it had seemed like such a good idea — only a short hop to freedom.

But on closer inspection, the "short" hop had proven to be a lot farther away than she'd originally imagined, looming like a great terrifying chasm, which should she choose to jump would undoubtedly end in a wrenched ankle or worse.

She cringed at the idea. She hated pain and avoided it at all costs. Even something as minor as a paper cut could make her miserable for days.

But she couldn't afford to remain here indefinitely, not with Adrian on the other side of the antechamber door demanding she let him inside. Either she needed to take her chances and leap to the ground despite the possibility of broken bones, or else hoist herself back inside the room, dust off her skirts and unlock the door to accept her fate.

Assuming she even had the strength to lever herself back inside. Her arm muscles were trembling, aching from the strain of holding herself in place. While her heart beat bird-fast in her chest, the hard-edged stone sill cut uncomfortably into her stomach.

Oh, what to do? she agonized. *Meet the ter-*

ror facing me below? Or meet the one await-
ing me inside the church?

She was still debating the conundrum
when a large, clearly male hand wrapped
around her ankle. Squealing in surprise, she
kicked her feet.

The grip tightened.

She squealed again, male hands reaching
higher, then settling firmly around her
thighs just below her hips.

"Come on, lass. Push off. I'll catch you."

She twisted her head sideways and tried
to glance down. "O'Brien?"

"None other. Whom else did you imagine
would be laying his hands upon you in so
familiar a manner?"

"If I had known for certain, I would not
have asked."

"Well, now that we've resolved the mystery
of my identity, you'd best come down from
there. Looks a mite uncomfortable, if you
ask me."

Blast the man, she cursed silently. He'd
not only discovered her before she could
make good her escape, but had caught her
smack dab in the middle of the process. She
could only imagine the picture she must
present, dangling with her backside promi-
nently exposed out a church window!

Much as she wished she could hoist

herself back up and into the antechamber, she hadn't the ability, leaving her no choice but to let him help her to the ground.

"You are sure you won't drop me?" she questioned, nerves making her voice pitch high.

"Sure as I can be under the circumstance."

"That hardly sounds reassuring."

"Trust me, lass. I've got you firmly in hand."

Yes, she mused — all too aware of the sensation of his big, powerful hands upon her body — she believed he did. Easing herself a tentative inch off the sill, she squeezed her eyes tight and let go. Her stomach did a sickening flip as she plummeted straight down. Then he had her, arms locked with tensile strength around her hips and waist, her back pressed to his chest. A single broad palm ran up and over her frame, pausing momentarily to cup one of her breasts before setting her onto her feet.

Her body tingled, nipples puckering beneath the cloth of her bodice in a way she hoped he didn't notice.

"You may release me now, sir," she said when he failed to loosen his hold.

"Aye, but should I?" he murmured into her ear. "Where was it you were off to, *a ghrá?*"

Spoken in his deep, lyrical voice, the foreign words sounded almost like an endearment. She considered the phrase anew, decided it was more likely a curse. Though he didn't sound angry. He sounded almost tender, even understanding.

But surely he must be cross. How could he be otherwise, having caught her trying to run off, attempting to jilt him at the altar? She wanted to turn, wishing she could see his eyes to judge his mood, but he held her steady, her back still pressed against his front.

"I . . . I don't know," she confessed with unexpected candor.

"Do you not? Just away, was it, then?"

"Yes, away."

Gracious, he was right. She'd had no plan, acting solely on instinct, exclusively on fear. If she had been successful in her escape and had managed to flee, where would she have gone? Certainly she could not have returned to her cousins' house nor to her parents, not if what Violet said was true. Her great-aunt Agatha would no longer take her in either, and as for Violet and Adrian . . . well, they had made her options quite clear.

When she considered the matter, she had no one. No one but Darragh O'Brien. Her shoulders sagged.

As if sensing her defeat, he turned her gently in his arms. He traced the side of a finger over the curve of her cheek. "Does it pain you so, then, the prospect of being my wife?"

She swallowed, nerves taut inside her throat. "No, but in so many ways you and I are still strangers. What do we really know of each other?"

A forbearing smile lifted his lips. "More than you might suspect, I imagine. Once we're wed, we'll have the pleasure of learning each other's ways, an exercise that will only add spice and adventure to the years that lie ahead."

"And what if it adds acrimony and regret instead?"

"We'll have to work hard to make sure it doesn't." Stepping back, he offered his hand. "Lady Jeannette Rose Brantford, I know we didn't come to this in the normal fashion of things, but will you step inside this church and do me the honor of becoming my bride?"

She stared at his hand. Strong, steady, resilient. Able to craft and create. Able to take on whatever needed to be done no matter how tough or how hard. A woman could do far worse than to accept the hand of such a man.

She trembled to imagine her future life with him. She trembled to imagine it now without. Accepting, as she never thought she would do, she laid her hand in his and said, "Yes."

CHAPTER FIFTEEN

"We'll pass the night here then be off for home come morning," Darragh said, escorting his new bride up the staircase into Lawrence McGarrett's drawing room.

Jeannette glanced around at the pleasant decor, an arrangement of shield-backed walnut Hepplewhite chairs and matching sofa upholstered in buttery soft tan leather. Flanking the sofa were a pair of inlaid satinwood Pembroke occasional tables. A tall liquor cabinet stood to one side, opposite the wide fireplace. Pastoral prints graced walls that were painted a warm, soothing blue.

She hoped the shade would have a beneficial effect upon her nerves. Needing the distraction, she busied her hands by drawing off her gloves. "And where exactly is your home, other than the West?"

"Our home now," he corrected her with a tender smile. "Near the banks of the Shannon estuary where the river meets the sea. 'Tis a place of rugged beauty I expect you'll like."

"We shall hope," she murmured softly. Crossing to the sofa, she sank down onto the cushions, finding them surprisingly comfortable. She folded her hands in her lap. "So this is Mr. McGarrett's house? Your best man, the one with the red hair?"

"That's the one. I've been lodging here while I finished your cousins' renovations. Lawrence offered to clear out for the night so we could be alone."

A sensation like the brush of butterfly wings fluttered in her stomach. "Did he? How very generous."

"That's Lawrence. Always willing to be of aid to a friend."

"He seemed rather severe to me."

At the wedding breakfast the man had been politely civil, but not much else, hardly speaking — at least not to her. He'd been loquacious enough with everyone else, including Kit Winter, whom he'd kept entertained with one outrageous story after another.

Darragh looked uncomfortable for a long moment. "Pay him no mind. The fellow's tongue knots up sometimes around the lasses, especially a lass as beautiful as your-self."

He crossed, leaned down to take her hand and press a kiss upon its top. The worst of her lingering pique over the matter melted beneath his touch.

"His tongue seemed fine to me," she remarked before deciding to accept Darragh's explanation on its face. If Lawrence McGarrett didn't like her because she was English and had wed his friend, then that was his problem and no one else's. She would dwell upon it no longer.

"At least his house is comfortable, if rather on the small side." Her father owned a hunting box that was larger, but she supposed she could be only so choosy about her accommodations now that she and O'Brien were wed.

Spinning the wide gold band encircling the third finger of her left hand, she wondered what his home — their home — would be like.

"What would you care to do?" he asked.

Her head jerked up at the interruption. "Do?"

She tossed a quick glance at the mantel clock, saw the hands at half-past three. Gracious, she and Darragh should have remained at the reception longer, but as bride and groom it would have looked odd for them to linger too long.

She'd already said her farewells to her family, knowing she was to leave in the morning and not likely to see them again for some time to come. Amid tears and hugs, she'd given Violet a letter for their parents in which she'd begged their forgiveness and asked for their blessing of her hasty marriage. She'd also made a point of seeking out Wilda and Cuthbert to thank them for their hospitality.

"You have been the best part of my time here in Ireland," she told them before startling Wilda by flinging her arms around her in an unexpected embrace. After a long moment, the older woman returned Jeannette's hug with genuine affection. Just before they separated, Wilda gave her a warm kiss on the cheek.

"Just be happy, dear," her cousin advised, patting her hand. "Write and let me know how you go on."

Jeannette had nodded, swallowing against the knot in her throat. "Yes, I will."

She only hoped she would be happy, cast adrift as she now was, with Darragh her only anchor. Her arrival in Ireland all those weeks ago had been daunting and scary. This time it would be worse, since there would be no reprieve waiting to send her home.

She shivered, grateful she would at least have Betsy and her familiar, reassuring routine to make the transition less frightening.

"Are you hungry?" Darragh asked. "Could you do with a cup of tea?"

She laid a hand across her stomach. "Oh, no, I couldn't eat another bite." If she did, she thought, she might become ill. "After the breakfast we had, and the cake afterward, I am more than well satisfied." She paused. "But if you would care for tea, I can ring, of course."

"No, no," he said, preventing her from rising to her feet. "I am fine. You're right, too much cake." He rocked slightly on his heels and stared down at the brown and blue rug on the floor. When he looked up again, he caught and held her gaze. "Shall I show you to the bedroom, then?"

Her lips fell open, her heart kicking into a fast, unsteady gait. "But it's scarcely mid-afternoon." Even to her own ears, her voice sounded weak and breathy.

For an instant, he appeared surprised. Then a smile moved over his mouth, humor warming his sky-colored eyes. "I meant so you could change and bathe, but we can get on with the other if you'd prefer. I like making love in the daylight."

She sprang off the couch. "Tonight in the dark will be soon enough. But I do believe I will retire to my bedchamber to bathe and change and take a brief rest, as you suggest."

Grinning, he stalked forward and snagged one of her hands in his. Exercising gentle pressure, he curved her arm behind her back, moved in so their bodies touched. "I'm disappointed now. Are you sure I can't talk you into letting me have my way with you, after all?"

She swallowed and trembled, imagining the two of them lying naked on a bed with nothing but a spill of sunlight to cover their entwined bodies. She throbbed, aware of his long, powerful frame pressed against her.

"Q-quite sure," she lied.

"Ah, you're a cruel one, lass, to torment a man so, and your new husband at that. I see I shall have to content myself with dreams of this evening. But I agree, you'd best have that nap you mentioned."

"Should I?"

"Indeed, for it's a promise I'll be keeping you awake nearly the whole of the night."

While she was still gasping at his prurient pledge, he swooped down and claimed her lips in a swift, sweet kiss that turned her knees to jelly, her toes to toast.

She swayed when he set her free.

"Shall I escort you to your room, or would you rather find it on your own? It's just past the landing, third door on the right."

"Under the circumstances, I had better find it on my own."

"Supper's at six and don't be late. And Jeannette?"

"Yes?"

"Wear your hair down. I've a fancy to see it around your shoulders."

"You said you had been to Italy, but I didn't realize you had visited Florence and the Uffizi Gallery," Jeannette remarked, pausing to quaff a delicate mouthful of red wine. "Such an impressive collection of works — paintings, sculpture and the wonderful architecture itself. Seeing it was one of the highlights of my sojourn to the region. That and all the shopping and parties, of course."

"Oh, of course. And you've the right of it. The gallery is a fine sight, well worth the trip and the trouble." Darragh flipped his silver dessert spoon over and back, then over and back again against his discarded linen napkin in an absent, yet methodical rhythm.

"Great-aunt Agatha and I were supposed to visit the Pitti Palace too, but the Grand Duke fell ill unexpectedly and our evening's entertainment had to be canceled. Alas, we had to journey on two days later and there was not the time to reschedule." She released a tiny sigh. "More's the pity, since I had so been hoping to see the Pitti." She paused then giggled. "Oh, listen to me, I believe I just made a pun. A pity about the Pitti. Get it?"

Darragh smiled across the dining room table at her. "Aye, lass. Very amusing."

"So I suppose both of us were forced to make do with outside views of the palace and gardens, instead of having the pleasure of seeing it from within."

Actually, Darragh mused, he had enjoyed a private tour, viewing the palace from every imaginable direction, as a friend and honored guest of Grand Duke Ferdinand III of Lorraine. But, Darragh decided, he would have to save that tidbit of information for a later conversation. A much later conversation.

Sprawled casually in his chair, he watched his new wife spear a minuscule bite of apple tartlet with her fork. The silver tines slipped in and out from between her rosy lips with unconscious yet suggestive provocation.

His loins tightened, fresh blood flowing to parts of his body that had nothing to do with digestion. Ordinarily he would have been interested in pursuing their conversation about art and architecture and travel, but not tonight — their wedding night.

He bit back a sigh and wondered if supper would ever end.

For the past hour and a half she'd driven him half mad with desire and frustration, toying and prodding and picking at each dish set before her. All the while, she'd chattered, talking as she lingered over one interminable course after another.

At first he'd tried to keep up, participating in the conversation with any number of observations of his own. Eventually, he'd fallen all but silent and let her rattle away. He knew she liked to talk — and she surely could argue with the best of them — but he'd never heard her prattle on as she was doing tonight.

Was she anxious? Slowing the meal in an attempt to delay the trip upstairs? But why? He knew she had a liking for his kisses. Sweet Mary, isn't that what had landed them in the marriage thicket in the first place, their inability to keep their hands off each other? So, it couldn't be a maidenly fear of intimacy that had her spooked.

If not, then what?

Bridal nerves, most like. A fear of the new and the unknown. Perhaps 'twas cruel of him, his plan for their immediate future. Perhaps it was wrong not to admit the full truth to her and put the worst of her worries at ease.

But an instinct that ran bone deep told him to keep his secrets and his silence. Told him he had but this one chance to curb her spoiled, flighty ways and teach her there was more to life than prestige and possessions. That simple things like happiness and love could be had, and once found were worth fighting for, as he was fighting for them now.

He stopped twirling his spoon, laid it aside.

Enough of delays. He wanted her. Now. And if she wouldn't come eagerly to his bed herself, then he'd lead her there and make her glad he'd coaxed her to agree.

Shoving his chair back, he stood.

She glanced upward, fork poised halfway between her lips and her plate. She followed his movements with a questioning gaze as he ambled toward her.

Circling around behind her chair, he stopped, running his gaze over her hair. He'd asked her to leave it loose, but she'd only partially complied. Her long, golden tresses were neatly brushed and tied with a length of pink silk ribbon that was looped in a bow against her nape.

He tugged it loose, that bow, slipping the knot free. With a gentle tug the ribbon came away in his hand. He tossed it already forgotten onto the linen-draped table, then slid his fingers up and into her soft, shiny hair.

Her fork clattered against her plate. "W-what are you doing?"

"What I've been wanting to do since nearly the first moment I saw you. You've lovely hair, did you know? Thick and silky, the kind that tempts a man to bury his face and breathe deep."

He did just that, leaning down to catch the healthy scent of her locks, clean and smelling faintly of apple blossoms. Gathering her hair together again, he twined it around one wrist to expose the curve of her neck, elegant, pale white and surprisingly vulnerable.

He skimmed the tip of one finger along its length and felt her answering tremble. Then he kissed her, caressing the sensitive spot where her neck met her shoulder.

Jeannette bit the edge of her lip and forced herself not to jump beneath his touch. She'd been anxious all evening, simmering with worry and nerves since earlier when she'd been dressing for dinner and Betsy had quite casually remarked about needing to set out a white night rail for Jeannette's bridal bed.

A white gown to signify the innocence of the bride.

Only the bride wasn't innocent, Jeannette thought with a mental wince. Though she wasn't what anyone would call experienced either. But the number of times she'd made love — once to be exact — was immaterial, since there would be no virgin's blood spilled this night.

That's when her belly had clenched and she'd begun to panic.

Why, she bemoaned, had she ever let that bounder Toddy touch her? She'd known it was wrong at the time, but he'd been so persuasive, making her promises of love and devotion and, one day, marriage.

Only, marriage to him had never come, and her innocence had been lost.

She knew it was unfair to Darragh, knew too that she ought to find some way to tell him. But how did a bride tell her new husband that it wasn't her first time? She wished she could turn back the clock and be the virgin he expected. The best she could offer him now was faithfulness.

Of course, it would all be so much easier if he didn't know she was not innocent. Did men automatically recognize such things or might he somehow be left in sweet, blessed ignorance?

Should she tell him? Should she stay silent?

The weight of her uncertainty had plagued her through the evening. Buzzing with anxiety, she had endeavored to stall their eventual ascent upstairs, all the while chattering like a magpie. Nervousness always made her talkative. Eating slowly, she had drawn out each dinner course, encouraging Darragh to drink rather more wine than he ought in the hopes he might become drowsy and fall asleep.

But she could see now that her plan had failed. Darragh was wide-awake and keenly alert, his Irish head obviously so hard he had remained sober as a tea-drinking granny despite all the alcohol he had imbibed.

And with his mouth making delicious forays across her neck, she knew he could not be put off much longer. The moment of truth was nigh and there was little she could do to prevent it. Still, a girl could try.

"Darragh, don't," she protested, her words high and breathless, as she wrinkled her shoulder to dislodge his eager lips.

"Why not?" he soughed against her skin, not the least bit discouraged. He caught her earlobe between his teeth, gave the curve of flesh a tiny nip. "Do you not like it?"

"I . . . I . . ." *Oh, Lord, how could she lie, when everything he did felt so divine?* "Yes, I like it but . . ."

"But what? Why should I stop?"

"Because this is . . . this is . . . the dining room."

"Aye, and so it is."

Darragh felt the rising heat in her, as he curved an arm across her chest, smiling as he filled his hand with one of her lovely, pliant breasts. Her nipple puckered through the cloth of her bodice. Teasing her flesh with his thumb, he relished the sensation as it beaded even more. "What better way to finish a meal than for a man to make love to his wife?"

"But the servants," she protested half-heartedly. "One of the footmen might return any moment to clear. What would they think?"

"That we're a pair of newlyweds who can't wait long enough to find the bedroom." He paused, pressed his mouth to her cheek, her chin, then let her go. "But perhaps you're right and we'd best continue this upstairs."

Pulling out her chair, he stepped to her

side to assist her to her feet.

She swallowed, her nervousness apparent on her face. "But I haven't completed my meal."

He eyed the barely eaten tartlet on her dessert plate. "Have you not? At the rate you were going, I estimate it would take you past midnight to be done. If you're so fond of that pastry, perhaps we should carry it upstairs. You can nibble on it later to regain your strength. After I've had my chance to nibble on you, that is."

"Mr. O'Brien, you are outrageous."

"I am that, Mrs. O'Brien," he said with a wink. "And so are you. 'Tis the reason we do such a fine job sparking off each other. Now, come to bed." He took her hand, dropped a kiss onto her palm. "Come to *my* bed."

Her pupils dilated, encircled by brilliant sea-colored rings, her lips parting as if she was thinking to delay yet again. Then she closed her mouth and let him help her to her feet.

With her small hand tucked comfortably inside his large one, he led her from the dining room and up the stairs.

Jeannette's lady's maid was waiting when they entered, the bedroom cozily warm from the lively blaze burning in the fireplace.

A half-dozen candles stood on the mantel and end tables, lighted to push the deepest of the night shadows away from the honey-colored walls and polished pine furnishings. A four-poster bed dressed in forest green bed curtains sat positioned in the center of the far wall. A thin lawn nightgown and robe lay in a frothy wash of white across its matching counterpane. Sweet beeswax and the womanly fragrance of dried lavender perfumed the air, a bridal bower waiting for its bride.

Betsy jumped to her feet and bobbed a curtsey, glancing inquiringly between him and Jeannette.

Jeannette moved to free her hand, but he held on.

"Go on to your own bed," he told the maid. "I'll see to your lady tonight myself."

Betsy stared at him for a long, surprised moment, then at Jeannette. She dipped her knees seconds after. "Very good, sir. Good night, sir. Good night, my lady."

His bride faced him the instant the door closed at her maid's back. "You should have let her stay to assist me."

"Why? Do you not think I know how to unfasten a woman's dress?"

"I am sure you do, but . . ."

"But what?"

She looked about to raise another protest, then abruptly dropped her shoulders in surrender. "But nothing."

Lifting her hair out of the way, she turned and presented her back to him.

As promised, he nimbly worked open the run of tiny buttons on her gown, saying not a word as he lifted the garment off over her head. After draping her dress across the padded arm of a striped settee, he returned to unlace her stays and loosen the tapes and ties of her chemise.

Stripped down to only one thin petticoat, she folded her arms over her breasts. Clearly, she thought to hide herself. Instead, her action only increased her cleavage, making her breasts appear fuller and more enticing, as viewed from his height and perspective. She shivered, goose bumps rising on her delicate skin.

He stroked his hands over her shoulders and arms, then slowly turned her, tucked her against him. "Why the nerves, lass? We're not in the dining room any longer, no one about to disturb us. Surely you know you've nothing to fear from me."

She raised her eyes to his. "I know, but it's our first time."

He cupped her cheek, pressed his lips tenderly to her mouth. "Aye, and your first time as well."

Her lashes fluttered for a moment before she lowered her gaze.

"We'll go slowly," he promised. "I'll make sure it's everything you could wish."

Darragh kissed her again, gentle and undemanding, expecting nothing greater than she could give, nothing more than she wanted to give.

She stood in his arms, her posture rigid. In a random pattern of leisurely, unhurried touches, he dusted his lips over her face. From forehead to cheeks he roamed, over closed eyelids that fluttered like fairy wings against his mouth, onward across her nose, down to her chin, across to her ears and along the divine curve of her neck.

He saved her lips for last, returning only after he had completed a most thorough tactile exploration of her features, leaving her skin warmed by a glowing, pink flush of desire. Her breath came in rapid puffs, breasts rising and falling against his chest in a most enticing way. He resisted the urge to bite her lips as he longed to do, forcing himself to go easy, to keep it simple and light.

She sighed and slid her arms around his waist to pull him closer. He knew she must feel his erection, straining thick and hard beneath his breeches. But she didn't flinch or show any sort of dismay, holding him tight as she responded to his kiss.

Encouraged, he eased some of the restraints he'd placed upon himself and intensified their embrace. Stopping just short of ravishing her mouth, he coaxed open her lips and slipped his tongue inside to play hot, dark, wet games.

She answered back, taking everything he had to give and offering more. He delighted as she traced her hands over his back, his shoulders, caressing him through the cloth of his shirt and coat. He moaned when she slipped her hands beneath the tails of his coat to ease the tips of her fingers beneath the waistband of his breeches. Anchored there, she held on for long, long moments before sinking the tips of her nails into his shirt and the skin beneath.

Half stunned, he quaked, his aching groin hardening even further. On a muffled oath, he broke their kiss.

Curving an arm behind her knees, he swept her off her feet and carried her across the room to the bed. He bent and yanked back the counterpane, then set her onto the cool white sheets.

She lay there, silent and watching as he tugged at his clothes. He had no wish to frighten her, to hurry things along like some green boy ready and eager to take his first woman. So he forced himself to slow, to behave as if he weren't yearning to simply toss up her chemise, part her legs and plunge deep inside.

'Twas hard controlling the beast, harder than a man of his age and experience should find it. Hard as well not to give in to the impulse to act the impatient fool and rip off his coat, yank at his neck cloth, kick free his shoes and pop every bloody button from his shirt and waistcoat and breeches in a frenzy to be naked.

Instead he took his time, draping each garment upon a nearby chair as he divested himself of his clothing. Her eyes widened as he revealed himself to her, inch by bare inch. To her credit she didn't look away, not even when he stood completely naked, his arousal jutting forward in a manner many an untried bride might have found alarming.

Remembering her earlier reticence concerning making love in the light, he blew out all but one candle. Near darkness spread over the room, leaving the bed bathed in concealing shadows. Setting a knee upon the mattress, he slid in beside her.

Wanting her relaxed and eager again, he

351

set to kissing her, softly, slowly, then with increasing hunger. She feathered her fingers into his hair and kissed him back.

Her unfettered sighs and breathy moans played like music in his ears, making his pulse stutter as his hunger arced higher and hotter.

His hands went to her chemise, drew back the slim ribbon that kept her breasts from his touch. Parting the fabric, he ran his fingers over her warm flesh, tracing her shape, savoring her texture. On a groan, he buried his face between her breasts, thrilling to the sensation of her lush female form against his cheeks, the intoxicating scent of her dizzying as a drug in his head.

Turning his face, he fastened his lips upon a single nipple, licking, teasing, suckling her in a way that made her fingers fist in his hair, her legs shift restlessly against his hip. She moaned when he opened his mouth wider to draw even more intensely upon her. He paid equal homage to the other breast, her hands shifting over his arms and shoulders, caressing the side of his cheek, the back of his neck.

Exercising careful control in an effort to increase both their pleasure, he slid lower, dappled lazy kisses and tiny licks all over her skin. Hands and arms, neck and shoulders, the undersides of her breasts, across the flat plane of her smooth belly.

Reaching down, he pushed the skirt of her chemise up to her waist then bent to lavish the same attention there, beginning at her feet and working his way back up. With hands and lips and tongue, he caressed her until she writhed against the sheets, his name a murmured prayer in the air. Skimming his hand over the velvety skin of her inner thighs, he parted her, felt her jerk as he slid a finger inside of her. She surrounded him, hot and wet, her fragrance filling his nostrils. She sighed and relaxed, vulnerable muscles quivering as she accepted his intimate touch, granting him her ultimate trust.

His arousal throbbed, so much so he nearly gave in to the temptation to settle himself between her thighs and put a whole lot more than his finger inside her. But she wasn't completely ready, not enough that she would be able to ignore any pain his initial entry might cause. Putting aside the knowledge that he might shock her, he spread her thighs wider apart, leaned closer and replaced his finger with his mouth.

She froze against him in obvious dismay, her hand reaching down to push him away. But she didn't push for long before she began to moan, panting in a litany of high keening cries that signaled her pleasure, her delight, in everything he did. Gripping his skull, she pressed him closer, urged him on. He smiled and applied himself more fully to the task of teasing and tormenting her to distraction. And then he did a thoroughly wicked, utterly immoral thing with his tongue that made her arch and shake, her release strong and satisfying for them both.

Knowing he could wait no longer, he moved up and over her body. Crushing his lips to hers, he poured out his hunger and want, demanding she match him, meet him, take him gladly into her mouth and her body.

Positioning himself, blood thrumming like a drumbeat between his temples, pulsing in his heart and loins, he eased himself inside her. Her slick, inner warmth wrapped around him, tight and snug as a hot velvet glove. The urge to plunge deep and hard roared through him. He held back, teeth clenched, jaw tight, muscles quaking. Pushing forward inch by deliberate inch, he allowed her to adjust to his size, waiting to encounter the resistance of her virgin barrier and gently ease through.

She shuddered and shifted beneath him, arms and legs curled around him, her face buried against his neck. He felt her tense slightly around him as he forced himself deeper, and deeper still.

For a second he thought she was stiffening against the pain of his penetration. Then he realized her reaction stemmed from something else, something for which he had not been prepared.

Shock poured through him as he lay fully sheathed inside her, deep and tight as he could go. The truth dawned slowly, sinking into his bones.

Jeannette, his dear, innocent, inexperienced, virgin bride, was no virgin at all.

CHAPTER SIXTEEN

Jeannette sensed the change in him instantly, swallowing hard against the rushing return of fear and the anxious worry he'd driven from her mind with his exquisite touch.

As soon as he'd taken her in his arms, kissed her, stroked her, coaxed her passion to the boiling point, she'd forgotten everything save him. He'd brought her to heights she wouldn't have imagined herself capable of reaching. Even now, pleasurable aftershocks sparked inside her body, fresh desire on the verge of stirring to life again.

But his tender entry had stopped, his body grown still. Easing her head back onto the pillow, she watched him, watched his expression and flinched.

He knew. Dear Lord in heaven, he knew.

Maybe she should have told him the truth first, after all. But it was too late for that now. Far, far too late.

His blue eyes shone hard and humorless even in the low light. Strain contorted his face, radiating inside the body he had lodged so powerfully, solidly inside her. Lowering her arms and legs, she started to slide free of his embrace.

But he would not let her go, pinning her in place by settling his full weight upon her. He might look lean to the casual observer but he was pure, solid male muscle, heavy enough to drive a good measure of the air from her lungs.

She gasped, then gasped a second time when he positioned his broad palms upon her hips and shifted her with silent, unmistakable intent. His action spread her wider beneath him, forced her to accept even more of his hard length as he pushed deeper.

"Darragh, I —"

Whatever she'd been about to say, he cut her off, obviously in no mood to hear. Covering her lips, he ravished her mouth, forcing his tongue between her teeth at the same moment he eased back to plant himself inside her again.

He thrust into her at a swift, relentless pace, all his earlier restraints gone. He took her without his earlier tender gentleness, yet even as he did, she realized he was careful not to hurt her. Quite the contrary, thrusting into her in a way designed to maximize her pleasure, to reawaken her sexual hunger and bring her to peak.

She sensed he was determined to force her surrender, to compel her body to perform for him in the manner he desired, to react and behave, to obey as he saw fit.

Aware, she resisted. Or tried to resist. But it was no use, as she lay helpless beneath his relentless sensual assault. He bit at her lips and pounded harder. She felt him shaking and knew he was near the edge of his own release.

Determined to win, he reached between them and flicked his fingers over a spot that set her instantly afire. She shook and arched into him as she crested again on a loud, mewling cry.

She could do nothing but feel, her mind devoid of coherent thought as he pumped furiously in and out of her for a few more strokes. He stiffened abruptly, frame quaking in violent reaction as he followed her over the edge into bliss.

Lungs heaving, he collapsed across her, his skin damp with heat and perspiration. He lay atop her for a full minute, then pulled out and rolled away.

An ominous silence descended, broken only when a log popped in the grate and sent up a minor shower of sparks.

Suddenly chilled despite the warmth in the room, Jeannette pushed the skirt of her chemise down over her legs. She covered her breasts next, fingers shaking as she tied the closure of her bodice. Plucking at the sheet, she pulled it over her then stared into the dark.

"Darragh, I'm sorry," she whispered.

He said nothing, just lay staring up at the bed canopy.

Tears stung her eyelids but she refused to let them fall. She sniffed. "I should have told you . . ."

He rolled his head on the pillow, eyes blazing. "Aye, I think you might have mentioned it. Did you think I wouldn't know?" His accusation struck her like a lash.

She'd hoped he would not know, for this very reason.

"Well?" he repeated in a clipped tone.

"I knew you'd be angry, so I —"

"Grew goose-hearted and couldn't tell me? Or did you deliberately set out to deceive me?"

She bristled. "No. How dare you suggest —"

"Under the circumstances, I think I have a right to suggest a great many things." Huffing out a full-blown sigh, he curved an arm above his head and lay silent.

She shivered. She thought about trying to explain, but what was the point when he would not want to hear?

A pair of minutes passed.

"Who was he, then?" Darragh demanded. "And you'd better not say your damned brother-in-law, or I may have to ride over to your cousins' estate and beat him bloody."

She felt her eyes go wide in astonishment. "What? Raeburn, do you mean?"

" 'Tisn't such a great stretch considering he was once your fiancé."

"It's true, we were engaged, but if you knew the duke better you would realize he's far too honorable ever to do such a thing. No, it was not Raeburn. You can set your mind at ease on that score and keep your fists to yourself."

He pinned her with a penetrating look. "Who, then? Tell me of this dishonorable fellow who stole your virtue."

She resisted the urge to squirm. "Not stole, precisely . . ." Seeing the angry flash in Darragh's eyes, she stopped, realizing what she'd revealed.

And really, what was she doing defending Toddy? His actions and behavior were indefensible, *stole* a far more accurate term for what he'd done, now that she could look back upon the past with a more sanguine eye. Despite the Town bronze she'd acquired after two Seasons as a London debutante, she knew now she'd been nothing but a naive innocent. A dupe willing to be preyed upon by a flattering tongue and debonair manner. How pathetic she'd been, willing to toss away her future in belief of his glib promises and practiced lies.

"Then what, precisely?" Darragh persisted.

She sat up, drew the sheet high against her chest. "Does it really matter? What existed between him and me is long since dead."

"That's reassuring to hear," he said, sarcasm dripping from his words. "So when did it end, this whatever it was? And where? Did you know this man in London?"

She picked at the bedcovers with the tip of her fingernail, and hung her head. "Yes, in Town. The particulars aren't important."

"Oh, I think they're very important. I assume he is a gentleman, or at least what passes for a gentleman." Speculation clouded Darragh's eyes. "He didn't by chance have anything to do with the scandal that got you sent here, did he?"

"No."

He cornered her with a look that had her

blurting out the truth. "Well, not directly."

"Indirectly, then? Is he the reason you jilted Raeburn? Secretly traded him over to your sister, as it were?"

Her gaze flew upward, pulse leapfrogging in her throat. How could he know that? How had he guessed? To this day, not even her parents suspected the full truth. Only Violet and Adrian and his inquisitive brother, Kit, were privy to all the facts.

One of Darragh's hands tightened into a fist. "Do you love him?" His tone was glacial, icy and impenetrable as a deep mountain lake.

"No, not now. I thought I did, once, before I learned what he was truly like."

"Where is he now? Still in England?"

She shook her head. "The last I knew, he was on the Continent, living off the largesse of a wealthy contessa. Wherever he is now, I most certainly do not care to know." She picked again at the sheet, awash in gloomy self-recriminations. "So now that you know you've received damaged goods, will you be wanting an annulment?"

He raised a single, reproving eyebrow. "I don't see how we could get an annulment considering we've already consummated our union. Even now you might be carrying my child."

Her gaze jerked to his. Mercy, he was right. She hadn't even thought of that. The one and only time she'd lain with Toddy she'd worried for two weeks after that she might have conceived despite the French letter he'd donned for protection against such a misstep.

To be honest, she hadn't enjoyed the experience all that much. His kisses and touches had been nice, but as for the rest . . . she could have left *that* well enough alone. Making love with Toddy hadn't been like tonight with Darragh. Or the night in the conservatory. He fired something deep within her, drew forth a feverish ache that refused to be denied. Left her with a pleasured satisfaction, the likes of which she'd hardly dreamed possible.

"What, then? Shall you repudiate me? Cast me aside?" Even as the words fell from her lips, she quaked in horror. What if he said yes?

"I am not the blackguard you obviously imagine."

"But —"

"I'm angry and have just cause to be. That doesn't mean I'm cruel. In retrospect, I suppose I should have read the signs."

"What signs?"

"The facts. For one, that you'd been

kissed before. Another, that you didn't faint dead away at some of my bolder moves, moves that would have sent many an untried girl running for her ma."

"If you're saying I'm a —"

He raised a hand, cutting off the ugly epithet. "I'm not saying anything of the sort. Just observing that I shouldn't have been so stunned to discover the truth."

She blew out a breath. "Where does that leave us?"

"With some repairing to do, I suppose."

"I've said I'm sorry. What more can I offer? What's done is done."

"Aye, and so it is."

Tears returned to her eyes. She brushed one away, a sudden rebellious fury rising within her. "It isn't fair, you know."

"What's not fair?"

"Society's double standard about women having to come to their marriage beds pure. It's not as if I'm *your* first, after all."

"And you ought to be glad you're not. Otherwise, I'd have still been fumbling around trying to figure out which part to put where. Blasted uncomfortable for you and damned embarrassing for me."

A smile built slowly inside her, the image of him as an inept, inexperienced lover painting a vivid picture in her mind. She struggled to keep the smile from forming, but it spread over her mouth nonetheless.

He tipped his head to one side, his own black humor slowly easing. "I guess I shall have to forgive you."

"Can you?"

He sat up, considering the question. "It all depends. You admit you once loved this scoundrel. Are you sure you are over him?"

"Completely sure. He is out of my life, never to return, exactly as I would wish."

A fleeting expression she thought looked like relief crossed his face. "If that is so," he said, "then I'm willing to put the past where it belongs and begin anew. But you'll have to promise to do the same."

"What do you mean?"

He reached out, caught a strand of her long hair between his fingers and began to toy with it. "Just that we're married now. I'm not ignorant of the fact that you had little wish for our union, nor that you nearly ran away this morning rather than take vows. But take them you did, and if I agree to think no more of this black fellow who took your innocence, an innocence that should rightfully have come to me, then I think I have cause to ask something in exchange of you."

Releasing her hair, he tucked a knuckle

under her chin and held her steady so she couldn't refuse his gaze. "I want a wife, Jeannette. A real wife willing to give our marriage a fair chance. We didn't start out under the best of circumstances, I'll admit, but that doesn't mean we've any need to continue that way. There's a spark between us. Even you can't deny that."

She shivered at his words, drew in a shaky breath, as he stroked a thumb across her lower lip.

"Aye," he said, "you feel it."

"And what if I do? It's nothing but lust," she charged, wanting to convince herself as much as him.

"Lust, is it? I'm not so certain. What if it's more? What if it goes deeper, lasts longer, has more meaning than a few heated weeks tussling amid the sheets?"

Her stomach did a queer little roll at the notion and the imagery as well. He was speaking of love. But she didn't want to love him, did she? She didn't want to be vulnerable and weak, open to giving her heart then later having it ripped in two.

She shook her head. "We wed for propriety's sake, no more, no less. In a few weeks, the passion will die down and we'll wonder what on earth we've gotten ourselves into." She shrugged. "But until then, you are right that we must make the best of an impossible situation."

"Then you'll give it a genuine try, our marriage?"

She could always refuse. Still, Darragh was her husband now, their marriage sanctified in the eyes of the church and the law. Given that, didn't she owe him an attempt at making something viable out of their union?

She sighed. "All right, I shall try. After all, we are married, whether we choose to embrace it or not."

He studied her for another moment, then smiled. "Speaking of embraces, you're much too far away, wife."

"But I'm sitting right next to you."

"Aye, but next to me isn't what I had in mind." Kicking off the sheet, he exposed his beautiful naked body and the rampant arousal protruding from between his legs. "Come closer, lass, and have a seat."

She eyed him, felt her eyes widen as he appeared to grow even larger and stiffer beneath her gaze. Blood warmed her cheeks. Quickly she glanced up.

He winked, a wicked grin on his lips. Then he patted one muscled thigh.

Gasping out a shocked laugh, she crawled

toward him and climbed aboard.

A painless whap across her quilt-covered bottom brought her awake the next morning.

Groaning, she cracked her eyelids open a faint slit and squinted against the early-morning light that shone in a cheery rectangle from around the window curtains. Cringing, she rolled onto her stomach and snuggled deeper into her pillow to resume her dream.

A large male hand curved over her shoulder and gave her a shake. "None of that, now. We need to get up and out and on the road. Arise, Lady Jeannette."

"Darragh?" she questioned in a groggy moan.

"Aye, and what other man would it be standing next to your bed?"

The scent of shaving soap and warm male skin teased her nostrils as he leaned close to press a kiss upon her cheek.

"Leave me 'lone. I'm tired." She raised a weak hand to push him away.

He chuckled in good-natured amusement, then captured her hand and kissed the center of her palm. "I am sorry not to leave you abed but we can't afford the delay. We've hours of travel inside the coach. You can sleep there."

Listening with only half an ear, and a sleepy one at that, she let her eyes drift closed again. But Darragh was relentless, using his hold upon her to tug her into a sitting position. The covers fell away, exposing her naked body to the cool morning air. Shivering, she huddled in a weary heap, covered by nothing but her long hair.

"Now, stay awake," he admonished. "I'll send Betsy in to help you wash and dress."

She listened to the faint thump of his boot heels striking the floorboards as he crossed to the door, the sound of the lock clicking as he let himself out. Alone once more, she flopped onto her back and yanked the counterpane over herself, head and all.

She was exhausted and it was all Darragh's fault. He certainly had a knack for keeping her from her rest. When he'd boasted last evening that he planned to wear her out, he had not been exaggerating. The man had stamina and more to spare, the night having been one round of energetic lovemaking after another interspersed with occasional minutes of sleep.

He would have taken her again just before dawn, she knew, but had restrained himself with a single kiss, realizing she was far too sore to accommodate him again. Tonight, he'd murmured, would be soon enough. Tucking her close, he'd let her drift into a deep sleep. So deep she hadn't even felt him leave the bed, nor heard him moving around the room as he shaved and dressed.

She'd just started another dream when the window curtains were yanked back to let in a stream of sunlight. The aroma of scrambled eggs and bacon wafted through the room. She roused enough to sniff, heard her stomach growl in response.

"Good day, my lady," her maid greeted in a happy tone. "I've brought you breakfast. Mr. O'Brien said he felt sure you would be hungry and in need of something more substantial than toast this morning. If you'll just sit up, I'll position the tray."

"Leave it, Betsy," she mumbled from under the covers. "I'll eat later."

"Mr. O'Brien said you might say that. I am to remind you that you need to be up and dressed and in the coach no later than eight. If you aren't ready by then, he said . . . well, you really ought to have your breakfast, my lady."

Jeannette flipped the coverlet off her face, squinted a look at her maid. "Why? What did he say?"

"Nothing, my lady. Now, I've brought you a lovely pot of hot chocolate, all rich and creamy just the way you like it. Let me pour you a cup."

"Not until you tell me what he said."

Betsy tucked her hands against her plain skirt. "Very well. He told me to tell you that if you aren't dressed and ready on time, he'll come up here and carry you out to the coach wearing whatever it is you have on."

Jeannette's lips firmed. Why, the barbarian. He knew full well what she had on, which was absolutely *nothing,* since he'd removed every last stitch of clothing from her body last night.

Carry her out to the coach naked, would he? Well, she'd like to see him try.

Then again, knowing Darragh, he would make good on his statement simply to get his own way, and devil take the consequences. *Dratted man.*

Sitting up, she beat at the covers in irritation at her defeat. "Very well. I will have my breakfast now."

Betsy turned, a relieved smile on her face.

"And extra jam for the toast. Lord knows after the last twenty-four hours, I deserve the indulgence."

A good meal and a warm bath went a long way to improving her mood and restoring her diminished energy levels. Allowing Betsy to assist her into a sprightly yellow-and-white-striped traveling dress helped even more. At her direction, her maid completed the ensemble by fitting fawn-colored half boots onto Jeannette's feet and perching an adorable, short-brimmed jockey hat with matching striped ribbons atop her curls.

Jeannette felt almost herself again by the time she descended the main staircase at thirty-one past eight. She was late and not the least bit repentant about it, having blithely ignored Darragh the two times he'd thumped up the stairs to "check" on her.

When she'd heard him come to the foot of the stairs and bellow up something about "getting her blasted little backside moving," she decided she'd pushed him as far as he would go.

She expected to find him awaiting her in the front entryway. Instead he stood outside, conversing with the coachman. Arranged in a mountain-sized lump at his feet sat Vitruvius.

The dog's ears perked, coming to attention the instant she exited the house, his lolling tongue retracting into his mouth on a slurping lick.

She came to attention as well. *Zounds*, amidst all the recent upheaval, she had completely forgotten about the beast.

But he obviously had not forgotten about

her, dark doggy eyes gleaming with pent-up excitement. Tail wagging, he jumped to his great hairy paws and started toward her at a lope.

A sharp whistle brought him to a halt. "Vitruvius, heel."

The dog stopped, whipped his head back and up in surprise. His shaggy body quivered in thwarted desire as he gazed expectantly up at Darragh, clearly hoping his master had spoken in error and would rescind the command.

Darragh patted his leg. "Come."

Vitruvius whined, gaze pleading.

"Come."

Seconds ticked by before the dog gave in. Head down, he padded back to Darragh's side. Obedient, he sat and accepted Darragh's words of praise, all the while raising sorrowful brown eyes her way.

She met those eyes, her heart softening in sympathy. *Silly lunkhead.* One would almost suspect he was pining for her.

She started forward, intending to pat him on the head, then let her hand fall to her side as she thought better of the action. After all, this was the same dog who had once knocked her to the ground, smothered her face with slobbery kisses and ruined one of her nicest gowns. A gown she could now ill afford to lose, considering her less than pecunious marriage. Heaven only knows how many weeks or months it would be before she set foot over the threshold of a suitable mantua-maker again. Until then, her present wardrobe would have to suffice.

Spirits dampened by the thought, she turned her sights back to the dog. "What," she stated in a dour tone, "is that big lolly-lob doing here?"

"You hear that, boy-o?" Darragh reached down, scrubbed a hand over the animal's wiry coat. "She thinks you're a big lollylob, and after all the hard work you've put in lately correcting your manners."

Vitruvius thumped his tail.

She walked closer, boots crunching on the pea-gravel drive. Stopping, she gazed pointedly at both man and dog.

The coachman murmured a greeting, then moved away to attend to his duties.

"Well?" she said to her new husband.

"Well what? If you're talking about the dog, Vitruvius is coming with us. You didn't think I'd leave him behind, did you?"

"No, of course not, but I had imagined by now that one of the servants would have taken him in hand for the trip." She tugged on her silk traveling gloves. "I assume he will be riding in the luggage coach. Unless you're planning to let him run alongside."

"I'd thought he would ride with us, seeing the luggage coach is nearly full, packed high and wide with your belongings."

Her brows shot upward. "Oh, no, he can't ride with us."

Only imagine all the dog hair, she thought, with a delicate shudder of distress.

"But your maid has the only empty seat. There won't be room for them both in there."

"Then he can ride up with John Coachman." She nodded, the discussion concluded as far as she was concerned. "Now, since you have done nothing but complain about the need to depart ere these many minutes past, I assume you would like to be off."

He looked as if he would like to argue further about his dog, but decided to keep his comments to himself.

She moved toward the carriage, only then noticing a crest painted on the side that depicted a stylized Celtic bull and lion. "Whose coach is this? I had assumed we would borrow one of my cousins' coaches for the journey."

Darragh stilled, stared for a moment. "What? No. The only vehicle the Merriweathers own isn't suitable for long trips."

"So where did this one come from?"

"This one?" He rubbed a finger along the side of his face. "Well now, this one belongs to . . . a . . . um . . . local landowner near home. He heard about our marriage and had it sent."

She folded her hands at her waist. "How very generous of him. Who is this man? He must be more than a landowner to have such excellent transportation as this, and to send it so quickly as well. Is he one of your patrons?"

An odd expression flickered through Darragh's eyes. "In a manner of speaking, you might say that he is."

"What is his name, this benefactor?"

"His name?"

"Yes, surely the man has a name, and a noble one at that, judging by his crest."

"What do you need with his name?"

She stared, puzzling at his peculiar manner. Why was he behaving in such a curious way all of a sudden? Mayhap, like all men, he had too much pride and chaffed to accept the charity of others, even when offered as a wedding gift.

"I thought when we arrive I might call upon him to express my appreciation," she explained.

He looked alarmed. "Call upon him? Oh,

no, you can't call on him because . . . because he'll be away. By the time we arrive, he'll have left again. Spends a great deal of time on the Continent."

"Oh. I suppose, then, I shall simply have to write."

"Hmm, you do that. In the meantime, we'd best be off. We've some miles to travel today."

A footman stepped forward, opened the coach door and let down the step. He assisted her inside.

She arranged her skirts around her hips, then leaned back against the comfortable silk upholstered seat.

Darragh joined her in the vehicle.

"So, what is his name?"

He scowled. "Whose name? Oh, that." He paused. "Mulholland. The Earl of Mulholland."

"Thank you. Now, was that so dreadful?"

"No, and neither will this be." Leaning out the open door, he whistled.

Seconds later, Vitruvius sprang inside the coach.

CHAPTER SEVENTEEN

Four grueling, travel-weary days later, they arrived at their destination, the nights spent in Darragh's arms the only thing that made the trip bearable. Her new husband, she had rapidly discovered, was a man possessed of deep passions and appetites. Some of them nearly insatiable, as he had taken to showing her, much to her nocturnal delight.

Speaking of appetites, Jeannette thought as she felt her stomach rumble, she was hungry again despite the satisfying midday meal of roasted game hen and new potatoes she and Darragh had shared at an inn in the town of Ennis. But that had been almost five hours since. Five long, tedious, teeth-rattling hours spent bouncing over rutted, uneven roads, watching mile after mile of endless green countryside pass by.

Green grass. Green trees. Flat green fields and gently sloping hills stretching as far as the eye could see. Then more green interspersed with rock-strewn patches of brown and gray, plus the occasional Celtic stone cross with its unique circular design that speared upward toward a cloud-filled blue sky.

A sky that looked glum and cheerless, threatening rain as evening swiftly approached. She peered out the window of the now stationary coach and felt a bewildered frown descend across her brow.

Obviously this could not be Darragh's home, she reassured herself.

Not this single-story, thatched-roofed cottage, its stone exterior covered with a fresh coating of whitewash. Some sort of bushy plant reminiscent of ivy grew up in a quaint semicircle around the entrance, the wooden door painted an intense, jocular yellow. A pair of four-by-four windows were centered on either side to let in light and air. In the foreground yard lay a small flower bed and herb garden, divided by a stone walkway and a curving path that meandered around toward the rear. There, an empty clothesline stood, just barely visible around the corner.

Clearly she was mistaken about their arrival, the place quite obviously the home of a villager — a farmer or laborer or some such person to whom Darragh must needs speak.

Her husband alighted from the carriage, preceded by Vitruvius, who sprang down with a loud, exuberant bark. He barked a second time before loping off toward a nearby stand of trees. She sighed and picked a wad of dog hair off her peach-and-brown-printed gingham skirt, wondering how much longer and farther their journey would be.

But instead of striding toward the cottage, Darragh turned back to her and extended a hand.

"Oh, no, you go ahead," she told him. "I shall wait here until you have concluded your business."

"What business?"

"*Your* business," she repeated with agreeable forbearance, "with whomever it is you have detoured here to see. Go in and I shall wait."

"I fear you're laboring under a confusion, lass. We haven't stopped to visit anyone. We're here. We've arrived."

She stared out the window again, saw nothing but the small cottage and its surrounding yard. "What do you mean, arrived? Arrived where?"

"At our dwelling." He gestured behind him with a hand. "Welcome to your new home."

She stopped breathing. For a long moment, she felt exactly the way she had the time she'd fallen off a swing at age seven and had the air knocked completely out of her lungs.

A dizzy buzzing started in her head. She swayed slightly on the seat and grew faint from a lack of oxygen.

Looking alarmed, Darragh reached in and gave her a shake.

She sucked in a rasping breath and blinked twice. Exhaustion from the trip, she concluded. That's what it must be. Or maybe her ears were clogged with wax and needed a thorough cleansing. Whatever the reason, she must have misheard him.

"W-what did you say?" she questioned, fighting to slow her thundering heart.

"I said welcome home. Now, I know it's likely not quite what you were expecting, but if you'll just come inside you'll find it quite pleasant."

She stared, stunned. So it wasn't a mistake. This really was his house — his *cottage!* His whitewashed, thatched-roofed peasant's cottage that was smaller than some of the homes her father rented out to his tenant farmers in Surrey. Darragh expected her to live here? Here in this . . . this pea-shell-sized hut?

"Oh, no," she said, frantically shaking her head, "this will not do. This will not do at all."

"Well, I'm sorry for your disappointment, but it'll have to do. This is my home and all that I have to offer. Now, come down from there and take a look inside. You'll soon see your imaginings are turning the place into something far worse than it really is."

A knot of dismay tied itself tight inside her chest. "But surely you cannot be serious. You're playing a joke upon me, aren't you?"

Mercy, she prayed he was playing a joke upon her!

But her chest tightened further when he didn't start to grin or laugh, or unbend enough to confess to his prank. Slowly she realized he was completely serious.

"But it's a cottage," she sputtered.

He crossed his arms and leaned a shoulder against the coach door. "Aye, it's a cottage. A clean, tidy, well-constructed cottage with six rooms, including a spacious kitchen that boasts the newest in modern cookstoves."

Six rooms? And all the size of a matchbox, no doubt. Did he seriously expect her to live in a six-roomed, matchbox-sized cottage?

Folding her arms over her breasts, she leaned back against the upholstered coach squabs. "Take me back."

"Back where?"

"To my cousins. I wish to go home, to England." Her lower lip quivered. "From my cousins' house, I should be able to contact my parents and procure a passage home."

"Don't be daft, woman. We've been on the road for half a week and I'm not taking you back moments after we've arrived."

"Fine. Then take me to an inn. I shall stay the night there then make arrangements in the morning for my return journey."

He let out a snort. "And what'll you use for money to pay for this return trip, since I won't be giving you any of mine?"

She wrinkled her nose in consternation. *Money?* She hadn't even considered money. All she had in her reticule was a single half-crown coin, a silver card case, her etui, a vinaigrette and a pair of lace handkerchiefs. Certainly nothing of enough value to pay her way back to her cousins' home.

"I have jewelry," she said, blurting out the thought the instant it sprang into her head. "I shall sell some of that."

"You could try, but folks around these parts have little use for fancy baubles. You'd do better if you had a cow to trade."

She gaped. *A cow?*

"Besides, I believe you're forgetting one essential point."

"Oh, and what, pray tell, might that be?"

"The fact that you're my wife, honor-bound to remain at my side, to let me care and provide for you the best way I can. Before we came here, you gave me your promise you'd try to make our marriage work. Have you forgotten that promise already?"

"N-no," she sputtered, "but surely you can't expect me to live in that." She flung a hand out toward the cottage. "After all, I am still a lady."

"Aye, you are, and living in that dwelling will not change that fact. Wherever you reside, humble or grand, you shall always be a lady and the person you were born to be. Now, come down with you and let me show you our home."

His words left her feeling churlish and every inch the snob he'd once accused her of being. But it wasn't right that she should have to live in such a meager abode. She'd known Darragh was a commoner, but not *this* common. She'd expected a house with at least two stories and a comfortable number of rooms. Something a member of the gentry, for instance, might be satisfied to own.

Surely working as an architect provided a more lucrative income than this tiny cottage in the middle of nowhere? Surely he could afford to build something better, bigger, finer, since clearly he knew how. Until now he'd been a bachelor, given to traveling for his profession. Maybe the cottage had suited his needs and now that he was wed he planned to construct something larger and more genteel. Or could it be he had another commission already arranged and did not plan for them to remain here long? She brightened at the thought.

Either way, she supposed she would have to make do for the time being.

Thank God none of her friends or acquaintances could see her now. How they would stare and deride her, shaking their heads in pity before turning away. Even her best friend, Christabel, would sniff and cast sad, reproving eyes upon her.

"Does Raeburn know?" she said, blurting out the question nagging at the back of her mind.

"Know what?"

"About this? About our . . . circumstances?"

He met her gaze, his expression oddly enigmatic. "Aye, he knows."

So, her jilted beau had found the means

to have a bit of revenge upon her, after all. It must seem a great joke to him, well deserved and fitting in a perverse sort of way. Well, she wouldn't give him the satisfaction of begging for his assistance, probably what he was expecting of her. Likely all of them were waiting for her to run back home, which she conceded she had been only too ready to do a mere two minutes ago.

But despite her pampered upbringing, she was made of sterner stuff. She would show them, every last one, of exactly what Jeannette Rose Brantford O'Brien was made.

The footmen and coachman had been busy while she and Darragh talked, unloading Darragh's compact travel valise then her trunks and bandboxes and hat cases, one after another after another.

She crossed to the front door, Darragh at her back. When they reached the threshold, he stopped her with a hand and moved around to her side. Turning the knob, he pushed the door open on silent hinges. Then before she knew what he meant to do, he bent and swept her off her feet.

She cried out in surprise, her arms looping instinctively around his sturdy neck.

"Tradition, *a ghrá*," he murmured in his deep, lilting voice. "To bring us luck."

Her pulse stuttered and for an instant she lost herself in the brilliant blue of his eyes.

The moment passed as he strode forward and set her on her feet. She looked around, heart plummeting to the soles of her fashionable boots. Gazing along the central hallway, she spied four doors, two on either side. He'd said there were six rooms in the house, and just as she'd feared, they were far from spacious. If she wasn't mistaken, she believed the whole cottage would fit into the family drawing room at Wightbridge House and still leave room to spare.

She gulped against the new lump wedged in her throat.

At least he hadn't lied about the place being clean. The floors were neatly swept and scrubbed, furnishings and decorative items neatly arranged, with nary a speck of dust anywhere to be seen. On the air, the scent of polish and sweet dried herbs — rosemary and thyme. And beef stew cooking in the kitchen, if she didn't mistake.

Her stomach ached with hunger, reminding her that a hot meal would not go amiss. But first she wanted to wash away her travel grime, change into fresh linens and a clean dress for dinner. She might reside in a true backwater now, but that didn't mean she intended to forget her manners.

"If you will excuse me, sir, I believe I shall retire to my room, if you would be good enough to show me where it is."

"Of course, darling." He nodded down the hallway. "Our room is just there in the back, to the right."

"*Our* room? So we shall be sharing?"

He tossed her a clearly amused look. " 'Tis the usual way of things for a wedded couple, would you not agree? Most particularly a newly wedded couple."

Not among her class, who generally kept separate bedchambers. But she supposed new sleeping arrangements would be yet another adjustment to which she would have to accustom herself.

"Please send Betsy to me if you would, and inform her I would like a bath as soon as one can be arranged."

Turning on her heel, she started down the hallway.

"About Betsy," he called toward her retreating back.

She halted, swung around to face him. "Yes? What about her?"

He dug his thumbs into his waistband. "She . . . well, she isn't here."

Her stomach lurched in sudden dread. "What do you mean, she isn't here?"

"I've been scouring my mind, since this

morning, trying to think how to tell you, but there's just no easy way. I am sorry, lass, but I had to let her go."

"Let her go?" she repeated, the tenor of her pitch rising with each word. "What do you mean? As in release her from my employ?"

Alarm shot through her at his nod.

"But how could you?" she said, aghast. "Betsy is a wonderful maid. Why would you dismiss her, especially without consulting me? It wasn't your right to send her away. She was my maid and my responsibility. You will send a rider back immediately to wherever it is you abandoned her and bring her back." She stomped her foot against the floor on a wave of rising hysteria, and sudden, unreasoning fear. "Bring her back now."

He crossed his arms. "I can't bring her back. She wasn't dismissed for poor conduct. There simply isn't the money to keep a lady's maid, nor much need for her services any longer."

She goggled at him in disbelieving horror. "Of course there is a need for her services. Who will keep my clothes? Who will tend to my toilette and arrange my hair? Who will help me dress and disrobe?"

"I can help you with any buttons or laces

you can't reach yourself, and manage the occasional pin or two, if you've trouble doing your hair. And since it isn't likely we'll be holding any fancy parties, you can wear simple gowns that don't take so much work nor care."

Reeling at his blasphemy, she pressed a hand to her chest. "None of my gowns are simple!"

"Then mayhap you'll have to stitch a few new ones that aren't so troublesome to maintain."

"Stitch? As in sew? Me?"

"You sew, do you not?"

"I *embroider*. I do not sew clothing."

"Then it's past time you learned." He gestured with a hand. "And for what it's worth, I didn't just abandon your maid. I gave her glowing references and put coins in her purse to pay for travel expenses to England plus two months' wages besides. 'Tisn't as if I'm a monster, after all."

At this moment, Jeannette decided, he was far worse than a monster. Far, far worse. She blinked against the pressure that built up behind her eyes, that made her nose and eyelids sting.

She would not cry, she willed. She would not let him see her reduced to a torrent of tears. But that's exactly what happened seconds later, a single, harsh sob bursting uncontrollably from her lips. Pressing a fist to her mouth, she whirled and ran toward the bedroom.

Darragh winced as the door slammed shut behind her, the sound reverberating with the fury of a thunderbolt through the cottage.

Well, he mused, that had gone about as well as expected, though he'd hoped she wouldn't cry. The wrenching misery of her weeping rang out, tearing at his vitals, twisting knife-deep.

Jesus, he hated it when women cried, their tears more caustic than a vat of quick lime. But after years living with three younger sisters, he'd long ago learned that there are all sorts of tears and just as many reasons for them to be shed. Female tears ran the entire emotional gambit from joy and relief, to anger and frustration, to sorrow and despair and even to pure, premeditated manipulation. When used effectively, a good cry could reduce the most hardened man to a puddle of mush, make him willing to do anything, no matter how foolish or unreasonable, if only to make the tears cease.

But he refused to be coerced. Not that he believed for an instant that Jeannette's current distress wasn't honestly felt. He'd given her a shock, several of them, and it was only natural she was in their bedroom crying her eyes out. But once she stopped, once her anger cooled, her panic eased, then there would be a chance for her to learn to look beyond her pampered upbringing, her social prejudices, and see something more. See him for the man he truly was, and see herself for the woman he knew she could be.

What if it doesn't work? a little voice whispered. *What if she never comes to love you the way you want? The way you need? What if this game of yours is only a conceit and does nothing but drive a wedge between the two of you that will never again be healed?*

A fresh wail carried down the hallway.

He set his teeth against the sound and the needle-sharp stab of guilt that followed.

It wasn't too late. If he wished, he could put an end to his plan right now. Explain that the cottage actually belonged to a friend and he'd just been having a bit of fun with her, a harmless little tease. She'd be angry at first. But then relief would set in, a smile appearing on her lips when she saw his real home, learned his true identity.

But then he would never know, would he? Forever left to wonder if she did indeed love him as he hoped, or whether he was just fooling himself, her love stemming from a pleasure in the material things he could provide.

Even with his wealth and title, if he revealed himself to her now she would always carry with her a sense of superiority. After all, she was English, he was not. The English as a group uniformly considered themselves better than the Irish, regardless of an Irishman's lineage. This would hold especially true for the pampered daughter of an English peer, a woman so beautiful she could have had any man in the realm. Even, it seems, a duke.

He tightened a fist at his side, resolved to continue on with his scheme. *Let her cry. Let her rage.* Tumbling her off her lofty pedestal to live like ordinary folk for a while could only do her good. And in a few weeks, after she'd had a chance to acclimate to her reduced circumstances, he would see if his plan had been unwise. See if he'd succeeded in finding a way into her proud heart, as she had already done to his own.

Jeannette placed the tray with its empty dishes that had contained a meal of beef stew, buttered soda bread, apple cobbler and tea onto the floor outside the bedroom. Shutting the door, she took angry satisfaction in turning the lock behind her.

Darragh O'Brien could find himself another bed to sleep in tonight. And tomorrow night as well, since her present unhappiness wasn't likely to have passed by then. If it ever did.

Just thinking about this cottage and his callous treatment of her made her livid and weepy all over again. She had cried for nearly an hour straight, leaving her nose stuffed, temples throbbing, eyes heavy and red-rimmed. If Betsy were here she would have brought a lavender-scented cloth for her head. But Betsy was gone. Dismissed by that insensitive brute of a man.

Her hands tightened into balls. He'd had no right. No right at all to release her lady's maid from service and send her home. She needed Betsy. A shiver ran through her at the thought of being without the other woman's familiar, comforting presence.

She hadn't even had a chance to say goodbye. And Betsy had been her last, her only remaining link with home and the life she once had led. Now she was alone. Stranded in this new, unfamiliar place, with only Darragh for company.

She padded to the bed and sank down onto the mattress in dejection.

Since delivering his infamous news, Darragh had only come near to ask if she wished to join him for supper. She'd refused, using silence as a weapon, waiting until his footsteps finally moved away.

Sprawled across the bed in the dark, she'd fallen asleep until sometime later, when his knock startled her awake. He announced he was leaving a tray for her outside her door. She'd wanted to refuse that as well, but intense hunger had driven her to accept his offering once she was sure he was gone.

The meal was delicious and left her feeling marginally better. But now that it was done, she had nothing to do and no reasonable idea of the time, since there were no clocks in the room.

By the light of the single tallow candle she'd found and lighted, she gazed around the modestly sized, modestly furnished room. Plain white walls, simple oak furniture — bed, bureau, wardrobe and cane chair — a large multihued braided rug spread over the wide-plank pine flooring. Ordinary blue curtains covered the single window, a yellow and blue quilt spread across the bed. The only decoration was a wooden cross hung on the wall next to the bureau, and near the door a small oil painting of an Irish country village.

She supposed she ought to go to bed. And

she would, if only she could figure out a way to unfasten the back of her dress. She'd tried, and all she'd been able to manage were the top three pearl buttons.

Wounded outrage burned afresh in her blood. She would sleep in this gown, she vowed, before she asked Darragh for help. She might well end up rotting in it before she asked. And to think all this had begun when she announced she wanted a bath.

A tear trailed over her cheek. She couldn't even tidy her hair, since her brush was still packed up and she had no idea where to find it. That had been Betsy's job, to unpack all her belongings, to see her clothes laid out, her toiletries arranged and available for her use. Yet another demerit to add to her husband's ever-increasing tally.

As if he'd known she was thinking about him, the doorknob turned and stopped. "Jeannette. Open the door."

Even though he couldn't see her, she glared and stuck out her tongue.

"Enough now, lass. Let me in."

"Has Betsy returned?"

"No, you know she has not."

"Then go to the devil," she shot back.

She expected him to rattle the knob again, issue another set of demands.

Instead, nothing. Not so much as a muttered curse.

A full minute of silence passed, quiet so palpable she could almost hear him breathing where he stood on the other side of the door. What was he doing out there? Why wasn't he arguing with her, demanding again that she let him inside?

She waited, tense and ready for his next salvo.

Then she heard him move away, his footfalls fading in a hushed tap as he trod down the hall.

Well, that had been easy, she thought. Too easy. Then again, maybe he'd realized she wasn't going to budge and had chosen to save himself the trouble of a strained voice and simply admit defeat. Let him sleep in the guest room — assuming there was a guest room in this pea pod — and in the morning she would decide whether or not to emerge. Whether or not to speak.

For now she supposed she ought to try to get some sleep. With that thought foremost, she twisted her arms behind her back for another wrestling match with the buttons on her dress.

She squirmed and strained, tugging at the material as much as she dared in an attempt to reach one of the quartet of buttons at the center of her back. Her arm muscles quivered, fingers straining in an agony of frustration against her overarched spine.

Contorted like a sideshow act in a circus, she wasn't fully aware of the sibilant squeak of the window gliding upward on its runners until it was too late. Turning her head, she met Darragh's triumphant gaze as he threw a leg over the windowsill and ducked his head to climb into the room.

Flabbergasted, her fingers slipped off the button she'd finally managed to reach.

Straightening to his full height, he planted his hands on his narrow hips. "Can I offer you some help getting out of that dress, darling?" he drawled.

She firmed her jaw. "Go away."

Shrugging, he turned to close and lock the window, arrange the draperies. "If you change your mind, you've only to say the word."

With her looking on, he raised his long arms above his head, gave one of those shivering all-male stretches that would have heated the blood of a nun. Replete with raw, understated strength, Darragh exuded virility the way other men shed their shirts, unthinkingly and with ease. He fairly reeked of it, his ordinary, loose-fitting clothes doing nothing to disguise the hard, agile frame Jeannette knew lay underneath. Supple limbs, wide shoulders, sturdy chest with its dark covering of hair that seemed custom made to pillow a woman's head. And clever, long-fingered hands that could both stimulate and soothe, depending on the occasion.

Luckily for her she was in the mood for neither, too unhappy to let his display affect her. At least not much.

"Well," he said in a mild tone, "bed and sleep sounds good to me. The day has been a long, hard one, and no doubt of that." He slipped off his jacket, then began untying his neckerchief.

"Did you not hear me?" she questioned. "I told you to go."

He tossed his neck cloth onto a chair, went to work opening his waistcoat buttons. "So you did, lass. But this is our bedroom and that piece of furniture you're sitting on is our bed and I've every intention of sharing it with you. You're my wife. We'll sleep together."

She sprang off the bed, as if the mattress had suddenly caught fire. "Oh, no, we won't, not tonight. Just because you pulled your clever little stunt and crawled through that window doesn't mean I'll let you crawl into bed with me."

Hurrying to the door, she twisted the key in the lock and wrenched open the door.

"Now, for the third time, *go!*"

He peeled his shirt off over his head, tossed it atop his growing stack of garments. His intense blue gaze locked upon her own. With slow deliberation, he lowered his fingers to his trouser fastenings, his message clear.

She felt her whole body quiver as temper flashed hot. "Fine. Then *I'll* go. There must be somewhere else to sleep in this house."

She whirled and started through the door.

"There's no room in the second bedroom to sleep, it's so full of your trunks and band-boxes and other assorted paraphernalia," he called after her. " 'Tis doubtful you'll even reach the bed. As for the sofa in the sitting room, you'll have a rough night of it there. Ropes need tightening, I'm afraid."

She bristled, but kept walking.

"And I'll only follow you," he said, startling her by striding up close behind. "Where you sleep, I shall sleep too."

She did her best to ignore him as he trailed after her, hope wilting as she inspected one room after the other, only to discover he was right. There was nowhere even remotely comfortable to sleep except their bedroom.

Her journey drew to a halt in the sitting room, where she turned a baleful eye upon an old, narrow sofa that even Vitruvius didn't wish to occupy. Curled on a thick rug near the fire, the dog opened a single eye and thumped his tail in greeting. Yawning, he closed his eyelids again, went back to his secret doggy dreams.

Darragh folded his arms across his bare chest. "So, will it be the pair of us on the sofa, then? Or shall we spread a blanket out over the floor next to Vitruvius? I suspect we can manage to roll up together snug as fleas."

If they rolled up next to Vitruvius they probably *would* have fleas! Utterly frustrated, she repressed the urge to give a very undignified kick to the couch.

Her shoulders drooped, a weary sadness sweeping through her. "Very well, you win. We'll both sleep in the bed. But that is *all* we are going to do tonight. Sleep. Is that understood?"

"Completely. So long as you can keep your hands off me."

"I believe I'll manage."

She led the way back to the bedroom. Darragh followed, closed the door and shut them inside.

"Now then, let me see to those buttons of yours," he said, coming up behind her.

She gathered her pride around her like a

cloak. "Thank you, no. I am fine."

He tsked, took her by the shoulders and turned her back around. "I saw how fine you were when I climbed through the window. You'll be miserable if you sleep in your dress and stays. Don't be so stubborn, woman. You won't be hurting anyone but yourself."

Why, she cursed, *did he have to be right?* If she refused him, she would be the one to suffer while Darragh slumbered peacefully as a babe at her side. When she really considered it, he ought to have to do all the things Betsy had done, since he was the reason her maid wasn't here.

"All right," she relented. "But I need a few things from my traveling cases."

"What things?"

"My nightgown, for one. My hairbrush and pin box as well."

His brow wrinkled. "Do you know which trunks they're in?"

She shook her head. "Betsy always arranged my things." *And you dismissed Betsy,* she thought on a sorrowful retort.

"I could be in there for hours searching. I'll look tomorrow."

She stuck out her lower lip. "But I want my night rail."

His fingers began freeing her gown. "You

402

can sleep in your chemise tonight."

"You are insufferable, do you know that?"

"Aye, so you tell me."

With a minimum of fuss, he helped her off with her gown, unlaced her corset and freed her petticoat ties. He left her to remove the pins from her hair on her own.

She was finger-combing her long tresses when he approached and offered her one of his brushes. Part of a matched set, it was round with no handle, its silver top engraved with his initials. She considered issuing a rebuff then decided to accept, drawing the soft boar bristles through her hair in long, soothing strokes.

By the time she finished, he was in bed, one long arm tucked beneath his head as he lay watching her. She tried not to stare, his beautiful, powerful body very obviously naked beneath the sheets.

Crawling in beside him, she rolled over onto her side and faced away from him. He sat up, leaned over her. She tensed, expecting him to demand a kiss and more. Instead he only reached across to the nightstand, blew out the candle.

Darkness engulfed the room.

"Good night, my Little Rosebush," he murmured in a warm, velvety tone.

"Little Rosebush!"

"Aye. I've thought for a long while that you're like a rosebush. Guarded by thorns but much too beautiful to resist."

"And I think you're a bully. And a devil."

Her taunt only made his chest shake with laughter.

She did not speak further, hugging her hurt to herself the way she hugged the blanket and sheet around her body. Even if he couldn't afford to keep Betsy, she thought, he ought to have discussed it with her first. He should have told her beforehand that he planned to let her lady's maid go, instead of behaving in such a high-handed, dictatorial manner.

Domestic arrangements were always the wife's purview, especially the hiring and firing of servants. But this was not an elegant estate with dozens of staff to manage, she reminded herself. It was a tiny cottage with only the two of them in residence.

The seclusion of it frightened her. She had never lived like this. How would she manage?

Day to day, she decided, the bed creaking lightly as Darragh arranged his large frame into a comfortable position beside her.

She listened to his breathing until she knew he was asleep. Only then did she relax. Only then did she allow herself to admit that despite everything he'd done, she longed to turn and snuggle close inside the warm shelter of his arms. Let herself be held so she wouldn't feel so lost and alone anymore.

Instead she stayed where she was, forced her eyes to close, her mind to clear to let the comfort of sleep take her away.

Desire burned like a brand between her legs when she woke hours later, the faintest hint of gray light creeping around the curtains into the room. She whimpered, disoriented and half-asleep. Her breasts ached, feeling heavy and swollen. Her bodice lay open, nipples damp and pinched tight, exquisitely sensitive, exposed to the cool morning air.

She barely had time to think about how she'd gotten that way when her hips arched upward, her head rolling against the pillow. Darragh's head was pillowed as well, on one of her thighs, as he kissed and suckled her in a place where until her wedding night she'd never imagined being kissed at all. Somehow without waking her, he'd positioned himself there, draping her other leg over his shoulder.

But she was awake now. God Almighty was she awake, lying helpless and enslaved beneath his mesmerizing touch. She remembered how cross she'd been with him earlier. How she'd turned him and his lovemaking away.

"Darragh," she murmured.

He heard her, pausing long enough to raise his head. "Morning, darling. Did I finally manage to wake you?"

"What are you doing?" she panted. "I didn't say you could . . . could, you know."

"I didn't know I needed to ask. Shall I stop, then?"

Her flesh throbbed, begging for a release only he could provide. Her pride urged her to say, "Yes, stop." Her body told her not to be a fool. Her body won, aching with a longing that was almost painful.

"God, no," she groaned. "Don't stop. Please don't stop."

He chuckled and went back to what he'd been doing.

It wasn't long before he brought her to an intense and incredibly satisfying peak, violent shudders racking her entire body. Before she'd even stopped shaking, he sat up, turned her over, raised her up so she rested on her hands and knees.

He gave her a couple light smacks on the bottom that made her gasp, not with pain but in heated arousal. Before she had time to adjust to his last astonishing move or the shocking novelty of their position, he came into her from behind, filling her to the hilt. And then she couldn't think at all as he moved inside her. Fast and deep, then faster and deeper, over and over until he had her moaning, all but incoherent.

She clenched the damp sheets in her fists, her head hanging down as he drove them both at a relentless pace. Raising her hips, she pressed back against him to take more. His groan rang harsh and satisfying in her ear.

He cupped her breasts, massaged them, giving them a gentle squeeze before skimming his big hands downward over her belly. Positioning one hand on her hip to steady her, he slipped the fingers of his other hand between her legs to play upon her wet, heated flesh. He stroked her there where she was most sensitive, scattering wild kisses upon her shoulder and neck.

Then before she had any idea what he planned to do, he bit her nape, his teeth clamping down just hard enough to send her hurtling over the edge.

She cried out and let the fierce satisfaction sweep her away.

He claimed his own pleasure soon after, quaking against her, around her, within her — so brutally, she felt his release almost as if it were her own.

Sated, they slumped together against the sheets. Rolling to his back, he tugged her close and tucked her against his chest. With a smile curving her lips, she fell asleep, locked inside the safety of his arms.

CHAPTER EIGHTEEN

Jeannette awakened in a profoundly mellow mood, well rested and deliciously revitalized by the residual glow of good lovemaking.

She stretched and sat up, a surprised smile coming to her lips when she saw the change of clothes laid out for her at the foot of the bed. Her toiletries were there as well — hairbrush, comb, pin box, perfume, even the milled soap she preferred — all neatly arranged on the bureau next to Darragh's shaving and grooming implements. A nightgown and robe were also draped over the back of the chair, just as she had requested last night.

She rose, found fresh, warm water waiting in a large china pitcher, soft clean towels nearby. Her upset over Betsy's dismissal eased, fading beneath the magnitude of Darragh's thoughtful consideration. Clearly, he'd gone through her trunks and unpacked the items he thought she would want immediately. Then he'd carried them in, managing somehow not to wake her.

Under the circumstances, she supposed it would be spiteful not to forgive him. And with his assistance, mayhap she could learn to do without a lady's maid for a time. At least until she could persuade him to rehire Betsy.

Cheered by the idea, she washed and dressed, the blue muslin morning gown he'd chosen one she was able to don and fasten on her own. Her hair presented a different challenge. It took three tries before she finally managed to pin the heavy mass into a reasonably acceptable knot on top of her head. With an indulgent smile on her lips, she went to find her new husband.

Ten minutes later the smile had vanished, along with her nascent good humor. She stared at Darragh over a bowl of lumpy oatmeal, her spoon forgotten in her hand. "You expect me to do what!"

" 'Tis only the two of us, so the cooking shouldn't take up too much of your time. As you can see by our breakfast, I'm not a great hand in the kitchen. As for housework, you'll only have to clean and straighten on the days Aine Murray isn't here to take care of the heavy work, scrubbing floors, washing the laundry and such. She's young, but she's a good girl. You'll like her."

Jeannette jammed the spoon into her dish. "Have you lost your senses? I am not some peasant housewife who bakes bread and dips candles and stitches quilts. I am a lady, trained to manage a large household and direct servants, not cook and clean and sew."

"Aye, but since I haven't a large household nor lots of servants, you'll have to try your hand at the other. I'm not saying it'll be easy at first but you've a keen mind. I know you'll figure things out quickly enough."

Despite having thought much the same thing last night regarding the lack of servants and her duties in that regard, Jeannette could not help but goggle, her eyes bulging in their sockets. "I do not wish to *figure things out*. I am your wife, not some servant you hired." She crossed her arms. "I refuse."

"Then we'll be a sad and hungry pair for certain." Lifting a spoonful of the oatmeal, he let it plop back into the bowl in an unappetizing heap. "Can't say I'd like to eat this for every meal."

"What about last night's meal?" she challenged. "The fare was simple, but quite delicious. Who made that?"

"Aine's ma, but the meal was a special

411

treat sent over in welcome. We won't be getting another of her suppers tonight."

"I fail to see why not. Hire the woman to cook for us. And engage more servants as well, ones who can live in and work every day, not just a few days out of the week."

"I'm sorry, darling, but I can't afford to keep a permanent staff of servants such as you're used to. Never mind the fact there wouldn't be the room to house them all. As for Aine's ma, she has seven other babies at home, all of them younger than Aine. Mrs. Murray doesn't have time to come and cook."

"Surely with eight children she could use the money."

"Why do you think she's hired Aine out along with her other two oldest children? Plus, Mrs. Murray is in the family way again, due to deliver another babe come spring."

Distressed, Jeannette tapped a fingernail against the wooden kitchen tabletop. "Mrs. Murray ought to tell Mr. Murray to leave her alone."

"Aye, but think of all the fun they'd miss." He grinned.

She failed to see the humor. "This . . . this notion of me cooking and cleaning and taking care of this cottage, however small it may be, is an absolutely preposterous idea. I know nothing about that sort of work. I don't even know how to put a kettle on the stove, let alone how to light the blasted thing."

"I can show you. All it takes is a flint and some dry kindling."

"Well then, if it's so easy, you do it. Or better yet, hire some servants to do it." She crossed her arms. "You ask too much. Such labors are simply beneath the dignity of a titled lady."

"They're not beneath the dignity of my wife. And there'll be no servants employed other than Aine, and she's to clean, not cook. I'll make sure there's food in the larder. It's up to you to fix the meals."

"But I told you. I haven't the faintest notion how to cook."

He eyed the cold oatmeal neither of them wished to touch. "You can learn. Now, shall I show you how to work the stove and such?"

"No, since I will not be using it nor any other kitchen devise in this house." She pushed back her chair and jumped to her feet. "I am going to my room."

"Go, then, and pout all you like, but such measures won't make an anthill's difference to me. And they won't change my mind nor will they put food on the table. When you change your mind, let me know and I'll show you how to work the stove."

"I will never change my mind."

He pinned her with a look. "Fair warning, lass. Never is an awfully long time."

Three days later, Jeannette decided that as much as she hated to admit it, Darragh was right. Never was an awfully long time, especially when one's stomach was empty as an echoing cavern.

Hunger gnawed her insides with the sharpness of a small vicious animal, a reminder that she hadn't eaten a decent meal since the evening of her arrival. Holding fast to her vow not to cook, she had been subsisting on raw apples and carrots, along with some cheese and milk she'd discovered in the larder. But apples and carrots, cheese and milk as a steady diet simply were not enough.

She wanted food — meat and fish, butter and eggs and bread. Hot, succulent, satisfying food that melted in her mouth and filled the empty, aching hole in her stomach.

She'd been counting on Darragh to break, to toss up his hands in defeat and agree to hire a cook. But as each new day dawned and he didn't so much as whisper a word of complaint, she began to fret. He was stubborn enough to outlast her, she realized, no matter how long the siege might take. Worse, she suspected the wretch was cheating, privy to a stash of food she couldn't find. And if he did have additional foodstuffs, Lord knows how long he might be able to hold out.

When Aine arrived this morning, Jeanette had practically fallen upon the girl, all but begging her to cook her a meal. With wide, sympathetic green eyes and hair as black as midnight, Aine had bobbed an apologetic curtsey and explained that Mr. O'Brien had forbidden her from doing aught else but the cleaning and laundry chores as agreed. She'd said she could answer any questions Jeannette might have on how to cook, but that she wasn't to do any of the actual preparation herself.

Jeannette had choked down an oath and stalked back to the bedroom, infuriated all over again. She wasn't even permitted the satisfaction of twisting the key in the lock, since Darragh had secreted it away. He'd secreted them all away, hiding every single blessed key in the house. Despite her pleas on the subject, he had refused to return any of them. Not until he could trust her not to lock him out, he said.

And since she couldn't lock him out, she couldn't keep him out either. Not out of the bedroom nor out of her bed. She did her best to ignore him during the day, letting him know in no uncertain terms exactly what she thought of his loathsome edict.

But at night he was impossible to ignore. Devil that he was, he delighted in finding clever and ever more inventive ways to turn her desire against her, to make her eager and aching and yielding in his arms. The first two nights he waited until she was too sleepy to put up more than a token protest, quickly luring her traitorous body to override her mind. Then last night he'd simply leaned close and started dropping random kisses onto her skin. Refusing to be shooed aside, he persisted until he had her purring beneath him, had her quite literally begging for his touch, his name a breathless, fervid sigh on her lips.

She knew she ought to be ashamed for surrendering in his arms the way she did at night, when by day he exasperated her to the point where she could barely bring herself to speak so much as a civil greeting to him. But there it was, the odd ambivalence of their relationship. The inexplicable push and pull between them that stirred the full gambit of emotions from high to low.

As the day progressed, she did what she could to pay no heed to her empty, aching stomach, glad Darragh was occupied in his study drawing plans or some such thing. But by afternoon she knew she could stand it no longer. Still, she refused to ask for any quarter from her husband, seeking Aine out instead.

She found the girl in the backyard, long hair tied back in a kerchief as she hung wet laundry from the line.

"Excuse me, Aine," she said. "Could you help me, do you suppose? I need to light the fire in the stove, and I . . . well, I do not know how."

The girl looked up, a pleasant smile curving her lips. "Sure and I'd be that pleased to help you, ma'am. Just let me finish hanging this sheet and I'll be there in a nip."

As a servant, Aine ought to have called her "my lady." Even married to an untitled commoner as Jeannette now was, her hereditary title — the one that came to her through her father — was still hers to use. A correction hovered on her lips, but she swallowed it down. What did it matter here in this place whether or not this ordinary girl addressed her properly? What lady, after all, would be asking the assistance of a servant to light a stove in the first place?

Aine completed pinning the sheet, then turned with a lithe step and disappeared into the kitchen. Jeannette followed, and once inside stood by to watch and listen while the maid showed her how to add kindling and light the range.

"Is there a simple dish you might suggest?" Jeannette asked the girl once the stove was heating nicely. "Something flavorsome, but easy to cook?"

Aine considered the question. "Potatoes, onions and bacon make a nice quick dish. They'll fry right up in a skillet in no time at all."

Jeannette thanked the girl and watched her return outside to the laundry. Potatoes, onions and bacon did sound simple. Plain and homey and filling, a far cry from the elegant cuisine upon which she usually dined. But under the circumstances, such fare would have to do. And surely even she could cook such a dish — after all, how hard could it be?

Darragh followed his nose into the kitchen, pleased to find Jeannette at the stove, but not so surprised to find her looking less than happy.

Metal spatula in hand, she chiseled in clear desperation at something cooking —

or should he say burning — inside a heavy iron skillet. Cursing, she blistered the air with a litany of words he wouldn't have imagined a gently bred woman like her to know. He watched as she grabbed a thick towel off the counter and wrapped it around the handle to yank the pan off the heat.

"Ouch." She stuck a knuckle in her mouth.

He hurried across. "Did you burn yourself?"

She rounded on him, her translucent eyes flashing hotter than a boiling sea. "Yes, and I hope you feel badly about it, since it's all your fault."

"Here now, let me have a look."

She slapped him away. "Keep your looks to yourself."

He gathered up her hand anyway, saw a faint pink mark on her skin, relieved to discover the wound wasn't serious. "Shall I draw you a bit of cool water from the well to ease the pain?"

"Don't trouble yourself," she said in a martyred tone. "I will simply have to bear the pain until it heals." She glanced toward the skillet, her disappointment plain. "Oh, look at it. It's ruined."

Whatever *it* was. In its current sad state he couldn't quite tell, though he suspected the main ingredient might have started out as potatoes. Criticizing her first attempt at cooking, however, was no way to instill confidence.

"Looks delicious," he lied. "A mite crispy along the edges — but then, I like it that way."

Incredulous eyes met his own. "You like your potatoes burned?"

Ah, so he'd been right about that. If he could still recognize what it was she'd cooked, then surely he could eat it. At least he prayed he could.

He slapped his hands together, as if eager to begin the meal. "Let me gather up a pair of plates and in we'll dig."

She stood back as he did exactly that, setting places for them at the table in the small dining room adjacent to the kitchen. He left her to scrape the charred mass onto a serving platter and carry it into the other room.

She set the dish down with a *thump.*

Helping her with her chair, he took a seat opposite. He forced an enthusiastic smile, then spooned a hearty portion of blackened potatoes onto his blue-and-white-patterned china plate.

Good thing he was hungry, starving actually. He hadn't eaten a satisfying meal since the night of their arrival. She had to be starving as well, ravenous hunger clearly be-ing what had driven her into the kitchen, just the way he'd planned.

Still, he'd been worried, afraid she just might outlast him. Sainted Mary, he was glad Jeannette had yielded, since it had been near killing him not to go to Aine and beg her to cook them something, anything that didn't have to be eaten cold or raw.

But he'd resisted and had won the reward. Though, to be honest, the food presently on his plate didn't look much like a reward. But Jeannette had made it and that was the point. He only prayed he'd be able to subsist on her mistakes long enough for her to learn to cook. *If* she learned to cook. Well, if worse came to worst he'd muddle through, a bit thinner for the experience.

Wishing he'd thought to get himself a knife, he jammed his fork into what looked like a dark, flattened brick and chipped off a corner. The food crunched between his teeth, the taste of charcoal and something else, something greasy and slightly revolting sliding over his tongue.

Half-raw bacon, he realized. And overly seasoned. Dear God, had she poured an entire pot of salt into the skillet?

He chewed faster and gulped. "Delicious."

She raised a dubious brow, studied him as

he forced in another mouthful. He got a huge wedge of onion this time, burned on one side, raw on the other. Amazingly, despite their blackened surface, parts of the potatoes were undercooked and hard in the center. Without question, the dish was one of the most revolting he'd ever consumed.

But consume it he did, working his way through at a rapid pace. In between bites, he gulped swigs of the ale he'd poured himself, grateful for the relief it gave his abused throat and tongue.

For Jeannette's part, she poked at the congealing mass with the tines of her fork. After a sniff, she ate a single bite, her nose crinkling in disgust before she set her utensil aside.

Vitruvius ambled in, canine eyes pleading in the hopes of earning a treat. Instead of shooing the dog out of the room, she set her plate on the floor. Tail wagging, Vitruvius raced up and wolfed down a huge mouthful. Seconds later, his tail drooped and he gagged, hacking the food back out onto the plate with a retching cough.

For a long moment she and Darragh stared at the dog, looking on in silence as he whimpered and retreated from the room, as though stung.

"Well, I guess that told me," Jeannette

declared. Suddenly the humor of the situation caught her and she began to snicker, then laugh full-out.

Darragh joined her, a huge grin on his face. "He's a rude lad, he is."

"But an honest one. Poor thing, I feel like an axe murderer."

"Animal has no taste."

Downing a reinforcing gulp of ale, Darragh stabbed another forkful of the food on his plate and raised it to his mouth.

Jeannette's lips parted in horror. "For mercy sakes, Darragh, stop. Even the dog can't bear to eat it." She reached out a hand, laid it on his forearm to keep him from taking another bite.

His skin unusually pale, he wavered. "It's not so bad."

"Of course it's not, it's worse than bad. So dreadful that if anyone dared to serve me such slop I would have them hauled off to the gaol for committing a crime. Put your fork down."

Looking relieved, he did as she instructed.

"I don't know how you ate as much as you did," she said after a long moment.

He planted a fist against his chest, his stomach roiling aloud in protest. "I'm starting to wonder about that myself."

"You should just have said the meal was terrible."

"How could I now? Not after the grand try you gave."

"But it wasn't grand," she cried. "It was a disaster."

He lifted her hand, pressed a kiss onto the top. "Aye, a grand disaster that makes me proud."

"How can you be proud of being served such a disgusting, revolting mess?"

"Because you made it and that's enough."

Something in the region of her heart melted at his words. She'd failed, she thought, and failed miserably. She couldn't even cook a meal a novice should be able to make. Yet still he claimed to be proud. To her recollection, no one had ever been proud of her before. Admiring, perhaps. Dazzled and envious, even in awe, but never proud.

In her life, the attainment of perfection was the ultimate goal. To be more beautiful, more popular, more desirable and refined than any other. To use the trappings of privilege and wealth to achieve heights in status and prestige.

But Darragh cared nothing for such matters. To him an attempt was still worthy of praise, a failure something for which he could inexplicably still express pride.

He puzzled and warmed her all at the same time.

"Nonetheless," she said, suddenly uncomfortable with the emotions churning inside her breast, "I am hopeless in the kitchen, and if you persist in this plan of yours to have me cook, the both of us shall soon wither away to skin and bones."

"We'll be fine. I told you before, you'll learn, and this was only your first attempt. Don't be so hard on yourself."

"I'm not. It's my stomach that's doing the scolding for me."

"Well, if yours is scolding, then I suppose you might say mine is screaming." He grimaced. "Have a care with the salt next time."

"I was trying to give it some flavor."

"Flavor, was it now? More like swallowing down the ocean."

Her lips twitched.

His lips twitched back.

Both of them broke into smiles, then laughter.

When their mirth subsided, he laid a hand over his belly. "Oh, I think you've done me in, lass. Is there any buttermilk? A glass might prove soothing."

"In the springhouse, I believe. Shall I ask

Aine to get some?"

"Aye. Then after, tell her I'd like a word. I'll see if she can stay a bit longer this evening and come again extra in the morning."

"For what reason?"

"To show you a few things about fixing a meal, if you're agreeable."

"I'd be more agreeable if you'd simply hire a proper cook. I was not raised to perform common domestic chores, particularly in the kitchen." She paused, reading the stubborn resolve in his gaze. "But since you insist upon perpetrating this insanity, very well, Aine's assistance would be most welcome."

"Good," he said on a pleased look. "I'll see it done."

She waited for the gloating grin to form on his countenance. He had won this particular skirmish, asserted his male will over her own.

But no grin emerged and no gloating either. Just a comfortable smile that emphasized the long square lines of his jaw, the blunt angles of his forehead and chin and nose in a most thoroughly pleasing way. There were no two ways around it, her husband was an extremely handsome man. Of that she could have no complaint.

Rather than let him see the effect he had upon her, she stood. "Well, I suppose I should go find Aine."

"Aye. And Jeannette?"

"Yes?"

"Thank you."

"For what?"

"For being my bride."

With that, he gathered their plates, dropped a kiss onto her surprised mouth, and disappeared into the kitchen.

CHAPTER NINETEEN

That afternoon's thank-you was just the first of many Jeannette received from Darragh as the weeks passed, the last of September merging into October as fall settled like a crisp, cool blanket over the land. Whatever she cooked — good, bad or mediocre — her efforts were greeted with enthusiasm and unstinting appreciation.

Despite Aine's cheerful tutelage, learning to cook proved to be a daunting and difficult task.

All her life Jeannette had taken meals for granted. Food was something the servants prepared and served, something she and her family ate. With the exception of menu planning in consultation with the chef and housekeeper — one of her mother's duties, as mistress of the house — Jeannette had never spared more than a fleeting thought for where the ingredients were derived and what happened to those foodstuffs while they were being turned into dishes fit to be served at table.

But in quick order the blinders had been yanked from her eyes, leaving her with a new sympathy and understanding for all the kitchen staff who had ever dutifully prepared her a meal.

After the potato debacle, Aine started her out with something easy — scrambled eggs. Aine helped her cook sausages too — careful to make certain the meat didn't burn — and aided her in brewing her very first pot of tea.

After the girl left for the evening, Jeannette sat across from Darragh at the dining room table. Sighing in happy relief, the two of them worked their way through the platter of simple food with pure, unabashed delight.

Baking bread, simmering oatmeal, frying and roasting meat, boiling vegetables were next on the list of essentials that needed to be learned — her first attempts all colossal catastrophes. And though she wanted nothing more than to give up and tell Darragh they would have to go back to eating apples and cheese, she bit her lips and doggedly persevered.

As for Darragh, he worked during the day in his study, whistling as he sketched his plans, occasionally muttering under his breath as he researched various books and consulted previous designs. One morning a little over a week after their arrival, he announced he had business and would be away for a few hours.

At first, she'd been peeved. "Why aren't you inviting me along?" she asked, thrusting her lower lip out on an obvious pout. "Don't you think I would enjoy an excursion away from the house?"

"No," he'd answered, pointing out that besides her having the evening meal to prepare, his business would only bore her and make her regret her decision to come along.

Of course, she could have ridden after him; there was a second horse stabled in the barn. But she wouldn't know her way around the area, and frankly, from what she'd seen on a couple of the walks she'd taken, there really wasn't anything of interest to see.

Alone in the too quiet house, since it was one of Aine's days off, she set herself to baking bread. All went well until she opened the oven door to check on the baking loaves and saw they were flat and hard as brick bats.

"Oh," she cried, using a pair of steel tongs

to pull the pans from the oven, wisps of hair curling over her forehead from the heat.

Swiping a forearm across her perspiring skin, she stared at the miserable results of her day's baking, wondering where she had gone wrong. Her eyes fell upon a small blue jar and she knew, nearly smacking her forehead for her stupidity. The leavening! She'd forgotten to add the leavening. *Of all the idiotic mistakes,* she admonished herself. Dejectedly, she sank onto a kitchen chair and burst into tears.

Darragh found her still there half an hour later, her eyes red and swollen from all the tears she had shed.

"Here now," he said, crossing quickly to her, "what's amiss? Have you hurt yourself?"

"No." She sniffed. "It's the bread. I've ruined it."

He cast a glance at the sunken, miserable loaves, then turned and pulled her up and into his arms. "Then we'll do without bread and content ourselves with whatever we've available. Don't berate yourself so, lass, 'tisn't the end of the world."

She sniffed again and let him pull out his handkerchief to dry her eyes and wipe her nose. That done, he kissed her, brushing his lips, soft and gentle as a breeze, over her closed eyelids and her cheeks and chin.

Then he claimed her mouth with a sweet pressure that made her sigh in delight as he coaxed her back to lie across the kitchen table. Flour skirred into the air, dancing around them in a fine white cloud, as Darragh made slow, exquisite love to her — all thoughts of bread baking fading fast from her mind.

Much later that evening, he presented her with a cookbook that he'd purchased for her while he'd been out earlier that day. By rights she ought to have been offended by his gift, but once she put aside what remained of her battered pride, she realized what a godsend the book truly was.

Emboldened, she began to experiment and expand her repertoire from plain, simplistic dishes to something she might have found served at her parents' home. Without quite realizing when or how, she began to enjoy her newfound culinary abilities, skills that brought her a surprising amount of pleasure and satisfaction. Demonstrated the evening she poached her first salmon and served it with a creamy dill sauce that made Darragh grunt in delight and ask for seconds and thirds.

She had never considered herself a helpless sort of woman, but neither had she realized before just how capable she could be.

Learning to create all manner of things with her own two hands and doing a fine job of it too.

She also learned she could do without her elegant clothes — at least during the day, since she still insisted upon dressing for dinner as good manners prescribed. But her London gowns, she conceded, were far too lovely to risk ruin in menial tasks. So with Aine's assistance, and several yards of soft woolen cloth, she sewed four serviceable dresses to wear while she worked.

But of the myriad things she learned, her most surprising discovery came from the fact that she wasn't bored.

Perhaps it was simply a case of being too busy keeping house, too busy being a wife and striving to make her new life with Darragh a pleasant one, but she rarely gave much thought to her old routines and pastimes. She rose each morning eager to tackle a new day. And fell asleep each night satisfied by her day's achievements, her body usually humming from the splendid loving she'd just enjoyed with Darragh as she drifted off in his arms.

Yet as busy as her domestic chores kept her, she didn't spend all her time inside the house. She took a mid-morning stroll nearly every day, enjoying the fresh air and country sunshine far more than she had ever done in the past.

Often Darragh went with her. Strolling arm in arm, they would talk on all sorts of subjects, some serious, some silly, while Vitruvius loped happily behind, sniffing for rabbits and vermin, ever eager to give chase.

On one particularly bright afternoon, she packed them a meal of cold chicken, dried fruit, biscuits and wine, then gathered her watercolor paints, brushes and paper. Darragh hitched one of the horses to a small gig, stowed the food and her painting supplies in the rear and helped her into the seat next to him.

"You'll like the Shannon here in these parts," Darragh told her, "where the river meets up with the sea. Not long now and you'll catch the scent of brine coming up sweet in your nose. 'Tis a beautiful place for passing an afternoon."

And he was right, the grassy shoreline creating a lovely display. Seated on a large blanket, they dined to the accompaniment of birdsongs, the pair of them waving carefree as children at an occasional boat as it sailed by.

"Have you room for dessert?" she asked, pulling a current cake from the basket.

"I do if you made it." Darragh leaned on

his elbow and tossed her a lazy smile. "Why don't you feed me a piece?"

She cut a wedge and did as he suggested, holding out small bites for his delectation, letting him lick her fingers and scatter kisses across her palm in between helpings. She cut a small piece for herself and ate it, giggling as he pressed increasingly ravenous kisses to her lips.

Soon they tumbled backward, limbs and lips entwined as Darragh satisfied her every urge, loving her most thoroughly beneath the protection of an extra blanket.

Some while later, she took out her pencils and paints to sketch the water. Darragh pulled a small traveling folio out of his coat pocket, borrowed one of her pencils and did the same. Until she saw the book, she hadn't realized he possessed any marked artistic skills, though considering he was an architect, she supposed she ought to have known better.

At length, he set the folio aside and closed his eyes, sleepy from the meal and the lovemaking. Waiting until she could tell he truly slumbered, she picked up the book and began to leaf through it, amazed by what she found.

In drawing after superb drawing, she traveled the world. Rome and Venice and London, of course. Paris, she surmised, given the street names he'd written in small flowing script beneath the renderings. And Greece, looking hot and sunny and ancient beyond her imaginings, exactly as he'd once described.

And then on a pair of the last pages, she discovered herself. Her heart leapt in wonder. In one drawing she stood with Wilda in the garden, a distant expression on her face as she observed the older woman pruning her roses. In the other, she sat painting in the field near her cousins' estate, gazing toward the old Celtic cross. The drawing was rough and hastily completed, except for her. Her, he'd sketched completely, leaving no detail unfinished, leaving her the unmistakable focal point of the piece.

When had he done the drawings? she wondered. *How* had he done them without her knowledge? Hastily, before he awakened, she set the folio aside.

But the questions lingered on long after the pair of them returned to the cottage.

Could he possibly love her?

She trembled at the thought, the idea both glorious and terrifying all at the same time.

And how did she feel about him?

Truth to tell, she didn't know anymore, her wishes and needs all jumbled up inside.

The only thing she knew for certain was the contentment she felt in his arms and the dawning knowledge that she never wanted that feeling to end.

Several afternoons later, as Jeannette placed a leg of lamb into a large copper roasting pan for dinner, a knock sounded at the front door. Isolated as the cottage was from any immediate neighbors, the interruption came as a mild surprise.

The only people she saw with any regularity were Aine and an older man named Redde, who couldn't speak a word of English from what she could tell. He came twice daily to care for the horses, milk the cow, feed the chickens and collect the eggs. A tradesman also stopped by once a week or so to deliver a fresh supply of peat bricks for the stove and fireplaces.

Thinking it must be one of the men, she dried her hands on a kitchen towel and went to the door. Pulling it open, she discovered a stranger waiting on the other side.

Tall and sturdy, the man looked to be in his late twenties, with thin, almost delicate features and a head of thick, short-cut wavy brown hair. Dressed for riding, he wore a tweed coat, simple linen shirt, breeches and boots. He looked her over with blatant interest, an oddly familiar gleam in his silvery blue eyes.

Her hand tightened against the door frame. "Yes, may I help you?"

A corner of his lips tilted as he craned his neck to get a better look inside the cottage. "Aye, perhaps you can. Might there be a Darragh O'Brien in residence, by chance?"

"There is. What business do you have with my husband, if I might inquire?"

His lips dropped open. "Pardon me, but your husband, did you say?"

"I did," she affirmed. "Who are you, sir, and what do you want?"

He slapped a palm against one knee so hard she jumped. "Well, I'll be dipped in Guinness and set aflame."

Before she knew what he intended, he stepped forward and wrapped her inside a massive bear hug, lifting her feet clear of the floor. She screeched, then screeched again when he planted a smacking kiss right on her lips. Grinning ear to ear, he leaned back and let out a laugh.

Dear God, she'd let in a madman. *Darragh. Where was Darragh?*

As if he'd heard her silent plea, or at least her screams, heavy footsteps rang out in the hall. The sound of dog nails scrabbling on wood followed close behind, Vitruvius unleashing a pair of loud, deep-throated barks.

"What in the blue blazes?" Darragh said, only to break off. "Saints preserve us, Michael, would you set her down before you give her the death?"

The crazy man turned his head. "She's a pretty one, Darr, where did you find her?"

"On a faerie mound, where do you think? Now leave off before you crack one of her ribs."

"Oh, I'm not hurting her." Silver-blue eyes swung back to her. "Am I now, lass?"

"I . . . you might set me down. Please," she amended on a gasping breath, "if you would."

At her request, the Bedlamite, who apparently went by the name Michael, deposited her on her feet. Tossing her a winking grin, he bent to pet Vitruvius, who had rushed up between them.

She expected the gigantic dog to bite him or, at the very least, give a menacing growl. Instead, the silly animal turned into a quivering mass of ecstasy, as Michael scrubbed an enthusiastic pair of wide palms over the dog's wiry fur.

"Would you look how he's grown," Michael said. "Why, he was nothing but a pup last time I saw him. But you remember me, don't you, boy?" he cooed to the dog. "Yes, you do. You do. I know you do."

Vitruvius licked Michael's cheek, making him laugh. The man straightened, turned toward Darragh. "So, have you no hug for your brother after nearly a year away?"

Brother?

Jeannette stared between the men, suddenly seeing the resemblance lurking in their similarly shaped eyes.

Darragh took a step forward, spread his arms wide. He and his brother embraced, beating each other on the back with fists and hands before drawing apart.

Darragh turned to her. "I suppose it's a bit late for formal introductions, since Michael has a way of forgetting his manners. But if you can bring yourself to forgive him for molesting you, then I'd like you to meet my brother."

She forced herself to relax, ingrained politeness compelling her to nod and curtsey.

"Michael, my wife, Lady Jeannette."

A fresh grin split Michael's face. He bowed, caught her hand and dropped a kiss on the top. " 'Tis grand to have you in the family. I'd have brought a gift had I known there were nuptials to celebrate." He cocked a brow at Darragh. "Why didn't you send word?"

Yes, she wondered, why hadn't he sent word? Darragh didn't speak often of his family. She hadn't even realized he had a brother living in the vicinity.

"We're on our honeymoon." Darragh caught her around the waist to draw her close. "I wanted to keep her to myself for a bit before the whole lot of you descended to scare her away."

Whole lot? Exactly how many O'Briens were there? Though she guessed she should have known he would have a great many relatives, the Irish being known for their large extended families.

She tossed him a look. "But I should like to meet your relations, Darragh. Really, it would be vastly impolite not to make their acquaintance soon."

"And so you shall, love, when the time comes right for a visit," he said in an oddly evasive tone. "Michael's traveled quite a distance to find us, haven't you, lad?"

"Aye. I rode all day."

"Oh, then you must be quite fatigued from your travels." She slipped out of Darragh's embrace. "I would accompany you into the sitting room, but our maid is not in residence today. Why don't you two go on

441

ahead and I shall procure us some refreshments. Would tea be agreeable?"

Michael traded an inscrutable glance with his brother. "Aye, indeed, most agreeable."

"And if you don't mind a small delay, I shall put the roast on as well. You will stay for supper, will you not?"

"He can't," Darragh stated.

"Of course I can. Hope to stay the night too, if you've the room."

"We don't," his brother said.

"Darragh," she scolded, amazed at his rudeness, before turning her gaze on Michael. "We are using much of the spare room for storage, but if you don't mind a bit of inconvenience, then you are most welcome to stay. Isn't he, Darragh?"

Darragh seemed on the verge of disagreeing, then gave a curt nod.

"Please, have a seat in the sitting room," she invited.

She waited until the men did as she bade, then she returned to the kitchen.

"What in Saint Brigid's name are you up to?"

" 'Tis none of your concern," Darragh said in a low voice, switching smoothly from English to Gaelic, "and when she comes in here you're to tell her you can't stay, after all, and find yourself an inn for the night."

Michael replied in the old native tongue that was forbidden by the English, but still used nonetheless, especially here in the West. "There are no inns, not unless I ride all the way to Ennis, and that's hours off in the wrong direction."

Michael's jaw turned bullish. "Why are you so blasted eager to see me gone anyway? And speaking the *Gaeilege* besides? Is there something you're not wanting her to hear? I ran into Dermot O'Shay a fortnight back, who said he'd been traveling through these parts and saw you. Said you acted mighty peculiar and were not much given to talk. So being the curious sort, he trailed you back here."

Darragh growled. "Dermot O'Shay ought to be put to the lash, blasted busybody."

"Guess you'll be wanting to take a lash to me too, since I was curious myself," Michael continued. "Curious enough to travel all the way here to see why you'd come west, but hadn't seen fit to write a word to your family about it. I assumed this woman you were living with must be your mistress, and you were keeping her secret, but if she's your wife —"

"She is my wife."

"Then why are you hiding her? Is it

because she's English? Mary Margaret will need time to get used to the idea that you've not married an Irish lass, but me, I don't mind. And I can see why you'd be smitten. She's pretty enough to near blind a man."

"Well, keep your eyes off her and your mouth closed, especially around Mary Margaret. Does she know you're here?"

"No, and I haven't told any of the others. But you won't be able to keep them ignorant forever."

"I don't need forever. Just a couple more weeks."

At least Darragh prayed a couple more weeks would be enough. He thought Jeannette was close, on the verge of saying the words he longed to hear. Tender, whispered words confessing her love.

Their first days together had not been precisely easy, but lately he'd sensed a change in her. She smiled at him as she never had before. She conversed with him, relaxed with him, even pampered him, seeming to take surprising delight in creating new and inventive dishes to please his palate.

And the way she responded when they came together in bed . . . Well, there had to be more to her feelings than the simple lust she'd once claimed. Did a woman snuggle against a man all night, draping herself over him as if she couldn't bear to be separated, if there wasn't a measure of love inside her?

No, it had to be more. It was more, and soon she would tell him so.

"What happens in a couple weeks?" his brother repeated.

"Nothing."

"Nothing? Doesn't sound like nothing. Perhaps I should go and have a chat with her —"

Darragh shot out a hand, grabbed his brother's arm. "She doesn't know, all right? She doesn't know who I am."

Michael stared. "What do you mean she doesn't know who you are? I heard her say your name more than once, so I think she knows who you are."

"But she doesn't. It's . . . complicated, and I haven't time to explain it all to you, but the short version is, she doesn't know about my title. She thinks I'm just Darragh O'Brien. *Mr.* Darragh O'Brien."

"But I heard you call her Lady Jeannette."

Darragh shook his head. "Aye. She's an earl's daughter and a lady in her own right. She believes I've no title at all, and I've let her. She also thinks this cottage is our home, our only home, and knows nothing about the estate, the castle nor my lands. To

445

her, I'm a middle-class architect, and a rather impoverished one at that."

Michael continued to stare, amazement burning in his silver gaze. Suddenly he caught Darragh's head in his hands, jerked him forward and began to paw through his hair.

Darragh struggled, tried to yank away. "What in the hell are you doing?"

"Looking for wounds, lad, from the knock you've obviously taken to the head. Was it a horse that kicked you or did you take a tumble down the staircase of one of those great mansions you build?"

"Leave off, you idiot." Darragh wrenched away, rubbed his abused scalp.

"No, *you're* the idiot. Are you daft, man? Lying to your bride? If I'm not mistaken you've got her out in the kitchen of this tiny place, cooking, for Christ's sake. Who ever heard of an earl's daughter cooking? And an English one at that. Whatever possessed you to hatch such a demented scheme?"

"I have my reasons," Darragh said defensively.

"Aye, and she'll have your hide when she discovers the truth. You'd best tell her yourself, while you still have the chance. If she finds out on her own . . . well, you'll be lucky if she doesn't take a cleaver and lop

446

off your balls."

At the suggestion, Darragh felt his testicles draw up tight in an instinctual gesture of self-protection. Shaking off the reaction, he willed himself to relax. "Don't be an ass."

"And don't you continue to be a fool. Confess to her now, lad, while you've still got a wink of hope she'll forgive you."

Guilt squeezed inside him like a nasty fist. He knew Michael had the right of it, that Jeannette was bound to be angry when she found out he'd been less than candid with her. But wouldn't she also feel relieved, even grateful to discover she wouldn't to have to spend the rest of her life living in a humble cottage, cooking meals and sewing her own clothes? Would she not be delighted to discover she was actually a countess, their home a grand castle with plenty of servants, and he possessed of enough wealth to keep her in luxury for the rest of her days?

She'd fly off into a temper at first for sure. But afterward she'd see reason, understand he'd done what he had for them, for their marriage and future happiness.

At least he hoped she would.

"I'll tell her when I'm ready," Darragh declared, letting obduracy brush aside any lingering doubts. "Until then you aren't to say a word to her on the subject." Michael opened his mouth, but he cut him off. "Not a word."

Michael raised his hands in a sign of surrender. "Have it your way, boy-o. I haven't been to a good wake in a while, and your demise should prove fine entertainment indeed. And if by some miracle your wife doesn't flay all the skin off your bones, you've got three sisters who'll be ready to finish the job. Mary Margaret in particular will be in a huff you didn't include her in the wedding nor tell her you've been married all these past weeks. Siobhan and Moira will be hurt as well, not to have been flower girls."

"They can enjoy that privilege at *your* wedding."

Michael snorted. "They're in for a long wait, then. I'm contented with my veterinary practice, taking care of horses and dogs and the occasional ailing feline. I've no need to be burdened with the care of a wife too."

"When you love a woman, such care isn't a burden at all."

"Tell me that again once herself finds out what it is you've done." Michael brought the flat of one hand down across Darragh's shoulder. "You're a brave man, Darragh O'Brien. An idiot, but a brave one all the same."

A movement at the door caught their attention, as Jeannette appeared in the doorway, tea tray in hand.

"Let me help you with that, dearest," Darragh said, reverting to English.

With a grateful smile, she let him assist her, then sat to pour tea and pass plates of biscuits. "Now then, tell me everything I've missed."

Chapter Twenty

Darragh's brother stayed the night then went on his way the following morning. Michael said he had a man to visit about a horse, a mare that would make a fine addition to his bloodstock.

Once Jeannette had recovered from the unorthodox manner of his greeting, she'd found Michael O'Brien to be a pleasant, interesting man with the same wicked sense of humor running through his veins as his older brother. He'd had them all laughing over tales of his and Darragh's childhoods, coaxing her to share a few wild stories of her own.

After he'd gone she realized how starved she'd been for company, yet how oddly contented she was in her solitude with no one but Darragh to fill her days. Lately, she puzzled even herself, not understanding the change.

That night Darragh took her breath away,

loving her with an intensity that made her pulses throb like hearts in her wrists, her body ache with a need she knew no other man could satisfy. Or would ever satisfy.

Without him, she thought, she would be lost.

And that's when she knew. She loved him.

How had it happened? she wondered. And when? The emotion had come upon her so gradually she'd barely been aware, inching in like a slow addiction that, now established, would be nigh impossible to break.

She nearly told Darragh, the words hovering on her lips. She wanted to tell him, but the last time she'd told a man she loved him he'd crushed her heart. As warm and attentive as Darragh was, he never spoke to her of such tender emotions as love. What if she told him how she felt and watched amusement rise in his eyes? Or worse, pity?

They'd married out of necessity, in scandal and haste, a poor beginning for any marriage. Yet in spite of their less than enviable living arrangements, they had formed a bond. Perhaps love was the next step. Perhaps love would be the one thing that would make all the hardships worthwhile and keep them together.

She mulled over her new emotions all the next week.

Now, as she straightened the sheets, wool blanket and quilt on their bed, then gathered up one of her nightgowns and a pair of his shirts for the laundry pile, she wondered again whether or not to tell him about her newfound feelings.

After kissing her good-bye this morning, he'd ridden away on the long journey to Ennis to purchase some drafting and other hard-to-obtain supplies. He'd promised to post several letters she'd penned and check to see if any had been received. So far she'd gotten only a single missive from Violet, who wrote to say she and Adrian, Kit and Eliza had made it home safely and that she would write again soon. From Mama and Papa she had heard nothing, no doubt shamed by her notable fall from grace. But she was married now, and they would simply have to accept that fact, and learn to accept her husband as well.

So far Darragh had proven frustratingly reluctant to discuss their future plans in any detail — odd, that — but she knew he was bound to receive another architectural commission soon, here or on the Continent. Maybe even in England.

With her family connections, who knew what manner of work he might obtain. If Darragh earned enough they could leave this tiny cottage behind and build a proper home in England. Once there she would be able to work to reestablish a social presence — oh, not of the highest orders, to be sure, but satisfactory enough. And she would be there to assist Darragh in furthering himself and his ambitions.

But to begin, she would need to stop cowering behind her doubts and silence. Tonight, she decided, she would tell him. When he returned, she would open up her heart and let him know how much she loved him. If all went as she hoped, he would tell her he felt the same.

She vowed not to let herself dwell on any other alternative.

As a treat, she would make a special meal, turn the evening into a kind of celebration. Once the food was cooking, she would lay out the lace tablecloth she'd found stored in the dining room cabinet and set the better china with its pretty floral pattern.

Next, she would ask Aine to help her don one of her fashionable gowns and arrange her hair in a glorious upsweep. She would dot lilac water behind her ears and fasten a length of creamy pearls around her throat.

Wouldn't Darragh be surprised? Wouldn't he be delighted?

Humming a melody under her breath, she

began preparing a meal that would consist of chilled cucumber and mint soup, roast pork with cabbage, buttered carrots, and for dessert, an apple cobbler.

She was up to her wrists in butter and flour when a knock sounded at the door. Wiping her hands on a towel, she walked into the hallway, wondering who could be calling this time. Surely not another of Darragh's siblings, not so soon.

Preparing herself for whatever she might find, she opened the door, a pleasant smile decorating her lips. Even so, she couldn't help but stare at the quartet of refined older gentlemen waiting on her stoop. All of them were resplendently dressed in well-tailored breeches and tailcoats, their silk waistcoats intricately embroidered. Behind them in the drive stood a large black traveling barouche with a team of four.

Sporting a head of thinning salt-and-pepper-colored hair and a Van Dyke–style beard, reminiscent of more than a century before, the oldest of the group stepped forward.

He swept off his hat and made her an elegant bow. "*Mi scusi,* signora," he began, "I am Count Arnaldo Fiorello and these are my fellow travelers, Signori Pio, Guglielmo and Ficuccio. We come seeking the Grand

Signore. Please to tell him we beg his most honored indulgence and would speak with him, if he agrees."

Her eyes widened. Clearly these gentlemen had lost their way and arrived at the wrong house. "I am sorry, but you are mistaken. Whoever it is you seek, he is not here."

The older man's brow beetled. "But that cannot be. We were told to come. That the Signore, Lord Mulholland, he is here."

This time she frowned. Lord Mulholland? The name tickled forth a memory. Were these men looking for the aristocrat who had loaned his coach to her and Darragh as a wedding present? She never had found out where the man's estate was located, though she had written him a letter the day after her and Darragh's arrival at the cottage to thank him for his gift. A letter Darragh had posted on her behalf.

"Signori," she said, switching to adequate, though far from flawless Italian. "I recognize the name of the man you seek, but I am sorry to say he is not in residence, and I do not know where to find him."

The men relaxed at her use of their language. "You speak Italian?"

"A little, yes."

"Then you understand we have come to

talk to the great architect, Lord Mulholland. We too are builders, and ardent admirers of his work. The four of us have traveled all the way from Italy to consult his wise opinion. We were told he is living here for a time instead of on his estate."

She forced down a sigh of frustration. "Forgive me, but whoever told you that is mistaken. This home belongs to my husband, Darragh O'Brien, and myself."

The gentleman beamed as if the sun had risen more brightly in the sky. "*Sì*, Lord Mulholland, as I was told."

Now she was the one who felt confused and a bit stupid. An odd buzz tingled between her ears. "Maybe I didn't understand you correctly. My husband is Darragh O'Brien, not Lord Mulholland." She repeated the words again, this time in English.

The man gave her a puzzled look, replied in her language. "Yes. Darragh O'Brien and Lord Mulholland, are they not one and the same man?"

Suddenly, startlingly, the world shifted on its axis beneath her feet, as the truth clicked inside her head like a key opening a lock.

Early fall darkness was casting heavy shadows by the time Darragh arrived home from his journey north. Quickly, he stabled his horse, then rubbed the animal down before giving him water and feed. Gathering the supplies he'd purchased, Darragh hurried toward the cottage.

The delicious aromas of roasting meat, boiling vegetables and sweet pastry greeted him in a warm, fragrant cloud. He inhaled deeply, hunger leaping in his belly, anticipation for the meal to come making his tongue tingle. Letting his nose be his guide, he strolled into the kitchen.

Jeannette glanced up from her place near the stove, a voluminous white apron tied around what looked to be one of her good dresses. Fastened around her neck was a strand of pearls, her beautiful pale hair twisted up into a soft, feminine knot, adorable wisps curling at her temples.

She looked as delectable as her meal smelled. Moving forward, he bent to steal a kiss, but lithe and quick as a nymph, she danced out of reach.

"I was beginning to wonder if you had lost your way," she commented as she stirred something in one of the pots. "Supper is nearly ready. Go change and we'll eat."

He was about to try again for a kiss, when he noticed the dining room table. Obviously she had taken care to set it. The table looked elegant and pretty covered with a lace tablecloth. She'd used the good china and, instead of the usual tallow ones, she'd lighted precious, sweetly scented beeswax candles. "What's all this, then?"

"Oh, nothing much. I just felt like making the evening a little special." She gave the long-handled wooden spoon a tap and set it aside. Coming forward, she placed her hands on his shoulders and spun him around, adding a firm little push. "Go on, now. Get out of those clothes so you don't smell like a horse."

He ducked his head in apology. "Yes, dear."

Then before she could elude him, he swooped in for the kiss he'd been wanting, a quick touch of his lips to hers.

She didn't kiss him back, easing away after a few brief moments.

He paid no attention, deciding he probably did smell like a stable from a long day of travel. In the bedroom, he stripped, then poured chilly water into the basin and washed. Taking a cue from Jeannette's more formal attire, he dressed in one of his better suits, a dark blue superfine that complemented the vivid hue of his eyes. After brushing his hair, he used tooth powder on his teeth, then returned to the hall to retrieve the present he'd bought for her. A delicate gold locket with a spray of wild roses engraved on the front. For the inside, he planned to have miniatures of them both commissioned at a later date.

Sentimental, he supposed, but then, she made him feel that way.

A small tureen of soup was waiting on the table when he entered the dining room. "Shall I serve?" he asked.

"No," she said, bustling in from the kitchen. "Just have a seat and I'll do the rest."

He took his chair.

She ladled out a bowl, the pale, creamy soup looking delightfully appetizing. Chilled soups were a delicacy, so he knew she must have gone to some trouble, including making a trip to the icehouse so she could retrieve enough chips to cool the soup.

He waited expectantly. Bowl filled, she turned to place it before him. Suddenly, her wrist bobbled and over it went, a great minty river of pureed cucumbers splashing across his chest and down between his legs.

He bit out an oath and instinctively leapt to his feet, his chair hitting the floor with a bang. But the action only made the mess worse, soup seeping through the material of his trousers and shirt, while drops of it rained upon his shoes and the carpeting beneath.

"Oh, mercy," she cried, "are you all right? Lud, I don't know what happened. My hand must have slipped." She cast a chagrined glance his way and clucked her tongue. "You poor dear. I'm so sorry."

" 'Twas an accident," he said, taking up his napkin to dab at the wet stains. But his efforts did little good, the material chilling his skin, and worse, his groin. He plucked at his waistband but found the action did nothing to relieve his discomfort.

"Why don't you go change out of those ruined things," she suggested, "while I clean this up and serve the next course."

"What about the soup?"

"Oh, I only made enough for each of us to have a bowl. You can have mine, if you like."

"No, no, you enjoy your soup," he said.

On a rueful sigh, he quashed the disappointment he felt at *wearing* his cucumber soup instead of getting to eat it as he'd been hoping. Tossing his damp napkin onto the table, he began to turn away. As he did, he caught the faintest hint of what looked like a smile playing at the corners of Jeannette's mouth. But when he looked closer, the expression was gone.

His imagination, he decided. Walking gingerly, he made his way to the bedroom.

When he returned, everything was clean and tidy again except for a large wet spot that remained on the floor under his chair. Easing into his seat, he watched Jeannette emerge from the kitchen, a platter of sliced, roasted pork, steamed cabbage and carrots in hand.

She set it down, then took up a dinner plate to serve. "Feeling better?"

"Aye. Nothing like a warm, dry set of clothes to put the world right."

She'd poured glasses of red wine for them both. He reached out, lifted his glass to his lips as she placed his meal before him.

"I worked all day preparing this," she said. "I hope you like it."

He smiled. "Your cooking is always delectable these days, and this smells like heaven. 'Tis certain I'm going to love it." Hungry, he waited politely for her to serve herself before picking up his fork and knife. He sliced a piece of pork, put it inside his mouth.

Heat erupted like an inferno, blazing across his tongue, scorching the tender lining of his mouth. He coughed and blinked, moisture dampening his eyes, his nose stinging and running. An overwhelming urge to spit out the chunk came over him but he resisted, knowing he couldn't do it, not with her looking on in expectant anticipation. Instead, he swallowed, immediately regretting the action as the sensitive membranes inside his throat burned like tinder set to flint.

What has she put in this? he boggled. Not black pepper. Something else, then, something deadlier. Almost like . . . cayenne.

His jaw nearly dropped as she took a bite of the pork roast, chewed and swallowed without so much as an extra blink. *Was her mouth lined with tin that she didn't notice the heat?*

Deciding he'd better move on to safer territory, he speared a big mouthful of cabbage. But instead of the buttery, melting, caraway-flavored softness he expected, the steamed leaves crunched in a horrific scrape between his teeth. And kept crunching, over and over again as his jaw worked, nauseating grit reverberating in a grating crescendo inside his ears.

He gulped, watching as she ate her food in apparent contentment. Surely she couldn't be enjoying this? It was the worst meal she'd made since that very first disaster. Over the past few weeks she'd become a fine cook, impressing him with her deft skill and quick ability to learn.

How could she have prepared so many dishes so badly? Unless she'd done it on purpose. He squinted at the carrots, studying them as though they were deadly explosives, ready to detonate. What sinister act, he mused, had she perpetrated upon these small golden disks? And more to the point, why? What had occurred between this morning when he'd left the cottage and his return home tonight?

She met his gaze, outwardly angelic. "How is your meal?"

"It's . . . interesting." He set down his fork. "I'm not as hungry as I imagined, though."

"Well now, surely you have room for dessert? Apple cobbler, your favorite."

And what had she done to ruin that? His stomach growled, protesting his hunger and the terrible fare he'd swallowed so far. As tempting as apple cobbler sounded, he decided he ought not risk it. "Uh, thank you, but no."

"What a shame. Perhaps that's best, though," she said in a sweet tone, "since I let Vitruvius try it first."

"You what?"

"He dug right in. I had no idea dogs were so fond of apples. I suppose there's still a little left that I could scrape out of his bowl, if you don't mind sharing."

Having heard his name, Vitruvius wandered in and flopped onto the floor. He groaned, his hairy stomach bulging from the large serving of fruit and pastry he'd obviously consumed.

Mother Mary, Darragh hoped the animal didn't get sick all over the floor.

Jeannette ate another bite of pork and cabbage and sipped her wine. "How was your day?" she continued after a moment. "I had a rather interesting one. Some gentlemen stopped by looking for you. A count and his friends, who traveled all the way from Italy."

Dread plunged like a blade into his gut. "What did they want?"

"Why, to consult with the great architect Darragh O'Brien. Funny, though, they knew you by a different name." She tapped a finger against her cheek, as if in thought. "Let me see, what was it again? Mulholland. The Earl of Mulholland." She fixed a gaze upon him that blazed hot as the fiery spice she'd put in his meal. "Is that not right, *my lord?*"

Christ, she knows. "Now, Jeannette —"

"Don't you *now, Jeannette* me." She beat her hand against the table. "How dare you deceive me. How dare you hide who you are, when I am your wife."

He strove for calm. "I realize you're angry, but if you'd just let me explain —"

"Explain what? That you're a consummate, contemptible liar?"

The memory of Michael's words echoed in his ears. His brother had warned him that Jeannette might take a cleaver to his balls when she found out the truth. He eyed the cutlery and prayed his bride wasn't quite that bloodthirsty.

"I had my reasons," he said, climbing to his feet.

"What reasons could you have had? Didn't you think I might want to know a little thing like the fact that you're an *earl?* It's not as if you haven't had plenty of opportunities to tell me."

His shoulders straightened defensively. "I tried to tell you, starting the very first time we met. But you cut me off, presuming to know everything you needed to know about who I am."

"And afterward? What excuse do you have for that?"

"No excuse. I just didn't see why it mattered whether or not I have a title, so I decided to let you believe what you wanted."

"Even after we were married?" She waved an arm through the air. "And what of this cottage? The count tells me you own a castle! So why bring me here? Why tell me this is all we can afford? Which one of your tenants owns this quaint abode, by the way?"

"Not a tenant, but a friend." A dull flush crept up his jaw. "I thought this would be a quiet place to honeymoon, as well as a good chance for us to get to know each other without other distractions."

"What sort of *distractions?* Do you mean like servants and a chef?" She paused as a new thought occurred. "And you dismissed Betsy!"

"It's not as bad as you —"

"No, it's worse. You made me *cook!*"

Disturbed by the fight, Vitruvius sat up, let out a single nervous woof.

Darragh calmed the dog with a brief murmur, then returned his attention to Jeannette. "You like to cook. You told me so yourself only the other day."

"Whether or not I derive any pleasure from the task is irrelevant. A lady does not labor, and as a titled gentleman, you ought to have known that. But then, you have never behaved as a gentleman ought, have you?"

"That'll do, lass," he warned in a soft voice.

"Will it? Or what? Do you have some new

form of humiliation dreamed up with which to torment me?" Unshed tears of fury and anguish glistened in her eyes. "Why did you do it? Revenge? Was this your way of punishing me for being forced into a marriage you obviously did not want? You must despise me to have played such a cruel and calculated trick."

Darragh cringed. This wasn't going at all the way he'd hoped or planned. She was twisting everything, turning it into something vile, when that hadn't been his intention at all.

He reached out a beseeching hand. "It isn't like that. If you'd just let me explain."

She brushed aside his hand, her lashes sweeping down as if she could no longer bear the sight of him. "I think you've explained more than enough. Whatever you say, how do I know it won't be another lie?"

"Jeannette —"

"I'm tired and believe I shall retire."

"All right. Go on and we'll talk there."

"No. You are not welcome."

"Welcome or not, you're still my wife."

Her lower lip quavered. "To my everlasting regret."

Even knowing she spoke in hurt and anger, her words stung. "Be that as it may, we are married. 'Til death us do part, just as the vows say." He paused. "If you'd take a moment to consider, you'd see you ought to be pleased."

Her mouth tightened. "For what, pray tell? Being turned into a scullery maid? Or being lied to?"

He wished he could retract his words, realizing by her severe expression that he was only making matters worse. Yet knowing himself damned either way, he plunged ahead.

"You wanted a title and you have one, you're now the Countess of Mulholland." He raked a hand through his hair. "You wanted a fine home and you'll have that, a grand old castle known as Caisleán Muir. You wished for servants and money. Well, there's plenty of both. All in all, I should think you'd be relieved."

"Given that tally, I suppose I should. Or rather, I *would* be, were that all I wanted."

"What else, then?" he demanded, frustration rising inside him like a surging tide. "What more could you want, unless it's to be a duchess? And that, I'm afraid, I cannot provide."

A startled look shone in her gaze before sorrow descended. "No, you can't give me that either, can you?"

His brows crinkled in puzzlement as she

spun and hurried from the room, a small, muffled sob trailing in her wake. Seconds later, the bedroom door closed, the lock clicking home echoing clearly after.

Finally found the key, had she? And already barred the windows as well, no doubt.

What a debacle.

Whirling, he kicked the corner cabinet and set the china rattling inside.

Vitruvius whined and thumped his tail, head bowed over his paws.

Darragh's anger drained suddenly. Bending, he beckoned the dog forward, then stroked the big, sleek canine head, giving comfort to them both.

"Well, lad, looks like we'll be bunking in together. I only hope it won't be for the rest of our natural lives."

CHAPTER
TWENTY-ONE

The next morning she awakened, tired and unrefreshed after a night spent crying quietly to herself so as not to let him hear. She'd slept little, the awful events of the day repeating themselves over and over again in her head.

Just past dawn, when she could stand it no more, she washed and dressed, then went into the kitchen to fix herself a pot of tea. She expected to find the room a disaster, the remains of last night's supper stuck to the plates, clinging to the unwashed pots and pans. But Darragh had done most of the cleaning for her, tidying and straightening, storing what food had been suitable to save. If he'd thought such minor acts would patch her wounds, he was very much mistaken.

After what he'd done, how could she ever trust him again? Believe him again? Love him? He'd stripped her down to the core, leaving nothing behind but hard, bare bones.

Just the reminder of his deception made her emotions rattle like the water steaming in the teakettle. She toasted a slice of bread, banging the metal range lids and the arched hearth-toaster as loudly as she pleased. So what if she awakened him? She hoped she did. Hoped she made him as miserable as he'd made her.

What a pitiable fool she was to have imagined he might love her.

Darragh came to the doorway not long after, and stood watching her, his face drawn and haggard-looking. She pretended not to see.

Vitruvius padded in and sat patiently waiting for his morning meal, as had become their recent custom. Having no quarrel with the dog, only his master, she prepared a bowl of cut-up pork from last night's supper — careful to make sure it was free of the cayenne pepper she'd liberally sprinkled on Darragh's portion.

The dog seen to, she put her tea and toast on a copper tray and returned to their bedroom, all without ever acknowledging Darragh's existence. She remained in her room the rest of the day.

The coach did not arrive until early the

following morning. To her chagrin, she discovered that the vehicle was the same one she'd traveled west in, the Mulholland crest emblazoned upon the door like an insolent slap. If she'd had any lingering doubts about his identity, they vanished the moment the vehicle arrived, the coachman jumping down, quietly greeting him as "my lord."

Her trunks were repacked and loaded into a wagon. Aine arrived, dismayed by their abrupt departure. The girl promised to clean and tidy everything, wash the sheets and see the furniture covered with protective cloths.

Jeannette gave all the perishable food to her and Redde, the old man smiling for the first time since she'd known him. The livestock belonged to Darragh's friend, who'd loaned him the cottage, and would be well looked after.

With Aine playing lady's maid, Jeannette dressed in one of her elegant traveling gowns, feeling almost herself again for the first time in weeks. Yet as she looked at the girl who'd been such a help to her, Jeannette knew she wasn't the same person she had been when she'd arrived. Without letting herself think through the action, she pulled Aine into her arms for a hug, then thanked her for her kindness. She promised the girl a job as well, should she ever find herself in need. Just come to Caisleán Muir, Jeannette told her, and she would be well looked after.

Then it was time to depart. She ignored Darragh and he wisely let her be, having decided to ride his horse instead of travel with her inside the coach.

She knew she should be glad to dust her feet of the place, yet as she looked upon the cottage one last time, all she felt was grief and regret.

The sun had reached its zenith and was descending into evening by the time they arrived at their new home. Towering in a massive sprawl of ancient gray stone that dominated the surrounding fields of verdant green, the castle was everything Darragh had said it would be, a fact that only increased her misery.

By no means the largest castle she'd ever seen, the structure remained formidable even so; three stories high with rectangular lines and narrow windows, each stacked one upon the other from ground to top. On the far east side stood an immense tower house, clearly added during a later period, lush emerald ivy clinging to the walls and creeping up to the parapets.

And in the near distance, next to a small cemetery and the ruins of what must once have been a church, rose a conical-shaped round tower. Spearing upward in a kind of austere glory, the structure announced, without explanation, its ancient purpose of protection in the face of an unwavering enemy.

Half numb from her unhappiness, she barely had time to take everything in, as the coach-and-four drew to a halt. With the assistance of a footman, she descended the carriage steps. Suddenly, she recognized a familiar face waiting among the servants, who had assembled near the stairs, and nearly cried out her pleasure.

"Betsy," she exclaimed, hurrying toward her maid. "Oh, it's so good to see you. I thought . . ." she paused, having to force the words past her lips, "my husband . . . had sent you back to England."

"Oh, he did, my lady, for a splendid visit with my family. A month entire in Cornwall. Then it was back here to Ireland to wait for you." Betsy lowered her voice, leaning in on a whisper. "Though I didn't realize until after I arrived at Caisleán Muir that Mr. O'Brien isn't a mister at all, but a titled gentleman. An earl, and you now a countess. You never said, my lady."

"No, I did not," she murmured, failing to add that her omission was because she'd learned the truth herself only two days ago.

So he'd lied about dismissing Betsy as well, she thought, adding another falsehood to his growing list of deceptions. Plus, he'd sent her maid on an extravagant holiday that she would likely cherish for the rest of her days. By now Betsy probably imagined him a saint.

Hmmph, Jeannette scoffed, *patron saint of tricksters.*

But had she once been any better? Trading places with Violet, pretending to the world that she was her sister while she lied to her family and friends. Darragh's lies seemed a kind of poetic retribution seen in that light. The ultimate irony of the deceiver being deceived.

Still, her past misdeeds didn't make Darragh any less wrong for his own. Did they?

She wondered if this was how Adrian must have felt when he had learned the truth. Had his heart been crushed? His dignity shattered? His trust in his spouse — the one person he ought to be able to trust above all others — abused and betrayed?

If so, she owed him a profound apology.

"And how was your honeymoon?" Betsy

475

inquired in a happy voice. "Was it grandly romantic?"

Is that what Darragh had led the girl to believe? That he'd whisked her away to some intimate, romantic locale where they'd spent an idyllic time alone? A month ago she would have blurted out the details of her ordeal and openly wept on Betsy's shoulder. Instead she held her emotions inside and said nothing. The less known about the humiliation and hardship she'd suffered, the better.

"It was . . . secluded," she said.

A girlish squeal rang out as a willowy figure rushed out of the castle doors. A single black braid flying behind, the child launched herself at Darragh, ankle-length skirts swaying as she leapt into his arms. "Darragh, you're home!" the girl exclaimed before lapsing into an incomprehensible torrent of Gaelic.

Darragh laughed, swung the girl in an exuberant circle. Kissing her on the cheek, he replied in the same strange tongue, finally setting the girl onto her feet.

She laughed, then turned to cast a curious glance at Jeannette, giggling as she murmured something more in Darragh's ear. Young, eleven at most, she had a heart-shaped face and large, lovely green eyes.

Cat's eyes. Bold and inquisitive.

As Jeannette watched, Darragh tucked the girl's hand inside his and led her forward.

"Jeannette, if you haven't guessed already, this impetuous scamp is my sister Siobhan."

"Lady Siobhan," Jeannette greeted.

The girl giggled again, then grinned. "You've a pretty speaking voice for an *English.*"

Jeannette raised a brow, but before she could marshal a suitable reply, three more O'Briens joined them on the drive.

Moira, not quite fifteen, Jeannette guessed, was an auburn-haired beauty on the cusp of womanhood, her eyes the same shade and shape as Darragh's, her face a slim, feminine version of her eldest brother's. More reserved, and with better manners than her youngest sibling, she made Jeannette a respectful curtsey and greeting.

Finn was next. Brawnier than any of his brothers, he looked like he could easily fell a tree — probably with his bare hands — and at only nineteen or so, he was still coming into his full height, she assumed. Presently, he stood just an inch shorter than Darragh. Despite herself, she liked his kind green eyes and the careful way he bowed over her hand.

And then came Michael, whom she knew already.

He gave her a wink and a kiss. "Welcome to Caisleán Muir, though I didn't expect to see you again quite so soon."

"No, I expect you did not, nor *Lord Mulholland*," she replied in an arch tone.

He had the grace to look sheepish, then relieved, as she murmured for his ears alone, "Just be glad it's only him I hold responsible."

"Of that you may rest assured, my lady."

The two other O'Brien siblings, Hoyt and Mary Margaret, were absent, so she was told. Married, with homes and families of their own, they no longer lived on the estate, but would be stopping by for a visit soon.

Remembering apparently that he had yet to introduce her to the servants, Darragh came forward, wrapped her hand in his. She wanted nothing more than to wrench herself free, but instead let him thread her palm over his bent elbow, aware of their large and interested audience.

Seeing the two dozen servants he employed — including the bona fide French chef he had on staff — hit her with the impact of a flaming match tossed into a saucepan of brandy. She endured the introductions, which thankfully did not last long, then moved inside the castle with the family.

Expecting dark, cold and antiquated, she was astonished by the cheerful, modern interior. The crisp cream entrance hall boasted glorious swags, and spirals of intricate stuccowork that graced the walls and complemented the beautifully turned balusters on the grand staircase. Escorted by the whole O'Brien clan, she was led through the castle. Room after elegant room was revealed, including a great gilded ballroom and a long portrait gallery that contained paintings and tapestries, broadswords, armor and artifacts of O'Brien ancestors.

She learned that many of the family antiquities had been saved by their late mother, who had hidden them away years before rather than see them go to pay debts and taxes.

Darragh's brothers and sisters regaled her with one story after another, pride ringing in their every word and gesture as they told her how Darragh had worked to restore the castle from near ruin to the grand, stately home it now was.

Finally, they departed, leaving their eldest brother to show her to the master suites located in the old tower house. The moment she and Darragh were alone, she slipped her hand off his arm and took a step away.

He gave her a penetrating look, but didn't push the matter, turning his back to let her follow on her own.

The countess's quarters, she discovered, consisted of three spacious rooms — bedchamber, dressing room and bath — that took up the entire top floor. Airy and feminine, the suite was done in pale shades of pink and cream with occasional dashes of crisp green thrown in for accent. Rich-hued walnut furniture made the rooms warm and inviting. And though she wasn't about to let Darragh suspect she in any way approved, she immediately fell in love with the beautiful decor.

He informed her his own quarters lay one story below, connected to her own through a small spiral staircase that wound up and down inside one corner of the room. He offered to lead her below to give her a tour.

"Thank you, no," she replied in a quiet voice, quickly pocketing the key she discovered in the stairway door, before he had a chance to do the same.

He merely smiled and shook his head. "A little key won't keep me out, lass, if I'm of a mind to get in."

"Then you'd best not be of that mind,

because you are not welcome in my rooms. Go visit your siblings, one of them may be pleased at your company."

"Jeannette, let me —"

"Send Betsy to attend me, please. Unless you have decided to dismiss her again for *lack of funds.*" Turning her back, she strolled toward one of the windows and gazed out. But she saw nothing of the landscape beyond, her heart clenched tight.

He sighed. "We need to discuss this, whether now or later. But, for present, I'll wait."

She remained silent, refusing to turn until she finally heard him leave. Head lowered, she wiped a single tear from her cheek.

Darragh gave her a week. Enough time, he hoped, for her anger to cool, her hurt to ease sufficiently for her to agree to sit still long enough to hear him out.

Mercy, but she could freeze a man out better than a raw north wind, leaving him stunned and shivering, wondering if he'd ever be invited into the warmth again.

To everyone else in the house, Jeannette was smiling and pleasant. Even Mary Margaret, who came for a visit with every intention of disliking her brother's English wife, soon warmed to Jeannette's graceful charm and inviting manner. And artistic Hoyt, who lived for his stories and his poetry, hadn't stood a chance, instantly mesmerized by her beauty, despite his obvious and enduring love for his own dear wife.

Given the parameters of their past association, Darragh'd never really seen Jeannette work a drawing room before. But after less than an hour he understood why she had been crowned the belle of London Society for two years in a row.

She poured tea, handed out sandwiches, conversed and entertained, making each person in the room feel as though they were her especial friend. A radiant sun bestowing brilliant light upon all within her orbit.

All, that is, but him. Him she ignored the way she would a pox-ridden beggar, though he had to give her points for concealing her displeasure with him when they were together with his family.

Still, some of the strain must have shown. Especially to Michael, who cast him periodic sympathetic glances interlaced with I-told-you-so shakes of his head. Darragh ground his teeth and did his best to be patient and give Jeannette time. Time to settle into her new home, time and enough distance to realize that perhaps what he'd done back at the cottage hadn't been so very bad, after all.

It wasn't as if he'd intended to keep her in ignorance forever, which he would already have explained if only she would unbend enough to listen. But as he had come to learn, when Jeannette felt wronged, she was about as unbending as a length of hard-forged steel.

Which left him at a crossroads. Either he could allow the rift between them to stand and possibly grow wider, or take decisive action to end it. So tonight, whether Jeannette liked it or not, they were going to have it out. And afterward, she was going to let him into her bed again.

After weeks of steady, satisfying, fabulous sex, doing without was proving a torture. A torture frequent cold baths weren't doing much to relieve.

Darragh held his council through supper, gritting his teeth as Jeannette chatted gamely with his family — everyone, that is, but him. Michael remained the longest at table, finishing his conversation with Jeannette while he nursed a glass of port.

After a time, he caught Darragh's stare and took the hint.

"Ah, well," Michael said, "if you'll forgive me, I think I'll follow the others and turn in for the evening. I've a . . . new . . . um . . .

veterinary journal to review."

"Oh." Jeannette set down her teacup. "Well, in that case, I suppose I shall do the same. Pray enjoy your reading, and sleep soundly."

Michael stood, bowed. "And you as well. Good night, Jeannette. Darragh."

Darragh came around to help her with her chair. She stiffened and climbed to her feet. Behind her, Darragh nodded to Michael, who mouthed the words *good luck* before Darragh followed his wife from the room.

He trailed after her, as she went up the stairs, following close on her heels so she wouldn't have an opportunity to get too far ahead. She did a fine job ignoring him until she reached the landing that would take her up to her suite of rooms.

When he made to follow, she turned. "Pardon me, but where do you think you are going?"

"Upstairs with you."

She shook her head. "Your rooms are just down the corridor, my lord. I suggest you find them."

Her formality irked him, exactly as it had every day since they had arrived at Caisleán Muir. Her new penchant for calling him "my lord" 'twas another thing he planned to put an end to tonight. By tomorrow morning, *Darragh* would be soughing from her lips once more, assuming all went as planned.

"This trouble between us has continued long enough," he said. "We need to talk, and this time you're going to listen. I thought you'd be more comfortable doing so in your quarters, where we won't run the risk of an audience."

"We will talk later. I am tired and wish to retire."

Knowing what she really meant was "I don't wish to talk to you tonight or ever," Darragh reached out and caught her arm before she could turn away. "We'll talk now."

Defiantly, Jeannette met his gaze. The force of his resolve rolled over her along with the strong, sensual magnetism of his appeal. She could smell the heat of him, the raw impatience that simmered just beneath his skin. Despite their rift, she knew all it would take was a single intimate touch for both of them to go up in flames. But she had done without him and the pleasure she knew his touch could bring all these many days, and she could do without him for that many more.

She held her ground. "Let me go, my Lord Mulholland."

His jaw tightened together with his grip.

"You can't freeze me out forever, Jeannette."

"Maybe not, but I can certainly try." She yanked her arm from his grasp. "Good night, my lord."

"You can tell me that again *after* we've talked. Please," he invited, motioning toward the staircase, "ladies first."

Irritation sparked inside her. "You are *not* coming with me."

"I am your husband and this is my house. I'll go anywhere I please."

Standing toe to toe with him, she became aware of her chest rising and falling fast beneath her bodice, the tops of her breasts quivering with fury and a passion she cursed herself for feeling. His eyes lowered, gaze lingering on her trembling flesh. Inside that gaze, she recognized a ravenous hunger, a blue flame that burned both hot and wild.

Knowing she dare not tempt fate an instant longer, unless she cared to be ravished right there on the stairs, she gathered up her skirts and ran.

Darragh paused for an instant like a predator scenting game, enjoying the sight of her pretty ankles flashing as she raced up the stairs.

Letting loose an impassioned growl, he gave chase.

He caught up to her on the top floor, capturing her elbow to bring her to a halt. Whirling, she struggled against him and raised a hand to strike. But he captured her wrist in his fingers before she could make contact.

"Now, now, haven't I already told you there'll be none of that," he scolded. "Seems you haven't yet learned your lesson."

"Bastard." She twisted, trying to wrench herself free.

He secured an arm around her waist to keep her from doing him any harm. "If I set you loose, will you come along nicely to your room?"

In answer, she kicked his shin.

He sucked in a painful breath. "As you like, darling. We'll do it your way." Bending at the knees, he hoisted her up and over his shoulder.

She screamed, beating a fist against his back as she dangled head-first toward the floor. When she hit him near a kidney, he smacked her bottom through the padding of her petticoats and skirt.

Her lady's maid was waiting wide-eyed and speechless as he sauntered through the door, her mistress draped like a hunting prize over his shoulder. "Good evening to you, Betsy," he greeted.

"G-good evening, my lord. M-my lady."

"Her ladyship won't be needing you tonight. I'll see to her needs myself."

"He'll do no such thing. Send for one of the footmen," Jeannette ordered, her voice half muffled against his shirt. "Send for Michael or Finn, anyone you can think of strong enough to make this barbarian unhand me."

"We're just having a bit of a spat, Betsy, nothing serious, mind you. She's as safe as a babe in my arms. Go on with you now."

The maid hesitated in a long moment of obvious indecision, then bobbed a quick curtsey and scurried from the room.

As soon as the door closed, Jeannette gave him a fresh punch, which drove an extra breath from his lungs.

"How dare you intimidate my maid," she said. "Now let me down."

"I guess I'd better or else I'll end up maimed," he said, his back smarting from where she'd planted her last blow.

Crossing to the bed, he flopped her onto the mattress, where she bounced twice. He stepped quickly out of reach as she righted herself, coming up furious as a wet cat.

"Get out!" she spat.

"Not after I only just got in. Besides, we haven't had our talk."

Eyes ablaze, she scooted off the bed and strode past him. Reaching her dressing table, she dropped down onto the padded seat. "You want to talk? Then, fine, talk. But make it quick, because I want to go to bed."

The corners of his lips curved up. "You can go to bed anytime you like, lass. I'll even help you disrobe."

"Keep your hands to your yourself, jackanapes."

"That's a fine one. Don't think you've called me that before."

"I'll call you that and far worse if you do not leave. Get out, O'Brien."

His eyebrows arched. "Back to *O'Brien,* are we? Seeing how you're such a stickler for social niceties, *Mulholland* would be more accurate."

She shot him a killing look. "Do not remind me, *my lord.*"

In quick, short tugs, she began yanking the pins from her hair, flinging them down, where they made tiny pinging noises on the polished, inlayed surface of her dressing table. Coiffure loosened, her hair swam in a golden cloud around her shoulders and down her back.

One glance and desire settled low and heavy in his loins. Her scent, lilac and apple blossoms, now clung to his shoulder where he'd carried her, all but driving him mad.

She reached for her brush.

On silent feet, he crossed to her. Without thinking, he bent, pressed his lips to a spot on her neck where he knew she loved to be touched. She whapped him with the brush.

He drew back. *"Ow!"* His eyes met hers in the dressing table mirror.

"I thought you wanted to talk," she said.

"Aye, I do," he grumbled, rubbing his forehead. "But I'd like to do the other as well."

"You can forget about *the other,* not after what you've done."

"And what is it I've done that's so very terrible, lass, except bruise your pride a bit?"

"Is that what you think? That I'm upset because my pride is wounded?"

"Aren't you? You said yourself you felt humiliated having to do the cooking and a bit of light housekeeping. But you didn't feel that way while you were doing it, did you?"

"I would have, had I known how I was being used."

"You weren't being used. You were just being my wife."

"Your wife is a countess, not a maid. You lied to me, Darragh. You tricked me in the worst possible manner."

"And you've never tricked anyone?"

A flush spread over her skin, his accusation hitting its mark. She turned again toward the mirror.

He continued. "I know I deceived you about who I am, and about the cottage as well. I'm sorry if I hurt your feelings, but I thought we needed time together, time alone without all the trappings that come with being the Earl and Countess of Mulholland, including my family and this castle and an army of servants watching us around every corner."

"So why didn't you just tell me that? Why set up some elaborate charade and dupe me into believing you are someone you aren't."

"I've never lied to you about who I am. The title perhaps; the man, never. In all the ways that matter, I have always been honest about who I am."

"And so have I. I am a lady. A woman who has been raised with certain expectations about how her life should be lived. A life that, for right or wrong, does not include performing menial labor. You're right, you did wound my pride. In fact, you stripped it from me, deliberately debased me. Why is what I still fail to understand."

"I didn't debase you. I taught you a lesson and a well-needed one at that."

Her mouth dropped open, anger return-ing. "You are a bastard."

"And you're spoiled and self-indulgent. At least you used to be. Before our time together in the cottage, I doubt you ever stopped to think about anyone but yourself, except upon occasion your friends and your family, but even then only when it suited your own needs."

She jumped up from her dressing table and pointed toward the door. "I have heard enough. Leave now."

He crossed his arms. "I'll leave when I'm ready. From the very first, you made it plain I wasn't good enough for you. You, the refined English beauty. Me, the lowly Irish architect, who might be all right for a stolen kiss or two, but who would never be worthy of your genuine respect and regard."

"That isn't true."

"Isn't it? Didn't you, just hours before you nearly gave yourself to me at the ball, tell me I ought to leave because I wouldn't 'fit in'? That those people were not part of 'my crowd'?"

"That isn't fair. How was I to know you were a gentleman?" she defended.

"Why should you have to know? We'd met. We'd conversed. We'd argued. I once even slept next to you on a lawn blanket, as I recall. Over many weeks, you'd had plenty of opportunity to take stock of the sort of man I am. Why should everything about me change simply because I possess, or do not possess, a title?"

Her brow furrowed, glancing downward as she hugged her arms around herself.

"You want to know why I decided to take you to that cottage," he stated. "I did it not to debase or demoralize you, but to give us time to be a simple married couple without all sorts of conditions, be they based on the status of commoner or peer. And there is one more reason," he said, his voice deepening. "Perhaps the most important reason of all."

"And what is that?"

"Love."

Her eyes, beautiful as a Grecian sea, glanced upward to meet his own.

"I wanted to know that you could love me. Not my title or my lands or my money, but me, the man you wed."

For a moment, she looked startled, thoughtful. Then something in her expression hardened again. "And you thought stranding me in some secluded wilderness, making me cook and clean and take care of your needs like some happy little farmer's wife, would make me love you?"

"It did, didn't it? Admit it, lass. You love me. I know you do."

She laughed, but it was a sound without mirth, one that sent a chill of doubt racing through his heart. He ignored it and reached out to wrap her inside his arms. "Go on. Tell me you love me."

She wiggled her arms up between them and flattened her palms against his chest to push him away. "But I don't. Let me go."

"Now you're the one who's lying," he said, refusing to release her. "Since the first day we met, there's been an electricity between us, a connection neither of us can seem to sever."

"It's called desire. I believe we discussed this topic once before."

"Aye, it is desire, but it's something more besides."

She lowered her gaze, pale lashes fanning evasively against her cheeks. "It's nothing more."

"Then what were all those little games we waged at your cousins' house, if not a court-ship ritual, unorthodox as it may have been? And why did you let me kiss you that time in the Merriweathers' garden and again that day beside the pond?"

She shook her head, made a muffled noise beneath her breath. "I told you. Desire."

"And why on the evening of the ball, when you knew you would be free of me in only a handful of hours, did you let me do all those delicious, wicked, passionate things out there in the dark in that conservatory?"

"I didn't *let* you."

"Did you not? A Society belle, who knew how to conduct far more than an innocent flirtation, allowing herself to get caught with the likes of me. From what I can see, you wanted to get caught."

Her eyes flashed. "Preposterous. Your entire theory is nothing but stuff and nonsense."

"Is it now? Then why are your nipples puckered tight as a pretty pair of beads?" He reached between them, flicked a thumb over her bodice and the taut flesh beneath.

She sucked in a breath and tried to yank herself out of his grasp.

He held tight, ducking his head to take her lips in a kiss both bold and persuasive. For an instant she yielded, meeting his demand. Then as though she remembered herself, and what she was doing, she turned the kiss around and bit his lip. Hard.

He drew back, tasting blood. His eyes narrowed for an instant, need making his head buzz. He swooped in and bit her back, nipping her lower lip just hard enough to sting but cause no lasting harm.

She jerked her head away, breath labored and heaving in her lungs. She stared, her gaze locked with his in a passionate war of wills and needs that radiated off her like sweat. Then just when he feared she might refuse him and herself, she gave an odd, strangled whimper and captured his head between her hands.

Moaning in relief, he let her drag his mouth down to savage his lips with her own.

CHAPTER
TWENTY-TWO

The taste of him filled her mouth, inflamed her senses, his short hair thick and springy beneath her fingers, a handhold to keep his lips locked to hers exactly as she wished. She accepted his tongue, matched his hot, slick thrusts with sensual thrusts and parries of her own, kissing him with a forceful, ravenous fervor.

Part of her wanted to push him away even now, deny him this pleasure of the flesh he coveted with such obvious desperation, the evidence of his arousal pressed like iron between them. But to deny him would be to deny herself and she could not bear the privation, her body desperate for the fevered ecstasy she knew his touch would bring.

In this they were matched. In this they were equals. Each of them hungering and craving, clamoring for the same end, one that would best be served by full and equal participation.

Without letting herself think, she tore at his shirt, yanking the tails out of his trousers so she could race her palms across the warm, hard planes of his chest. She threaded her fingers into the dark curls that grew there. Touched him in wide, greedy strokes before pausing to tweak his flat nipples in a way that made him growl and shudder.

Then she reached lower, delving beneath his falls to find him thick and rampant. Caressing him, she elicited a tortured moan that made his flesh leap and pulse in her grasp. She gloried to know that in this, at least, she held sway.

But before she knew what he was about, he turned the tables, crushing her lips to his in a fresh, tempestuous kiss that left her knees weak, legs shaking. As if she had unleashed a rapacious beast, he slanted his mouth over hers and claimed her as though he could not get enough.

Without her even being aware, her bodice sagged, sliding down her arms. Down went her chemise as well, tumbling her bared breasts into his waiting hands. She cried out as he fondled her with supreme skill, then again as he bent and used his mouth and tongue to equally devastating effect. Blood beat behind her eyelids as he feasted upon her, a yawning emptiness that demanded to be filled settling deep in her core.

Caressing his head, she freed him of his shirt so she could trace his shoulders and along the firm, slightly moist skin of his muscled back and arms.

Her dress, stays and petticoats landed in a sudden, silken pool at her feet, leaving her wearing nothing but her stockings. She moved to slip them off but he stopped her, straightening to his full height before lifting her into his arms.

He lay her on the bed, her legs over the edge. Shucking off the rest of his clothes, he spread her thighs, then stepped between. She expected him to come into her. Instead he leaned across, planted his big, wide hands on either side of her head and plundered her mouth. He left scarcely an inch between them, their naked bodies touching along the peaks and angles that glided together and apart with heady, tantalizing friction.

Savage hunger and torrid yearning clawed inside her. Catching him, she squeezed his buttocks as she tried to pull him down and in. But he resisted, using his greater strength to keep his body just out of reach.

She growled, her answering kiss turning brutal, demanding, possessive. He returned it with an unflinching carnal intensity that further incited her need. Breaking away, he showered kisses across her body, pausing to lave and nibble and suck on her skin in a manner she knew would leave marks.

His mark, as if he was trying to brand her. And perhaps he was. Hadn't he already staked a claim? One that went far deeper than only her skin?

Just when she could stand it no more, he separated her knees a few inches more and clasped her hips in his strong, male palms. She cried out as he pumped himself inside, plunging her fast and deep into a world of wanton sensuality, making her mind go dim from the bliss.

Her body welcomed his, instantly accommodating his large, familiar length, delighting in the sensation of being stretched exquisitely full. But instead of setting a rhythm and pace, he locked an arm under her back and rolled them over.

Suddenly on top, she stared down, breath panting from between her parted lips. He glided his hands over her skin. Shoulders, breasts, waist, hips and thighs, setting every nerve ending in her body atingle.

"Tell me you love me, lass," he murmured, his accent husky and thick as he continued caressing her.

Tell him? She sighed, her thoughts punch-drunk with pleasure.

He pumped once inside her, the movement drawing a moan of longing from deep in her throat. "You know you love me. Say it, sweetheart."

"I, *ooh . . .*" She bit the edge of her lip, whimpering as he rocked inside her.

"Say it. I want to hear."

He thrust again, tendrils of delight spiraling through her frame.

"Say 'I,' " he commanded gently as he thrust.

"I," she murmured.

" 'Love.' " *Thrust.*

"Love," she repeated, her mind in a whirl.

" 'You.' " He thrust again, deep enough to stimulate, but not quite satisfy.

"You," she whispered. *Oh, God, what had she just said?*

"You what? You love me? Tell me, Jeannette."

"Yes," she cried as he pumped, wringing a fresh moan from her lips. "I do."

Thrust.

"Love you!" Her heart skittered at her admission, but she was too overwhelmed to care.

He smiled, drawing her down for a sweetly savage kiss. "Now show me, darlin'. Show me how you feel."

Unable to prevent herself, she did show him, kissing him with raw, naked, unrestrained need. Flexing against him in undulating rolls and bouncing, shuddering shimmies as she drove them both half mad.

Faster and faster she raced, gasping at the frenzied pace as she sped them toward completion. When, at the very last, her strength gave way, he reached up and grasped her hips to carry her to the finish. Spine arching, fists braced on her quivering thighs as he flexed deep inside, he hurled her into oblivion. She screamed from the unbridled force, rapture cascading through her in a violent, mind-spinning flood.

Her body was shaking still, aftershocks flashing in wild pings and twinges when he stiffened and claimed his own fierce satisfaction. She collapsed over him, exhausted and shaken.

At length, she slept, cradled inside the security of his arms, warm beneath the sheet and blanket he drew over them both.

Yet when she awakened near dawn, it was not with a sense of happiness and peace.

What had he done to her? Why had he made her say it?

Tell me you love me, he'd demanded. *Show me you love me.*

And she had, giving him exactly what he wished.

And yet he hadn't said the words back. Hadn't told her he felt the same.

Chilled, she sat up, gazing down at him as he slept, a boyish smile on his lips.

Did he love her? Or had he only wanted her to say the words in order to assert his will over her? To bind her more fully to him, as their vows decreed.

She could ask him how he felt. Wake him and say, "Darragh, do you love me?"

And if he said "Yes," what then? Could she believe him? His deception had shaken her faith in him, made her doubt where once she had felt only trust.

Another man had lied to her too. Toddy, who had whispered endearments and promises of forever into her ears, only to reject her and cast her aside.

Might Darragh one day turn from her as well? True, he hadn't been unfaithful, but there were more ways to deceive a person than with sex, as he had so recently proven.

She loved him. Of that she had no doubt. Yet was it enough? Because she knew if she let down her guard and gave her heart fully into his keeping, another betrayal would surely destroy her.

Covering her face with her hands, she

fought for clarity. *What should she do?* She felt so confused, felt in some ways as if she no longer knew herself, or what she really wanted.

Home.

How lovely it would be if she could go back to England to the safe embrace of her family. Violet would help her, she knew. Being with her sister would let her catch her breath, would give her a chance to sort things through. Despite their differences in the past, Violet had always been there for her, willing to provide a comforting shoulder as well as a compassionate ear and sympathetic heart. And maybe she could help Violet. She must be nervous, with the birth of the babies so near.

Beside her, Darragh stirred, shifting sleepily beneath the covers. She didn't react as he stretched up a hand and laid it upon her shoulder, tracing the unusual kitten-shaped birthmark that dappled her skin. His fingers skimmed lower, her traitorous body arching of its own pleasured volition. Knowing how easily she might be tempted to succumb to his wiles, she got to her feet.

Crossing the room, she retrieved the dressing gown Betsy had laid out for her last evening, shrugging into the soft flowered wool.

She sensed Darragh watching her, heard the rustle of the sheets as he climbed from the bed. Moving to her dressing table, she picked up her brush. A few strokes later, she located a ribbon in one of the drawers and tied her long tresses back at her nape.

His bare feet silent on the carpet, she didn't hear him approach, shivering faintly in surprise as he pressed his lips to her neck. Slowly, he straightened and extended his hand into her line of sight.

On the flattened surface of his palm lay an oval locket, gold glinting in the pale early light. "For you, *a stóirín*."

She stared for a long moment, hesitating before accepting his gift. Engraved roses trailed over the surface, simply yet beautifully etched.

"Do you like it? I bought the piece on that last trip to Ennis. When I saw it I thought of you because of the roses, that being your middle name and all."

She stiffened at his mention of Ennis, skimmed a thumb over the design. "Yes, it's lovely."

And it was. An enchanting, thoughtful gift tainted now by the knowledge of what he'd done. Of the lies he'd told, the elaborate ruse he'd fabricated to deceive her. Her fingers curled around the jewelry, metal links biting into her skin.

"Why don't you try it on, see how it looks," he suggested on a throaty murmur. "Then come back to bed."

She moved to put some space between them. "I would rather not."

"Why? We've plenty of morning left to us. No one will mind if we stay abed a while more."

"I would mind."

"What is it, Jeannette? What's wrong?"

"Nothing. Everything." She spun to face him, rubbing her hands over her arms. "I have been thinking and . . . well, I want to go home."

He frowned. "What?"

"Yes, I want to go home, to England. And since I know you have sufficient funds, it should not present a hardship."

His eyes darkened and for a second she thought she saw a flash akin to panic, then he blinked and it was gone.

"Will you make the arrangements or shall I?" she asked.

His expression hardened. "No."

"What do you mean, no?"

"Exactly that. I won't have you going to England."

"But I want to go. Besides, Violet is near

her term and will wish me to be present for the birth."

"Has she written to say so?"

"No, but —"

"Then she'll do fine without you and you'll do well enough here. Anyway, this isn't the season for you to be traveling abroad. Perhaps we can reconsider in the spring."

From his tone, it didn't sound as if he planned to reconsider, ever. "I don't want to go in the spring," she declared. "I want to go now."

His jaw tightened. "Well, you aren't going now, so I suggest you do your best to get used to that fact."

"You're a bully and I detest you."

"That isn't what you said last night."

For a second she stood stunned, unable to believe he would use the confession of love he'd wrung from her as a weapon.

"Get out! Get out and take your damned trinket with you." Putting the strength of her fury behind the throw, she hurled the locket at his chest.

He grabbed it in a neat catch, curling the gold inside his fist, a glimmer of hurt on his face. "If you didn't want it, you had only to say."

"I don't want it," she lied.

Or you.

Her last words lay between them, as clearly as if she had spoken them aloud.

"As you wish." Jaw tight, he bent to scoop up his trousers from the floor. Stepping in, he jerked them up around his hips, fastened the buttons in quick, short movements.

"What I *wish* is to go home," she said.

A black glower descended over his face. "You *are* home. *This castle* is your home, and you had best remember that fact. The day you took my name as your own is the day you became part of this place. The day you became Irish."

She considered arguing, but saw the chill that glinted like an icy winter lake in his eyes. She'd never seen Darragh lose his temper before, not like this, and decided she didn't care to test him further.

He yanked his shirt over his head, grabbed up his shoes and coat. "I had hoped matters between us would be resolved this morning, but I can see they are not. So I shall bid you a good day, Lady Mulholland, and see you again when I am less likely to do you a harm." Striding to the connecting door, he stopped, dug into his coat pocket and came up with a key.

She felt her eyes widen at the revelation, took note of the answering scorn in his gaze.

508

"Aye, that's right," he said. "I've a spare key that I could have used any night I wished. And should I wish to use it in the future, don't bother trying to keep me out. I proved to you last night just how useless such measures are. 'Twill not be hard to prove it again."

Flipping open the lock, he disappeared into the darkened stairwell that lay on the other side, shutting the door hard enough to rattle it in its frame.

Trembling, she slumped down onto the bed and began to cry.

Darragh stormed down the stairs to his bed-chamber.

So she wanted to go home, did she?

Apparently last night had meant nothing. The words of love he'd coaxed from her merely cries of passion, after all. She'd as much as said she wanted to leave him. His gut clenched at the idea as he stalked into his bedroom and slammed the door.

Perhaps he should let her go, if that's what she wanted. Let her journey to England to be with her sister for the birth of Violet's twins. But what if Jeannette decided, once there, that she wanted to stay indefinitely? What if her old life appealed to her so much she refused to ever return?

And that, he knew, was the real reason for his blunt refusal. The soul-deep fear that if she left now, she would be leaving him for good.

He could always go with her, he supposed. A move to England would no doubt make her beam with delight. But he didn't want to live in England, not permanently. Sighing, he tossed a fresh pair of peat bricks onto the fire, then sank down into a nearby armchair.

Over the years, he had enjoyed traveling the world, had thrilled to see new places, and meet new and intriguing people. But always he had known he would be returning to Ireland. Here to the land of his birth, where the cool, soothing green and ancient quiet replenished his soul as nothing else could. To do without . . . well, he couldn't do without, not indefinitely, and he had a frightening premonition that was exactly what Jeannette might have in mind.

Even if her plans were only for a temporary sojourn, he couldn't afford to accompany her. Not right now. He'd already been away from Caisleán Muir far too long. A mountain of estate concerns with which he needed to deal had piled up, and then there were his young sisters to consider. Moira and Siobhan would be devastated if he left again so soon. Guilt rode him, as it was, for being away all these months past. Especially since he knew both girls still sorely felt the loss of their parents, Ma in particular, and needed his guidance and support.

Which meant that Jeannette would just have to acclimate to life here at the castle. Maybe if she gave her new situation a little time she would grow to love the place. Maybe if she gave their marriage a chance, she would put aside her wounded feelings and actually come to mean the words of love he'd compelled her to say last night.

His lips tightened. He was hurt that she obviously had refused to forgive him for the cottage. Couldn't she understand that he'd done it for them? That they *had* grown closer because of those quiet, secluded weeks together? He knew lying to her had been wrong, but he couldn't regret what he'd done. Just as he didn't regret his decision to keep her here with him now.

She was his wife. This was her home, the place she belonged. Perhaps in the spring he might reconsider, surprise her with a trip across the sea to visit her family. Until then, she would simply have to adjust.

Over the next weeks, Jeannette discovered

she wasn't the only one capable of dishing out large helpings of silence. Darragh, she found, was every inch as talented at the trick as she.

Around his family he treated her with genial care and solicitousness, acting for all the world as if he doted upon her every word. But in private, he was often distant, behaving as though she was the one who had hurt him, instead of the other way around.

Of course, it didn't stop him from coming to her bed in the dark of night. Once there he seemed to delight in taking her at a slow, gradual pace, whipping up her passion to a knife edge then tormenting her until she writhed and begged him to give her release. And when he finally did, he punished her further by making sure she wailed out her completion at such a mortifying volume that she worried the whole castle could hear.

Without ever voicing the thought, he made it clear the situation between them was hers alone to rectify. All it would take would be for her to say she no longer wished to go to England, and all would be forgiven.

But she couldn't say that, not without lying, and that she would not do. She might have her shortcomings, but in this instance, she had done nothing wrong. Darragh was the one at fault, only he refused to admit it. And so she endured his coldness by day, then burned inside the heat of his irresistible carnal torment by night.

Otherwise, life took on a pleasantly full routine, daily growing more familiar with her new role as Darragh's wife. As countess, she assumed responsibility for managing the household and the servants.

"About time the master took a bride," the housekeeper, Mrs. Coghlan, declared during their first consultation. "About time he quit roaming and started raising a brood of young ones. You'll be wanting a large family, I'm supposing?"

To that Jeannette decided it wisest not to reply. Children? Yes, she thought, she wanted children. A brood? Well, raising her own cricket team was most decidedly not in her plans.

When she wasn't occupied with household affairs, she passed the time embroidering, painting, writing letters and playing piano in the music room. When it wasn't raining, she enjoyed taking afternoon walks with Darragh's sisters, who despite their youth proved lively, interesting companions. In the evenings, Finn or Michael would often suggest a game of whist or hearts. She quickly discovered all of the O'Brien men had a clever knack for cards. Especially Finn, who contrary to his large, innocent appearance kept count of the deck like a seasoned sharp.

Despite her worries that she was living in a complete social vacuum, a few visitors did come to call. The local vicar, Reverend Whitsund, and his wife arrived first, spending nearly the entirety of their visit reminiscing about their old life in England, while prodding her for information about "home." Although glad for the company, she found so much talk of England a painful reminder of her present difficulties with Darragh, her mood sadly blue-deviled by the time they departed.

Then there were the MacGintys, a bluff, horse-mad couple with eight children and a prosperous stud farm that she learned kept Michael gainfully employed. As a wedding present, they brought her an all-black kitten with huge amber eyes, an adorable creature that snuggled instantly into her lap and began to purr. While gazing down upon the small cat, hearing his tiny, adorable mew, something warm and maternal stirred in the vicinity of her heart, and to her surprise, she found herself accepting the gift with a glad smile.

She named the kitten Smoke, and welcomed him into the house. At first, she worried about introducing the little cat to Vitruvius — the wolfhound large enough to bat Smoke around like a ball. But the tiny kitten and the huge hound took one long look at each other and became instant best friends.

Now, nearly two months later, she gently untangled a skein of thread from Smoke's playful paws before placing the length safely inside her sewing basket, where the kitten could not find it. She didn't want the little cat accidentally swallowing the thread. She'd just tossed a small, velvet-covered ball made especially for the cat, when a knock sounded on the family drawing room door.

"Come," she called, smiling as she watched Smoke give chase.

A footman entered bearing a letter. After thanking the young man, she turned over the heavy cream vellum, discovering the red wax seal of the Duke of Raeburn. Slitting open the missive, she quickly read the splendid news that Violet's babies had been born.

Twin boys, Adrian wrote, delivered after a merciless fifteen-hour labor that he had feared, for a time, Violet would not survive. But his darling wife had pulled through magnificently, as had the babies, who had their mother's smile. They had decided to name them Sebastian and Noah. Being the eldest by seven and a half minutes, Sebastian was now the new Marquis of Ashton.

With Violet still recuperating, Adrian hadn't waited for her to write, but had done so himself, wanting to get word to Jeannette as soon as possible. He invited her and Darragh to visit anytime they liked, and sent Violet's love and his regards.

Jeannette set the letter down in her lap, her mind full as she gazed in absent distraction across the room, with its airy decor and cheery lemon yellow walls. If only she felt as cheery as the room. If only the joyous news didn't leave her the tiniest bit melancholy.

She had so wanted to be there for the birth. Had wanted to share the happy event in person instead of through a letter. Despite knowing it a fruitless endeavor, she'd tried again, four weeks ago, to broach the topic of traveling to England. But as soon as she began speaking, Darragh had turned frosty and ended the discussion. Now, because of his intransigence, she had missed the birth entirely.

And his moody, dictatorial behavior of late wasn't helping her resolve her true feelings, the two of them living in an odd limbo of sorts. How long, she wondered, could they go on as they were?

No nearer an answer than ever, she reread Raeburn's letter, then folded it and tucked it into her sewing basket for safekeeping. She would write to Violet directly to wish her happiness and congratulations. Of her own difficulties, she would continue to say nothing. Now was not the time to concern her sister with anything but the babies. Doing so in person might have served, depending upon Violet's health, but letters would only frustrate the matter and leave her twin to worry. So, Jeannette decided, saying nothing would be best.

A gift would need to be sent, she mused. But what? And where to purchase something suitable? It wasn't as if she could buy from the shops in London — well, not with ease anyway. Perhaps she would consult with Mrs. Coghlan to see if she had any ideas. Mayhap there were some native products, a beautifully woven set of blankets or lace-trimmed christening gowns whose handicraft Violet would admire.

Jeannette sighed. She'd just risen to go pen her reply to Violet, Smoke having vanished off into another part of the house, when a footman tapped again on the door. "My lady, a visitor has arrived asking to speak with you."

"Did this visitor give a name?"

The footman opened his mouth to reply when a disturbingly familiar voice, one she had never thought to hear again, did the honors for him. "He did provide a name," the voice declared, "though as I told this boy, there is no need for introductions, since you and I are old and dear friends. Is that not right, *cara mia?*"

Jeannette's lips parted on a surprised O, as Toddy Markham, the man who had once stolen her heart along with her virtue, strode into the room.

Lean and dangerous as ever, Toddy stopped before her and executed a bow stylish enough to impress the Queen. Catching up her hands in his, he dropped a pair of warm kisses onto her knuckles. Overly warm, overly intimate kisses that made her pull her hands aside, aware of the young footman looking on with overt interest.

"You may go, Steven," she informed the boy, waiting until the servant withdrew before turning her attention to her former beau. To look at him, one would never guess he was often one sovereign short of insolvency, his attire impeccable, immaculate, the height of fashionable good taste.

Today he wore precisely creased buff pantaloons, white shirt and starched cravat, buff waistcoat and a bottle green coat she was sure had been cut by no less estimable a personage than the great Weston himself. His Hessians were polished to a high gloss he'd once boasted of achieving by using a mixture of boot blacking and twenty-year-old French champagne. A sapphire signet ring she knew he'd won in a long-ago card game winked on his right hand.

His hair was brown, well cut and well styled, his pleasant, patrician features not what one would ever describe as handsome. Yet he possessed a magnetism, an aura that drew people in, men and women alike. Once he had been able to draw her in using those penetrating amber eyes. But never again.

"What are *you* doing here?" she asked.

He had the effrontery to look amazed. "Well now, that's a fine greeting, isn't it? And after I traveled all this way to see you. Jeannette, my love, this backwater is obviously having a deleterious effect upon your spirit."

"My spirit is fine, and I am not your love. I'll thank you to remember that, Mr. Markham."

"So formal. You were warmer the last time we met."

"We were in Italy. Of course I was warmer."

His lips quirked. "You know what I mean. Now, now, I know you're vexed with me and justifiably so, but I've come to make amends."

"Why? What happened to your contessa? This time of year, the two of you should have been making your way south."

A wry glint flickered in his gaze. "Carlotta and I decided to part ways." At her continued stare, he shrugged. "If you must know, her brothers apparently took a dislike to me, and persuaded me to rethink my affections for their sister."

"They threatened you?" Toddy wasn't the sort of man to back down from a fight. "How many were there?"

He laughed. "Eight, and a pair of uncles. I could have handled them, but the Italians have a nasty habit of starting vendettas. Seemed more trouble than it was worth."

He was also nothing if not pragmatic. "So you sailed away and came here to me."

"Actually I stopped off in London first. You might imagine my amazement when I heard you had gone off to Ireland. I decided I could not leave you to suffer a moment longer."

"Perhaps you did not hear the whole of it. I am married now."

"Yes, I know. Countess Mulholland, is it

not? I also know you did not wish to wed, that it was a hurried match to avoid yet another unfortunate scandal. How horribly disconsolate you must be."

Reaching for her hands again, he graced her with his handsomest smile. "My darling, I am so sorry. I should never have abandoned you as I did. Truth to tell, I've missed you. Adore you still. Foolishly, I let greed stand in the way of true love. Please forgive me and let me make things right between us again. Let me take you away from this heathen wilderness. We'll go back to the city, to London, where you can shine again as you so rightly deserve."

A year, even six months ago, she might have fallen for his blandishments, believed his lies. With very little additional persuasion she would likely have fallen into his arms. But no more. Now she could see him for exactly what he was, a cad and a user.

She could see another truth as well. Despite his practiced, winning ways, his power over her was done. She did not love him anymore. She did not love him because she loved another.

"Toddy, I —"

"Steven tells me we've a visitor."

Her gaze flew to the doorway where Darragh stood.

Zounds, how long had he been there? More to the point, how much had he heard? Enough, she surmised, to put a vicious gleam in his usually genial eyes.

She winced imperceptibly as Darragh's gaze lowered to her hands, hands still held inside Toddy's grasp. Loosening them quickly, she took a hasty step back, hating the fact that her withdrawal must make her appear guilty, when she had nothing about which to feel guilty.

Darragh stalked into the room, moved to stand beside her. "Introduce us, then, love, if you'd be so good."

Masculine possessiveness and animosity arced through the room like chain lightning, the two men inspecting each other the way wolves from rival packs size each other up before a fight. She almost expected them to snarl.

"Allow me to present Mr. Theodore Markham. Mr. Markham, my husband, the Earl of Mulholland. Mr. Markham is an acquaintance of mine from London, Darragh."

The men nodded, but did not shake hands as amiable politeness demanded. Then again, there was nothing amiable between them.

"Acquaintance, you say?" Darragh asked.

"Yes, old friends, actually." Toddy flashed her a warm smile. "Much too old for tedious formalities. What's this *Markham* business, my dear? I was *Toddy* only a moment ago."

"Well then, *Toddy,* what is it brings you to Ireland?" Darragh said, his tone like steel covered in silk. "And why travel all the way to the West at such an unlikely time of year? Englishmen don't usually have the stamina to withstand our bluff, raw winters."

"Oh, I have plenty of stamina," Toddy drawled. "Haven't I, Jeannette?"

Darragh's entire frame tensed beside her, barely veiled fury streaming off him in an invisible wave. She shot Toddy a look of reproof, unable to believe he would make such an indelicate and overt innuendo.

Deuced take him, what was he about? Was he deliberately trying to make Darragh believe there was still a relationship between them? Was he trying to provoke Darragh into issuing a challenge?

As insane as it might be, another glance convinced her such a result could indeed be his plan. Toddy might dress the part of a clothes-conscious fop, but he was lethal with a sword and equally deadly with a pistol. As for a bout of fisticuffs, she couldn't easily pick a winner, since she felt sure Darragh could scrap with the best of them. Suffice it to say, she had no interest in finding out.

Determined to stem any potential bloodshed, she stepped between the two men. "Mr. Markham, you must be weary after your long journey. Why don't I call one of the servants to escort you to your bedchamber, then I'll send up tea. You can rest for a few hours before dinner. We keep country hours here and dine at six." She crossed the room, pulled the bell.

"I remember when you and I dined at ten, sometimes later for a midnight supper dance."

"Yes, well, we are no longer in London."

"More is the pity."

A housemaid arrived.

"Please show Mr. Markham to the red bedroom. He will be staying with us for the night."

"He can go to a bloody inn," Darragh growled.

She glanced at Darragh, keeping her voice deliberately gentle. "There are no inns, as you well know." She turned back to the servant. "Nora, show Mr. Markham to his room, please."

Wide-eyed, the girl stared between the three of them, as if they were a prime carnival act. Recovering, she curtseyed.

"Aye, my lady. Sir, if you'll follow along with me."

Amber eyes gleaming, Toddy came forward, took Jeannette's hand. "Until dinner, my dear." Bending, he once again pressed a warm, far too familiar kiss upon the top. She pulled her hand away before he could give Darragh even more reason to complain.

Toddy straightened, angled his chin toward Darragh. "Mulholland."

Darragh showed his teeth. "Markham."

The instant the other man exited the room, Darragh swung around to confront her. "He isn't staying."

"Of course he's staying. You said yourself it's winter. We can't very well turn him out to freeze in the cold."

"He can sleep in his coach. With that fine, inflated ego of his, he'll stay more than toasty."

"And what of his servants and his animals? Would you condemn them to a night exposed to the elements?"

He glared. "Considering the man, it might be worth it." He set his fisted hands onto his hips. "Fine, let him stay, but only for the night. In the morning, out he goes."

"We shall see," she said, irritated by Darragh's overbearing command.

He froze, set narrowed eyes upon her.

"There's no *seeing* about it. He's going, at first light if I've my way." A pronounced silence fell. "He's the one, isn't he?"

Her heart took a leap. Devil take Toddy for running his mouth, and quite deliberately too. "The one what?" she repeated, deciding to pretend ignorance.

"*The one.* The blackguard who took your innocence, then left you to deal with the aftereffects. You told me it was over."

"It is over."

"Then why is he here? Why would that blighted knave travel across two countries and a sea, if not for good reason?"

"I have no idea."

"Do you not?" His eyes narrowed. "Or do you simply not wish to say?"

Stricken, she countered his cold look with one of her own. "I have nothing to say, if you are indeed implying what I believe you are implying. Retract your statement, my lord."

"I'll retract nothing until I've a satisfactory answer. Did you, or did you not, write and ask him to come here?"

His accusation drove into her heart like a dagger. After everything, he would now accuse her of deceiving him, cuckolding him? Before she knew what she intended, her

526

hand flashed up and she slapped him across the face.

The scarlet imprint of her palm mottled his cheek. His gaze afire, he covered the burning stain with his hand, rubbing the spot. "I'll not have him in the house above the night, and if I catch him anywhere near your room, he'll be dead. You tell that to your lover."

He spun and stormed out of the room.

Shaking, she went to the sofa and collapsed upon it. Her lips quivered and she pressed her fist against them, fighting to stem the tide of her misery.

Dinner was a tense and unpleasant affair.

Toddy spent his time flirting with her and regaling her with the latest on-dits from London, remarking on who did what and had she heard about so and so? and do you remember when?

After five minutes she wanted to strangle him. She toyed a time or two with the idea of jabbing the tines of her dinner fork into his hand to watch him yelp and make him shut up. But other than resort to violence or an outright scene, there was little she could do to stem what she knew to be his deliberately provocative behavior.

And all the while the others looked on.

Darragh's siblings were arranged silent and watchful as spectators at a very taut tennis match. She and Toddy presided at one end of the table, while Darragh sat at the other, brooding darkly into glass after glass of bloodred Bordeaux.

Darragh wasn't given to heavy drinking, as a general rule, and to her recollection this was the first time she had ever seen him get slowly and thoroughly inebriated. Dangerously foxed in a way that had even Michael minding his tongue by the conclusion of the meal. Luckily, this being a casual family dinner, there was no need for the ladies to leave the gentlemen to their after-dinner port and cigars. Instead, Darragh stalked off to his study while the girls made their way upstairs.

The prudent action would be to retire as well, she mused, but the evening was young and she refused to scurry away like some timid mouse, cowering beneath Darragh's displeasure. He wasn't the only one displeased tonight, her emotions abraded by his obvious lack of faith in her.

She had not sent for Toddy, and there was nothing between her and her old lover anymore. She had told Darragh that, but if he chose to believe otherwise, then so be it.

Into the drawing room she went, letting

Toddy lounge beside her and talk, his conversation reminding her with each word of her old life and everything she had left behind. The memories he awakened stirred wistful longings inside her, longings for all the parties and entertainments, friends and relations with whom she could even now be mixing and mingling.

She had been rusticating in Ireland far too long, she told herself. Just because her life here at the castle hadn't been nearly as grim as she would once have imagined, that did not mean she wished to become permanently immured in the countryside.

She had a right to fun and frivolity. A right to participate in the social whirl and rejoin Society should she wish, especially considering she was now a countess. A few of the loftier members of the Haut Ton might sneer down their noses at her Irish title, but they wouldn't have the gall to cut her outright, as she once had worried they might. With careful planning and positioning, she could still conceivably rise among London's social hostesses. After all, is that not what she had always wanted? Is that not what she had always planned?

If her relationship with Darragh were better, perhaps those things would not matter so much. Then again, if their marriage were better, she argued to herself, wouldn't he want those things for her? Wouldn't he want only to see her happy?

He spoke of love — hers for him. But not the reverse. His seemed a one-sided kind of affection, expecting obedience and devotion from her without any expectation of a similar commitment from him. Was it pride holding him back or did he simply not love her beyond the obvious physical pleasure he derived from her body? And if he did love her, why could he not admit it and apologize, beg her pardon and promise never, ever to lie to her again?

But he had not.

As she and Toddy continued to converse, her brothers-in-law sat over the chessboard, each of them pausing every now and again to shoot her separate, disapproving glances. Finally she decided she had had enough — of them, and of Toddy too — and rose to her feet, excusing herself for the evening.

Toddy followed her into the hallway, reaching out to stop her with a light touch. "Consider my offer, my dear. England is little more than a week away. You have only to say the word and I shall be your grateful escort, the instrument of your triumphant return to Society's bosom. I can see you are unhappy, and despite your Irish philistine of a husband, I shall not leave until you have bade me do so." He bowed, kissed her hand. "Think on it, *ma petite.* You deserve better than to molder away in obscurity, locked inside some forlorn old pile of Celtic rock."

Frowning, more troubled than she wished to admit, she murmured a brusque good night and continued on to her bedchamber.

Hours later, lying in the murky umbra of full night, she roused from a shallow sleep to find a man standing beside the bed, cloaked in heavy shadows. Her heart skipped before settling into a more natural rhythm when she recognized his size and stance.

Darragh.

She waited, expecting him to come to her bed, unsure how she would respond, given his earlier state of intoxication and temper. Instead, he did nothing, just stood with a single fist wrapped around the bedpost, gazing down upon her. She said nothing, making no movement, as if she slumbered still.

Long minutes passed before he flung himself away, striding out as soundlessly as he had come, his catlike footsteps silent as he disappeared down the steps of the connecting passageway.

Disquieted, she curled on her side, where she lay the remainder of the night, weary but unable to sleep. Thoughts and feelings raced like a turbulent river through her mind, and not long after first light she decided what she must do. What she had to do for the sake of herself and her own dignity.

Once she knew her maid was awake, she rang for Betsy. Unnaturally calm, she ate a simple breakfast of toast with lemon curd and drank a cup of the strong Irish tea she now preferred. Afterward, she bathed and dressed, comfortable in a gown of mulberry velvet, a plum-colored cashmere shawl draped around her shoulders for added warmth.

Hugging the material to herself, she made her way through the castle in search of Darragh. She found him in his workroom, his face pale and drawn, eyes tired, as if he too had not slept. His overindulgence in wine from last night no doubt playing havoc, she concluded.

He glanced up, pencil caught in absent distraction within his grasp. "Jeannette."

"I would speak with you, my lord, if you might spare a moment."

Carefully, he placed the pencil on his drawing board. "Aye, of course. Would you care for a seat?" He hastened toward a chair, reaching to sweep aside the stack of books and scrolls piled on top.

She stopped him with a quick shake of her head. "No, please, I prefer to stand." Without giving herself time to hesitate, she plunged onward, her hands clasped before her. "I have done a great deal of thinking and I have come to a decision."

"About what?"

"Going home."

His brows drew together. "We have discussed —"

"Yes, and you have made your feelings on the subject more than clear. But circumstances have changed."

"What circumstances?"

"My circumstances. I have options now that I did not have even a day ago, but I thought it only fair to ask you one last time. Darragh, will you take me to England?"

CHAPTER
TWENTY-THREE

Darragh stared at Jeannette out of narrowed eyes, his head throbbing mercilessly from all the wine he'd drunk the evening before. As if that weren't bad enough, a nagging, almost bone-deep fatigue weighed upon him like a leaden sinker. He had barely slept, despite the drink he'd consumed, the alcohol failing to produce a sedative effect and lull him to sleep. Instead he'd found himself awake and alert throughout the whole long night, nursing a fury quite unnatural to his usual temperament.

Jeannette was the cause, he knew, able to ignite his temper in ways no one else of his acquaintance had ever done before.

She and that bastard Markham, that is.

How dare that popinjay come here to this house. How dare he sit at Darragh's table, eating *his* food, drinking *his* wine, and practically make love to *his* wife under Darragh's very nose, with everyone, including his little sisters, looking on.

How dare the man.

And how dare Jeannette for allowing it.

It had been all he could do not the reach out and throttle the life out of Markham, wrap his hands around the other man's throat and squeeze until the English scoundrel's face turned ruddy as a boiled beet, then just as lifeless.

Instead he had tossed back glass after glass of wine, letting the liquor attempt to numb his pain. Only it hadn't. It couldn't. He'd been teetering on a razor's edge later, when he'd gone to her room, suspicion whipping his jealousy into a froth. Half convinced when he went inside he'd find Markham in her bed.

But he hadn't. She'd been asleep, alone, slumbering as peaceful and innocent as a child. Not trusting himself to touch her, he'd forced himself to leave, when what he truly yearned to do was lie beside her, lose himself inside her sweetly scented warmth.

Now here she was, telling him again that she wanted to go home. Could she still not see that's where she already was?

Massaging the bridge of his nose, he repressed a sigh. "We've been through this before. This isn't the time for travel, not with winter coming on. In the spring perhaps we'll talk of it again."

Her lips firmed. "I wish to talk of it now. I haven't had an opportunity to mention it before, but I had a letter yesterday from Raeburn. My sister delivered her babies, twin boys, both of them healthy and robust. Violet, I understand, is recovering well."

A genuine smile creased his face. "That's magnificent news. We'll not delay in sending them a fine gift."

"I would rather give them one in person. If we leave now, we could stay a few weeks at Winterlea before traveling on to London around Easter; that way we would be there in time for the start of the Season."

Easter? Easter was months away. His headache gave a hard kick against the inside of his skull.

Apparently encouraged by his silence, Jeannette continued. "I was thinking we might take out a lease on a townhouse in Mayfair. I suppose Berkeley or St. James's Square is a bit out of our reach, but Jermyn Street might do. Mount Street or Upper Brook Street are very elegant addresses as well. Yes, any of them would be more than acceptable. We shall have to find a land agent to make the necessary arrangements. I'll ask Raeburn who he might suggest."

Darragh gripped the back of his chair and

stared at her. Surely she wasn't suggesting what he thought she was suggesting? In his present condition, he could think of no way to finesse the issue, so he would just have to say it out plain.

"If by all this talk you're proposing we move to England for the next half year or more, you'll have to put that notion straight out of your head. For one, I can't leave Moira and Siobhan again, not so soon after I've been away these many months."

"Then let us take them with us. Finn too, if he wishes. As a young man, he could do with a layer of Town bronze. Michael shall have to stay behind, I suppose, because of his animals. A shame, since he would enjoy the adventure."

His pulse increased, an unfamiliar tension rising inside him. Last night at dinner, he'd seen the way her eyes had lighted at memories of her time in London, had seen how quickly she'd been seduced by nothing more than Markham's words.

All the fears he'd been nursing these last weeks returned. Once in England, back among her old friends and her old haunts, she would likely sink again into the life she had been used to living. Her new home here in Ireland, for which she'd barely had a chance to gain an affection, would fade further and further away in her memory until it barely existed at all.

Then there was Markham himself, who would no doubt come sniffing back around her skirts at the first opportunity. And who knows what other men. Jeannette was an incredibly beautiful woman. Even now his gut churned, wondering if he'd been right that she had indeed invited her old lover here. She'd been outraged at his accusation, but still . . .

"London is no place for the girls," he told her abruptly, his tone firm and deliberately dismissive. "As for Finn, he'd likely land himself in a world of trouble in a place so big. No, I've work to do here on the estate, and a design to start for a new client who lives little more than an afternoon's ride from here."

Posture rigid, she studied him for a long moment. "Your answer, then, I take it, is no."

He forced his gaze to hers, cringing inwardly at the stricken expression he saw shimmering back. "That's right. The answer is no." Discussion over, he turned away and picked up his pencil.

"You offer me no choice, then," she said.

"What's that?"

"If you will not take me, then I shall go

without you."

"You'll not be traveling alone. I won't permit it."

"Don't worry, I will not be alone. Toddy has offered to escort me."

A muscle jumped near his eye. "*Toddy* offered, did he? Well, I believe you missed him, since I saw his coach roll down the drive not long after first light."

"He is waiting just beyond. He said he would not depart until after I gave him my leave." She raised her chin. "Shall I send him word that you plan to accompany me, or shall I go with him instead?"

The pencil he'd forgotten in his hand snapped in two. He tossed the fragments aside. "Is that what you want? To run off with your lover?"

"He is *not* my lover, and we are not running off."

He cast her a vicious look.

"He is simply escorting me home."

"This is your home."

She shook her head. "Is it? Some days I can't help but feel isolated, cut off from everything familiar to me, including my family. At those times, I become very aware that this is an island."

"England is an island too."

"But it is *my* island, just as this one is yours."

Panic beat a tattoo beneath his ribs. He could not let her go. How could he, when he wanted to sweep her into his arms and beg her not to leave? Tell her how much he adored her and wished their quarrel at an end. But his pride remained strong, urging him to hold firm and not give in to her demands.

She was his wife; her place should be at his side. If she loved him, she wouldn't be talking about traveling to England without him. If she cared about their marriage, she wouldn't be indulging her old lover and threatening to run off with the man. Instead she ought to be kicking Markham out and smacking her hands clean of his dust as he went on his way.

The thoughts fired Darragh's temper, his aching head shortening an already dangerously short fuse. "I forbid you to leave, and that's the end of it."

"And how do you propose to stop me? Do you mean to keep me behind lock and key?"

Her words took him aback with sudden stunned dismay. Abruptly, a weariness stole through him, harsh as a January wind.

"Nay," he said. "If you truly cannot bear to live here, to live with me, then I'll not see you imprisoned. Go if you want. Go with him, if that's what you've a mind to do."

Jeannette's limbs quivered, shock turning her weak as if the earth shook beneath her feet. She had known she was taking a risk, trying to force his hand, and yet she had never honestly expected him to tell her to go. Somehow she had hoped her declaration would push him to act, would make him admit at last that he could not do without her. In her imagination, he reached out to draw her into his arms, murmuring endearments as his lips came down upon her own. Then he would tell her that, of course, they must go to see Violet, then on to London it would be, if that was truly what she wished.

Only, she was the one who had been pushed into a corner, leaving her with a pair of unpalatable choices. Either cede every last scrap of self-determination and admit her threats were empty — that she didn't want to go anywhere without him — or else carry through with her ultimatum and depart exactly as she had said she would.

A small crack formed in the vicinity of her heart as she made her decision. "Very well. I shall pack and depart today."

Darragh stared sightlessly down at his drawing table, not wanting her to witness the hell he knew must be visible in his eyes. "As you like, but don't imagine this sets you free."

"What?"

"Wherever you may live, you are still my wife. I will never grant you a divorce, no matter how miserable the pair of us may be. You and I are locked together for life. So if you were hoping you could be done with me and marry your lover once you return to England, you can put that notion from your mind."

Her pretty visage was pinched with sorrow. "I have no such intentions."

"Go, then, if that's what you want," he ordered in a rough voice. *Go,* he whispered in his head, *before I fall on my knees and beg you to stay.*

She paused for another long moment, then whirled and fled the room.

Slumping into his chair, he set his head into his shaking hands and wondered if he would ever see her again.

"My lady, I am sorry to wake you, but we have arrived."

The gentle cadence of Betsy's voice cut through Jeannette's somnolent haze. Opening her eyes, she gazed out the coach window to see the immense, elegant stone façade of Winterlea, principal residence to the Winter family for over 250 years. One of the grandest homes in all of England, the stately house stretched outward like a great lion at rest, regal and proud, mighty in its bearing and scope and architectural grandeur.

Darragh would find the structure fascinating. And he could be studying it right this minute, if only he had agreed to accompany her here to Derbyshire.

A bitter lump collected beneath her breastbone. She still could not believe it had all gone so dreadfully wrong. Yet perhaps it was for the best. She could never have agreed to reside permanently in Ireland. Always she would have longed to return to England, for part of the year at least. And even if Darragh had no interest in joining the social whirl in London, she did. She had never tried to disguise her wishes in that regard. He'd known who she was, the background from which she came, when he married her.

But, ah, she forgot, he had not wished to marry her. Instead he had been trapped, just as she had been. She only wished in the process the price had not been her heart.

Well, it made no matter. She would recover somehow and take solace inside

Society's arms just as she had always planned. In time her present unhappiness would fade and she would feel herself again. Once she had a chance to settle in and let her life resume its full and natural course, she would quit wanting to weep at the least provocation and scarcely give Darragh O'Brien a passing thought.

And who knows, in a few years she might decide to take a lover. But for now she wanted no man, particularly not Toddy Markham.

Four days ago, the pair of them had parted ways at a coaching inn in London, much to his visible displeasure.

"Jeannette, dearest," Toddy said, folding her hands inside his. "Stay with me. Let me make you happy. I wronged you before, I know, and I am more sorry than I can ever express. Please give me a chance to set things right." He kissed her knuckles, one hand then the other. "Remember all the fun we used to have? We'll have that again and more. I'll lease a house, something close to you. It won't be so hard to see each other, especially with your husband living an entire country away. Mulholland's a fool, you know, to have let you leave."

She tugged her hands from his grasp. "Perhaps so, but he is still my husband and

I will not betray him by lying with another man. I do thank you, however, for bringing me home."

His lips thinned. "And that's to be it? A simple thank-you-for-escorting-me-home and nothing more?"

"There is nothing more. We're finished, Toddy. We have been finished for a long time."

He reached for her again, but she eluded his grasp.

"I refuse to believe that," he said. "You're hurt, jealous. I love you, Jeannette, and you still love me."

"I'm sorry, but I don't. Not anymore."

His skin paled, and for a moment she actually thought real pain shone in his gaze. Then he blinked and with shoulders straight made her an elegant bow. "I hope that buffleheaded husband of yours comes to his senses soon and pleads for your forgiveness. He truly does not deserve you."

And then Toddy was gone.

She gazed across at Betsy and shook off her reverie. "Finally we are arrived. I am most glad, as I am sure you and Smoke must be too."

When she'd left Caisleán Muir, she'd decided to take the kitten with her. Except for a bit of meowing from inside his wide wicker basket, he'd proven a good traveler. Trusting him to the care of Betsy and a footman, she made her way into the house.

March, Winterlea's stately majordomo, welcomed her with all the deference due her rank, making her realize how used she had grown to the far more relaxed, informal nature of the staff back in Ireland. Not that he was unfriendly, merely precise, the epitome of everything the head servant of one of the finest families in England should be.

"I shall inform the duke of your arrival. The duchess is in the library, my lady," he advised. "I will show you the way."

She knew the way, but said nothing, etiquette demanding she be announced, even to her sister.

Count on Violet, she mused, to be back among her beloved books, even after having just given birth to twins. Ensconced in a cozy leather armchair, Violet peered over her wire-rimmed spectacles as they entered the room, an astonished smile lighting her features.

"Lady Mulholland, your Grace." March bowed and left the sisters to make their welcome.

Setting down her book, Violet hurried to her feet with far more agility than the last time they had met, her figure lush yet clearly on its way to returning to its usual slenderness. They exchanged a warm embrace. "Gads, what are you doing here? You said nothing about coming for a visit."

"When I received Adrian's letter about the babies, I simply had to see them and you. My turn this time to drop by and surprise everyone."

"Well, you have, and delightfully so. You've just missed the family, though. Everyone was here, as usual, for the holidays, even though Adrian wanted to break with tradition this year because of the birth. But his mother wouldn't hear of it and really I did not mind. The hoards will descend again in a month for the christening, but until then Adrian has shooed them out. He says I need rest and quiet to recover my health, but in truth I think he's the one in need of recovery." She grinned and glanced toward the doorway. "So where is Darragh? Lagging behind with the coach, or has Adrian found him already to bend his ear?"

Jeannette strolled toward a small table, picked up a book that lay on top, then immediately set it back down. "No. He . . . um . . . he could not accompany me. Estate business and one of his architecture clients, you know."

She could have confided in Violet, as she had been wanting to do for such a very long time. But now that the opportunity was upon her, she hesitated, reluctant to reveal the shameful truth of her disastrous marriage.

"Oh," Violet said. "Well, perhaps he can join us later, for the christening."

Jeannette refused to meet her twin's gaze. "Hmm, perhaps."

"You traveled all this way alone, then?"

"No, I . . . um . . . I was accompanied by my maid." She decided not to mention Toddy, knowing Violet's less than favorable opinion of the man. "And my kitten. I have an adorable new kitten. You don't mind if he sleeps in my room, do you?"

Violet tossed her a bemused smile. "Of course not, I love kittens. What is his name?"

"Smoke. He was a wedding present from one of my neighbors." No longer her neighbor, Jeannette realized, since she no longer resided in County Clare and might very likely not do so again.

"What's this about smoke? Is something on fire?" Garbed in relaxed country attire, yet still managing to look every inch a duke, Adrian strode into the room.

Violet laughed. "No, not at all. Jeannette was just telling me about her cat."

Adrian bowed over Jeannette's hand, murmured a quick hello. "You have a cat?"

"I do. He's a dear creature and a wonderful companion."

She saw Violet and Adrian exchange a curious glance, but decided not to let it trouble her. She had far too many things over which to be troubled without adding another item to the list.

"It is so very lovely to be here at last," Jeannette continued. "The journey from Ireland was quite exhausting."

"Of course it was," Violet said. "When did you last eat? You must be hungry and thirsty. Why don't we all go into the drawing room and I'll ring for some refreshments."

Jeannette agreed and the three of them walked upstairs, Adrian pausing first to slip Violet's arm through his own, obviously still cosseting her, despite the fact that she seemed well recovered from the babies' delivery.

"Where is Mulholland?" Adrian asked after they entered the drawing room and took seats — she and Violet side by side on the sofa, Adrian across from them in a chair. "I assume there's no longer any need to call him O'Brien now."

Jeannette's lips tightened at the reminder

of Darragh's duplicity. "No, no need at all. His true identity has been most thoroughly revealed, as I related to you in my letter. Of course, you already knew the truth well before any of the rest of us, did you not, your Grace?"

She met Adrian's gaze.

He returned it with an unflinching one of his own. "I admit I did. At the time, it seemed rather a case of tit for tat. One deception exchanged for another."

She paused for a long moment. "Then I guess you might say that each of us knows the other's pain. In appreciation of that, it would seem I owe you an apology. Being hoodwinked is far from a pleasant experience, is it not?"

Surprise crossed his face. "You are right, it is not pleasant."

His gaze shifted and settled upon Violet, turning warm and rich with a love so profound Jeannette was forced to avert her own gaze, feeling suddenly as if she were intruding.

"But I find I no longer mind. The rewards I've received," he murmured, "have more than made up for any discomfort along the way. I would not trade a moment of the journey that led me to the life I have today."

Violet beamed and reached out a hand.

Adrian took hold, squeezing tightly before releasing her hand.

Then he turned his attention back to Jeannette, nodding his head to silently accept her overture at ending the hostilities that had stood between them since their aborted wedding day.

Jeannette drew a breath. "So, in answer to your original question, no, Darragh did not accompany me. He . . . had work in Ireland."

Nothing more was said, a discreet tap at the door coming at just the right moment. A pair of housemaids bustled in bearing a laden tea tray and another tray stacked high with an array of delectable foodstuffs.

"Ah, good, the refreshments have arrived," Violet declared. "Kit will be sorry to have missed this."

"Yes, where is Lord Christopher?" Jeannette drew off her gloves.

"With friends up at a hunting box in Yorkshire. He'll be back in time for the christening, however."

Having learned the skills of a good hostess, Violet poured tea and arranged plates of food for each of them before handing them around.

Jeannette sipped her tea and ate a single triangular sandwich before setting her plate aside. "I hope you will not take it amiss, but

I am rather dreadfully tired all of a sudden. Would you mind terribly if I retired to my room to rest and change out of these traveling clothes?"

"Oh, of course not. I should have thought." Her sister made to rise in order to ring for the housekeeper, but Adrian forestalled his wife and crossed to pull the bell himself.

"Later this afternoon, I would love to see the babies," Jeannette said.

Radiant pleasure spread like sunshine over Violet's face. "That would be wonderful. I usually feed them at two. Why don't you join me in the nursery about two-thirty."

"Two-thirty it is."

At half-past two, Jeannette climbed the stairs to the third-floor nursery. Bathed and rested and changed into a fresh gown, she felt far better, far more in control of her volatile emotions.

Tapping softly upon the door, she entered the room. Cheery and pleasant with bright spring green paint on the walls, rich walnut floors and furnishings, the nursery was a place of security and contentment. Two large cradles were set up at a perfect angle to the fireplace and windows so the infants would have plenty of light and warmth, yet be sheltered from any unhealthful effects.

Violet sat in a nearby rocking chair, one of the babies at her breast. Jeannette exchanged a smile with her twin, then gave Violet time to finish feeding her child without the interference of conversation.

A young, rosy-cheeked nursemaid appeared, crossing to help Violet with the baby once he was done eating. Violet buttoned her dress into place, then let the maid carry the sleeping baby to his cradle to tuck him in next to his brother's. As soundlessly as she had arrived, the maid departed.

"They are beautiful." Jeannette stood at the foot of the cradles, gazed down at the two slumbering infants.

Violet joined her, voice low. "Perhaps it's motherly conceit, but I think so too. I think they are the most adorable boys on the planet. They have Adrian's eyes."

"And his stubborn chin, I see. I swear they're as alike as we are. Can you tell them apart?"

"Only by the hair on Noah's head. He came out with a big hank growing right on the crown. While little Sebastian is as bald as an egg."

Jeannette looked closer, and sure enough, one of the babies sported a tuft of black hair that peeked out from beneath the tiny white lace cap on his head.

"Once they both grow hair, I'll have to think up a new way to tell one from the other."

"No switching, hmm?"

A tiny grin curved over Violet's lips. "Definitely no switching. Any chance you might be expecting one of your own?"

Jeannette gazed at her nephews, unexpectedly wistful. "No. No chance at all."

During her journey to England, she'd gotten her menses. It should have come as a great relief, since a pregnancy now would have only complicated matters further between her and Darragh. Still, gazing down upon the babies, her heart squeezed with sadness.

"Would you like to talk about it?" Violet asked after a long silence.

Jeannette's fingers tightened on the crib rail. "Talk about what?"

"The real reason you're here. The reason your husband isn't."

She considered sticking to her earlier story and pretending everything was just as it ought to be, but even as she opened her mouth to do so, the whole sordid tale came tumbling out. Violet listened, saying nothing as she let Jeannette give voice to her troubles.

". . . and so we have . . . well, I suppose you might say we are separated. He and I have different wants, different needs, and our marriage has never been easy, even from the start. He wishes to live in Ireland and, well, I wish to live here. I ask you, is it so unreasonable to want to live in your own country?"

"No, for either of you. But Jeannette, he is your husband."

"Which is why I gave him every opportunity to come with me. I practically begged him and he refused."

"Do you love him?"

She nodded. "Yes, but what does it matter? He and I are worlds apart and not likely to meet anywhere in between."

"Perhaps it's not so hopeless —"

"He doesn't love me. Sometimes I've thought he might, but he's never said the words. Oh, Violet, I think my marriage is over."

Violet laid a hand over hers, gave it a gentle squeeze. "Then I am sorry. Is there anything I can do?"

Jeannette flipped her hand, squeezed back. "Yes. You can let me stay here. Just for a while until I find my feet and arrange my affairs. It won't take me long, I promise. A few weeks perhaps."

"Take as long as you like, as long as you need."

"And Adrian?"

Violet shrugged. "What about him? You are my sister. Adrian will simply have to get used to dealing with more than one set of twins in the house."

CHAPTER
TWENTY-FOUR

Jeannette remained at Winterlea for four weeks.

While there she spent time with Violet and Adrian and the boys, enjoying the babies far more than she would ever have imagined. Placing them on a blanket on the drawing room floor in the afternoons, she liked to fuss over them until she earned a smile from each. And once she thought she heard a giggle from Sebastian, though no one believed her, since Violet had been asleep in a nearby chair at the time, exhausted after a fractious night with the twins. Despite the necessity of hiring a wet nurse, Violet wanted to breast-feed the boys as much as she could, insisting the intimacy created an irreplaceable bond.

For her part, Jeannette resumed her old habit of sleeping late and letting Betsy and the other servants see to her every need. She was aware of their efforts, though, as she had never been in the past, careful to thank them for their service and not ask too much of them in the way of extra duties.

Which is why when she had trouble sleeping, as she often seemed to lately, she went down to the kitchen and made herself a cup of hot milk. She even banked the coals in the stove afterward, and scoured clean the pot and cup so no one would know she had been there.

She had Darragh to thank for that, she supposed, for giving her the knowledge and self-sufficiency to do something as ordinary as heat up her own cup of milk. She had him to thank as well for her inability to sleep, memories of their time together tormenting her in the dark, quiet hours, when she was not occupied enough to hold such thoughts at bay. Yet whatever regrets she might harbor, she refused to let them dissuade her from her chosen course.

The babies were christened during the final week of her visit, family traveling from all parts of the country for the event, including her and Violet's parents.

Their initial reunion was awkward and strained, her parents deluging her with a barrage of questions about this mysterious Irishman she had married. Why, they demanded to know, had she not said in the first place that he was an earl? And why had he only sent a gift and card for Violet and Adrian, instead of attending the christening himself?

Two hours into the visit, however, her mother's cool demeanor began to thaw, then warmed to an easy flow over a discussion of the latest fashion pages in *La Belle Assemblée.* By that evening, it was as if none of the unpleasantness of the past months had occurred. Jeannette was forgiven.

She was also forgiven by her friends, who wrote to her in droves. By the end of her stay at Winterlea, she had invitations to four country-house parties and a winter fête in Bath. She chose one of the house parties, an entertainment hosted by her dear friend Christabel Morgan, now Lady Cloverly.

Christabel, it seems, had married in August while Jeannette had been in residence at her cousins' house in Ireland. Christabel's new husband was an older gentleman, a widower with a half-grown daughter and need of an heir to carry on his title. In addition to an attractive estate in Kent, he owned a luxurious townhouse in London, where he spent the majority of his time as an active member of the House of Lords. Christabel loved that she would be living in London and professed to be overjoyed by her prosperous alliance.

Clearly, Christabel's marriage was not a love match, as Jeannette witnessed for herself only a short time after her arrival in Kent. But just as her friend would never experience love's highs, she would also never experience its lows. And Lord Cloverly was not a bad man, neither cruel nor unkind, simply more interested in his work and his legacy than in entertaining a new young bride.

Determined to enjoy everything now that she was back among old friends, Jeannette threw herself into the house party with gusto. She and the other fifteen guests rode horses and participated in target practice — archery for the ladies, pistols for the gentlemen, weather permitting. On the days it was too cold to venture out-of-doors, they played cards and charades, and listened to the ladies, including herself, perform a variety of musical selections — activities that continued well into the evening.

Christabel's party was precisely the type of entertainment Jeannette had always adored. And she was having fun. Of course she was. She spent half the day laughing, did she not?

Yet somehow all the frivolity held a hollow ring, an emptiness at its core that she could not seem to fill. And as each day drew to a close, and she lay in bed waiting to fall asleep, a sense of dissatisfaction would sweep through her, where only weary contentment should have been.

It was Darragh's letter that was draining away her enjoyment, she decided. Just before she left Winterlea, he'd written to her, a hard, crisp businesslike missive that had left her frozen for a time in her chair.

In the letter, he informed her that he'd set up an account for her in London on which she could draw, providing an allowance generous enough that she could have no cause for complaint. Included as well was the deed to a townhouse in Mayfair that now belonged to her, together with a rudimentary staff that she could manage in any manner she saw fit. If she did not like the house, she had his leave to locate another; arrangements would be made for its purchase and sale of the first. Horses, a phaeton and a coach would be provided as well. Had she need of anything further, she was to contact his man of business in London to see to the matter.

Along with his letter, he enclosed notes from Moira and Siobhan, who wrote to say they missed her, asking when she was coming home. From Darragh, there was nothing of a personal nature. He'd said there would be no divorce, but his actions felt like one nonetheless.

She'd cried for an entire afternoon and evening after his letter arrived, twisting around and around and around the gold band he'd placed on her finger on their wedding day. The next day she'd dried her eyes and determined to put him from her mind, and her heart.

She should be ecstatic. She had everything she wanted. Her own townhouse in London, a generous stipend and the freedom to move about in Society as she willed, now that she was a married woman. It was the life of which she'd always dreamed, and she didn't even have to put up with a husband to have it. He would live in Ireland, and she would live here. What could be better? And should he decide sometime in the future that he wanted an heir, she would do her duty and find it within herself to provide him with one.

But she wouldn't dwell on that now. Now was the time to make merry. And she would, especially once the Season began. Entertaining as Christabel's house party might be, it was still a country affair. She needed the city again, Jeannette told herself. London, where there was never a lack of thrilling things to do and see.

Once Christabel's party ended, Jeannette had another house party to attend, and one after that. By then spring would be in the air, and with it Society's return to Town. That's when her new life would truly begin. The moment when she would be happy once more. At least, that's what she hoped.

"Your move."

"Hmm?" Darragh murmured.

Michael shifted in his chair. "I said it's your move, lad, and if you don't start minding the game, I'll be capturing that rook of yours in another pair of turns."

"What?" Darragh roused himself from his mental wanderings, stared hard at the chessboard.

Blister it, he thought, *I have no idea what move to make.* He couldn't seem to keep his head in the game. Couldn't seem to stay focused on much of anything these days. Knowing his brother was waiting, he forced a decision and slid a black marble knight forward to capture one of Michael's white pawns.

His brother clucked his tongue, making a quick move of his own that let him sweep two black pawns off the board and left his queen in a position to take Darragh's rook, as promised, on the next play. "Why do you not admit you're miserable and go after her?"

Darragh shot him a scowl. "And why don't you mind your own bloody business and keep your nose out of mine?"

Michael raised his whiskey glass to his lips, took a swallow. "I would if you weren't driving us all mad with these blue-devils of yours. Your temper's so short these days I could use it to light my cheroots." He lifted the cigar in question and drew on it, releasing a long, slow puff of smoke into the air. "Yesterday you made Moira cry."

"I apologized to her for snapping. She understood."

"Aye. We all of us understand. You need your wife back. So quit stewing in your own sour juices and go get her."

If only it were that easy, Darragh thought. Since Jeannette had gone away, he had been wretched. At first he'd held on to the fragile hope that she might change her mind, make that scoundrel Markham turn the coach around and return. But she hadn't. One day melted into two. Five into a week. Three weeks into a month, then more, as winter cast its chill over the earth before relinquishing its grip to the inexorable greening warmth of spring.

In all that time, he'd had only a pair of letters from her, each of them brief. The first informed him that she had arrived safely in England and would be residing for a time with her sister and brother-in-law at their Derbyshire estate. The second letter arrived weeks later, thanking him for the generous allowance he'd provided and for the London townhouse, which she described as "attractive and comfortable."

She made no mention of her feelings toward him. Said nothing about whether or not she was still seeing Toddy Markham. And gave no indication she had any intention of ever returning to Ireland.

Of course, he'd said virtually nothing in reply to her either, too angry at first, then too desolate to make the effort.

He tossed back the last of his whiskey, taking grim satisfaction in the discomfort that burned along his throat. " 'Tis plain she doesn't want to come back. She made her wishes clear enough the day she left."

"Then you're a fool to have let her go."

"And what would you have had me do to stop her? Chain her in the old dungeon? Lock her in the round tower? She wanted to leave. What choice had I but to set her free?"

"Did you think to tell her you love her?"

"She knows my feelings."

But did she? Had he ever once actually said the words *I love you?* He had thought them dozens of times, he knew. He had expressed them in countless ways, especially when they made love. But perhaps because of their troubles since arriving at Caisleán Muir, that particular sentiment had gotten lost. Maybe if he had told her straight out how much he cared, she might have stayed.

Still, after all they'd been through, could she really believe he did not love her? With the depth of passion that raged between them, it seemed impossible.

"What does it matter?" Darragh demanded, thumping his glass against the table hard enough to make the chess pieces shift on the board. "She says this isn't her home, that she wants to live in England. Well, I want to live here. Where is there any room in that for compromise?"

"There's always room for compromise, if you want a thing badly enough. The question is, how much is she worth to you? Do you love her enough to set aside your worries and your stubborn Irish pride? Or will you give her up and let her go for good? The choice is yours."

■ ■ ■

Jeannette whirled in the arms of a handsome lord, surrounded by the light of a hundred burning candles and the warm press of the three dozen other couples squeezed onto the dance floor. Clove-scented honey water and an attar of roses competed with the effervescence of champagne, hair pomade and human perspiration, to make for a rather intense mix.

The soiree was what one might term "a sad crush," guests packed in the way sheep were herded into a market pen. Precisely as the hostess desired, since her entertainment would now be deemed a complete success. Who had attended, what they had worn and ate, who danced with whom and how many times would all be written up in tomorrow's Society column, fodder for the Ton and the masses alike.

It was the kind of party Jeannette had always adored, but tonight she admitted that, once again, she was not enjoying herself as she ought. Seven weeks into the Season and the myriad fêtes, soirees, musicales, card parties, breakfast parties, suppers and routs were all beginning to run together into an indistinguishable blur.

She'd had an entirely new wardrobe made, but the novelty had waned already. And the pleasure of calling upon her friends to take afternoon tea and gossip about the latest happenings and scandals had grown into a wearisome chore. She didn't even enjoy the eager attentions of the dozen attractive men all vying to become her *cisisbeo*. She had no interest in taking any of them as a lover, and after a while even the most elegant of the pack were turning into bores.

She'd been so sure London would cure her ennui, lift her flagging spirits. And initially it had, as she reveled in the fast pace and hubbub of city life, thrilling to the sights and scents and sounds. But far too soon she had begun to grow tired of it. Seeing the same faces, playing the same games, doing the same sorts of activities day in, day out. The parties were of the highest caliber, and yet they were sadly tedious. Many of the people vapid and shallow in a way she had never really noticed before.

Is this to be my life, then? she wondered. *An endless merry-go-round of parties and social calls? Is there to be nothing else?*

But what else did she want? Wasn't this exactly the kind of life she would once have given her soul to have? So what had changed?

Darragh, she thought, his name whispering in her head. *Darragh and Ireland are what had changed.* And because of him, because of the place, she was no longer the person she had been even a year ago. It was as though a curtain had been yanked aside, showing her life from a completely different perspective. Unquestionably, she still loved parties and people, but without Darragh by her side, everything somehow seemed washed in gray.

The music came to an end, the dance done. She thanked her partner after allowing him to escort her from the dance floor. Nearly one o'clock, she saw by the tall casement clock standing along a nearby wall. Not late by this crowd's estimate, but late enough tonight for her. With a dispirited sigh, she went in search of her mother, who had shared a carriage with her to tonight's party.

"Mama, I am going home."

Her mother raked concerned eyes over her. "But why? Are you unwell, dear? Have you come down with the headache? The air is very close in here tonight, what with so many guests. Sheila really ought to open a few windows, but you know how she is about drafts."

Their hostess, Lady Farnham, had a

notorious fear of colds and disease. Consequently, she kept her windows sealed and her rooms far too warm.

Jeannette shook her head. "No, nothing like that. I am simply a tad fatigued. If you would like to stay, I can have the carriage sent back for you."

"No, no, let me say my good nights to a few people, then we'll be on our way."

Mama's good nights took nearly an hour, leaving Jeannette more than a little vexed by the time she and her mother climbed inside the carriage for the journey across town.

Jeannette leaned back against the satin squabs, stared out the darkened window, the quiescent *clip-clop* of the horses' hooves resounding against the street pavers in a soothing cadence.

"Well, that was a most satisfying evening," her mother declared, tucking her fan inside her reticule. "And despite the crush, one can never fault Sheila Watt for her hospitality. Her food is quite the best I've ever had. Stole the Oxneys' chef out from under their noses, don't you know. An Austrian fellow, so I understand. I hope you tried the medallions of beef, and the brandied squabs. Your father would have enjoyed himself at table tonight, you know how he loves fine cuisine.

But he *would* insist on going to his club." She gave a derisive sniff. "Men. One can do nothing with them really. Most unaccommodating creatures."

Jeannette remained silent, well used to her mother's opinion on the subject.

"And speaking of unaccommodating males, you really must write that husband of yours. Imagine leaving you without an escort during the Season, and in your very first year of marriage. There's been talk, you know. And were it not for your established popularity among the Ton, I fear some might have turned their backs on you."

Jeannette turned her head. "I beg your pardon, Mama?"

"Well, I don't mean to upset you, love, but truly, what can you expect? That man you married is *Irish*, after all."

Jeannette felt her lips tighten. "There is nothing wrong with being Irish."

"So you say, but if he were English, he would have the manners to present himself to his in-laws and to Society at large. Why is he hiding himself away? There are many whispering, wanting to know."

Jeannette's fingers curled in her lap. "He isn't hiding. I've explained before, Mama, he is a very busy man. He . . . he simply could not come at this time."

"Yes, his architectural pursuits, was it not?"

"And his estate business."

"Estate business can be handled by a bailiff, for the length of the Season anyway. As for this other business, this architecture of his, it really will not do, Jeannette. It's rumored he has received payment for his services," she finished in a scandalized tone.

Jeannette's chin came up. "Yes, he has. To aid his family."

Her mother let out a soft gasp. "Well, he must give it up immediately. Dabbling in architecture as a pastime is quite one thing, but to be earning money from it . . . well, no true gentleman *earns* his living."

Temper simmered through her. "Darragh does. And I see no shame in it at all."

"Jeannette —"

"What he does is honorable and useful and, yes, even beautiful. The new wing he built for our cousins is magnificent. I have never seen work any better. And what he has done to improve his own property, his castle that once lay nearly stripped to its bones, is nothing short of breathtaking. He trained and studied and sacrificed in order to restore his family's wealth, his family's name. And if he accepts payment for his efforts, I see nothing shameful in that despite his being born a gentleman."

"No English gentleman would accept money in trade."

"No, he would marry for it instead. A far less honorable way of replenishing the family coffers, if you ask me."

Her mother set a hand to her bosom. "What in heaven's name has gotten into you? Truth be told, I haven't wanted to mention it, but you have not been entirely yourself since you returned from that savage place. Nor since you wed that obviously uncivilized man."

"Darragh is very civilized." And suddenly she realized the truth of those words. Darragh, in his own unique way, was very civilized. Perhaps the most civilized man she knew. A man of conviction and resolve, who did things not because of what he'd been told to do, but because of what he believed he should do.

"If these are the kinds of notions he's been planting in your head," her mother continued, "then I am sincerely glad you have returned. He is not a proper influence on you. Best perhaps if he does not come to London, after all. He would only drag you down."

"He would do nothing of the kind. He is the Earl of Mulholland and my husband,

and I would be proud to stand at his side, anywhere, anytime."

"Even if he becomes the ruin of you? Think, my dear, you have always longed to be a leader of Society. Should certain details about him be revealed, that dream will slip out of your reach. You will never be the woman your grandmother was."

Jeannette waited for the pang, the old sense of inadequacy to hit her. Instead she felt nothing. No regret. No disappointment. Only a peculiar kind of relief, as if a great burden had suddenly been lifted from her shoulders. Her goals, the things she had always assured herself she wanted, no longer seemed so important. And as for Society, well, it could think and do as it liked and so would she.

"I don't want to be my grandmother. She was beautiful and popular and everything a Society matron should be. But underneath she was brittle, rather cold and unhappy."

"Jeannette!" her mother scolded. "You should not say such things."

"Why not? Is it not the truth? Did you never wish, just once, that she would reach out and hug you, tell you you were all right exactly as you are? Did you ever wonder if living up to other people's rules might be overrated? Violet has. Violet does. Oh, she conforms enough to be accepted, but at her heart she acts as she sees fit, Society be damned. And so does Darragh. I'm only now beginning to understand they're both of them right."

"As soon as we reach Wightbridge House, I'm sending for the physician," her mother wailed.

"I don't need a physician, Mama. I need my husband back, don't you see? That's why I haven't been happy here. Why none of this satisfies me as I once thought it did. I love him, and I miss him, and I walked out when I should have stayed and worked through our differences, instead of running from them."

But first, Jeannette supposed, she needed to forgive him for his deceit, for his tricks and lies at the cottage. He'd said he'd set up his hoax for them, and at the time she'd thought his statement utter nonsense, a flimsy excuse made to cover up the insensitivity of his scheme.

Yet maybe he had not meant his decep-tion to be cruel. She could see now that some of his assertions about her had been true. She had been dreadfully spoiled and self-centered. And she had been a snob, more concerned about his outward status than about the man he was inside.

But could she trust him? He had lied to her about his entire identity. Could she put his falsehoods in the past and move forward? Let herself love him with a full and open heart? She might end up hurt. Yet was she not hurting now? Was she not miserable without him? And if she must be miserable, then why do so alone? Trusting him was a risk, but one she realized she would have to take if she ever hoped to find happiness. And wasn't love at its very core a risk?

What if he didn't love her?

Her spirits sank for a moment, then her optimism returned. If he didn't love her, then she would have to convince him he did. He desired her, she knew that, and once she really turned on her charm, Darragh O'Brien wouldn't know what had hit him. Before she was through, he would wonder how he'd ever survived without her.

"I will make this succeed," Jeannette murmured softly.

"What's that? What are you saying?" her mother asked, her brow wrinkled with alarm.

"I'm saying I'm going back to Ireland. I'm going back to Darragh to save what's left of my marriage. I love him, and until this moment I hadn't truly realized why. It's because he lets me be myself like no one else in the world. With him there is no pretending, no pretense. Just me and him being the people we are. I want that back. I want another chance. And with any luck, he'll soon discover he does too."

CHAPTER
TWENTY-FIVE

"Betsy, did you remember to pack my peach silk gloves in the valise instead of the trunk?"

"Yes, my lady. I laid them alongside your handkerchiefs and hair ribbons."

"And the gifts we boxed up yesterday? You reminded the footmen those cases contain breakable items? A pair of Meissen dresser sets for the girls, and a Sèvres tea service for Mary Margaret? The men's gifts I'm not so concerned about, since there is little chance of damage to those. Although the horse sculpture for Michael could suffer dents if not properly handled."

Her maid wrapped tissue around one of Jeannette's evening gowns. "I spoke to each of the footmen personally, my lady, and pointed out which boxes require special attention. Thomas, the head footman, assured me every care will be taken for their safe transport."

Jeannette gave a satisfied nod. "Thank

you, Betsy, efficient as always. I don't know how I would get on without you."

Pleasure warmed Betsy's eyes at the compliment. "I suspect you would do quite well, my lady, but I am glad to know you are pleased with my service."

"I am, and glad you shall be accompanying me back to Ireland. Well, I shall leave you to the rest of the packing. We depart early tomorrow, as soon as Lord Christopher arrives."

Kit Winter had surprised her with his offer to escort her as far as the Welsh seaport town of Swansea — at Violet's urging, no doubt. Still, it was very decent of him to agree. Once in Wales, Jeannette, Betsy, and a trusted manservant would make the long sea journey to Cork, then hire a coach to drive them north to Caisleán Muir.

Over the past few hectic days, she'd penned hasty excuses to friends and family, canceling all her upcoming social engagements, while she and the servants made ready to close up the townhouse. This morning, she had left word with her butler that no further callers were to be received, since she'd been deluged with friends and acquaintances, all eager to know why she had decided to make such a precipitous mid-Season departure. She had no time or interest in indulging their curiosity further.

Betsy laid one of Jeannette's gowns into an open trunk, then reached into the huge mahogany armoire for another.

Jeannette tapped a finger against her side. "Oh, I just remembered that my sewing basket is in the front drawing room. Best not wait to retrieve it, or else it shall be forgotten in tomorrow's rush."

Betsy paused, a pelisse draped over one arm. "Would you like me to go now, my lady, or send one of the housemaids?"

"No, don't trouble yourself. You and the others have enough to do, and it won't take above a minute. I'll go myself."

On a swish of lilac-hued skirts, she exited her bedroom and made her way through the house to the drawing room. Warm midday sunlight poured in through a set of tall sash windows. A green jasperware Wedgwood vase stood on a side table, filled with a bounty of fresh pink roses to sweeten the air. Next to the sofa, exactly where she'd left it the night before, waited her sewing basket.

Only, the basket now had an addition. Her cat, Smoke, was curled in a perfect circle atop her embroidery, black fur gleaming like midnight as he slept.

She bent close. "Naughty puss. You're get-

ting fur all over my cross-stitch fire screen."
Instead of shooing him out, she reached
down and stroked a hand over his velvety
fur. He opened a single golden eye and
began to purr.

A knock sounded at the door. "My lady,
pardon the intrusion," her butler said as she
straightened, "I know you are not receiving
callers, but there is a gentleman who insists
upon seeing you. He says he is your —"

"Husband," declared a deep, musical
voice from behind the servant.

Her heart leapt in her breast. *Darragh!"*

At first glance, he appeared thinner, taller,
and broader of shoulder than she recalled.
Handsome and powerful, he commanded
the room from the instant he stepped over
the threshold. She drew a breath, finding
herself suddenly short of air. Nerves beset
her, heart beating at the speed of hum-
mingbird wings beneath her breastbone.

*What was he doing here? Why had he
come?*

She was barely aware of the butler as he
bowed and withdrew from the room, her
eyes riveted upon Darragh. She wanted to
rush into his arms and smother his face with
kisses. Instead she tucked her hands at her
sides, her mind crowded with all the things
she longed to say, yet somehow couldn't

seem to express now that he stood only inches away.

"Good day to you, Jeannette. You look well. That color suits you."

She plucked at her skirt. "Oh, this? It's new, I . . . thank you. You look well yourself." He looked tired, somber, yet oh so dear. "Why have you come?"

"I needed to see you. I . . ." He broke off, glancing down to his feet, where Smoke was rubbing his furry body against his trouser leg, purring and butting his head. The cat let out a plaintive meow and gave a little hop. "Is this Smoke? My how he's grown."

"He has. He's no longer such a kitten. Smoke, come away now," she coaxed, patting her thigh.

"He's fine." Darragh bent and lifted the cat into his arms, stroking a broad hand over the animal's sleek frame. She wished he might do such a thing to her.

After a long moment, he set the cat onto the sofa and turned back. "My apologizes for coming without so much as a word of notice, but to be honest, I wasn't sure what kind of reception I'd receive. I've taken rooms at a hotel, so you don't have to worry I'll impose myself upon you here."

She bit her lip. Was the situation so grim between them he couldn't even bear to stay in the same house? But if that was the case, why come all this way? Unless he'd come because he had to present himself in person. Because he'd decided he wanted to end their marriage, after all, and needed to petition the courts here in London. Her stomach pitched like a rolling sea, panic slicing at her throat.

"Darragh, please, I —"

"No, don't," he implored, raising a hand. "Let me speak first. I've been thinking about this, about what I'd say to you, these many weeks past. But now that I'm here, well, it's all flying straight out of my mind."

He raked his fingers through his hair, leaving it disheveled. Looking up, his gaze locked on hers. "I've been a fool, lass. An arrogant, stupid, opinionated fool. Even if I thought my intentions sound, 'twas wrong to lie to you, to trick you about the cottage, and about myself as well. I worried you'd see nothing but the trappings if I was honest, but mayhap I underestimated you, lass. You have my sincerest apology, late now though it might be."

Her lips parted on an astonished breath.

He took a step forward and grasped her hands, dropping down onto one knee. "My only excuse is that you stir something fierce inside me, something that makes me act half crazy whenever you're near. I should have told you as soon as I knew, but then you really would have thought me mad."

"Told me what?" she murmured, gazing into his brilliant blue eyes.

"That I love you. That I've loved you from the moment I laid eyes on you, watching you swat that cursed fly while you sat in your coach, wheels stuck fast in the mud. You were the proudest, most beautiful, most magnificent creature I'd ever met. You fair took my breath away."

"Darragh —"

"But I knew you didn't want me, not to start. And later I feared you still wouldn't, even if you knew the truth, so I kept it from you to prove something foolish to myself. But it's all gone wrong. I've mucked it up, driven you away, when I should have held on, should have told you exactly how much you mean to me. I've been miserable, driving everyone to despair with my melancholy and my temper since you left. Which is why I've come, to win you back. Will you give me a chance?"

He swallowed, agony in his gaze. "Unless it's too late. Please tell me it's not. Or do you love that bast— that Markham fellow?"

"No," she hastened to reassure him. "There's nothing between him and me.

There hasn't been, not since we parted ways last year in Italy. He's the one who came to Ireland to find me. I didn't ask him, I swear. I didn't want him. Don't want him. I sent him away the instant we reached London and haven't seen him since."

Relief washed over his face, and at her urging he climbed to his feet and drew her into his arms. "Perhaps we can start anew, then. Perhaps you'll let me court you again, properly this time. I'll send you huge bunches of posies, take you for carriage rides in the park, escort you to all the parties you like. There's a few weeks left in this London Season of yours, time for us to learn to know each other all over again."

She opened her mouth to speak, but he hushed her again, laying his fingers over her lips for a brief moment. "I know this is where you want to be, and so that's where we'll stay. Here in England, near your friends and your family. I'll have to go back to Ireland on occasion, but we can make our home here most of the year, if that's what you wish. I'll bring Siobhan and Moira over to live with us, since I can't leave them to grow up in the castle alone. Finn and Michael, well, they can do on their own."

"You mean you'd move here to London, to England, for me?"

His face sobered. "Aye, if that's what it takes to have you. I thought perhaps I could manage without you, lass, but it just won't do."

She flung her arms around his neck, love welling inside her, so intense she felt as if she might burst from the pressure and the delight. "Oh, Darragh, I love you so much! I've been miserable without you too. And I was wrong, so wrong. You were right all along to say I was too proud, too haughty and selfish and, yes, spoiled. I should never have left, not without telling you how I felt, not without telling you again how much I adore you. I'll admit I struggled against it. I didn't want to love you, but I just couldn't seem to resist. You're everything I thought I didn't want, and everything, I now know, that I love and need."

He cupped her cheeks. "Shh."

"I've been desolate since we've been apart. Let's never be apart again."

At her declaration, he crushed her tight in his arms, kissing her with a savage, unbridled hunger that left her gasping, her heart thundering at a dizzying pace.

"Have you a bedroom anywhere in this house?" he asked in a husky voice.

"Yes, but I fear we'd shock Betsy if we used mine, since she's in there packing."

His brows drew together. "To go where?"

"To Ireland. I was coming back to you, sweetheart. If you'd arrived tomorrow, you'd have found me gone, traveling back to where I belong. Didn't you see the boxes in the hall?"

"Aye, but I didn't imagine . . . I don't understand —"

"I thought London was what I wanted, but it's not. I don't belong here, not anymore, not without you."

"But you can have me, and this place. I want you happy."

She smiled. "And I will be. At home with you in Ireland."

His eyes widened in surprise and awe.

"I want to be your wife, Darragh. In all ways your wife, forever and always. Please say you'll have me."

"Of course I'll have you. But you needn't sacrifice so much. I came here prepared to compromise, so what do you say we meet in the middle?"

"What do you mean?"

"Part of the year here, part of the year in Ireland, or anywhere else in the world we've a fancy to visit."

A slow, beautiful smile curved her lips. "Are you sure?"

"So long as you're with me, I'll have

everything I could ever need."

"Oh, Darragh, I love you so. Kiss me again, please, before I faint from want."

And he did, holding her safe in the circle of his arms, the two of them in the one place they would always most long to be.

ABOUT THE AUTHOR

Tracy Anne Warren is the author of *The Husband Trap*. She grew up in a small central Ohio town. After working for a number of years in finance, she quit her day job to pursue her first love — writing romance novels. Warren lives in Maryland with a pair of exuberant, young Siamese cats and windows full of gorgeous orchids and African violets. When she's not writing, she enjoys reading, watching movies, and dreaming up the characters for her next book. Visit her website at www.tracyanne warren.com.

The employees of Thorndike Press hope you have enjoyed this Large Print book. All our Thorndike and Wheeler Large Print titles are designed for easy reading, and all our books are made to last. Other Thorndike Press Large Print books are available at your library, through selected bookstores, or directly from us.

For information about titles, please call:

(800) 223-1244

or visit our Web site at:

www.gale.com/thorndike
www.gale.com/wheeler

To share your comments, please write:

Publisher
Thorndike Press
295 Kennedy Memorial Drive
Waterville, ME 04901